the

WEIGHT

of RAIN

the
WEIGHT
of RAIN

MARIAH DIETZ

Cover Design © By Hang Le byhangle.com

Edited by Murphy Rae with Indie Solutions by Murphy Rae

Interior Designed and Formatted by

www.emtippettsbookdesigns.com

Other works by
MARIAH DIETZ

The His Series
Becoming His
Losing Her
Finding Me

For Lisa Greenwood, my strength, my confidence, my humor, and such a large and essential part of my life.
And for my boys. I will always love you too.
Dream big, my loves.

chapter

ONE

"Ben, Brian, Benny, Brent, Bailey?"

"Isn't Bailey a girl's name?" My eyebrows draw down in question, though I'm tired of playing this game.

"No, I've known guys named Bailey. It's one of *those* names." Charleigh twists in the driver's seat, eyebrows arching knowingly. I catch her glasses sliding down the bridge of her nose and her hand brushing blonde hair from her face before I turn to watch the road.

"One of *those* names?" My voice is surprisingly even as we dangerously near the median.

"Yes. One of *those* names. You know, where a boy *or* a girl could have it. Like Charleigh."

"It wasn't Bailey. I would have remembered that name for sure."

"You were pissed! You can't even recall how you got home!"

"Drunk," I reply automatically. "I was drunk."

"Drunk, pissed, same difference."

"Only you Brits think pissed means drunk. Here in America, we all think it means angry. We've gone over this."

"Yeah, yeah, stop changing the subject. Brandon, Brad, Bobby, Benedict?"

"Benedict?" My neck snaps to face her.

"Yes, Benedict."

"Who names their kid Benedict?"

"Plenty of people!"

Raising my eyebrows, I look at her with disbelief, which she returns with a glare.

"Did he tell you where he lives?" Charleigh asks, undeterred by my attempt to change subjects.

My index finger slams against my chest. "Drunk. Remember?"

"At least you remember what counts, I suppose."

"I don't remember *his name*, Charleigh!"

"But you remember that he made you see stars!"

"Stop! You make me sound like a floozy."

"You were a floozy. You got pissed and slept with a complete stranger with good teeth."

"He did have great teeth," I agree.

"At least we know he has good hygiene. That's a plus." I groan, slapping a hand across my eyes to hide from my own embarrassment. "I'm just teasing. I'm proud of you, Crosby. You finally got a piece! It's been over a year since the last time someone dusted your hallway."

"Stop!" My objection is met with laughter, which has my eyes rolling.

"Don't get your knickers in a twist. I'm just teasing you. I'm glad you found someone you're interested in." Her focus moves back to the windshield for a moment and then turns to me, her lips pressed tightly into a hopeful smile. "We could try changing the last two digits and dial the number, see if we get anything."

I look down at the palm of my left hand that's been scrubbed clean. Two weeks ago I woke up with a pounding headache, a hazy recollection of events that involved meeting a guy with auburn hair, warm amber eyes, and some of the straightest, whitest, most even teeth I've ever seen—along with a phone number that was half smeared/half worn off my palm. I vaguely recall mentioning to him that it was hard to read at the time and him smiling at me, offering me more water. My memories contain blurbs including people dancing and me laughing, but the bright smile, and eyes that held so many unspoken words—that I vaguely recall trying to pull out of him—are the most potent.

Images became clearer and clearer as the night went on, including one where I definitely remember convincing him I was sober enough to have sex.

I, Lauren Crosby, convinced a complete stranger to sleep with me at a house party.

On someone else's bed.

He was quite possibly the hottest guy I've ever seen. There's no way that, had I not been drinking, I would have spoken to him. Liquid courage alone led me to trace my tongue along the python snake tattoo that wrapped around his bicep and over his shoulder. I know we exchanged numbers in such an outdated fashion because I'd been wearing a dress and left my phone with my roommate, Kenzie.

"I doubt he even remembers me," I mumble.

"Lauren, I swear to God, if I hear you say that again, I'm going to kick you in your loaf of bread."

"Your cockney threats don't scare me, they just confuse me."

"I'll kick you in your head! Make that brain of yours start working!"

"I'm sure I gave him my number too. He hasn't called," I object, meeting her hard stare. "It wasn't like I was the only person interested in him. Trust me."

"I think we should ask around some more."

"Ask what?" My tone expresses my exasperation.

"Someone had to have seen you both at the party!"

"Charleigh, I'm giving up. It would be so weird to find him now, anyway. I mean, what am I going to say? 'Hey, remember me? I'm the girl you gave water to because I was too drunk to take care of myself. Then I talked you into sleeping with me.'"

"You could tell him you're pregnant."

My hand flies out, connecting with her shoulder. "That is seriously the worst joke ever. Plus, Aunt Flo arrived this morning, thank you very much."

"I know. You're grumpy as all hell, and you ate a Snickers for breakfast."

"Stalker."

Charleigh laughs, shaking her head. "Did you try describing him better to Kenzington? She knows loads of people." Only Charleigh insists on calling Kenzie by her full name—Kenzington.

"Like five times."

"What about the others?"

"I've asked everyone I know. I'm beginning to look pathetic."

"Stop being such a stubborn arse," Charleigh orders, but the lilt in her voice makes it hard for me to take it as more than a suggestion.

"Can I be a cranky arse and tell you to just drop it? It happened, it's over, we're moving on."

"But you liked him, Lauren! You really liked him!"

"Charleigh, I don't even remember the entire night. Beer goggles make everyone seem amazing."

"Well, let's see Mr. Stars without the beer goggles, then."

"Let's focus on you staying on the right side of the road. The more you talk, the more you forget that we drive on the right side of the road over here."

"Don't be a twat."

"I'm going to give you a pass and pretend I don't know what that means. Meanwhile, I'm going to nap."

"You're going to make me stay awake and drive while you rest?"

"It's better for both our nerves."

"You're a nightmare."

"Dressed like a daydream."

"Don't you dare!"

I lean my seat back and start humming the popular song, eliciting a growl from Charleigh that makes me laugh before she reaches forward and drowns me out with the sound of a new song. Smiling, I close my eyes and imagine the warm brown eyes I saw that night, and the chestnut hair with a natural wave that somehow managed to fall perfectly in place, unlike mine when I leave it in its naturally wavy state. There are dozens of partial memories I have from that night, but sleeping with him is as clear as crystal. Every breath, sound, stare, and touch is flawlessly etched into my memory, and I'm struggling to decide if I am grateful or rueful for it.

I stir as the car engine stops, grateful that I missed Charleigh's parallel parking job. "Since you're working a half shift, I'll just take the bus home," I say, unbuckling my seatbelt.

"What time are you off?"

My hand grips the cloth strap of my messenger bag, pulling it into my lap so I can securely fasten the flap. Rain is coming down in sheets. It distorts the images of people and storefronts, bringing a slight itch to my brain that has been absent. It's the desire to create.

"Lauren." Charleigh extends my name like it's several syllables, and I shake my head and turn to face her.

"Sorry. I'm off at ten."

"I was going to head over to the library. I've got some homework I need to work on, and I can't go home and do it. It's English, and I can't focus on reading and books when I'm surrounded by fabrics and designs."

"The library closes before ten."

"Then I'll just come by and have some nachos."

"Charleigh, I'll be fine."

"I know."

"Then why are you acting all mother hen on me?"

"Because you get distracted when she rings."

"When who calls me?" I ask absently.

"Did she talk about coming to visit again?"

I shake my head and watch the blurred shape of a person jog across NE Martin Luther King Boulevard. "No. She said she wants to try again in November. She's been busy."

"But you're her daughter."

My nails rake across my forehead, likely leaving a red pattern across my fair skin. "I know. She'll come eventually. Summer's a busy time for her work." I straighten in my seat and reach for the door handle. "I'm serious though—don't hang around downtown for four hours. Go home. I'll catch the bus."

"I can come back. It's a short drive."

My chin drops and my eyes blink and then slowly open. "I'll. Be. *Fine.*"

"Call me, then. I want to know when you leave and when you get home."

"You know, I was doing this a long time before I met you."

"Too long." My eyes dance across her lips that are turned down at the corners. Her gaze won't meet mine. "Alright, at least text me. I get anxious."

"Alright, I will text you when I leave, and again when I get home. Seriously, you're worse than the possessive boyfriend type."

"Damn right. I got a key to your flat after knowing you for only a week. I move fast."

"Did I mention you're a stalker?"

"You can't stalk the willing."

"Only willing with you."

Charleigh leans forward and kisses each of my cheeks and reclines back and opens her door. "Later, love. Don't forget to text me!"

"Don't forget to stalk Allie."

"I already know she's at her friend Katie's, working on an empire waist dress that is going to look fab on you. Now get to work. You're going to be cutting it close." She slams her door closed as I stand on the sidewalk.

The rain quickly finds every fraction of exposed skin, including my wrists and the back of my neck, sending a tingle down my spine. I give Charleigh a parting wave before putting my head down and making a run for Sonar, the small Mexican restaurant I work at.

"Hey, Lo!" I smile at Mia as I make my way through the back entrance that leads directly into the kitchen. "Guess what? Julio and Kendra are making mole and sopapillas tonight! Do you smell it?"

I stop and take a deep breath through my nose, taking in the tingling sensation from the spices and the sweetness lingering with the heat. "I was hoping for tamales, but mole is a good second."

"The best." Mia's lips, which are painted a bright orangey-red, lift into a wide smile. Then she turns, heading over to the prep counter where she expertly begins dicing lettuce. She's been working here since she was eighteen, and her thirtieth birthday is next week. She knows this place better than everyone aside from Estella, the owner, and helps with all functions.

"Hey!" I call, heading farther into the kitchen, passing several waiters, bussers, and cooks.

"Hey, Lo!" a chorus echoes in response.

"It's crazy out there tonight," a new waitress says, stopping in front of me. Her brown eyes scan her notepad as she shifts her weight to the other foot. "My feet are killing me." She's still trying to wear cute shoes with heels rather than practical ones for all the moving we do.

"I'll have some mole ready for you as soon as you're on your break, baby," Mia assures her.

"Mole and a foot rub?"

"Mole and a shot of tequila," Mia counters.

"Deal."

My laughter joins Mia's, a woman who has become one of my closest friends since moving out here three years ago, and head over to clock in. With the few minutes left before my shift, I fix my hair, pulling the loose brown strands back up into a messy knot on my head, and tie a black apron around my waist.

"Lo, you're on one through eight tonight. I may need you to take nine and ten too. The new guy isn't working out so well. The more tables he gets, the more mistakes he makes." My manager, Estella, appears from the front of the restaurant, her long black hair parted and braided around her head and her lips a dark maroon. I used to sketch her on my breaks because she has one of the most parallel faces I've ever seen, but lately, all I sketch are hands—the same hands I managed to memorize the most minute and subtle details of.

"I'm on it," I assure her.

"And Lo." I turn, my eyebrows high with surprise that there's more instruction when we generally communicate with so few. "Find your smile for me tonight. I miss it."

My lips lift obligingly, and I shake my head before I head out to table four. My hands fish through my apron to ensure I haven't notoriously grabbed the one apron with no pens again, and work begins.

chapter
TWO

"You've got to move out, Lauren."

"Tell me about it," I grumble, dropping my pillow and sleeping bag to the small bedroom floor.

"Lie up here with me." Charleigh extends the same offer each time I come in, and each time I reject it.

"I'm fine."

She's learned to stop arguing.

"Was it the same guy? The crier?"

"No. This guy kept making her call him daddy. If I didn't already have daddy issues, this would have done it for me."

"That's sick," Allie murmurs.

"Sorry, Al. I didn't mean to wake you guys up."

She releases a long yawn before I hear her roll over. "No worries. I sadly use your bad luck and stories about Kenzie to feed my boring life." Another loud yawn fills the quiet space. "But do you ever worry about your bed ... and if they use it."

"I hadn't … until now."

Allie's giggles are muffled as she pushes her face into her pillow, making my lips instinctively curl, but the idea of some strange man sleeping in my bed—very possibly naked—makes me feel the need to burn my sheets first thing tomorrow. At least I always bring my pillow with me.

"Daddy huh? Like, *Spank me, daddy*?"

"Charleigh, you need to get laid," Allie says. I release a quiet chuckle as I roll to my back, feeling the hard floor bite into some of the tension in my shoulders from having been hunched over my easel all afternoon.

"No, I'm not turned on by it. I just want to know in what context he wanted to be called daddy," Charleigh says, her thick British accent heavier with sleep.

"I don't know. I was sleeping and woke up to heavy breathing and 'Call me daddy.'" I've woken up to my roommate having sex in our closet of an apartment more nights than I haven't since we moved in together a few weeks ago. The first time it happened, I froze. I had no idea what to do. Our beds face each other, but thankfully I was rolled toward the wall when the noises woke me up, so I dipped below the covers and tried to discreetly move so I was covering my ears and started trying to remember the lyrics to every Backstreet Boys song I used to dance around to in my room.

We hardly knew one another other than the awkward pauses and extended invites we each doled out, our schedules only burdened with work and social engagements with it being summer. The guy thankfully left after he found what he came for, and Kenzie fell asleep soon after the door shut. I stayed awake all night, trying to determine what had happened. I expected her to be mortified about what had transpired the next morning, or suffering an extreme hangover, because really, who would do that sober? I was shocked to find her glowing, happier and even more chipper than she normally was.

It was two days later that I was awoken by similar sounds. There was no way I was going to remain in there and pretend I didn't hear what was going on.

I rolled over with the initial intent of telling them to go somewhere else, but they had turned on the desk lamp, and when I turned, I got a view of my roommate fully exposed on her hands and knees, with a guy I didn't know behind her. He heard my sharp intake of breath and for a split second, I saw a look of panic cross his face. His expression quickly turned lazy and then for several long, awkward seconds, he moved into her while staring at me. I had never felt so inferior in my twenty-two years. It took thirty seconds for me to grab a sweatshirt, my pillow, and book bag, and get the hell out of there.

It was still late June, and although there was a slight breeze, the night air was still warm as I made my way down the stairs of the apartment building. My eyes scanned over the parking lot in an attempt to go unseen, because I was wearing a pair of blue fleece pajama pants covered in moose and polar bears on skis that I'd received from my grandma at least five years prior. They were hideous and too short, but they were also soft and comfortable, and I was suffering a slight case of homesickness.

As I made it to the ground level, a car pulled into the space in front of me. The dome light lit up the interior as female voices filled the silence.

"Are you lost?"

My eyes widened as I looked between the girls, holding my pillow a little lower so I didn't look like a lost ten-year-old. "Sorry?"

"Are you lost?" she repeated, a heavy British accent joining each of her syllables into a song.

"No," I replied, shaking my head. "I was just taking a walk."

"At midnight? In your pajamas? With your pillow?" With each question, the lilt in her voice diminished, making each sound more like a statement rather than a question. "Are you hurt?"

Shaking my head, I gripped my pillow a little tighter, wishing she would stop staring at me. "No. I'm okay, really."

"Do you want something to drink? Some tea maybe?" she continued, taking a step closer.

"Thanks, but I'm good," I replied.

"Clearly you're not. You're creeping around after midnight in your pajamas. You aren't a mugger, are you?"

"A what?" I asked.

She looked across the hood of the car as her friend began to giggle. "She asked if you're a burglar," her friend said, a light southern drawl accompanying her words.

"No!" The word popped out of my mouth with enough force to reach the opposite side of the apartment building. "No," I said again, softening my tone. "I'm not a burglar."

"Then what are you really doing?" the British girl asked.

"My roommate has a male friend over."

"These flats are studios. There's no privacy!" I noted the lack of the "a" as she spoke the word with emphasis, making me mentally repeat it a few times myself, *privicy*. "That's awful."

I lifted a shoulder and moved my pillow to my side, dipping my free hand into the pocket of my hoodie.

"We have a couch you can sleep on," the friend said, her accent lost.

Normally I would have declined the offer and sought out a place to sit where I could watch for my roommate's guest to leave, but something about her kindness, or possibly her persistence, had me nodding in agreement and taking my hand back out of my pocket as I took a couple of steps closer to them.

"I'm Charleigh, and this is Allison," the British girl said as I got within a couple of feet.

"Allie," the dark-haired woman corrected her instantly, her tone agitated, like this was something she repeated often.

"What's your name?" Charleigh asked, ignoring Allie's correction.

"I'm Lauren. It's nice to meet you both."

"It's nice to meet you too, Lauren. Come on, then."

I followed them back up a flight of stairs to the studio apartment below mine where I was met with fabrics of all shades filling nearly every surface of the small space. My eyes tracked several of them, a new one beginning before the last ended.

"We're going to school for fashion and design," Allie explained from my side. I turned to look at her and nodded a couple of times before my attention was caught by something that resembled the fur of a long-haired cat, only fuchsia pink. Eyebrows slightly raised, I moved my focus back to Allie and Charleigh.

"You'd make for a great model." My eyebrows lifted even higher as I looked to Charleigh. "You have that willowy look to you. But we need to work on your posture." With that as her warning, she pressed her right hand to my breastbone and her left to the center of my shoulder blades, pushing down, making me stand taller.

"There you are. That's perfect. Right, Allison?"

"You would be pretty great. How tall are you, anyway?"

"Nearly five-eleven."

Allie blew a low whistle between her bottom lip and her two front teeth. "You can sleep here anytime if you're willing to model my final project."

"Yeah, I sort of need a hazard sign on my back when I wear heels."

"That's okay. We have months to get this right. We'll have you walking the runway like you own it." Allie turned toward the small inlet of a kitchen and quietly began singing "On the Catwalk."

My gaze moved to Charleigh seeing her give me an assuring smile. "You'll get used to it. Besides, she'll be on to her next thought in like five seconds. She's totally ADHD."

"I can hear you," Allie sang as she turned off the tap from filling a tea kettle.

"I intended for you to," Charleigh returned in the same sing-song tone.

"What's your poison, Lauren? Coffee or tea?"

"Coffee, please," I replied as my eyes started following another bolt of fabric. "You guys have so much stuff. School hasn't even begun."

"What are you studying?"

"Art restoration and composite drawing," I replied.

"And you don't have any supplies upstairs in your apartment so you can work whenever you please?"

I looked at Charleigh, noticing her eyes were a beautiful grayish blue, almost the same color of the skies before they turn dark with a storm. "Touché," I said with a smile, turning my attention to where she was staring at my hand with the charcoal stains that never fully washed away, regardless of using a hand brush or special soaps.

"We're artists. We've been living and breathing fashion and designing our own clothes since long before we enrolled here." Charleigh's words made perfect sense to me. I never went anywhere without my messenger bag, which always contained at least one sketchpad, multiple pencils, and random pieces of charcoal rolling around the bottom.

"Coffee for you, and tea for you." Allie extended two giant mismatched mugs to Charleigh and me.

"I can't believe I haven't met a single American who likes tea."

"You're in the Pacific Northwest, babe. Land of great coffee and the best garage bands in the world," Allie explained, reaching for her own mug, a cup with yet another design and shape.

"Are you from Portland?" Charleigh asked, looking up at me.

"No." I shook my head and carefully set my cup on the small table beside me, watching as billows of steam evaporated into the air. "I'm from Montana, actually."

"Montana?"

"Yup."

"Is that where your roommate is from as well?" I repeated Charleigh's question in my head a few times, memorizing the notes as she spoke.

"No. She's from here."

"How did you meet her?" Charleigh took a seat beside me, her eyes wide with interest.

I took a deep breath and released it nearly instantly. "I replied to an ad."

"You found your roommate through an ad?" Allie turned her full focus to me "That's crazy! She could be all single-white-female crazy." Allie's brown eyes were wide, and I could tell her imagination was starting to run with possibilities as to why I had truly left my apartment.

My soft laughter was inevitable. "I don't think she's that kind of crazy."

"You never know." Allie's eyes were still stretched, catching on the light of the lamp, leading me to inspect the chestnut shade with amber tints around the edges. I couldn't help it. Art has always been something I have loved and always led me to carefully inspecting every color, shape, texture, and movement that many disregard.

"I guess it's a good thing I can model my way onto a couch, then, right?"

They both laughed, and I traced their faces, noting Charleigh's upper lip, which was slightly more pronounced than the lower—became even fuller when she smiled. And that Allie's nose bunched up and her nostrils flared in an endearing fashion.

"As long as you can learn to walk in heels," Allie said, nodding to my flip-flop exposed feet.

"Heels … right."

I roll over and try to get comfortable. It was only a few days later that their couch became an important surface to store materials with such limited space, thus leaving me to the floor. But I don't mind. The friendly memory tickles my mind as I search for sleep.

THREE

"Hey, Lauren, would you be interested in going to dinner with Celeste and me? We're going to that Chinese place you like."

I look over to Kenzie and try to hide my surprise. It's been over a month since she has made an attempt to be friendly toward me. Most would likely think this is because I complained about her disgusting habit of inviting strange men over, leading me to sleep downstairs on the floor, but it's not. I don't know why I still haven't voiced my objection. Actually, I probably do. I'm sure it has something to do with the fact that I can't afford to live in Portland by myself, don't know anyone looking for a roommate, and as lame as this sounds, I want her to like me.

I'm still not certain why she was looking for a roommate, because according to Charleigh, she can afford this place on her own without a problem based upon her wardrobe. Her clothes are all designer, made to look vintage and worn. I may have eventually noticed that all of her clothes were laden with popular and expensive names, but it was Charleigh who noticed one day while she was up visiting me as I finished a portrait of her that I was working on.

Kenzie had returned home and was changing her clothes, throwing her dirty clothes in a pile on the floor. Charleigh's jaw dropped. Initially, I thought it was because Kenzie was naked; she had little concern for modesty. Then Charleigh's eyes moved across the room. "How did you get the winter collection already? It's not out until next month!"

My charcoal hovered over the surface of my canvas, and I followed Charleigh's eyes over to Kenzie. I have always loved fashion. I guess it goes with being an artist—my clothes are yet another form of art—however, my clothing budget has always been sparse, forcing me to be creative with used clothing stores and sale racks, intermingled with a few more expensive items that I can mix and match. Charleigh smiled with appreciation, and the two discussed designers and brands that I had never heard of as I finished my drawing.

I guess you could say Charleigh in many ways bridged the relationship between Kenzie and me because, after their conversation, Kenzie started to spend fewer nights going out and more of them with Allie, Charleigh, and me.

A month later, Kenzie invited us to the party that changed way too much, and yet nothing, for me. It's where I met *him*. Charleigh and Allie weren't able to attend—they had a previous engagement with some other design students— but I chose to step outside of my comfort zone and go along.

The next several days following the party, everything was normal between Kenzie and me. She would tell me about her dates. Charleigh would try to make different teas in an attempt to convert us. The three of them discussed fall fashion trends. Everything was following what had become a familiar and comfortable routine. Then one day, it stopped. Kenzie's tone became petulant when directed toward me, and she avoided eye contact with me at all costs. She started spending less time at the apartment again and more time avoiding my calls and messages as I worked to apologize for whatever I had done.

"I can't go tonight. I had to get more canvases for class. It's Top Ramen for me until I get paid next week. Thanks for the invite, though."

Something flashes across Kenzie's face, and her eyes narrow in question. "Do you like kids?"

"I don't know if I want my own, but other people's I like."

My eyebrows draw down as her brown eyes grow wide and bright. "I have the perfect job for you!" she cries, jumping up from her bed.

"I have a job."

"Yeah, but this one pays more."

"What is it?"

"A nanny!"

"I have no experience being a nanny."

"It doesn't matter! You just need to make sure she doesn't hurt herself. She's totally easy. You'll love it!"

"I have a feeling there's a lot more to it than making sure she doesn't hurt herself."

Kenzie waves away my objection. "Trust me. I know what I'm talking about." She grabs her phone and focuses on the screen for several seconds while I try to process if this is something I might be interested in. And why she's had the sudden change of heart.

"They'll need you a few nights a week and some weekends. It will be super easy. It's just one kid."

"So you know the family? Have you babysat her before?"

"Yeah, a few times. Don't worry, she's chill."

Chill? Is there such a thing as a *chill* kid? "How old is she?"

"Like ten."

"Where do they live?"

"Not far. I'm sure you could walk it."

"I'm sure I could walk to Seattle if I had to—it doesn't mean I'd want to."

Kenzie's chin drops to her chest as she lowers her phone. "There's probably a bus that goes close to their house. Don't you still have your bus pass?"

"Yes …"

"Great. Problem solved."

"Kenzie, I never agreed to this. I want to meet them first. What if the kid doesn't like me? What if I don't get along with her parents? What if I can't commit to how many hours they need me?"

"The job pays twenty bucks an hour." Her words match the bored expression on her face.

"Twenty dollars? An hour? Who pays twenty dollars for a babysitter?"

"I'm done playing twenty questions with you. Do you want the job or not?"

"Don't they want to meet me first?"

"I know them. This is fine."

"How?"

"Lauren—" Kenzie's eyes narrow "—do you want the job or not?"

"Yes. I mean I think I do, as long as everything works out."

"You'll figure it out."

I mentally start tallying the things I need to ask as Kenzie reverts her attention back to her phone.

"Perfect. You start tomorrow at three."

"I have class until three thirty."

"Every other day they won't need you until four. I'm sure you'll figure it out. You're smart." With that, she stands up and leaves.

"Apparently not smart enough," I mumble, collapsing on my bed and focusing on the plastic glow-in-the-dark stars that decorate my ceiling.

The address Kenzie texted to me is nearly two miles from the bus stop. I know I'm supposed to be heading south, but apart from that, I'm clueless. Portland is a big enough city that even though I've been around numerous parts, I'm still not intimately familiar with most of it, including this area that's boasting large homes and wide sidewalks that have grass and trees painted along both sides as well as down the median.

I grip my messenger bag and pull it higher on my shoulder as I try to figure out my directions app for walking.

Thirty minutes later, annoyance and frustration are clawing at my nerves.

It's cold and damp out, the sky a misty gray, yet I've been picking up the pace in hope of not being late, and now sweat is making me feel sticky and making my bag and jeans rub uncomfortably. My hair is adding to my irritation, heavily weighted as it actively attempts to strangle me. I still have no idea where I am, but I'm positive I've passed this house already. It's lime green, making it stand out. The house is beautiful. I'm sure most architects and artists would consider it a masterpiece with a long wraparound porch, wide-paneled siding, and an intricately carved bargeboard along the roofline that looks like it was hand carved. There are matching gablet windows on the second story that make me yearn to curl up with a sketch pad and cup of hot chocolate in this cold drizzle. I can't imagine why they painted the damn thing such an intrusive color; it nearly matches the lichen moss that blankets several of the large rocks in the front yard.

"You look lost." My head jerks from the rocks that rest against the sharp contrast of the garage doors, which are painted a crisp white, to where an older man is standing with a small smile that, even with his unfamiliarity, I can see reaches his eyes.

I brush the small wisps of hair clinging to the sides of my forehead—likely curled and sticking out at dangerous angles, making me look both younger and homeless. I try to paint a smile on my face and nod. "Yeah, I keep getting turned around. I'm supposed to be on Cedar Drive. Do you happen to know where I can find it?"

"Cedar Drive? You looking for the Knight residence?" He takes a few steps closer to me, letting the screen door fall shut behind him.

Relief makes my smile grow. "Yes."

"You're not too far. You're just going to head up two blocks, take a left on Washington, and head that way three blocks. You'll see Cedar on your right. It's a narrow road, easy to miss."

"Left on Washington, right on Cedar?" I repeat in question, ensuring that's all there is to remember.

"That's it. You'll have a small trek to get to their house, but you'll probably be there in about twenty minutes or so."

I don't have twenty minutes to spare—I'm supposed to be there in four. "Thank you so much for your help. Have a great day."

"You should try smiling more." I have to turn to look back at him because I'm already moving quickly in the direction he pointed. "Smiles like yours make this world a better place."

I intentionally don't smile at his assessment. Instead, I redirect my focus and pick up my pace to cut my time, hoping his twenty-minute prognosis is an estimate of how long it would take *him* to reach the house.

Each of my breaths stretches into white clouds of lace as I jog down the road, my ears and lungs burning from the cold though my muscles are too warm. The road is narrow, only wide enough for a single car to pass at a time, and both sides are covered with an encroaching green mass of trees and moss that has made the road both darker and slicker. I haven't passed a single house since I turned onto Cedar, like I've entered another part of Oregon, something closer to Mount Hood, where it's typical to find houses surrounded by nothing but wildflowers, heavy curtained fir trees, and single dirt roads that you can get lost down for days.

A turn of the narrow road breaks the monotony of green, and a large cabin-styled house appears with a dark green roof and wide driveway. A loud sigh emits another large billow of white as I hurry toward it.

Stopping at the front door, I feel the cold roughness of my jeans clinging to my calves from soaking up the water from the road. My heart races as my finger connects with the doorbell while my eyes slowly rove around the porch. It's stained a dark brown to match the house. The front door matches the dark green roof and is detailed with carvings of small squares and thick lines, bordered by much finer lines that make the door look subtly expensive.

The door opens as I'm studying the wooden blinds covering the windows facing the porch, all of which are drawn shut. My attention snaps to where a little girl with dark brown hair lying in waves down her petite frame, is staring at me. Her eyes are wide and a sea green that makes me think of an ocean painting I'm currently working on for a class—it would be the perfect hue for the caps of the waves, right before they turn opaque as they hit the surf. Her lips are folded against her teeth as she stares at me. It's not in wonderment. No, I've seen this look; she's judging me. Mentally berating me, likely for being late and my appearance if I look half as bad as I feel.

"Hi, you must be Mercedes. I'm Lauren."

Her small hand remains wrapped around the doorknob as she continues staring at me, and I turn to glance in the same direction to ensure there's not something or someone behind me that's holding her attention. There's only the same looming trek of forest that I ran through to get here, though.

"I'm really sorry I'm late. I kept getting turned around. Cedar Drive isn't marked, so I thought this was just a driveway or a dead-end road."

"Are you from another planet?" Her voice is gravelly for being so young, but it's her words that come as a surprise.

My eyes widen in confusion and my head tilts. "Some days it feels like I am, but as far as I'm aware, no. Ten toes, ten fingers, one belly button." I'm not sure where this explanation derives from, but I regret it instantly as I see her face contort with obvious repugnance.

"Are your parents home?" I ask in an attempt to change the subject.

"My mom's dead." I'm fairly certain my eyebrows are lost in the mass of curling wisps clinging to my forehead. There is no emotion behind her words; it's simply a statement.

"I'm sorry." My voice is much softer, making my already quiet tone come out so low I'm not sure she can hear me.

"Why?" Her eyes narrow again, but this time she looks like she's angry rather than curious.

I stare back at her in confusion for a moment and then shake my head ever so slightly. "Because you lost your mom."

She lifts her shoulders and focuses her eyes over my shoulder. "Shit happens. Right?"

I leave her question unanswered, not sure if I should reprimand her for swearing when she's all too right. Then her eyes come back to me, seeking validation, and I swallow though my mouth is still too dry from my run and the cold temperatures. "Shit happens," I agree.

Her eyes warm, stretching to their natural almond shape, and I see the corner of her lips twitch as she fights a smile. Mercedes takes a few steps back, her hand dropping from the door. "Do your friends call you Lauren?"

I hesitantly step forward, trying to keep my eyes on her rather than the mess surrounding us. "Most of my friends call me Lo. But you can call me either."

"What? I'm not allowed to be your friend?" My eyes skirt from the large wad of laundry against the wall to Mercedes' eyes that are narrowed once more.

"No, call me Lo."

"No, you don't want to be friends, no?" She fists her small hands and then slams them on her narrow hips.

"That's not what I meant. You're welcome to call me Lo, or I'm cool with you calling me Lauren. It doesn't matter. I'm still your babysitter, but I like the idea of us being friends."

"You're my nanny."

My shoulders shrug and my eyebrows knit slightly before relaxing again. "Same difference."

"No. It's not. I don't need someone to babysit me. I can take care of myself." She leans her chest toward me and raises her voice with each word.

Thoughts of revenge against Kenzie are multiplying, not only for giving me shit for directions, but for setting me up with this miniature diva that's trapped inside a ten-year-old's body. "Look, I was hired to come and babysit. I ran for over forty minutes, and let me tell you, I hate running. My clothes are wet, my hair is—"

"Your hair's a mess."

My eyes narrow on her this time as my chin drops. "I know. Because I was *running. For forty. Minutes.* If you don't want me here, say the words, and when your dad comes down, I'll leave."

She rolls her green eyes. "Stop being so dramatic."

I shake my head and blink heavily a few times as she spins on her heel and heads down the hallway.

"Are you coming?" Her tone isn't welcoming, nor is the scowl on her lips.

I'm considering zip tying every item of Kenzie's in place like my older brother, Josh, did to me several years ago on April Fool's, as I follow her, blandly paying attention to the clutter that seems to be drowning this house.

When we reach a large room, it takes me several seconds of looking around to realize we're in a living room. At least … I think we're in a living room. There's a TV hanging on the far wall, but no seating is near it. The only couch is against the opposite wall and piled high with clothes. A chandelier hangs from the ceiling ahead of us, but there's no table below it. Instead, my eyes search over wheels that look like they belong on bicycles, and boxes that are precariously balanced with bubble wrap flowing from each of their tops. Bags that appear both empty and full are haphazardly mixed in with endless amounts of laundry, toys, a few pillows, food wrappers, packing materials, magazines, and even shoes.

"So what do you want to do?"

I turn my head to Mercedes. She's unaffected by the mess and doesn't seem to care at all that I can't stop staring at it, feeling slightly horrified that anyone could live in such chaos. I can't tell if it's because she's too young to understand this would commonly be considered a social faux pas, or if she simply doesn't care. "What do you normally do?"

She rolls her eyes again in an exaggerated fashion, her fists slamming back to her non-existent hips. "What do *you* normally do?"

I tilt my chin, wondering if she's seeking sarcasm, but I attempt honesty. "I go to school and work. When I'm not doing that, I'm usually with my friends, Charleigh and Allie."

"What do you do when you hang out with them?" There's still an edge to her tone, but her eyes are filled with curiosity as she watches me.

"They go to school for fashion design, so sometimes we talk about art stuff, sometimes we watch movies and make Charleigh try American food, other times we just hang out." I shrug once again.

"American food? Is Charleigh not from here?"

"No, she's British. A tea drinker," I add, noting an empty Starbucks cup littering the ground.

"How very Mary Poppins of her." I feel the edges of my lips lift into a smile and note the way her lips mirror mine for a second before they stop and turn into a forcible frown.

"What do you know how to cook? I'm hungry."

"Want a sandwich?"

"Try again."

Raising my eyebrows, my tone becomes indifferent. "Cereal?"

"No way! It's afternoon."

"Mac and cheese?"

"Seriously?"

"What's wrong with any of those?" I ask, following her into a kitchen that is shockingly clean. The surfaces are empty and wiped down. Even the floors look as though they've recently been washed.

"We have basil. Can you make pesto sauce?"

I narrow my eyes, drawing my eyebrows together. "Not unless it's in a jar that I can open."

"What about scallops?"

"I thought you were ten."

"I am."

"What ten-year-old eats scallops and pesto sauce?"

"Ones with refined taste buds that didn't grow up on Cream of Wheat," Mercedes quips.

"How about scrambled eggs?"

"Do you know how to cook *anything* that requires more than one ingredient?"

"Not many, no." My frankness is not well received. Her eyes become tapered once more and her jaw clenches.

"Let's pray there are leftovers," she says, doing a quick spin on her heels and moving toward the fridge.

The afternoon passes at an alarmingly painful crawl. I can't express my relief when I hear the front door close and a male's voice call, "Mercedes, I'm home!"

The first genuine smile I've seen from her passes her lips, and she drops the small gadget she has been playing with for the past hour, on the floor amongst the maze of clothes and toys in her room, and heads toward the greeting.

"Hey, buttercup! How are you doing?"

"Why are you home so late?"

"Sorry, I had a long meeting with Stan." His attention shifts to me as I trail into the room, feeling a new sense of unease. Not only have I had a terribly awkward afternoon with his daughter, but I don't know the guy, and he's attractive. Like ridiculously attractive. "Hey! You must be Lauren. I'm Kashton," he says, extending a hand.

His smile is warm, inviting me to reply with my own. "It's nice to meet you," I say, taking a few steps closer to the man who doesn't look much older than me.

"Yeah, you too. You came highly recommended." His hand feels slightly rough, but it's the warmth of it that distracts me. It feels as if he just emerged from the hot sun rather than the cooler rain that has made an early appearance. As our hands slide apart, I notice several small nicks and scratches across his knuckles.

The impulse to object about my qualifications dances across my tongue, so I bite it. I bite harder when the desire to question him about not meeting me prior to allowing his daughter for the afternoon enters my mind.

"Did you guys have a good day?" he asks.

"She doesn't know how to cook." Mercedes announces the fact like this has been the biggest issue we've faced today.

Kashton's eyes meet mine. They're a warm brown, reminding me of well-worn leather, but are a similar shape and depth to Mercedes. "Maybe your uncle can teach her." His voice is playful, accompanied by a smile that assures me the thought is more for Mercedes.

"He will have to; otherwise, I'll starve."

Kashton laughs and ruffles a palm over Mercedes' head, triggering the same look of disdain she's been sending me for most of the afternoon.

"We'll see you tomorrow, then, Lauren?" Kashton asks.

"Yes, at four, right?"

He nods and shoves his hands in his pockets, rocking back on his heels. "Yeah, I'll be here tomorrow, but I'll be out in the shop, so four will work great."

I nod in response and then jerkily move forward to grab the strap of my messenger bag, still leaning beside the door, and pull it on.

I'm already near a large SUV in the driveway when I turn around and wave. "I'll see you guys tomorrow, then."

"Yeah. Nice to meet you, Lauren," Kashton calls in reply.

"You too. Bye, Mercedes."

"Bye." I hear her voice, quiet and lacking warmth or amusement, then watch as she closes the door with a bang.

"So how was your first day of the new job?" Even Charleigh's warm voice sends chills of frustration through me that make my teeth grind.

"I'm pretty sure Lucifer has a daughter, and her name is Mercedes."

Charleigh's loud giggle goes from a sound to a vibration as she wraps her arms around my shoulders, hugging me from behind. "Was it that awful?"

"Worse."

"What were her parents like?"

"Her dad is young. Really young. And he's a total slob."

"Did you meet the Queen?"

I shake my head slowly and avert my eyes back to my sketch. "No, I guess she passed away."

"Oh, that's awful. Maybe that's why she was so difficult?"

I shoot her a glare that says *I don't care what her excuse is.*

"Why don't we go get something to eat. Something totally bad for us. We'll put in a movie and watch our pant sizes grow."

"I'm not hungry."

"You are cross, aren't you?"

I rub a palm over my eyes that have gone dry from staring too long, a side effect of my art.

"That's Lucifer's daughter?" Charleigh keeps one hand wrapped around me while the other snakes out and hovers over my drawing. "She's lovely."

"I'm sure Eve thought the apple looked really delicious too. That's why looks are deceiving."

"You know, I learned in my history of religion class that they don't believe Adam and Eve ate an apple. Before the seventeenth century, all fruit was referred to as an apple besides berries and nuts."

"That really doesn't change anything."

"I know, but I didn't think I'd ever be able to use that useless fact again, and you just happened to set the perfect stage for me."

I release a deep breath and drop my head to her shoulder, not having the energy to continue this conversation. "You're so weird."

"It's why you love me."

"Something like that."

"Come on. I'll let you pick the movie this time. I've got my mind made up on this. We're going."

"And you can't,"

Charleigh growls, cutting off my words as she stands from my bed. "You know I hate when you do that! That song is going to be in my head for days."

I'm not in the mood to be around anyone, even Charleigh, but I grudgingly stand up and grab a clean hoodie from my closet. As much as I don't want to see anyone, I know if I see Kenzie, I may lose my shit and actually punch her after the afternoon I've endured with Mercedes and her crazy amounts of attitude and sidelong glances that kept mocking me.

chapter

FOUR

"Lauren!"

I turn from where I'm holding an empty laundry basket midair, staring at one of the thousand piles of laundry that literally cover this house. My eyes find Mercedes and dance over the too-short skirt she's wearing over a pair of tights, which are covered with stripes in every color, and a black T-shirt that says "It's hard being a ten" and is covered in rhinestones and skulls. When my eyes meet hers, they're narrowed again, her hands back on her slender hips. I have been babysitting for three weeks now, and little has changed between us. I grew up having only an older brother and an often times aloof father. My brother and I helped our dad from the time we were young, doing chores that included taking care of the land and the animals because there was always more work than hands. We had several men who worked on the farm for my father, and a woman named Nell who lived with her husband Alan—our foreman who takes care of the animals and machinery—in a small home situated an acre away from our house. Nell is great. She's been around since before I was born and has played a large role in my life, participating in events my mom missed with her frequent absences. Our 300-acre cattle farm lies between Helena and Missoula, and although the town I grew up in is small, both nearby cities were large enough that I have seen and experienced a lot of people in my life. But I've never dealt with anyone quite like Mercedes.

Over the past few weeks, there have been moments when I've wanted to get an inch from her face and start screaming at her for acting so rude. Other times that I've wanted to walk away and quit. Then there have been moments when I have realized this ten-year-old girl who is acting like nothing in the world phases her, is trying to be tough for reasons I don't understand, and it worries me that she will become hardened for life. Cold and ignorant to all of the small beauties and blessings that too many already miss. Those small windows are why I've lasted this long. Well, that and the fact that I'm making double what I was.

"You're not paying attention. I almost hit you in the face!" Mercedes' voice comes out petulant, her face distorted with anger.

"Yeah, I'm done." I drop the empty laundry basket she's been aiming a miniature basketball at. Her chin juts out, becoming more prominent as she clenches her jaw. "Why don't we clean up some?"

"I'm not done," she says, keeping her face locked in a silent threat.

"Well, then you're going to have to find out if you have an actual basketball hoop that goes with your ball. If we start cleaning, we might find it by next week."

"You're not funny."

"Good, I wasn't trying to be." Growing up, my room usually resembled the aftermath of a tornado. With clothes rarely ever being put away, but rather in heaps on the floor, across my desk, desk chair, and bed, along with CDs and books and the occasional stray piece of silverware that my foot always seemed find in the middle of the night when I was heading to the bathroom.

It took dorm life to learn simplicity and organization in my personal space, and it's become even more prudent now that I'm living with Kenzie. My shoulders sag as a loud sigh leaves my lips. This house is a mess. Dead bodies could be concealed under these piles, and the carpets are covered in crumbs and dirt, bringing a personal rule to always wear shoes in the house.

"I know. Let's ride bikes! The shop isn't finished yet, but we can ride around outside. There are tons of trails." The rubber basketball falls to the ground without a sound because it hits one of the many miscellaneous piles of junk.

"Not right now."

"I do. Not. Clean. I'm ten."

"Everyone cleans. It's one of those universal rules: if you're old enough to play, you're old enough to clean. Besides, we have nowhere to do anything." Mercedes' eyes follow my arms waving around at the mountains of toys that are shoved against walls and piled on the couches along with more clothes, and several bikes and random metal parts that keep getting added to the space.

I look back at her, thinking she finally understands as she shakes her head. "I'm not cleaning. It's not my job."

"It's *everyone's* job."

"No one else has to do it."

"Wouldn't you rather have space to play, and watch movies, and do things other than crawl over piles of stuff?"

"It doesn't bother me."

I fight to keep from rolling my eyes as her hand swings to her hip. She has more attitude than someone twice her age, and I don't doubt for a second that she's never been forced to clean up after herself. I can probably find a collection of toys from when she was three under one of these piles.

"Mercedes, I'm not playing with you until you help clean up."

"I don't need you to play with me. I can play by myself just fine. All of my other nannies just watched TV or played on their phones."

"How lonely."

Her back straightens and her eyes slit so I can't see their ocean-green color. "I don't need you." Her answer is automatic, her tone filled with something that makes my heart hurt slightly because I don't know why there's so much vehemence.

"You can't play with me *or* by yourself until you help me clean."

"Then I'm going to get you fired."

My shoulders rise with indifference at the conviction behind her words. "That's your choice."

She turns again and stomps to her room, her small feet echoing down the hall. I stretch my neck a few times, rubbing what's become a constant nagging knot where my shoulders meet.

It takes only a minute to fill the laundry basket we'd been using as a basketball hoop, so high I can hardly lift it without random articles of clothing tumbling down the sides. I head out to the hallway, trying to carefully hold it at an angle that allows me to see around it, and pass Mercedes on my way to the basement. She's sprawled across her bed, diligently ignoring me as my foot slides on a towel. Her snickers follow me down the hall, and I realize how much I'm starting to loathe my job.

I've never been down to the basement. Mercedes gave me a tour of the entire house my first day, but all she mentioned of the basement was that it was her uncle's stuff and the laundry room. I'm in a small hall with only two doors, one of which is closed, and the other is open with clothes strewn about. When I turn on the light, I realize the entire room is packed full of clothes. There are so many I can hardly move. I've never seen anything like this. There must be thousands of dollars worth of clothes in this house. I drop the basket outside the door and carefully wade through the laundry, trying to steady myself as my feet shift with the moving garments. White and colored shirts are tangled with jeans and shorts. Pairs of socks and boxer briefs are strewn out, with bright pink shirts and flannel dotting the piles.

I sit down on a large pile with a sigh and close my eyes. I need to look for another job. I'm not equipped to help Mercedes, and this is becoming draining for me not only with all of her attitude and demands, but with less time to work on homework and the commute time to get out here each day. Plus, I've been missing my Comparative Art History class every Wednesday because I would only be able to attend for a few minutes before having to catch the bus out here.

The combining effects of not getting along with Kenzie, the school stress, and now the added strain of my job makes me question so many things about this year.

I drop a final shirt onto the mass of clothes that I've spent the last hour separating, and look around. I don't know where to start. At home we run anywhere from eight to ten loads of laundry a day. It's not like I'm not used to having mass amounts of dirty clothes, but this is unreal. I gather a pile of Mercedes' laundry and shove it into the washer while making a mental game of guessing how many loads are down here. Opening the cabinets that line the washer and dryer, I find the first clean and empty spaces in the house, and shake my head with the unveiling of a whole new issue: there's no detergent.

My neck drops back so I'm staring at the bright lights overhead. "What did I ever do to you?" My words are intended to be rhetorical, said to no one in particular, except perhaps fate so she'll give me a small break.

"Give up yet?"

My head feels like it weighs too much as I look at the doorway and see Mercedes wearing a gloating expression that instantly becomes the singular look I hope to never again see on her face. If we were on the farm, I'd probably throw her in the lake.

"I'm too stubborn and stupid to give up. Ask my roommate."

"My dad doesn't care about cleaning. He says life's too short to worry about having everything perfect. Fun is what matters."

"But you also have to appreciate what you have. Throwing all your stuff on the floor and not taking care of it isn't appreciating stuff, or having fun."

"Why are you so uptight?"

I clench my teeth to keep angry words from spilling out, and her eyes turn back to the familiar narrowed glare she's fit for me.

"Go ahead, Lauren. Do you have something to say?"

I need this job. I hate that I need this job, but I need this job. Twenty dollars an hour is twice what I make at the restaurant. "You need to learn to appreciate things, otherwise, you're never going to have fun because you're never going to realize what you have."

"I don't have anything." She turns with a final glare, and her feet stomp back up the stairs.

"If it doesn't work out, we'll find a place for you here, Macita."

I wrap my arms around Estella and squeeze. Leaving the restaurant is relieving for the fact that I will no longer have to work closing hours, and horrifying because it means I'm fully committing myself to being Mercedes' nanny.

"Thank you. I really appreciate that."

"At least I know you'll be returning to finish my mural," she says, stroking my hair in a motherly fashion that makes my body itch with the need to move.

"That and you have me addicted to your pollo asada. I swear you're lacing that stuff with something that's not legal."

"Yeah, my love," Estella retorts, leaving me in a fit of laughter.

"We have to do a going away party!" Mia announces.

"We're not having a party." Estella shakes her head. "We only have parties when we're glad they're leaving. Lo's coming back to visit. Weekly."

chapter

FIVE

Mercedes' comment about having nothing is still haunting me three days later as I make the twenty-minute trek on foot to the Knight residence. It's like being around her has heightened this maternal instinct in me, making me wish to shield her from any conceivable pain or ugliness, yet in the few weeks that I've been working at the house, I have seen so little that could constitute as experiencing pain or ugly.

"Hey, Lauren!"

I turn toward the kitchen as I manage to get my key free from the lock, and see Kashton along with a woman and another guy, leaning against the kitchen counters. "Hey," I call back. My voice is soft and comes out cracked, causing my cheeks to heat. I pocket my key and head over to where the three of them are facing me.

Kashton smiles in greeting and lifts a hand to the man on his right. He's tall, a few inches taller than me at least, with hair as dark as midnight and two rings that curl around his lower lip, and another in his eyebrow. He's wearing a light gray beanie that brings out the darker shades in his blue eyes, making them resemble the storm clouds outside. "Lauren, this is Parker." His elbow twists and his hand rotates to the woman on his left. Her hair is long and auburn with unnatural shades of red and purple peeking through. Not surprisingly, she's smaller than I am, looking petite and beautiful in a pair of designer jeans and a hoodie. It reminds me of French design, almost messy, yet sophisticated and feminine. Her entire face is set with indecision as her clear green eyes scan over me. "This is Summer. Guys, this is Lauren."

"The kidlet was right. You are pretty hot." Parker's compliment—if you can call it that—only makes me feel more uncomfortable.

Summer takes a few steps closer to me, extending her hand. I take it and swallow my unease. I loathe standing beside small women. I feel like it only accentuates how large I am. Drawing visual comparisons to how much longer my legs are, how much bigger my hands are.

"But jeez, you're tall," Parker comments, confirming my very thoughts.

"Don't be a dick." Kashton looks at me, his lips turned down as though he's embarrassed as well.

"It's nice to meet you guys. Do you know where Mercedes is?" I ask in an attempt to skirt the discomfort.

"Yeah, I think she's in her room, but do you mind if we chat real quick?" My eyes stretch and my pulse quickens as I look to Kashton, and it isn't because my boss resembles a male supermodel.

I'm going to get fired.

Sweat quickly coats my palms, making me feel even more uneasy and self-conscious.

"You guys mind meeting me out in the shop? I'll be out there in a few," Kashton says, turning to acknowledge both Summer and Parker.

"Yeah, take your time. It was nice meeting you, Lauren," Parker says, pushing off from the counter.

"Nice meeting you too." Weaving my fingers together in front of me, I try to meet their eyes as they pass, and then hastily wipe them across my thighs as the front door shuts.

"I just want to touch base and see how things are going. Kenzie assured me that you're responsible and great with kids, so I know Mercedes is in good hands. I'm just used to hearing a few things by this point."

I try to hide my surprise by forcing a smile. I don't know what has me more off kilter, the fact that I don't think he's trying to fire me, or that Kenzie said nice things about me. "That's okay. I totally understand that you're busy, hence my being here." I scratch my eyebrow, wondering what kinds of things previous nannies have shared. "Things are well, though. We're ... working on getting acquainted."

Kashton presses his lips together and edges them up ever so slightly as if he's trying to smile but can't. That twinge of unease in my belly seems to burn brighter. "I hope this doesn't make me sound like an asshole, but whatever you see or hear in this house, or outside in the shop, is confidential. It doesn't leave."

My eyebrows draw downward, knitting with confusion as my mind races, wondering what in the hell he's referring to. Could he be a drug dealer? A money launderer? What's in his shop? "Don't you work on bikes?"

Kashton's eyes grow wide and his lips part for a second and then lift into a genuine smile that makes his brown eyes relax. "She was right. You have no idea."

I turn my head to glance in the direction of the front door. The action is instinctual, as though I need to measure the space to know how fast I need to run.

"I sound like a fucking crazy person. I'm sorry. That's what happens eventually, I guess." Kashton raises a hand and runs it over his short hair, then clasps the back of his neck for a moment before straightening. "I'm not crazy or dangerous, and neither are those guys. We're BMX racers."

"Like BMX bikes?"

Kashton nods, looking slightly sheepish. "Yeah. You'll see other racers around too, and the team. They're all harmless, but we take our privacy seriously, and here at the house, we're not on. We don't worry about the shit we say or what we're doing. We just like to work hard and have a good time."

"That's cool." I swallow, trying to understand what that means exactly when I know absolutely nothing about BMX racing or what that world entails. "And you don't have to worry, I won't say anything."

He smiles, and while it doesn't look like he's reassured yet, it still helps me relax. "Okay, so now that I have one awkward thing out of the way, let's move on to the next." Rubbing his palms together, he settles his gaze on the counter behind me. "Everyone who's ever watched Mercedes has been from an agency. You're the first person that I've ever hired from a reference. Yesterday I realized I don't know much about you. I don't need to run a background check on you, I guess, but I just feel like I should know more. I mean I'm leaving you with my daughter."

It relieves me to hear that Kashton is realizing how informal and fast our relationship has progressed, but it spotlights how out of character this seems for a parent, which makes me wonder if Mercedes is feeling like he doesn't care enough about her.

"My brother, King, usually takes care of all of the business stuff. He's my manager and does all the paperwork and arrangements, but he's over in Switzerland right now for an ad campaign, so I went with Kenzie on this. Don't get me wrong..." his hands span in front of him "...I'm really glad she referred you. You've been great! I'm just not used to this stuff."

"I understand." My words are a lie, but for some ridiculous reason, I suddenly want to protect and comfort Kashton as much as I do Mercedes.

"King will be back soon, and that will help, but yeah ... If you don't mind, just share some things with me. I don't know," he says, running a hand across the back of his neck again and wincing just slightly with the movement. "What do they normally ask on a job application?"

My eyes widen, trying to recall the last one I filled out. "Do you want my address?"

"No, I already know where you live."

My eyebrows knit together and Kashton shakes his head. "I mean, since you live with Kenzie, I know."

I nod a couple of times though that still seems odd since I've never seen him come over. "Do you have my number?"

"Yeah, do you have mine?"

I nod once more. I've never used it, but it's one of the few things Kenzie provided me with.

"What else?" he asks.

"I can give you a list of references, previous jobs, my dad's address."

"That's probably a good idea. Let me grab some paper really fast."

I lean against the counter as he jogs to the door adjacent from the kitchen, one that I haven't ventured to open after Mercedes announced it as the office. While he's gone, I look around the kitchen that has become messier as the weeks have gone by. It was so clean when I got here, leading me to initially believing it wasn't used, but now, I realize it must have been used by previous nannies.

"Okay, um, I found this old application, and here's just some paper." Kashton passes me several sheets that I set on the edge of the counter. "Sorry, I forgot a pen, hang on."

"That's okay, I have one." I dig through my bag, grabbing a handful of long cylinders to see what I've managed to catch, and sift through several pieces of charcoal and a couple of pencils. I drop them back in my bag and fish again, grabbing a new handful that has several colored pencils, another piece of charcoal, and a pen. I hold on to the pen, drop the other items inside, and look up to see Kashton watching me.

"Kenzie said you go to PSU for art."

"Yeah."

"That's cool. Do you practice art? Or are you learning about it?"

"Both." I shift my weight so I can lean against the counter. "I'm studying art history as well as taking several classes with the creation of art and restoration."

"No shit. Maybe I can see some of your work sometime? I keep wanting to have a mural done out in the shop."

I smile because I can tell he's saying this out of obligation, and turn my attention to the papers.

"You don't have to fill them out now. Just get them back to me when you have the chance."

"Alright, I'll get them back to you tomorrow."

"Thanks, I would appreciate it. Sorry to start your shift with this…"

"Don't sweat it. I completely understand."

He smiles and then rubs a hand over the back of his neck once more before he turns to head out the front door.

chapter
SIX

"What are you doing?"

Turning to Charleigh as she comes through the door of my studio apartment, I look over her outfit that is overdressed even for her. "Homework. What are you doing?"

"I thought we were going to that dollar cinema tonight for the three showings?"

I bring a hand to my face with a near silent groan. "Oh, Charleigh, I completely forgot! I'm sorry. Let me change really fast and we can go."

"No problem. If we miss the first movie, I won't mind. It's not really something I care about," she says, coming around to sit on the couch that butts against the end of my bed and extends just into our small kitchen.

"You're drawing him again." Charleigh's words are quiet, as though she only intended to think the words.

I stand from my stool and clear my throat before flipping the cover of my large sketch book closed. "No, these are old, actually. I was just working on some shading techniques with colors. You know, since I usually stick to black and white." My answer is only a partial truth. I truly found the unfinished sketch when I was looking for something to motivate me. You often hear about writer's block in the art world. What you don't hear about very often is that artists who sculpt, paint, draw, and create, also face these same empty stretches where nothing holds our attention, or seems adequate nor inspiring. I've been facing this stretch of black for several weeks—since I met *him* at that party in July. Today I saw an old sketch of his eyes, the shadow of his brow, and the slight bridge in his nose, and all I could see was him as I put my charcoal to the paper. It was his hands that I was working on when Charleigh arrived. I am amazed at the details I can remember about him when I can't remember something as important as his name. Nonetheless, some of these details seem more significant. I can recall the line of his jaw, the way his hands were stained from working outdoors, his lips that curved into an uneven smile, and the scar that carved a long path up his forearm. Yet even those details pale in comparison to what I can remember about how he made me feel. I have stored to memory his warm breaths against my cheeks and the solidity of his muscles as he flexed while inside of me, and the exquisite way he seemed to know exactly what I wanted and needed without me ever giving direction.

A heat that has been less familiar as of late with me trying to forget about him makes my body tingle and my face flush as I face my closet and pull out a clean shirt to exchange the old sweatshirt I threw on when I got home. Artists have two wardrobes: the one we wear to work in, and the rest of our clothes. It doesn't matter how careful I am while I work; charcoal dust always gets on me, and paint is worse. I hate having to worry about it. That's why I always change while I'm working and bring extra clothes to change into before I leave school to watch Mercedes.

"We could bring it up to Kenzie again? Maybe she'll think of someone new to ask."

"I'm not asking her again. We've been down that road several times. Do you know how embarrassing it is to ask for the name of the guy I slept with at a party? Not only that, but now I sound like I am completely hung up on him because it's been over three months! There's no way, Charleigh. I'm over it. I was just sketching. It's no big deal."

"Maybe—"

"Charleigh, no. Don't make me sing. You know I will."

"You're going to do that anyway."

"And you love it."

"No I don't, because you don't actually sing the words. You just say them. And I now have this awful habit of turning other people's words into songs. It's terrible!"

A small laugh has Charleigh standing with her arm raised, ready to strike at me. "It's not funny! Stop laughing!"

"I'm teaching you American music."

"We have American music in England."

"American culture, then."

"That isn't American culture, it's Lauren culture," Charleigh objects as she follows me to the door.

"Same difference."

"No, you're crazy."

I open my mouth to say words that will turn her words into another song.

"Lauren!" Charleigh groans, following me down the stairs. "Stop, or I will ask Kenzie."

I stop and turn to flash her a smile before I start humming the tune.

"Come on."

"What?" Mercedes asks, looking up from the pile of toys she's been making a valiant effort to shrink.

I stand up from where I've been sorting small bolts and screws from across the living room into buckets that I found out in the garage, and look at Mercedes. Over the past week we've barely spoken, but she's slowly become less and less despondent about the idea of cleaning and has started to join in my efforts. By Halloween we might be able to see the floor. "I think we need a break today."

"What does that mean?"

"Let's go somewhere. Get some fresh air before it's too cold to go outside."

"It's raining."

"You won't melt."

Mercedes doesn't bother with a retaliation; she simply rolls her eyes upward and stares at me through her lashes. "Fine, but we're staying inside."

"Come on, I'll take you to the donut shop my friend works at. You'll fall in love."

"Donuts?" I notice the glint in her eye and the softening of her jaw as she repeats the word.

"Grab your coat."

"I don't understand how you don't have a car." Mercedes' tone is back to being annoyed as we trudge down the long drive.

"I live in the city. There's not much use for one."

"But what do you do when you go grocery shopping?"

I glance over at her and watch her dodge a large puddle that has become a constant on the road. "I bring a few bags with me."

Her eyes meet mine as we continue. "Are you poor?"

A small smile rounds my lips. "I'm twenty-two. Of course I'm poor."

"So you can't afford a car?"

"I probably *could* afford a car, but with the additional costs that come with it and parking it downtown, I'd rather spend my money on things I need and enjoy."

"How poor are you?" I meet her eyes once again and see worry cross her small features. "It's okay that I ask, right? I mean … I'm not saying anything bad, am I?"

I shake my head and shove my hands into the pocket of my sweatshirt as I smile at her with assurance. "I don't mind, but some people probably wouldn't appreciate the question." I kick a small rock with the toe of my shoe and watch as it sails a few feet in front of us and rolls to the side of the road. "My dad owns a cattle ranch, so money has always been kind of tight. Farming has changed a lot over the years."

"What do you mean?"

"There's a lot of competition now. People like my dad who own their own farms are being forced to lower their prices because there are so many commercially owned farms now. It makes things really hard for the smaller guys."

"Do you want to own a farm someday?"

I shake my head and turn my face skyward, allowing a few cold drops to splash across my cheeks and forehead. "No I don't."

"What do you want to be?"

My hand slides up to readjust the hood of my sweatshirt and then falls back into my pocket as Mercedes and I skirt around another large puddle. "I want to do something with art. That's what I'm going to school for."

"What kind of art?"

"Ideally"—I look over to Mercedes, catching the way her attention is rapt for the first time, truly interested in my words—"I would like to become an independent artist and sell my work to galleries."

"Is that hard to do?"

My eyebrows rise and my chin tilts as her question brings forth memories of my dad and the countless times I've heard him tell me that art is a hobby, not a career.

"It's difficult to break into the circle."

"So what are you going to do if you fail?"

The word fail has the temperature of the air lowering as it coats my throat. "I guess we'll see." I don't chance looking over at her when she doesn't respond. Regardless of her expression, I am pretty certain I don't want to see it.

"Our bus will be here in just a few minutes," I say, tracing the time schedule on the wall of the small enclosure.

"So you ride this every day?"

"Yup."

Mercedes keeps her hands shoved in her pockets and her face down as we wait along with a couple of guys who look to be in high school and whom I dutifully ignore, positioning my body between them and her.

"They were checking you out," Mercedes hisses as we find a couple of empty seats across from each other on the warm bus.

"They were just talking."

"They were checking you out."

I pull off my hood and tighten my ponytail, ignoring her comment as the bus moves forward. She doesn't mind. She moves her attention to the other passengers, sometimes staring too long at a person, bringing their attention to her. When this happens, she doesn't look away. She keeps their gaze, and I watch as each person who meets her stare, smiles. It's as though the gesture is inescapable. Today Mercedes' long hair is once again winding down her back, dark as coal. Her skin is becoming a lighter shade of olive as we spend more and more time inside with the rain becoming a constant. It's her eyes though that catch everyone off guard, with the clarity and rare color that is such a stark contrast against her dark complexion.

"You're staring again. It's weird." I blink a few times to stop focusing on details and take in her expression. When I attended my first art class that Nell signed me up for when I was ten, the teacher came over to me. Her hair was wiry and gray, falling to the small of her back, and she always smelled of coffee and stale cigarette smoke. Her voice was gravelly and her eyes were coated with too many shades of blue eye shadow, but there was something I innately liked about her, and when she leaned beside me and said, *"You have the attentiveness of a true artist. I can see it in the way you watch people,"* I felt like she understood me.

"I want to go to the mall first," Mercedes says, looking out the bus window.

"What do you want at the mall?"

She shrugs and turns to look back to me. "Whatever I want. I'm not poor."

Her comment is delivered as an insult, but it doesn't make me blink. Not having money isn't something that I'm ashamed of. It doesn't define me. However, the fact that she obviously believes that this creates a division between her and others bothers me for several reasons.

We get off at Pike's Place Square and follow a train of people to her desired destination, my thoughts stuck on wondering how she has become so jaded.

We wander through several stores in the mall, Mercedes pulling farther and farther away from me with each new store that she rummages through.

I'm staring at a large photograph on the wall of kids wearing nicer and more adult-looking clothes than I own, and notice Mercedes shrink behind a clothing rack. I peer around the store, looking to see what could lead to a reaction like this, and notice a couple of girls around Mercedes' age coming toward us.

I look back to Mercedes and find her eyes fixed on me with a scowl that has me taking two steps back and raising my hands in surrender. I've never been the quote unquote cool kid, but I was never seen as a social leper before either. Babysitting is not only honing my cleaning skills, but it's also thickening my skin and teaching me how to brush off being looked at as a loser from a ten-year-old.

"Is there something I can help you find?" an employee asks from my other side. She's around my age, and like so many here in Portland, her outfit screams fashion.

"Thanks, but I'm okay. I'm just waiting on…" I whirl around, searching the entire store, coming across the girls who entered, but not finding Mercedes. "Oh, God."

I dash out of the store and whip around, looking in each direction for her dark hair. "Mercedes!" I yell, catching sight of her on the escalators across from me. She doesn't look up, keeping her attention focused on squeezing past a man in front of her.

"What the hell?" My nearly silent question is meant for both of us as I race toward the escalator and mutter apologies as I step around people, working to not trip and watch where she's heading.

"Mercedes!" I yell again as she sprints toward the exit doors of the mall. She doesn't stop. She doesn't even slow down.

The air is cool and wet as it's carried against my skin by a strong gust of wind that has my eyes instinctively closing. I shield my face with a hand and look each direction before I spot her.

"Mercedes!" My steps increase of their own accord because I'm too frustrated to think clearly. "Mercedes!" I yell again, louder this time.

She stops and her head turns ever so slightly, making her dark hair shift.

Then she runs full out.

"You've got to be kidding me," I mutter, shaking my head. "I'm not chasing you!" I'm not sure if she can even hear my words over the wind, rain, and traffic. She certainly doesn't slow down to indicate she does. A heavy sigh empties my lungs before I grit my teeth together, considering a thousand ways to repay Kenzie for this job opportunity. Then, I run after Mercedes' small silhouette.

My long strides cover more distance, but she's fast and too young to be suffering a side ache after running down the escalator, outside, and a brief sprint. The idea of yelling her name again to see if she'll stop crosses my mind, but I can't waste my breath on calling out to her and keep running, so I gulp more cold air and feel a burning sensation along my shins.

Mercedes runs along the sidewalk, oblivious to the leaves swirling and rain pelting us from what seems like every angle. The rainfall here in Portland is like nothing else. The drops are the size of quarters and are so dense it takes mere seconds for your clothes to become sodden. Even my Toms have been penetrated.

The cars beside us begin moving with a wave of exhaust as they pass through the green light, and Mercedes follows with their movement, crossing the intersection without hesitation. A thick chunk of my wet hair wraps around my throat as I continue the race, making me feel nearly strangled by the combination of it and my obvious lack of conditioning.

A truck unloading a crate of boxes slows Mercedes' steps down and brings her head to jerk in each direction twice before I catch up to her and pull her thin jacket tightly in my fist. Her head falls, her long hair protecting her like a shield as we move forward at a slower pace. My lungs are burning, working so hard to try to hold air that I can't speak. It's probably for the better—nothing running through my mind is appropriate for her ears.

My heartbeat is pumping in my ears; it along with my heavy breaths drowns out the sound of the traffic that's becoming more congested with the late hour, and the slap of our footsteps on the wet sidewalk, until a sniffling sound mutes everything. I turn to get a better angle of her face, but her head is still down. My fingers begin to loosen with guilt, and my mind begins to wonder how to sound caring and authoritative at the same time.

"You can't do that. You can't run around downtown Portland, trying to get away from me. If you don't want me to be your nanny or whatever, just talk to your dad. Getting hit by a car isn't the right way to resolve this."

"It has nothing to do with you." Mercedes' tone is verging on angry, but the vulnerable side of her has won, making her words quiet and hitched.

"What happened?"

"What do you think happened?" Her seafoam-green eyes are rimmed with red as she flips her face toward me, and I shake my head, clueless and caught so off guard by how hard she's working to conceal her pain that it squeezes that maternal need building inside of me once more. "They hate me. They *all hate me.*"

"The girls at the store?" I think back as I pose the question, seeing the way Mercedes had recoiled. I thought it was directed toward me but realize I had absolutely nothing to do with her reaction. "What happened?"

"They call me a boy. They tell me I'm gay because I ride bikes. And say I have two dads."

My steps stop and my hand moves from her jacket to her wrist. I'm over a foot taller than Mercedes, and the thought of kneeling on the wet cement crosses my mind before I realize she will likely find the gesture demeaning. Instead, I shake my head again and rake a hand across my forehead until I feel a familiar purse of skin from a long-forgotten scar. "That's bullshit, Mercedes. Complete and total bullshit." My hand smooths the hairs that fell while I was running, and I look across the street, focusing on a trail of leaves blowing. "I don't know why the terrible things said to us are what we hear while we try to sleep, or what feed us when we're struggling and starved for encouragement. I guess it's because as much as we don't want to care what others think, we do." My eyes move back to her face and catch her gaze for a second before she drops it to my feet. "They're trying to get a rise out of you because that's how they feed their ugliness and insecurities. They're likely so afraid to be the next target, and their victims are too concerned with wondering if the attacks hold any truth that no one sees that the person behind the hurtful words is the one with the problems."

Her eyes look away from me. Either she has been told something similar, or she isn't ready to believe my words.

"If you're gay, that's no one's business but your own."

"I'm not gay."

"I'm not saying you are. I'm just saying that your sexual preferences are yours. God, what am I saying? You're ten. You shouldn't have sexual preferences." Mercedes' chin drops to the side, and she shoots a leveling look to me. "If riding bikes is something that you love, then you can't let them ruin it for you. Being different doesn't make you a freak; it makes you brave. And that bullshit about two dads? I don't even know where to start on that one." A chill shoots down my spine as I catch several drops of rain in the face from looking up, and I shrug before facing her again. "It doesn't matter if a person is purple, green, male, female, gay, or straight. All that matters is that they love you, protect you, and care for you. Hell, even with your brooding attitude and death glares, I've started to fall in love with you and feel these really weird surges of motherhood that scare the shit out of me because I don't want to have kids. Obviously you have something great in you for that to occur."

I feel like I'm modeling in front of a class of artists again with the way she's reading each of my features.

"Are you ready to go home?" I ask.

"Yeah." Her reply nearly gets lost in the sounds of the city, her voice is so quiet.

"Let's go. We'll order a pizza on the bus."

The two of us turn, my hand still firmly gripping her shoulder, now less because of my fear that she'll run and more because I want to comfort her.

"Hey, Lo?"

I'm sure my surprise at her calling me Lo is written across my face as a small smile turns her lips up. "I only like cheese on my pizza."

"I'm good with that."

Her smile widens, and I know I'll be sketching this expression in the near future. It's frame worthy.

chapter
SEVEN

I pull the third load of laundry for the day—a heap of white shirts—from the washer and shove them into the dryer. My hands freeze. I think all of me has. A familiar scent is tickling all of my senses, causing my thoughts to race in a void of blankness. I reach for the same pile of shirts and bring them to my nose. The clean, crisp scent of the laundry detergent is prevalent, but there's also the faint trace of men's cologne, or body wash—something male. I take another deep breath before dropping them back into the dryer. Maybe it's the same laundry detergent my mom uses? Or the cologne from someone I know? Or maybe it's simply the act of doing laundry that's making a piece of my mind think of home, but something has me feeling weak and dazed with nostalgia.

"Lo, you know you don't have to keep cleaning, right?"

I turn to acknowledge Kash. I've started calling him the nickname that the others all use in the last week, though it sometimes still rolls off my tongue a little strangely. My cheeks heat as my nails run along my forehead. "Yeah, I know." I don't see much of him, and when I do, Summer and Parker are usually close behind. The way Summer watches him, tracking his movements and always being a step ahead of what he seems to ask or think of, makes me fairly confident she has feelings for him, but Kash is difficult to figure out. He is flirty and kind to her, but he is with me as well. I think it's just his personality to be that way.

He smiles and takes a step back so I can exit the laundry room.

"How's it going? Are things working out with your professor now that you're attending your Wednesday class?" Kash tilts his head with a slight mock lighting his eyes. I finally had to approach him and discuss coming later on Wednesdays so I could attend my Comparative Art History class after being reminded by a friend that attendance alone is thirty-five percent of my grade.

"Yeah, thanks." My professor is still intentionally calling on me more than any of the other students to prove his point, but thankfully, I'm catching up.

"How have things been going here?"

"Good. Mercedes is in her room finishing homework, so I thought I would put in a load really quick," I say as we head back upstairs.

"Homework? I didn't hear any complaining."

"Yeah, I bribed her with ice cream."

Kash laughs, following me into the kitchen where he leans both elbows on the granite counter covering the bar. "So, I saw on your paperwork that you're from Montana."

Appreciative of the change in topic, I nod. He can't be oblivious to the fact that he's a slob, and I sort of fear that my efforts are being seen as intrusive, but thus far, he hasn't spoken to me about it until now. "Yeah. Have you been over there?"

"I went to Yellowstone once, as a kid."

"That's usually what people go for."

Kash returns the smile I'm giving him to show my statement, though true, is intended to be lighthearted. "What do you think of Portland?"

"I love it. I love the people and the buzz around the city. I love the peaceful tranquility you find outside, and the food and music. I even love the rain."

His head shakes as he quietly laughs. "Nobody loves the rain."

"There's something beautiful about it here. It's intense. Almost cleansing."

"Yeah, until you nearly drown in a puddle or get pulled down a river running down Highway 26."

My cheeks lift so high my vision is slightly obscured as I nod my head in agreement. "I do sometimes feel like I need a raft. But there's something special about this place. It just feels different."

"Is it all of the weirdos?"

My cheeks are still stretched as I shake my head. "No. I have learned in my three years of being an unofficial Oregonian to recognize the transplants. There's authentic weird, and then there's trying to be weird."

There's a quiet rumble of laughter from Kashton as he leans farther against the counter. "You don't seem to try to pose as weird. Are you sticking to your clean-air, backwoods Montana image?"

"Backwoods?" My eyebrows rise and my chin drops, making Kash's laughter increase. "I am the definition of weird! I go to school for art."

"I ride a bike for a living," he counters.

"I know, but that's cool. You do tricks, and jump, and..." my hands lift in the air to reflect movement, "...you do all that crazy stuff."

"You have no idea what I do, do you?"

I shake my head and fight my lips from turning upward. "No, I really don't."

"I'll show you. Next week I get to be in the editing process of some videos and images that are going with this Swiss campaign. You can come check it out. Give me your expert art advice."

"I would love to, but I know nothing about film or photography. That's a whole other world. Kind of like cooking."

He laughs again and then resituates his baseball hat as I see a thought cross his features. "I want to see some of your artwork. Kenzie says you're pretty good."

I try to mask my surprise by shrugging.

"Oh, so you're one of *those* people."

"One of what people?"

Kash shakes his head, curving his lips into a smile. "I'm not sure," he admits with a chuckle. "Your reaction didn't give me much. I was hoping you would either admit that you're really good or play it off and act like you suck." His eyes narrow slightly and then his index finger taps his temple. "I'll get you figured out soon enough. First, I need to see some of your work. Show me something."

"I don't have anything with me." I don't. My portfolio rarely travels with me.

"Bullshit. Open your bag and show me something."

"You think I'm bluffing?"

"No. I think you're ignoring the fact that I know what it's like to have a hobby that you love. You live it. You breathe it. A piece of it goes everywhere with you."

I nod a couple of times in silent understanding and then move to get my bag beside the kitchen table. Kash follows me, keeping a respectable gap between us, allowing me to choose what I want to reveal. I used to have a hard time showing people my work. There's something very personal about it. I'm not showing you a scene or a person; I'm showing you how *I see* a scene or a person. In the last two years, that discomfort has ebbed as I've been trying to circulate my portfolio in an attempt to get my name out into some different circles. For some reason, showing Kash my work is comfortable, almost easy.

His lips curl into a knowing smile as I lift a sketchpad from my bag and hold it out to him. Without hesitation, he takes the book, holding it as though he understands and respects the countless hours that have been poured onto the pages.

"Holy shit." His voice is barely audible as he stares at a sheet.

My curiosity is piqued. I move to look over his shoulder and see a drawing of Mercedes. Her hair is down, wrapped around her in curling vines, and her eyes are bright with a happiness that I've only recently been subjected to. Her mouth, however, is straight, reflecting little emotion as it does too often.

"You're an artist." His words are filled with admiration and a sincerity that makes me suddenly feel nervous. "This is insane!" He stares at several of the pages without a word, just silently inspecting each of them with a level of respect that makes me feel proud.

"These are really cool. Whose hands are these? Your boyfriends'?"

That damn flush returns to my cheeks and I shake my head. He can tell they're intimate even though there is nothing sexual on the page. "No. Nothing like that." I know what page he's looking at by catching sight of a heavily shaded corner. I had drawn a series of pictures with hands from all different angles. Every perspective I can still picture them being from that night: balancing a bottle, resting on his thigh, holding my hand, running along my sides. I have worked to block the memory of him but still find myself mindlessly sketching parts of him.

"These are amazing, Lauren. Truly amazing."

"Lo."

Kash and I both turn toward the hallway where Mercedes is standing.

"What?" he asks.

"Her name's Lo, Dad."

He smiles and nods. "Did you know Lo is a flipping artist?"

"They look like pictures taken from a camera, don't they?"

"Yes! It's crazy!"

Kash's form of artistry is a different realm altogether from my own, but his compliment feels nearly equal to hearing an accolade from Douglas McDougall or Anselm Kiefer.

chapter
EIGHT

"Hey, Lo. Are you ready?"

I turn my head to look over my right shoulder and widen my eyes in question. "Ready for what?"

"The shop is finally ready!" There's a giddiness in her eyes and voice that I haven't heard before, and it makes my heart swell, but it's the smile on her face that makes it feel like it may burst.

"Show me!" I don't even consider what we're going to do. I mindlessly follow her out into a light and steady late October drizzle. We pass the yard and continue on a well-worn dirt path to the large shop that can be seen from the house.

"Are you ready?"

"Want a drum roll?" Mercedes rolls her eyes with my dry tone, making me break into a smile. "Show me this world you love."

A smile creeps back across her lips as she turns and pulls the door open. My nose wrinkles with the assault of fumes as we step inside, but I don't focus on it. I can't. My eyes are trying to ingest all of the gray tones of cement and the wide path running around the parameter. There are long rails along a set of stairs, a large pit of foam, and two wide ramps that curve up in giant cement C's, all surrounded by bright white walls.

"This place is huge." My voice is an echo, getting lost in the vastness.

"Isn't it awesome?"

"Hey!" Mercedes and I turn and find Kash and Summer in the doorway. Kash is looking to Mercedes, obviously seeking approval. "What do you think? Pretty legit, right?"

"It's blowing my mind." Kash's smile grows with Mercedes' approval.

"Are you ready to break this baby in?" he asks, clasping his hands together.

"What about King?"

"He sent me a picture of the Alps yesterday. I think it's a pretty even trade. Parker will be here in five."

"Come on, Lo, let's pick a bike for you." Mercedes takes my hand, and I truly consider following her before I stop.

"Yeah, I think I'll break in the bleacher seat," I say, nodding to a long bench against the wall.

"What? No! You have to come ride with us," she objects.

"I haven't been on a bike in like ten years. I don't think my outer layer of skin is going to look very pretty on these new floors."

"Everyone can ride a bike." Her head falls to the side, daring me to disagree.

"Not well," I assure her.

"Come on, Mercedes. She doesn't want to, she doesn't have to," Summer objects. The fact that her eyes won't settle on me makes me realize her sentiment is lacking something basic. Her outfit is simple and easy: a pair of skinny jeans and a graphic T-shirt. Somehow, the way she manages to wear them makes me feel uncomfortable and underdressed in comparison, though my mint green pants and floral blouse were even marveled by Allie yesterday when I set them out. I could likely wear one of the beautiful dresses that Allie and Charleigh create and still feel inadequate. Summer has a presence I can't begin to compete with, let alone relate to.

"Yeah, remember? You never push someone's comfort zone on a bike. It makes Uncle King pissy as all hell to do all the paperwork that goes with broken bones." Kash looks from Mercedes to me and winks, leaving me to wonder if he's serious. "We can help get her comfortable with riding again by showing her how fun it is." His eyes are bright, and his smile has become wide and inviting. "I bet she'll want to join us soon!" He grabs a bike leaning against the wall and swings his leg over the seat. It looks too small under him, like it's made for a child. He grips the handlebars and pulls up, making the bike bounce on the back tire as he twists his body to turn it. The movement is clearly practiced. It's smooth and looks so simple, my brain tricks myself into thinking I've done the same maneuver myself in the past. Like I can feel the jars from the pavement as the front tire hits the cement again. Then he twists the bike below him, and suddenly, my eyes can't move fast enough.

Kash moves with a grace and elegance that doesn't seem possible. It leaves me mesmerized, watching as he glides through the air, turning and twisting, leaving me with an envy and appreciation I didn't know I would possess for the sport.

Parker walks in shortly after, joining Summer and Kash in perfecting moves that seem impossible. Mercedes rides for a while and then returns her bike and sits beside me, naming moves and spins, and telling stories about the group and her own experiences. This isn't the first time I get lost in her words and completely forget that she's only ten. The fact that she hasn't been treated like a child—given the ability to pretend that the world holds only hope and potential—saddens me and broadens that maternal instinct I feel toward her.

"Dude, you aren't watching! You're going to miss it!" Mercedes cries, plunging a hand forward to redirect my attention to the ramps. I oblige and within seconds feel her head resting against my shoulder.

It feels like the biggest accomplishment I've yet achieved.

"What are you doing?" I ask.

"Freaking out!"

I watch Allie pace her and Charleigh's loft. Her neck is stretched forward and her shoulders are hunched as her eyes intently move around the crowded tables and fabric-covered floors. "What are you looking for?"

"The fabric I picked up last weekend!" Her eyes swing toward me with a look of anguish that makes my eyebrows rise. "Sorry." Her apology is clipped, removing any trace of sincerity, but I accept it and move to the kitchen where I take a seat on a stool so as to be out of the way. It's moments like these that I really resent Kenzie and her male visitors.

"Remember telling me I have a long torso, so empire waists look..." She shakes her head. "I don't know what you said, but you said to wear an empire waist dress."

I track her as she rifles through her shared closet. Her hands are quick and aggressive but gentle as they shove the materials around.

"Yeah..."

"You know that silk we picked up last weekend when we were in Seattle that matched the cotton voile so well? It had the really big print with coral and black and gray? The cotton had the coral and gray with darker undertones."

I saw so many fabrics at the store last weekend, I feel as though I can picture nearly any possible pattern. I have always loved clothes, and while some of the patterns were both thrilling and inspiring, others were completely overwhelming. The passion for design that Charleigh and Allie share makes my love for the arts expand into new regions. Since meeting them, my closet has grown and small accessories have been added. They both enjoy talking to me about sizes, patterns, colors, and shapes—things all artists like to brainstorm about. Allie feels that my knowledge and experience with drawing so many people and figures helps me see patterns better. I'm still not sure she's right, but I've enjoyed working through some designs and the creation of some of her work. I nod absently and her eyes harden, recognizing it as a lie.

"How could you forget that fabric? It was gorgeous!"

"Do you know where Charleigh is? I tried calling and she didn't answer," I ask, deflecting her question.

"She was staying late to cut out some patterns."

I nod a couple of times and slide from my stool. "Alright, well I'll see you later."

"Sorry, sorry!" Allie turns toward me, her hands on her head. "I'm just so stressed out about the show now that themes have been announced, and I really want to make a dress to wear to the show that doesn't cover any of them to hopefully showcase another design." Her hands drop, followed by a loud sigh. "I think I need Drew Barrymore. Let's order Chinese and watch Ever After."

"You and Charleigh and food. It's like your comfort."

"Food is comforting to most people. It provides memories and a good reason to sit down and talk, or not talk and just fill yourself with yummy goodness. It's like whenever I'm feeling homesick, I always make English muffin pizzas. It's not because they're my favorite food or the best thing my mom made, but whenever my dad worked late, she and I would make them together." Allie shrugs and takes a seat on the couch. "Didn't you guys have food traditions?"

This time it's my turn to shrug as I think back. "Not really."

"Sunday dinners? Weekend breakfasts? After school snacks?"

"Not that I can remember."

"Alright, well, new tradition: Chinese food is now the comfort food to cure long days and stress."

"Deal," I say, sitting beside her as she scrolls through the menu on her phone before calling in our order.

"How are things going with the new job? You seem happier lately."

"I am. Things are improving. And that house was such a mess, and it's finally starting to come together."

"I can't believe you're still cleaning! It's been a month!"

"I know, but when you discover the sink isn't really taupe—it's white—it takes a while."

Allie's nose wrinkles. "That's disgusting."

I nod. "And slow moving."

"What's slow moving?" Charleigh's voice rings out.

"We're just discussing how Lo became a maid."

"I'm not a maid."

"It sounds like they're allowing you to be," Allie says, flipping on the TV.

"It's kind of weird, Lauren. It's not like your room is super tidy." Charleigh steps over my feet and sits beside Allie. The two of them have a special rhythm, a bond. Though they've become my best friends, I know they are best friends with each other, and I am their close friend. I try to not resent this because I don't want them to be upset, or worse, feel guilty for being so close. The two share a love for fashion, reality TV, expensive fabrics, and similar childhoods. I'm an artist, so I can join in many of their conversations, enjoying most of them, but our focuses are often as different as night and day.

"We ordered Chinese," Allie explains.

"Did you get it from Panda Box?"

"Yes," Allie answers, flipping off the movie and pulling up their DVR. "And I got you the beef and broccoli and sugar snap pea chicken, the two dishes that are as close to a hamburger as possible."

"Thanks, love. Lauren, how are you? You look happier today."

"That's what I said," Allie cries enthusiastically, sensing their shared bond.

"I am. I'm really starting to enjoy working with Mercedes, and school is falling into a comfortable rhythm, finally. Things are going in a good direction."

"Maybe you should ask Kashton out." Allie's words catch me so off guard it takes me a second to shake my head.

"No way. He's my boss!"

"So what?"

"Allie's right. You do seem to get along with him well," Charleigh adds.

"We do because we're *friends*. Besides, I'm pretty sure he and another woman he works with have a thing. That's really beside the point though, because as much as I like Kash, I don't have feelings like *that* for him." I don't. Sometimes I think I do, but each time I close my eyes and try picturing myself kissing him, nothing about it feels right.

"Because you're still stuck on Mr. Stars." My lips turn down in a frown as I look to Charleigh. "Sorry, I'm sorry. I know you say you're over him, and I know it's been months. I just still think it's possible."

"It's not," I say firmly.

"I heard there's a party this weekend out by the Gorge. What do you think? We could go and see if he shows up?" Allie is reading the synopsis of a show, missing my scowl at her suggestion.

"You guys aren't listening. I. Am. Over. Him. Nothing was even there to begin with!"

"Then why aren't you dating anyone?" Allie turns her blue eyes on me with a leveling intensity.

"I don't have the time to date!" My voice is exasperated, filled with annoyance for having to defend myself yet again about him.

"You don't have to get worked up. It's okay that you aren't dating. But it's also okay if you still have feelings for that guy, too. Look at Romeo and Juliet; they fell madly in love within a few days and then were ready to die just so they could be together."

"That's fiction!" I object. "The real world isn't like that. You don't fall in love with someone in just a couple of hours. That's called infatuation, lust, a crush. I had a crush on a hot guy that I had a good time with. I did not fall in love with him."

"My nan married my granddad after knowing him for only three days. It's not all fiction," Charleigh says, shaking her head.

The doorbell rings, and I have never been so appreciative of a distraction because as much as I don't want to, I want to believe she's right.

We settle in, Allie turning on Ever After like she had initially planned, while Charleigh carefully begins dissecting her food, ensuring there aren't any chili peppers.

"By the way, I think I remember his name."

"Whose name?" Allie asks as she impatiently hits the button to skip previews repeatedly.

"Mr. Stars?" Charleigh asks, her fork stopping and eyes widening with hope.

I nod slowly. "Yeah, I think it was Bentley, but I asked Kenzie, and she said she doesn't know a Bentley, so I'm still not positive I'm right."

"Bentley." Charleigh repeats the name and then says it several more times. "I like Bentley. Bentley and Lauren, that's cute."

"Don't make me regret telling you."

chapter

NINE

"We should try riding in the shop tomorrow." Mercedes' voice is filled with a hope that I hate being the one to break, but getting back on a bike has held little interest for me. Rather than feeling braver or more eager about the prospect, the mere idea makes my heart thrum and my palms grow sweaty. I had relented to the idea and rode around the backyard which is a mostly level expanse of wet leaves.

"I like watching you ride. Besides, I have to keep my arms out of casts since my job and education both rely on them."

"You can't scare yourself. You did so well!"

"I'm not scaring me. The giant cement pool does that."

Mercedes shakes her head, rolling her eyes. I know she's about to let the control freak in her spout attitude, because she's balled her small fists and stamped them on either hip. "You're being ridiculous. If you quit everything because it's scary, how far would you ever get in this world?" Her green eyes are wide, waiting for my reply.

"When did you start listening to anything an adult says?" I tease. "I have to get going. I have a scene I have to finish that I'm dreading. We can argue about this tomorrow."

Her scowl falls as the front door opens and a loud *hello* is called.

"Uncle King!" Mercedes sprints down the hall, her sock-covered feet sliding along the wood floors, nearly making her lose her balance, which elicits giggles, and rather than slow down she speeds up.

"Easy, monkey. No breaking bones on my watch. Remember?" His voice is deep and warm, with a slight trace of gravel, much like Mercedes'.

My heartbeat is still accelerated from watching her Evel Knievel sprint down the hallway as I watch her wrap around his waist, her head tilting back as she laughs. He's tall—taller than Kash—and wearing skater shoes, a pair of black and gray plaid shorts, and a black hoodie, along with a black baseball hat that's shadowing his face as he looks down at his niece.

"Are you hungry?" he asks. His voice paints an image of burlap in my mind with the soft roughness.

"Yeah, Lo doesn't know how to cook," Mercedes says.

"Lo?"

"My new nanny," she explains, sounding burdened by the question. "Come on, catch up."

"Oh, that's right. I forg—"

My eyes climb at the break in his words and find the same dark brown eyes I've been seeing everywhere over the past three months, staring at me. My heart wasn't racing solely because of Mercedes' daredevil race—it recognized his voice before my conscious mind did.

"King, can we order pizza?"

King?

"Yeah, yeah. Um, why don't you go pick a movie and I'll order."

"I don't want any toes on my pizza."

"No olives, got it," he says impatiently, his eyes still focused on me.

"And no mushrooms, or onions, or anything besides—"

"Cheese, yeah, I know."

"Last time you tried to sneak pineapple. None of that this time."

His head shakes and finally turns to look at her. "Cheese on top of cheese, nothing else."

"I want sauce, duh!"

"Watch the attitude. Go pick a movie."

"Maybe my uncle King can teach you to cook. He's really good," Mercedes explains, turning to face me again.

"Mercedes, get your butt in the game room and pick a movie."

"What's your problem?" Her scowl has returned, but rather than firing off a reply, she shuffles down the hall.

"Lo?" I can feel his eyes inspecting me, bringing my arms to cross over my chest.

"I thought your name was Bentley?"

"It's my middle name, but ... What are you doing here?"

My eyes widen. It seems that my reason for being here is fairly obvious, yet the explanation seems lost on me as well for a moment.

"I mean, I know why, but ... how? How did you find me?"

"Find you?"

"You never called. I thought..."

I don't know that I've ever been this embarrassed. The brown eyes that haunt me in my sleep are wide, making his hat rise slightly so I can see more of his face without shadows from the bill. He looks terrified to see me. Not only does he look afraid, but there's something else. When you draw people, you study them and learn there are certain expressions that are nearly unanimous. Humiliation has my eyes darting from his before I can grasp what other emotions are mingled with his surprise.

"King!" Kash nearly hits King with the front door as he steps inside, dressed in a similar non-cold-weather outfit. "What's up, dude? I didn't know you were getting home tonight!"

My neck snaps and my eyes stretch, replaying the word home.

"Did you meet Lo?"

"Yeah, we just met," I reply instantly, keeping my attention on Kash. "I have to go, but I'll see you tomorrow. Nice meeting you, King."

I grab my coat and bag from beside the door and barely notice the confusion on Kash's face as I clear the deck to create some space.

"Hey! Wait!"

I feel entirely too warm as my steps slow down, and turn to see King clearing the bottom two steps with a practiced leap. Still, I yank on my coat because of course it's raining again, and I know I will be freezing on the bus ride to my apartment if I'm soaking.

"That came out wrong. I'm sorry. I didn't mean I thought you had stalked me exactly…" His voice is wary, tinged with confusion.

"Exactly?"

"Well, it's just weird that I come home and you're babysitting my niece."

"That's funny because I was just thinking how weird it is that you told me your name was Bentley."

His gaze moves to the side of me, weighing my words, and I realize I still haven't objected to the fact that I've somehow stalked him.

"I didn't know you lived here." I blurt the words louder and more forcefully than the others, making his eyes return to mine. "I barely remember you. Whatever happened happened, but I wasn't looking for you. When someone told me about a babysitting job, the last thing I questioned was if I would see you here. That was what? Like three months ago? I didn't plan to ever see you again."

His eyes narrow, reflecting a similar expression to the one I so often received from Mercedes that is finally becoming a shadow to the smiles she generally greets me with. "Good. I just wanted to make sure things were clear between us."

"Crystal."

"Perfect."

My lips press together and I nod. "Great."

"Wonderful."

"Terrific."

"This is amazing." He shakes his head as he dips it low enough that his eyes disappear under the bill of his hat.

My eyebrows cinch with confusion that quickly relents to awkwardness for standing here, watching him shake his head after accusing me of stalking him. I shake my head and without looking back to him, head down the long driveway that's starting to darken with shadows.

The soft echo of his feet crunching on the gravel meets my ears over my own footsteps. His are louder, and I know part of that is because he's taking wider steps.

They stop long before my trip to the bus station does.

"I have wine and donuts." Charleigh pushes the door open with her foot and lifts two bags in the air to show me her treasures.

"Wine first. I want my stomach empty."

Charleigh cracks a smile and deposits the bags on the counter before making her way over to where I'm slouched at my easel.

"I thought things were getting better with Mercedes."

"They are."

"Then why are you in such a foul mood?"

Usually the sound of Charleigh's accent pulls my lips into a smile. Her sense of humor carries a warmth that I've become reliant on. But as she approaches me, all I can think is I want to be alone.

"I found him."

"Who?" Charleigh's brows furrow as she stops with several feet still separating us.

"*Him*," I say. "Bentley."

"Oh my God. What do you mean you found *him*?"

"I mean, I saw him today."

"What? Where? How? He remembered you … didn't he?" I try to ignore how hopeful she sounds.

"He thought I was stalking him."

Charleigh closes her eyes for a full second and then opens them wide, her long painted lashes becoming more pronounced as her eyes seem to stretch wider with shock. "He did not!"

I press my lips together and nod, fighting a smirk that doesn't feel appropriate for how terrible I still feel about everything that transpired today. It becomes a laugh that makes me cough. All afternoon humor has been at the very bottom of the emotions that I've been experiencing, but suddenly retelling my story to Charleigh is making me want to laugh and let the awkwardness of the afternoon fall like the rain.

"Where did you see him?" she asks, leaning closer to me.

"Oh, you're going to freak out."

"Tell me!" she cries, sitting beside my small stool, on my bed.

"I'm trying, patient one." Charleigh scrunches her nose and purses her lips. She wants to tell me off, but her need to hear about my seeing him again is outweighing her retort. My lips climb into a grin before I shake my head to clear my thoughts. King's wide eyes return to my memory, and with it, so does a frown and the embarrassment I've been treading all evening.

"He's Kashton's brother. Mercedes' uncle."

"*You're lying!*"

I shake my head again. "He came right before I got off. Apparently, he *lives* with them."

"He lives there!" I can tell by her tone that she thinks this is just as horrible as I do.

I slowly nod in confirmation. There really isn't anything to say.

"What did he say?" she asks.

"Not a lot."

"Then how do you know he thought you were stalking him?"

"He asked how I found him."

"What did you say? Did you tell him he was impossible to find?"

"No! Kash got home. And do you want to know why it was impossible to find Bentley?" My head cocks to the side. "It's because it's not his real name." My voice is raised to express just how ridiculous this all is. "His name's King."

Charleigh's eyebrows soar up her forehead and she stares at me for several long seconds. "His name isn't Bentley?"

"Nope."

"People are named King? I thought that was like American pop culture that brought this wave of strange baby names?"

"His brother's name is Kash, Charleigh."

She wrinkles her nose and smiles faintly. "What's worse is they're starting to grow on me and become normal names." She throws her head back and shakes her long dark hair before looking back to me. "That really doesn't sound like he thought you were stalking him though, love."

"You should have seen his face, Charleigh. He was not expecting to see me. And then I left and he followed me outside and down the driveway and said he wasn't trying to accuse me of stalking."

"You never tell someone you aren't trying to insinuate something! It automatically says that you are!"

I nod several times in agreement and she closes her eyes again, releasing a loud sigh. "So, are you telling me that Mr. Stars is just like all of the rest of the wankers?"

"He's a dude. The Y chromosome is crafted with the art of being an asshole."

"No, no. Not all Y chromosomes. Boys are wankers. You need to find a *man*."

My lips slide into a smile without me being able to consider it. "I don't need a man. I need to get some sleep because I have a test tomorrow in math that I'm predicting I'm going to fail."

"I'm so angry though, Lauren. Aren't you mad? He was so great, and then you find him and he's…"

"A wanker, I know," I say, standing up from the small seat that is far more uncomfortable when I'm not lost in creation. "I didn't expect to see him again, so I don't think I'm all that disappointed. I'm more dreading going back and having to possibly face him again."

"That is going to be awful."

"Not helping, Charleigh."

"Sorry! But it is!"

"I'm going to bed. I'll see you tomorrow."

"What about the wine and donuts?" Charleigh asks, standing from my bed.

"Allie probably needs them more. I stopped in to say hi to her earlier, and she's acting like a maniac. Carbs and alcohol will do her good."

"You might find carbs and alcohol to be beneficial as well."

"Not tonight. Thanks."

"Tomorrow, then?"

"Yeah, sure."

With a deep breath, I fall against my bed with enough force my hair bounces around me. I should turn off the lights. I should lock the door. I should eat. But my eyes are already closed, tracing over the memories of King from this summer, and seeing him again tonight.

I allow myself only the briefest of seconds before I roll off my bed, hitting the edge with a fist before stalking to the door and locking it, and peeling my clothes off as I head back to my bed, not caring about food.

"Lo, we need to talk."

Heart thrumming, I turn to face King and watch his long strides close the gap between us faster than what seems possible because my attention is focused on the muscles moving beneath the thin grey cotton of his tee. His slightly uneven smile confirms he knows I was admiring the fluidity and strength of his body. He exudes a confidence and sexual vigor that makes my stomach tighten and every cell in my body to divide with equal parts want and a struggle to deny that want. Trying to ignore the heat rushing through me, I hold my chin a bit higher and wait for him to continue.

The humor is still bright in his brown eyes as he stops in front of me and runs a hand across his chest, drawing attention to how soft the worn fabric appears. My fingers are itching to follow the same path but I clench them tighter at my sides. "You're so beautiful in the rain." Extending his hand, he trails his thumb over my cheek that is suddenly wet. All of me is. The rain seems to be literally falling from every direction. My hair and clothes are quickly dampening, sticking to my skin that feels sticky.

I don't know how to acknowledge or interpret his words. Rationally I'm accepting the compliment, bathing in it, clutching it like it's a physical object, one precious enough I want to both hide in my underwear drawer and show to everyone.

"What are you talking about? I thought you said…"

"You caught me by surprise. I never expected to see you when I opened that door. I think I just … I was really shocked." King's hand trails over my shoulder, lingering on the sensitive skin at the inside of my elbow before traveling down to the inside of my wrist. "I've been waiting for this."

"This?" My voice is embarrassingly low and breathy. King's lips climb back into his beautiful crooked smile, knowing his affect over me.

"You," he says, moving a foot between mine, bringing him so close I can feel the warmth of his chest through our wet shirts, causing my arms to feel colder in contrast.

I keep my chin level so that my lips are just low enough he will either have to bend or manipulate my back or neck to kiss me. I kind of hope he chooses the latter. I want to feel his hands on me, knowing how powerful and gentle they can be. My hips slide forward, manipulated by only his presence, willing to comply with anything, or possibly begging traitorously.

"Lo." My name is a whisper. A plea. An entire dedication to my heart that steals my breath and any lasting hesitation.

My chin falls back as one of his hands wraps into my loose hair and his other wraps around my back, pulling me closer to him. His lips are softer than

I remember, but the comparison vanishes nearly as quickly as it came when his tongue parts my lips and then slides purposefully against my lower lip, coaxing, encouraging, taking. I press up on my toes and tighten my grip around his neck, drawing me closer to him, deepening the kiss because I want him to take everything from me.

His warm, earthy scent sweetened by soap and something that is singularly him fills my lungs, bringing me higher, losing every sense of the rain and any concern that was planning a strike in my head.

His rough chin scratches mine as he bends to shift and lower me to the ground, which is surprisingly warm and soft for being the front yard. The warmth from his palms seeps into my skin like a dye, absorbing and stretching until I feel him touching me nearly everywhere. Everywhere except where I want to feel him. My groan of impatience makes King chuckle as his nose skims across mine. I don't care that he's laughing at my eagerness; it doesn't dampen my lust and need for him in the slightest. Reaching between us, I fist my shirt and pull it off, shocking both of us when I reveal I'm not wearing a bra.

King's hand runs over my belly, following the path where my ribs meet so that the curve of my breasts feel the barest of pressure, causing a new objection of patience to quickly be cried as my back arches.

I feel the weight of him against me everywhere, yet it's worse than having him not touching me at all, because I am so desperate to feel his skin, his power, and the relief my body is seeking, that I feel like another person. I want to immerse myself in this moment and get completely and utterly lost. I have not experienced a desire like this apart from when I first met King and we spent the entire evening lost first in conversation and later in sensations and emotions.

Twisting below him to bring him more firmly against me, I nearly whimper when the pressure of his body eases, becoming lighter and lighter until my body burns with exposure.

My eyelids slam open, meeting the darkness of my apartment. Over the thudding of my heart, I take in the silence, the emptiness around me, and am grateful Kenzie didn't bring a guest over as I reach for the shirt I had peeled off mid-dream.

"I hate you," I mumble, shifting to my side, flipping the weight of my blankets back over me, and nestling deeper into my bed.

chapter

TEN

The walk to the Knight residence seems longer today. I have no idea what I'm going to say, or how I should act around King. Ignoring him seems not only rude but impossible when he lives in the house. However, when I arrive, the driveway is void of all vehicles, and the garage and shop are both closed. I wander through the house, paying close attention as I go to ensure I'm alone before I take a seat at the kitchen table and pull out an art history book. The creative part of art comes fairly naturally to me—the book part of school does not. This year, my advisor informed me that not only was I a history credit behind, but also a math credit. These quiet times at the house before Mercedes gets home from her carpool have become a saving grace for me to allot time to the subjects.

I close my book, knowing Mercedes should be home at any second, and hear the door open and Mercedes releasing an indecipherable growl. "Hey," I call. "How was your day?"

I barely register her words as I enter the foyer, waiting to see why the door is still open behind her.

"… and Justin Davison puked all over the cafeteria at lunch. It. Was. Disgusting."

When nothing follows her but a gust of wind, I turn to Mercedes and grin. "I hope you don't get sick too. I have a rule about puking."

"What kind of rule?"

"My stomach doesn't like you to go through it alone."

"Gross!" she cries, dropping her shoulders with defeat.

I raise my eyebrows and nod. "I don't enjoy it either. Close the door and let's get homework done so we can play."

It's two days later that I finally see him, and I hate that it makes my pulse quicken and every one of my senses is heightened. He doesn't pay attention to me. Not a smile, not a word, not even a glance. Nothing. I decide it's better this way. It will be easier to forget that night and him if we both pretend the other doesn't exist. My brother, Josh, and I practiced this game for most of our lives—I'm proficient at pretending.

"Anything good in there?" I poke my head out of the fridge where I'm making room for the instant pudding Mercedes eventually gave in to making with me after pleading for us to make a dessert. She thought my cooking skills were lacking—she was mortified to learn my complete lack of ability to bake. Parker is behind me, his baseball hat flipped backward over his messy hair, with a scruffy jaw that clearly hasn't seen a razor in several days.

"Hey, Parker."

"How have you been? I haven't seen you much lately."

"Yeah, I was visiting my family over the weekend," I explain.

"In Montana?"

I nod a few times and hear the fan of the fridge kick on. He is too close for me to move out of the way without brushing against him though, so I remain standing in front of the open door.

"How did it go?"

"It was ... home." The word is so self-explanatory for me.

"Maybe I'll make the trip out there with you next time to see if they grow all Montana girls like you." His index finger is curled as it brushes down my cheek in a movement that's too fast to be sensual but too intimate to be a joke.

"Did King make this?" he asks, his eyes moving to something over my shoulder.

"Sorry?" I ask, taking a small step back and feeling the coolness of a shelf press against the back of my arms.

"Do you know if King made this?" His arm reaches forward, crowding me closer to the fridge. He pulls a plastic Tupperware from a shelf with a quiet scrape.

"I don't know..."

Parker lifts his gaze to mine, and a slow smile curves his lips into an easy smile. "It must not be. If King had made it, it would be gone. His cooking is better than sex."

"You have no idea what good sex is like if you believe that." King appears behind Parker, and his attention locks on me. It's unnerving, making me question what thoughts are occurring behind his brown eyes that are narrowed ever so slightly, making his dark eyelashes appear even thicker.

"But you're right, I *am* a good cook." King takes the leftovers from Parker's hand and pulls down a couple of plates from the cupboard.

"What is that shit? It looks good," Parker says, taking a step closer to King and allowing me to finally move.

Being anywhere near King still makes me feel uneasy, even with us ignoring each other. Just being in the house when I know he's here makes my shoulders tight, my ears strain, and my focus constantly stray. The effects seem to magnify with him being so close.

"You want some, Lo?" My name on King's lips intensifies it that much more.

I try to shake my head, but my neck is too stiff to make it appear natural. "No thanks, I'm good."

"No, dish her up some of that. If she hasn't had your food yet, she needs to check this out," Parker insists.

"It's okay, really. I need to get heading home, anyway."

"Hot date?" Parker's lips are still curled in the same familiar smile I've seen him wear since my first day.

"No, Charleigh and I are going to hit up an art store."

"When are we going to meet Charleigh?" Parker asks.

"Yeah. When are we going to meet Charleigh?" I raise my eyebrows, meeting King's stare. His head is tilted slightly to the left and his chin lowered just enough that I can tell he's annoyed. Blinking several times, I try to gain a cohesive thought and shrug as the microwave beeps. Thankfully Parker takes a step forward, breaking the path of King's stare.

I move to where my sweatshirt is folded over the back of a wooden stool and pull it over my head, bringing a shower of fine hairs to fall across my face. I'm grateful for straightening it this morning. If I had left it its normal curly/wavy/undetermined self, these wisps wouldn't be lying flat against my temple; they would be a frame of frizzy fuzz.

"Hang on, Lo. I'm serious about you trying this," Parker says, grabbing forks from the silverware drawer.

Raking my short nails across my forehead, I work to prepare another excuse. My words fall flat as he brings a fork to his mouth and lightly blows on it while holding his other hand below the bite. The gesture is something I've never experienced, and my mind fights to decipher if I find it to be parental or romantic.

He closes the short gap between us and I slowly lower my hand, keeping it midair in an awkward stance. My brain is yelling at me to object the offer, to make an excuse for food allergies or about being late, but the excitement dancing in Parker's wide blue eyes makes me swallow my words along with the bite of food.

It's some sort of rice mixed with vegetables, coated in a light sauce that is slightly tangy and aromatic against my tongue. It's delicious even as leftovers, assuring me that it was mouthwatering when King first made it.

"What do you think, Lauren? Is it better than sex?" King's voice is bold with the edge of a joke hanging on the word sex.

I can feel my face heat with humiliation. Concealing my embarrassment is something I've never been able to master. It's always been apparent by the deep flush that covers my cheeks and makes me feel like I'm in a sauna.

"Way better." My throat feels too dry from the bite and his shocking question, but my words are clear. Parker's eruption of laughter confirms they were also loud enough to be heard. My eyes move to King for a moment, my feet firmly planted in place to convey I'm not bothered by his innuendo.

"Really? So you're silent while you do the dirty, huh?" King asks.

A new wave of embarrassment burns my cheeks, and I catch him raise his eyebrows for a second, before they fall back in place. His lips quirk ever so slightly—so slightly I don't know that anyone would even catch the expression if they didn't know to look for the truth.

"Not when it's so good it deserves to be heard."

Rather than narrowing into a glare like I'm expecting from his previous reaction, King's eyes brighten with humor and he slowly nods a couple of times. Thankfully, Parker's laughter distracts me, and I look over to catch him with his head thrown back and his mouth wide as he laughs like my words merit the reaction. But it's only a second before my eyes turn back to King.

Lately I've begun sketching Mercedes here and there—something I have been grateful for after such a long dry spell—but my fingers and mind feel a familiar desire to draw King's reaction with every detail my eyes are soaking in. I haven't felt this buzz, this unattainable desire to draw and get every line I'm carefully storing to memory, for so long, I feel nearly drunk from it.

I need to go. I need to go now so I can draw while this yearning is still flowing through me. Even if King is my subject again, I need to feel the power only attainable when my charcoal is able to transform a blank sheet.

"I'll see you guys later." Without waiting for a reply, I head outside where the dampness from the air fills my lungs. It makes them feel heavier, stretched, like the air here weighs more because of how much moisture clings to everything surrounding me.

My thoughts are so consumed by everything I want to draw; I'm at the bus stop before it seems possible. I then watch everyone that passes me, noting details and sizes, shades, emotions—things I haven't been able to see clearly for months. It's nearly overwhelming, not just because there is so much to be seen, but because I am so relieved to once again see it.

The charcoal in my hand doesn't hover with indecision as it has for so many weeks; it glides across the paper with ease. It's as though I'm allowing myself to finally draw what I've been waiting to create for forever, though it's impossible, because I have only known King a short time. Somehow, every single detail of him is perfectly stored to memory. So familiar, I don't have to think to recall the line of his jaw or plains of his cheeks. I know each contour so well, it's as though he's been a constant throughout my entire life.

My back is tight and stiff up to my neck, and my wrist aches when I finish shading a final strand of hair. Still, I feel reluctant to stop. It feels so good to be able to draw once again. My eyes burn and my lids feel suddenly heavy. It isn't a conscious decision, but my eyes seem to blink far less when I work and always feel gritty and tired after a long session like they just endured.

I roll my shoulders and stretch my neck before standing and noticing it's after 3:00 a.m. I don't feel panicked or exhausted by the thought of having to wake up in a few hours. I'm far too invigorated for anything to get me down at this point.

chapter
ELEVEN

"Lo, come check these out." I pause and take a step back to the open office door and peer into where Kash is sitting beside King and Summer. "Come here. Remember the pictures and video I was telling you about? Summer's showing me the edits. I want you to check these out." Both King and Kash are turned to face me, but Summer's eyes remain on the screen as I slowly approach them.

"Summer's crazy good." Kash rolls closer to the desk and points to an image on the screen. "Show her what you did to this one."

Two images appear on the screen side by side. The image on the right has a background that has been muted while Kash's skin is brighter, enhanced. My eyes slowly trace over the differences between the two images, noting far more differences than I'm sure she thinks I can. The one on the left showcases a scar that's been erased on the image on the right, and though his muscles are larger in the enhanced image, the definition isn't as beautiful, and the shadows and curve along his spine are missing.

"Crazy, right?" Kash's question stops my comparison, and I move my attention to him and force a nod which feels too slow.

"Yeah," I quietly agree, trying to sound more persuasive.

King's eyes meet mine. They're narrowed with question and doubt, like he knows I'm lying.

"That's a really great picture. You have to let me know when you have an event. I'd like to come see one."

"Come back to the shop. We're going to be working on a new trick. It will make you question physics when you see this shit."

"Yeah, you should totally come out to the shop," Summer adds, turning to look at me.

I nod a few times, my neck feeling just as forced and awkward as before, when I meet her eyes. "That would be cool."

"You can even get on and ride, if you want." Her voice rises with suggestion.

"Absolutely! I can't believe I've been such an ass. If you want to, Lo, you can totally come check it out. Ride around with us."

I casually lift a shoulder. "Mercedes and I went on a path out back a few weeks ago, but I think I'm better being a spectator. The whole balancing thing has never been something I've excelled at."

"You're going to be my new project! You're going to love it, Lo. We'll get you comfortable and then let you experience some really sick shit that will make you fall so in love with it, you may forget your art." Summer's eyes flare with Kash's proclamation.

"I don't know how great of a nanny I'll be in a full body cast," I tease while taking a few steps back toward the hall.

"Don't worry. You'll start off on the little track, work your way up." Kash's voice is calm and measured, his attention back on the computer screen as he flips to the next picture. "But seriously, I want your opinion on more of these pictures. I was thinking of having you do some sort of black and white drawing or painting. I don't want it super clean. You know that sketch you had of all the hands? I want something like that with the harsh angles, all straight lines that still somehow seemed … I don't know how to explain it…" He turns in his seat to look at me, his brows furrowed, seeking an explanation or designation. "It was like harsh lines, but you could still see curves and almost a softness even though it wasn't."

I shouldn't be enjoying his description and appreciation of my work nearly as much as I am, but his lack of knowledge and technical jargon makes his accolade seem far more superior than those from my professors that often feel recycled and overused. Kash smiles and shakes his head. "I don't know how you do it." He turns back to the screen, but King's and Summer's eyes are both on me, sparking a familiar sense of unease that has me taking another step back.

"You doodle?" My jaw clenches at Summer's inquiry. This is one of the questions I have always loathed, more so when it comes from another person who likes the arts. It's as though they're looking for validation to see if I'm good enough at what I do to be considered an artist when really, who sets that criteria?

"I study art."

Kash's eyes move from the screen to my face, his eyebrows drawn. "You live it." He turns toward Summer so I can't see his expression. "Seriously, her art is amazing. I think she could make a really cool logo graphic to replace the current one we're working with."

"I thought you were going to have the team in Switzerland work on that?" Summer's discomfort with involving me is evident in the softness of her voice.

"I don't know. I can't get her work out of my head. I want her to paint every wall in this house."

Summer's eyes flash to mine and her lips purse ever so slightly. "If you want to meet up, we can go over the branding materials. I can be pretty flexible with my schedule since I know you have like four jobs."

My head shakes as I work to suppress my concerns of Summer thinking of me as competition for Kash, finding her fear almost humorous. "Why don't you guys discuss the other option first? I'm truly flattered, but I don't do marketing and logos. I don't even—"

"Stop selling yourself short. Meet with Summer. You guys can go have coffee or go to dinner or whatever, on me. Summer can fill you in on what we're gearing toward, and I want you to show her some of your work so she can see how good you are."

"We can go next week."

I turn to Summer, reading her indecision, envy, anger, and defeat even though she doesn't hesitate to extend the invitation. It makes me feel guilty and reminds me just how tightly knit this group is. "Yeah. No problem." I hope she's putting it out till next week to allow enough time to think of a good excuse to cancel, or at lease postpone, until Kash changes his mind.

"Look at these," Kash says, oblivious to our exchange.

I approach the desk again, standing a foot from King's shoulder because he's the closest one to the door. Kash clicks to the next image. It's an image of him upside down, holding his bike in place with just a single hand. The shot is amazing, capturing movement and the adrenaline rush he was feeling, but the finished photo has been softened so that it almost looks like a blurred thought.

"Is it an illusion?"

King shifts, looking over his shoulder at me. His lips nearly draw my full attention as they part. He grips the back of a chair, and I glance over to see the familiar scar that runs along the knuckle of his index finger. "This is supposed to look like a dream sequence." I process his words seconds after they're spoken because I'm realizing the scent I have been catching while doing laundry is his.

"That's a cool concept. I doubt many people can do … that," I finish lamely, pointing to the monitor.

"Don't worry, Lo, we'll have you doing some awesome shit by summer. Just you wait." Kash's grin stretches from ear to ear as he looks back at me. "Wait until you see this next one. It's my favorite."

The bike is midair and he's parallel to it, as if doing a pushup off the handlebars. It makes my eyes grow wider with disbelief. "That's amazing."

"Get your sketchpad, Lo," Kash says, his attention remaining on the screen. "We'll hammer this shit out now."

"I have to get going actually, but if you send me some of your favorite pictures, I can try to create something."

"Cool, okay, I'll text you then," Kash says, still lost in thought. I doubt he'll remember this conversation tomorrow based upon his attention.

"Sounds good. Um, Mercedes is working on a report in the dining room, I made her a deal that if she finished it tonight instead of waiting until Friday, I'd ride bikes with her tomorrow."

Kash's attention is torn from the screen, his lips turned up in a grin. "You're getting on a bike tomorrow?"

"Well, that depends on Mercedes, but yeah, it looks that way."

"We have that fucking meeting tomorrow with Spencer," Kash groans.

King shrugs, his attention shifting to me for a split second before moving away again, like he can't be bothered with looking at me—he's been doing this a lot lately. "I'm sure we can move it."

Kash grips his baseball hat and lifts the bill, leaving it raised as he scratches his forehead. "We can't. We've canceled on him the last three times. He'll start taking it personally if we do it again."

"I'll be here," Summer volunteers. "I can show her around."

"You guys know I'm planning to just coast around the perimeter, right? None of that..." I lift my hand to indicate the screen still showing the impossible move. I notice the corner of King's lips tip upward before he moves so I can't see his face.

"That's okay. It'll get you warmed up so you're ready to start doing shit like this soon enough," Kash says, pushing his chair back.

I raise my eyebrows but don't argue. I know what it's like to believe everyone should be as passionate about what you love as you are, but I'm sure like me, he realizes that is often untrue.

"See you guys later." I wave as I take a step back, watching each of their reactions to my departure: King looks indifferent, his face still hidden as he looks to the monitor, though his shoulders look tight. Kash looks slightly disappointed by the news, his eyes on me as he smiles warmly. Summer looks relieved, her posture becoming more relaxed as she takes a fleeting look in my direction.

I turn and try not to think about any of their expressions as I make my way down the long driveway.

"You aren't still looking for the Knight residence, are you?" I turn and notice the owner of the lime green house, the one who gave me directions my first day, out in his front yard. It stalls my steps when he takes a few in my direction.

"No, your directions were really good. Thank you for that."

He nods a few times, stopping when he nears the edge of his yard. "I'm glad. That family could use someone like you."

His comment catches me off guard. *Someone like me?* How does he have any idea who I am? Or if I can offer the family any benefit?

"I've known the family for years," he continues, reading the confusion on my face. "You're what they've been needing."

"As long as they don't need to eat."

He laughs, resting his hand on his thigh covered in worn denim. "It's not their stomachs that need fed; it's their souls."

I feel like I'm fourteen years old, caught with the indecision of making an inappropriate joke or asking if he's crazy. I strike out both options, knowing that neither is going to make me look like I'm a positive influence on the family, and try to stop looking so alarmed. Smiling would be good, but trying to hold back how bizarre I find this man is difficult enough.

His lips slide slowly up his face, pronouncing defined laugh lines that look well used. "Have a good day." He dips his chin, as if granting me the escape I've been searching for. I return the gesture and continue, my pace slightly quicker as I wonder who this man is and if he truly knows the family.

The bus ride home goes too fast. I'm lost in a trance of tipped up lips, shadowed eyes, and a scar that stretches across several knuckles. My materials are tossed in my bag haphazardly to not miss getting off at my stop, and on the way down the aisle, I pass each passenger, seeing only their hands in an attempt to bury the image I've been working to create.

My phone buzzes just after 9:30 p.m. as I'm sketching a face I haven't drawn before: Summer. I'm not sure why I'm drawing her, but I welcome the fact that it's not King. I release a heavy sigh as I reach for my phone, anticipating seeing a message from Kenzie. Instead, it's a picture message from Mercedes holding up a paper with a picture of a bike and a giant grin.

I'm now convinced I need to draw all night because tomorrow at this time, I'm going to be in a full body cast.

chapter
TWELVE

"Hey, Lauren! Ready for your first ride in the shop?" I look to Summer as I enter the kitchen, still in the midst of taking off my coat and setting my bag down. She's standing beside Parker and a guy I've met on a few occasions named Dustin.

"Thanks for the invite, but I have to see where Mercedes is first."

"Squirt's already in there," Dustin calls.

I'm grateful they're too far away to hear the loud sigh that accompanies my steps off the porch following their wake. The last thing I want to do is go into the shop. Actually, the last thing I want to do is go in there and ride a bike. Deals with ten-year-olds should never be made.

"We have to take it easy on her. She's a Mary." Summer's light brown eyes are taunting me, waiting for me to initiate in some sort of verbal fight that I don't doubt she'd consider making physical.

"You've never been on a bike?" Parker's surprise is evident with his tone. "Like ever?"

"I rode a few weeks ago, but before that it had been a while," I explain, purposefully trailing behind them in hopes that they'll exclude me from conversation.

Parker seems to realize the gap and stops until I'm beside him, then slides an arm around my shoulders. I know the gesture is meant to be friendly and inclusive, but it pulls my hair and makes the idea of doing this even less inviting when I know they're all going to be paying attention to me.

The shop is huge, likely as many square feet as the house. It's difficult for me to focus on any one object because there are so many things in the space that make my heart race with unease.

"Let's get you a helmet first." Summer moves to a cabinet against the wall and opens two doors, exposing shelves of helmets. "You kind of have a big head, so let's try this one."

No one laughs or comments on her words that strike me as an insult but sound almost factual, making me feel self-conscious as I reach out to accept it. Sadly, it fits like a glove.

"Lo!" Mercedes' tires stop inches from me, making my heart slam against my chest. "I'm so excited for you to finally try it!"

"You should probably start off with just getting comfortable on the bike again. Find your footing and timing," Parker says, placing a hand back on my shoulder.

"Yeah, we wouldn't want to scare you." Summer looks away as she fastens her helmet in place, which only makes her taunt that much more annoying. If you're going to deliver an insult, at least have the decency to serve it with eye contact.

My palms are itchy with sweat as I climb onto the bike Parker and Dustin picked out for me. It's black and has a sequence of numbers and letters along both sides that mean nothing to me. The seat feels too small; in fact, *everything* about this bike feels too small, making me once again feel all too aware of my size.

"Alright, this is easy. You'll remember everything with a few spins around the place," Parker assures me.

I notice Summer watching me as she mounts her bike, and then it's me watching her as she rides to the edge of a steep ramp and disappears for a second before becoming airborne on the opposite side. It causes an ugly feeling of envy to swirl around in my gut.

My feet push forward and the bike wavers almost violently as I begin, but it quickly becomes steadier, almost easy as I continue. The air in the shop is held at a temperature far cooler than the house, but it doesn't take long before it feels too warm and I stop to remove my sweater.

"Ready to try the small ramp?" I turn to Dustin with my eyebrows rising, making my helmet slide up.

"That's not a good idea. This is her first day back on a bike, and look at the shoes she's wearing." I don't know whether I want to thank Parker or refute his words because they make Summer and Dustin both laugh.

"She'll be fine." Summer makes eye contact with me, her chin tilted and eyes narrowed with calculation. "Unless you're not up for it." And apparently challenging.

I realize as I'm moving toward the ramp that I should have conceded to Summer. She's likely seeing this as me accepting a challenge much larger than this moment. Something that says I want to compete for Kashton since it's obvious she has feelings for him and is concerned about my relationship with him. I send a curse to my older brother and Kenzie for always making me feel like I need to prove myself, and then push my weight forward, triggering the bicycle's mechanisms to roll down the incline.

"Remember, just don't squeeze the brakes too hard!" Parker's advice is the last thing I consciously think of. The air whips across my face, and the exhilaration seems to fast forward the entire event until my shin painfully knocks against the pedal and I land on the other side, where I tentatively squeeze the brakes to a stop. The shop erupts in cheers and whistles that echo with the high ceilings.

"You have to do it again! The first time goes so fast, you don't get to appreciate it!" Dustin's words are so true it's almost frightening to know that I have just experienced something they know so well.

"You were made for this shit!" Parker calls, riding along the outer rim to join me. "That was perfection! You looked like a natural."

My eyes feel too wide as I follow him to where Dustin and Summer are standing at the beginning of the small ramp, their bikes lined up like a voting panel with Mercedes behind them.

"What's going on?" We all turn toward the entrance to see King. I first notice that he's wearing board shorts even though it's nearly freezing outside. Then I see his grimace, which is becoming more prominent as he approaches us.

"Uncle King, she's a natural. You have to check this out."

King's eyes don't even move in her direction. They're fixed on me, and then they slowly turn to Summer. "Did you guys take a stupid pill this morning? What were you thinking? When do we allow someone who doesn't know how to ride, to go down a ramp? Does that not sound like a liability risk?"

Parker shuffles his feet, and Summer's face turns downward with shame. I feel my own heat with embarrassment. "Sorry, King. This was my fault. I should have stopped this," Parker says.

"You're damn right you should have. All of you know better. I don't have time for this kind of stupid shit..." His words become inaudible as he turns, pressing a thumb and forefinger to the slight bridge of his nose and closing his eyes.

I want to look to the others for direction, feeling like I've just been caught in a very compromising position. However, I don't know any of them well enough to feel comfortable with doing so. So I stand still as a statue and wait.

"How did things go with Spencer?" Dustin doesn't seem nearly as concerned with King's obvious disapproval.

"I don't know. Kash went without me."

"To Spencer's?" Summer's voice is filled with confusion, and it's obvious King doesn't appreciate it as he turns back to face us, his eyes wide with a new challenge.

I try to make my movements as slow as I can and turn to see Mercedes. She's watching the scene play out like a sitcom. Her eyes move to mine, feeling my stare, and her lips purse slightly. "Uncle King, Lo and I are going to take some bikes out on the trails. Want to come?"

I feel my eyes go wide with horror. This is a terrible idea for so many reasons. My attention stays on Mercedes in favor of seeing her over the revulsion I'm sure to see on King's face. I'm waiting for him to tell her what a horrible idea this is but am distracted by Dustin discussing something with words and expressions that don't make sense.

"Lo." My neck snaps to face Mercedes again, my eyebrows raised with question. "Let's go." They climb even higher when I turn to the door and see King leading a bike outside.

I'd rather try my luck with the ramp again.

I wheel the bike outside, clipping my shin twice with a pedal, but thankfully both times the contact is only enough to cause a slight wince as I follow Mercedes to the side of the shop.

"Where do you want to go, monkey?" King asks, swinging a leg over his bike.

"Can we go into town?"

"Not today."

"You just don't want to wear a helmet," she fires, her chin tilted with accusation.

"Not if I don't have to." His tone is brazen, like he's not trying to show off but is unabashed to answer the question honestly.

"Want to go on a trail in the back, then?"

"That's what I was thinking. Why don't you lead? I'll take the back."

I feel my nose crinkle with this prospect, not wanting to be in the middle. "Why don't I go last? That way you guys can go at your own speed."

"Because I know what I'm doing."

"Exactly."

"Didn't you make this your deal? These are the terms."

It was of course. However, I thought it would entail spending the afternoon going in continuous circles while watching Mercedes ride. Never had I considered the idea of King being here. I had known before making the deal that the two were supposed to be gone today. A retort seems futile at this point, so I get back on the bike, my fears of falling and breaking my arms a distant memory replaced by how ridiculous I look on this bike and how much more embarrassing it will be to break both of my arms in front of King.

Several minutes later, I'm impressed by how well I'm keeping up with Mercedes. Though the trail is mostly packed from obvious use, it's narrow with roots, stumps, and rocks protruding like masked men at a corn maze, they hold my attention a little too long.

"Put more weight on your toes."

My bike swerves as I attempt to look behind me to verify if King's directions are intended for me.

"Don't look back! Watch where you're going!" he instructs, his voice raised.

"I didn't know if you were talking to me."

"Mercedes knows how to ride. You don't. Of course I'm talking to you."

I'm considering ten ways to flip him off when he breaks my train of thought. "It's easier to maintain your balance and use your muscles more efficiently when your weight is forward. Try standing a little to get the feel of what I'm saying. Then you can sit back down and you'll understand."

Stand up! Is he kidding? His directions only confirm he's watching me too closely, making his stare feel that much heavier. My knuckles turn white, straining to hold tighter to the handlebars as I slowly move to stand.

The bike shifts and my body jolts before becoming rigid, my knees and elbows both locking.

"There, feel that?"

"What? Terror?"

King's laugh nearly gets lost amongst my adrenaline rush and the breeze, but the hushed sound makes my muscles slowly retract. Before I can contemplate the fact, Mercedes' bike lifts off the ground, her front and back tire each going a different direction. I'm not sure if my scream is vocalized or simply in my head as I drop back to my seat and stomp on the pedals to get to her.

Before I can swing my leg off to dismount the bike, King is beside her, his knees buried in the mossy undergrowth and hands working to carefully withdraw the bike.

In a hurried rush I realize there's no kickstand and set my bike down, rush over, and take the bike from him. Mercedes is trying to conceal her cries, which are muffled in the crook of her arm, making that maternal itch become more prominent. I take a second to scan over her body, searching for blood or gashes before kneeling beside her and running a hand down her back.

"Mercedes, I need to know where it hurts, monkey." King's voice is steady, but his eyes reveal he's shaken as they continuously move over her, wide with concern.

"Everywhere." Her reply makes him move forward.

"I need you to roll over for me."

Slowly, Mercedes shifts onto her back, her sweatshirt rising, exposing her stomach up past her belly button and revealing the area is clear of any abrasions. King reaches forward and slowly peels her arm back, exposing blood that's smeared around her chin and neck.

"Alright, Mercedes, you know the drill. I need you to tell me if anything hurts worse than a bruise."

I consider this analogy for a second, thinking back to how painful some of the bruises I've endured have been. A bone bruise is easily at the top of my worst pain experiences, but then again, unless you're raised with horses, your chances of ever having been kicked by one are rare.

"I don't know. I hurt everywhere." Both of her hands move up and down, emphasizing her point. King seems relieved by the fact, however, and reaches forward to inspect where the blood is coming from.

"Looks like you're going to match Lo," he says, moving her chin slightly to examine a gash along her jaw. The comment makes my breath stall and my hand travel up to feel where the skin is grooved with a scar I got from climbing a fence when I was twelve.

King gets to his feet and easily lifts Mercedes, cradling her in his arms. "Can you stay here with the bikes? I'll get her in the house and be right back."

"Yeah, go. I'll bring them back up."

"No, just stay put. It's going to get dark and it's slick out. Summer can help get her changed."

Against my better judgment, I nod.

Where I grew up, you can see a few miles in all directions. Sure, there are hills and vegetation and such, so you can't actually see a person a mile away, but you can still see what's going on around you. But here in the woods, it's like being in a jungle. I'm surrounded by thick greenery that is so beautiful, yet so intimidating, holding the slight threat of so many possible creatures and predators. I wish I had at least thought to bring my cell phone with me. I may not get reception wherever I currently am, but at least it would offer me a little bit of light. I look up at the darkened branches, searching the sky for an idea of what time it might be, and idly wonder how things are going with Mercedes.

I move back to the path and find a long feather. My fingers brush the fine barbs lining the right side which are nearly completely matted with mud. Some separate into new clumps, while others remain sticking out at flawed angles from the weight of the rain and dirt. It never ceases to amaze me how beautiful such a tiny detail is.

This feather is now useless and undoubtedly flawed, but the quill is sharp, ending in a fine point that I run across the ground, which is soft from all of the rain we've been having. It leaves a vague line that I appreciate. I like that I'm making such a slight indent, one you have to search for. I lean closer, my knees growing damp with the residual wetness that moss always seems to hold, and I draw.

I notice the cast of the bright yellow lights before I register the rumble of the truck's engine. My fingers slowly release the tight pressure around the feather and I straighten, brushing my free hand that has become stiff from being cold and supporting my weight, and take a step back.

The passenger door opens first, followed by the driver's side. Parker and King head over to me, their profiles darkened by the light of the cab.

"Were you writing an SOS in the dirt?" Parker's tone is light, teasing. I feel that uncomfortable energy creeping through me, filling me with doubt. I never question that art is a profession, a necessity, a legitimately respected craft. I do, however, doubt that I'm deserving of those things. Even with the awards and recognition I've earned over the years, these familiar insecurities still crawl through me. I know I'm good. I just don't know that I'm *good enough*.

His comment has my nerves and thoughts stumbling, delaying me from taking the few steps to distort the image with a couple of carefully placed prints of my ballet flats.

"Wh … How … Shit, you're good!" Parker rattles. His shoulder brushes against mine as he stares down at the image. "She drew Mercedes, dude. Check this out."

King carefully steps up to the image, coming to the top of her head where her hair is blowing in an invisible breeze. His gaze remains down as he steps around the drawing to my other side. Without saying anything, he pulls out his phone and holds it forward, taking a series of photographs.

"It doesn't capture it. I need Summer," he says, frustration deepening his voice.

"It's too faint. She wouldn't be able to get anything much better," I assure him. He looks over at me, his eyes intense with focus. "I thought you didn't know anything about photography?"

"Just random bits from a high school elective, which believe me, isn't saying much."

"You're like the musicians that play all instruments," Parker says, pulling out his phone and capturing a few images as well.

"Hardly." My eyebrows jog up and down a single time with the thought. "There are so many different types of art; it would blow your mind to see them all. Just the different kinds of painting and drawing techniques can fill several books."

"Feathers are covered in parasites and bacteria. I thought being a farm kid, you'd know that." My attention flickers to King; his is on my hands.

"Parasites?"

"Viruses too."

Talk about the tempting fruit. It slips from my fingers before I consciously think of releasing it. It falls gracelessly to my feet where the already muddied barbs become covered with a new coat.

"It's the lice and mites you really have to worry about." King tilts his head, giving me a clearer view of his raised eyebrows that are assuming I've already contracted one or both and is telling me it was my own fault.

"It's obviously been out here a while. Bugs like that have to feed off of something," I counter.

"Parasites you mean." His eyes follow me.

"Whatever."

His eyebrows go up even higher, bemused by my disgust that I'm trying to mask with ambivalence.

"You go to school for art though, right?" Parker's question punctuates the silent exchange of threats and dares that King and I are locked in. I wonder if he just knows King well enough to ignore his behavior. I give King one last hard look and nod absently while voicing a confirmation to Parker, and then turn to the abandoned bikes. My footfalls echo in the silence of their thoughts and undoubted revenge King is masterminding.

"How's Mercedes?" I lift the bike I had been using and wheel it toward where the guys are standing, Parker with his phone still out and King staring at the picture I drew. I'm tempted to cross over it. Though I received the accolades I had been searching for, I now question the sincerity.

"I sent this shit to Kash. He's going to freak out," Parker says, still staring at his phone.

"He's already seen her work. He knows how good she is." King's statement makes it impossible for me to look over at him.

"Yeah, but this is in the dirt! Who can make a freaking picture with dirt and a feather!"

"We should probably go check to see how Mercedes is doing," I say, wheeling the bike so close to the picture, the tire creates a ridge around the top of her head.

If I look back, I'm fairly certain King would be staring at me, but I don't. I push the bike to the tailgate and lean it against my waist as I open the latch.

"Here, muscles, I've got it," Parker says with a teasing grin. He takes the bike and hoists it into the bed of the truck before hopping inside. I don't watch as he readjusts it, but rather I go in search of another bike.

King meets me by the hood of the truck, guiding a bike with each hand. I step closer, my hands extended to receive one of them. We do a strange dance, him reluctant for me to help, me refusing to stand here and do nothing. The pedal from Mercedes' bike bites low into my shin as I make a move to take it, ultimately stalling me, and making the entire process even more awkward.

"How's Mercedes?" I ask once more as Parker cinches a rope around the bikes.

"She's fine. Just that gash on her jaw. She'll likely have some bruising tomorrow, but nothing serious." I blink several times in an attempt to pull my stare from King. When he talks, his lips go slightly higher on one side, just like when he smiles. Most of the time, it's hardly noticeable, and at others, impossible. I find it entrancing.

"I'm glad. That fall looked painful."

"It's the nature of the beast," King replies, pulling on the knot Parker just secured.

"Is that where you got all of your scars from?"

King shifts his gaze to me, tilting his head. "What scars?" He can hardly keep the smirk off his face.

I should consider my next words, but I'm so concerned his smirk is to disguise offense from my loosely posed question that I don't. "The ones on your hands and arm."

"Oh, I thought you were talking about the ones on my chest and back, or the one on my thigh."

My face heats, and my jaw drops open slightly.

"You walking around the house in your skivvies?" Parker asks, hopping out of the truck.

"Just on the days he runs out of flannel." My tone is dry, attempting to create a warning.

"I'm pretty sure you've seen all of my—"

"I'm pretty sure you wouldn't remember what you wore yesterday considering how well-acquainted you and Kash are with the washing machine."

"Says the twenty-two-year-old that doesn't know how to cook anything besides boxed dinners," King says pointedly.

"Seriously. I can't believe you were able to finish all of that laundry! Where did it all go?" Once again, Parker's question leaves my mind reeling.

I can tell by the brightness shining in King's eyes that he's finding Parker's addition to be intrusive. He wants to make a dig back at me, but Parker's already talking about something else, his voice loud but his words inaudible. My thoughts are in a darkened bedroom, tracing over a map of both faint and distinct scars. They aren't ugly, not in the slightest. In fact, they're beautiful. A network showcasing dedication, endurance, commitment, and perseverance. "Where do you think it went, shithead?"

Parker barks out a laugh, returning a handful of expletives that don't reach me as I focus on a tire track from one of our bikes that the truck missed. Moving to the passenger side door, Parker releases another loud laugh that finally focuses my thoughts. By the competitive yet friendly way his eyes are turned up, I can tell King delivered a few more verbal punches. Parker unlatches the back door of the truck, and without instruction, I climb in.

The reason for the familiarly darkened skies begins to descend as the doors are shut. Rain splatters across the windshield and over the roof in a harmonious melody that encourages me to nestle farther into the seat and close my eyes for a nap.

"Good timing," Parker says as he cranes his neck to the side, attempting to look up into the patches of darkness. King puts the truck into gear without comment. Extending an arm behind him, he grips the passenger headrest, invading my space, followed by his even more invasive gaze. His eyes move from mine to the back window before moving his foot so that we're reversing.

I hadn't considered how we'd get out of here, yet backing up the entire way still comes as a surprise. I feel like I should offer to help, or turn and look as well so that I'm not so close to him, but I keep my composure and remain facing forward for the short distance back to the house.

While they unload the bikes, I head inside and immediately move to the bathroom where I lather and rinse my hands three separate times, careful to clean under each of my nails and scrubbing the sections of my skin that never return to their naturally pale tone.

"Let me see." I avoid Summer's gaze and move closer to where Mercedes is lying on the couch with a small piece of gauze pressed against her jaw while watching something on TV.

"It's not so bad." Her eyes are still rimmed with red, and her voice is shaky. I'm not certain if she's just recovered from crying or if she's working to hold it in.

"Let's go to the bathroom where it's brighter."

She doesn't argue, confirming it's the latter. I push the door closed, allowing only a small gap for her privacy. She sits on the closed toilet seat and peels the cover back to reveal her wound. It's swollen and already bruising. The gash is fairly long but not deep. With any luck, it will only leave a tiny scar if any.

"Did you guys clean it?"

Mercedes nods and a small tear falls down her cheek. "Summer got a wet rag."

"Okay, that's good. Let me see if there's something else. If we can get this really clean and put a little medicine on it, you won't even know it happened in a couple of weeks." Her tears increase with my assurance.

My knees hit the tile floor and instantly plea for me to sit back on my heels, but I ignore the protests and lean closer to Mercedes, my hands resting on her thighs. "I promise I'll be really careful and gentle. You'll barely feel anything." There's still dirt and moss and twig debris on her clothes and in her hair, catching my attention for brief seconds before I focus on her face.

"You aren't upset because it hurts, are you?" My voice is soft. Although I've broken many of Mercedes' barriers, she still has many more that prevent us from discussing a multitude of things I don't think either of us knows how to breach.

"They're going to tease me." With her words, I realize it's a multitude of things that will inflict physical pain on me to possibly hear one day.

A chill runs down my arms still resting on her legs, and I blink back tears I want to share with her. "If someone says something to you about this, Mercedes, they're going to rack up some serious points against karma, and let me tell you, karma returns with interest."

She doesn't respond, making me feel like my small bit of advice is neither helpful nor assuring. "People can be really mean. I wish I could tell you that they'll stop, or that you won't have to deal with this in a few more years, but unfortunately, you'll have to deal with bullies forever. You can't stop them or control what they say or do; you can only control what you do. Don't give them the satisfaction of letting their words hurt you. If they want to say something rude and mean, let *their* souls be scarred with that hatred. Let *them* drown in their own unhappiness. You're better than that. Don't even look their way. Don't allow their words to carry weight or merit. I know it's hard, I do, but you do it a couple of times, and they'll stop because without your reaction feeding them, that darkness that they've created—it starts to drown them."

Her green eyes are wide, heavy with tears, making my own itch with the return of moisture. "Did someone tease you?"

The desire to look away and keep my pride intact is my initial reaction. Ugly memories and taunts dance through my head before my eyes return to hers and I nod.

"How could anyone tease you?"

"I wonder that very thought a thousand times a day about you," I say before pressing my lips together, watching as her fears become sympathy.

"Let's clean you up and we'll make a kick-ass bandage for you to cover it with."

One edge of her lips quirks up, making her look more like King than ever before, and I turn to the medicine cabinet, which is well stocked with multiple sources of disinfectants and bandages.

"What are you making?" Mercedes asks again, this time more insistent, her patience worn.

I look over to where she's sitting on the couch again, seeing her eyes are vibrant and challenging. Involuntarily, I smile. Her eyes stretch with a growing frustration in return. "Watch your show. I'm almost done."

The front door opens as I'm capping my marker, but I don't turn. For several weeks instinct had me turning each and every time it opened when I first started, concerned about who was coming, but now it's become the norm to hear it open and close throughout the day as people come for food, supplies, to chat, or whatever else. I thought they were checking in on me since they can do most of this in the shop. Recently, I've realized that sometimes they leave the shop in order to think. I can turn away from my drawings—flip on the TV, go into the kitchen—but when they're in the shop, they're immersed in their world.

"Don't tell me you got road rash on your beautiful face!"

My eyes snap up.

"Isabelle!" Mercedes cries.

She's beautiful, and I'm nearly positive she isn't a fellow rider. She carries herself with a gracefulness that almost makes her appear like she's dancing. Her jeans are tight, too tight to ride a bike, and her shirt is a designer blouse that would likely tear if she stretched to reach the handlebars. Isabelle walks over to the couch where Mercedes is now standing with a giant grin, and hugs her.

"What are you doing back?" Mercedes asks.

"I'm just up for a long weekend to visit." She releases Mercedes and drops her hands to her thighs, rubbing the pads of her fingers across the material as though she's nervous. "Where is everyone?"

"The new shop."

"It's finished?"

Mercedes nods proudly, a smile spread across her face.

The front door opens again, and almost as if called, the three traipse back into the house with Summer in the lead. She smiles, but it isn't sincere. However, it still seems far more welcoming than the ones she greets me with.

"Hey, guys!" Isabelle calls.

King's gaze moves up from where he's following Parker into the house. A myriad of emotions passes over his face, ones that I focus on with the selfish hope of finding confusion, uncertainty, or disgust. There's definitely a shade of confusion, but joy is brighter.

They each greet one another with friendly hugs, further proof that they're all close.

"How is Seattle treating you?" Summer asks, standing taller as she faces Isabelle, making me wonder if Isabelle is an ex of Kash.

"It's good. Lots of cool bands, food, rain—it feels quite a bit like home," Isabelle says, raking a hand through her light brown hair streaked with blonde.

"Like home?" Parker scoffs. "You're forgetting to consider the awesome people here. No one is friendlier than an Oregonian."

"Or stranger." Isabelle's comment is met with laughter. Even my own lips are pulled into a smile before I press them into a firm line and scoot my chair back, drawing everyone's attention.

"I'm sorry. I didn't see you," Isabelle says, her blue eyes focusing on me.

"This is Lo. She's a friend of Kash and King's, and watches Mercedes." Summer's introduction has me turning slightly to regard her. She rarely even acknowledges me. "Lo, this is Isabelle. She's been a long-time family friend."

"That's great." Isabelle's tone is friendly and sincere.

"It's nice to meet you." I still don't feel relaxed. Whether it's from fearing for Summer or myself, I'm not sure, but I try my best to make my tone sound welcoming, and for my legs to move closer to the assembled group.

"I have to get going, but let's get this on real quick." Mercedes doesn't hesitate. Her eyes are down, trying to see my drawing before her feet propel her forward.

"How did you do that?" Her eyes slowly drag away from the image and up to me. They're wide with shock and a happiness that makes the embarrassment from the attention she's drawing toward me quickly diminish.

"We'll do a new one tomorrow after we change the bandage. You can pick the design. My professors will love you."

"Why will they love me?" she asks, tilting her chin to expose the wound already covered with medicine and gauze.

"Because I draw people." I tear off the strip of tape and carefully apply it to hold the dressing in place. "Plus this is only an inch wide and textured. You're making me work for it."

"Show me." King takes a step forward, craning his neck around to see the bandage. He stares at it for several seconds without blinking. Then Parker moves up beside him, slapping a hand on his shoulder before he stops. Their reactions are what encourage me to believe I can do this. I can survive in this world doing something that I love so deeply.

Parker's head shakes ever so slightly. "You have a gift." He swallows and then looks over to me. His lips are set in a serious expression, his eyes bright with a validation that has more value than a paycheck. The girls step closer as well to inspect the hawk with wings spread wide.

"She needed something nearly as beautiful as her while she recovers." I brush my thumb along the edge to make sure it's secure and then slides my hand across her back. "I'll see you tomorrow."

"Sorry for the sucky ending," Mercedes says quietly, her eyes falling.

I shake my head, waiting until she looks at me. "You have nothing to be sorry for."

She gives me a sheepish grin that tells me she's considering my words, and

I turn to the others before announcing a final goodbye.

"Hey, Lo, do you have anything going on tomorrow?"

I look to Summer with curiosity churning in my stomach.

"I'd like to meet up with you about the logo. You mentioned that Mexican restaurant downtown. Does that work for you?"

"Yeah, what time?"

"How about seven?"

"I'll see you then."

chapter
THIRTEEN

"You look nervous."

I turn to face Mia and smile. "I was going to come back and see you!"

"Yeah, well, it's been over a week since you've been by to work on the mural, so I was worried you were here to dine and dash."

"I know. Don't worry though; I'll be here all morning Thursday."

"I'll make you chimichangas."

"With extra guacamole?"

"Don't get greedy on me, Crosby."

I laugh, leaning into my seat. "I'll be around to the back in a few. I'm just meeting someone about a possible work thing."

"I'll send up a prayer." Mia turns and heads to the kitchen, her long red skirt flowing behind her.

I work to settle the comparison of meeting Summer to feeling like I'm about to meet an enemy. We aren't rivals. I need to find a way to ensure her of that so she understands I'm not going to be an issue, without revealing that I spend more time and attention on Kash simply because he isn't King.

"Sorry I'm late."

Summer's words startle me. Having the person I'm thinking about appear, even when expected, always catches me a little off guard. Her attention is focused to my side, nullifying the sincerity of her apology. She lays a large file on the table and then carefully removes her jacket and purse, and gingerly sets them inside the booth before scooting in beside them.

"I saw your new work today. That fish was pretty cool." I smile, thinking of the salmon I drew with colored Sharpies for Mercedes' new bandage shortly before I came here. "I heard you're also pretty good at drawing in the dirt."

"I'm better with paper."

Her focus moves to mine and I see that I've caught her off guard. Obviously my lack of confidence and discomfort was as clear to her as it was to me when Kash originally proposed this venture. "Can we clear the air really quick? You know that I don't *like* Kash, right? We're just friends."

Summer's eyes narrow with apprehension, and her shoulders square, her spine straightening. It serves to make her appear even more intimidating as I'm sure she intends for it to. "I mean Kash is great and all. I just don't have feelings for him like that, and I sometimes get the impression that you think I do." I stare at her for a moment as she listens intently. "He's just easy to talk to. We get along well."

"But King isn't?"

My eyes shift over the same table that I've cleared hundreds of times while being on the opposite end of this dining experience. "King's … I don't know. He's just…"

"Hey, Lo!" Relief fills me as I turn to Estella and see her smiling face. She stops in front of our table and her eyebrows furrow as she turns her attention to Summer. "Did you guys want anything?"

"Yeah, um…" I look over at Summer to see her menu is still closed and her eyes are wide, staring at me. "Can we have a few minutes?"

She smiles warmly, nodding her head ever so slightly before turning to another table.

"Oh my God. *You're Lo.*" Summer's voice is a strained whisper.

My eyes tighten, attempting to understand why hers are wide. "What do you mean?"

"You're Lo," she repeats quietly, her eyebrows arched.

My heart lurches. There's no conceivable way ... Is there? "I don't understand."

"Sorry." She clears her throat and diverts her attention to the menu. "So what's good here?"

"What just happened?"

Summer shakes her head as her attention remains focused on reading over the same meals I memorized three years ago. "Nothing. Sorry, I was just ... It's nothing."

"Who do you think I am?" I insist.

Summer slowly lifts her gaze to mine, searching my face with patience, not slow like an artist does to catch unseen details, more like she's looking at me for the first time. She clears her throat again and moves a hand to her forehead for support. Her throat moves with a swallow, feeling my stare. "King told me about that party in September, when he met Lo. You're her. You're Lo."

Everything seems to come to a halt as I focus on what she's just told me. About the fact that she knows about me. That King told someone.

"You don't ... I mean, we don't have to talk about it. I just didn't realize ... I didn't know you were *her.*" Summer's eyes have gone back to being sharp like her tone, which catches me off guard. If anything, it seems this secret should bring her some relief.

My mouth feels too dry as I swallow and turn my attention to the mural I've been working on near the back of the restaurant. A distracted part of my mind that doesn't ever know how to rest starts questioning the colors I've been considering, while the rest of my thoughts go around in a tailspin. "I'm not like that."

Summer raises her eyebrows, imploring me to continue. "I don't sleep around, if that's what you're thinking."

"Why would I think that?"

"I don't know. Why do you?"

She releases a sigh through her nose, her eyes moving down to the table, avoiding me. "Look. You seem like you genuinely care about Mercedes. I've never seen her connect with anyone the same way she has with you. And the fact that you have somehow managed to get the Knight house clean, and stay clean, is a miracle in and of itself. But King is like my brother. The fact that you screwed with him is not something I will be able to easily forgive."

"Screwed with *him*?" I lean forward as the words fly from my mouth. "He screwed with *me*."

"You didn't call him."

"*He told me his name was Bentley*," I cry. "I looked like a fool asking way too many times to way too many people if they knew a Bentley because when I woke up the next day, his number was rubbed off. He had *my* number. This wasn't me playing games and disappearing."

I watch each of my admissions run through a silent mental checklist. *What have I just confessed?*

"So you like King?" Her voice is quiet, trying to restrain what I believe to be hope, which confuses me even further.

I shake my head swiftly. "King and I..."

Summer leans forward, her neck stretching. "Yes..."

"We're, I don't know ... friends ... I guess. Part of the time I think he hates me. Others I think he likes having me around to torment. Occasionally he seems to just be cool with things."

"Friends?" Summer spits the word.

"I'm not getting involved in anything with King. We got along well when we met that night. Now we're starting to finally find some even ground, but there's no way in hell I'm going to hang out with him when he's spending time with someone that has feelings for him." I shake my head with more conviction. "No way."

Her whole face squishes with confusion. "What are you talking about? Isabelle?"

"Yes, Isabelle."

"They aren't dating. They've never dated."

"She obviously has feelings for him." Her words are slowly absorbing through my defenses, relieving me far more than I wish to admit.

"Yes, yes she does. Isabelle has known King forever. They grew up together. I told you this when I introduced you guys." Summer's neck retracts and her shoulders fall ever so slightly. "That was intentional. You shouldn't feel obligated to be a bench warmer because she likes him. King doesn't have feelings for her—not like that, anyway. And she knows it. They're friends and have only ever been friends."

I break her stare and look down at the table. Her encouragement is unsettling. This was the last thing I was expecting to hear, especially from her.

"Lo, King has feelings for you. But if you're going to date other guys and keep dangling that in his face..." I glance up and her lips are pursed, her chin tilted. "Sometimes I really like you, and then other times..."

"You hate me," I finish.

This time her eyes hold mine. "Sometimes, but not for the reasons you probably think I do. Kash never lets anyone get very close to him, yet he seems to really like you. I thought you guys were ... Well, you already know what I thought. And now that I know you're *her*"—Summer's eyes travel downward again, but I can tell by the stretched skin by her temples that they're widened—"my mind is a crazy mess of thoughts. Did you take this job because of him?"

"No! I didn't even know King lived there!" My objection is so loud a couple across the restaurant looks our way, making me duck my head.

"Are things with your boyfriend serious?"

"Boyfriend?"

"Charlie."

A laugh escapes my lips, followed by a giggle that makes me close my eyes and look out the window in time to see a full-sized SUV rear-end Summer's truck.

"Shit!" Summer shoots up from her seat, her jaw dropped and attention diverted outside. "Son of a bitch." Summer exhales the words. She swings her purse over her shoulder and then looks to me. "Write down his plates," she demands, and then she's gone.

I find a piece of charcoal in my bag and quickly pull my things out of the booth, following her out into the rain. I fish my arm back through my bag, searching for a pen, knowing the charcoal won't last long on my skin with this weather. I rip the cap off with my teeth and write the series of numbers and letters on the inside of my wrist before walking over to where Summer is talking with a raised voice to a wiry man with red hair who has his arms spread wide in disbelief or irritation. As I get closer I realize it's both.

I start to text Mia to ask her to call the police when my phone rings, Kash's name filling the screen. I consider ignoring it before accepting the call and pressing the phone to my ear. "Hey, Kash. Sorry, do you mind if I call you right back? There's kind of a situation."

"A situation? What, with you and Summer?"

"Someone just rear-ended her." At my words, the man flips around, his arms rising higher.

"She's parked over the line! This was her fault!" he bellows.

"Yeah, a situation," I repeat before turning my phone off and stepping up closer to the man, tilting my chin with disbelief.

"Did you guys exchange insurance information?" I ask the question, already knowing the answer is no.

"This is bullshit! I'm going to explain to them that you parked like a fucking idiot with half of your truck sticking out in traffic!"

I glance in the direction of her truck, noticing she is in fact slightly over the line, but not enough to impede another vehicle.

"Good thing they hire people to research accidents and facts," Summer says.

His face turns a startling shade of red, his eyes bulging with anger. "I want your name, your address, I'm going to destroy you!"

"It's just a car," I say, forcing his attention to return to me. "If this is how you handle all of your mistakes, let me give you a quick life lesson: you need to dial the asshole meter down." My words are spoken firmly, my eye contact never wavering from his.

His eyes grow rounder with shock. "Who in the hell do you think you are? I'm not talking to you! Unless it was both of you morons that parked!" His voice is alarmingly loud, and his comments make my blood heat and heart race, but I calmly blink to feign how unaffected I am.

Summer's head rears back with a retort, forcing my response to come faster than I wish. I want him to have to wait for my words. "Nice to meet you, asshole. I'm Lauren, the witness that is happy to complete my civic duty by reporting to anyone that wants to hear how you hit her truck. Now, I think you need to grab your license and insurance information because this moron already called the cops." I force my jaw to relax and my lips to loosen so I can continue the façade of being calm and unaltered by his behavior.

I notice Summer take a step away, and I want to see where she's going but refuse to break eye contact with this guy. It's a small gesture, but I will not be the one to back down.

"Good! I hope you did call the police!" His voice has turned vile, belligerent. His face has reddened even more, blanketing his freckles and kicking my heart rate up a few more notches. I steel myself, relaxing my mouth again to ensure I'm not expressing any emotion. His eyes narrow, noting my impartialness, and he takes a long step, bringing him close enough that I can smell his cologne. "You're such a—"

"Finish that sentence," King's voice demands in an explosion. He appears beside me, his shoulder moving in front of mine, nearly pressing his chest against the man. "Finish your sentence!"

Kash and Parker seem to materialize as I'm jostled back a few steps, both of them moving just as close as King.

"If you want to act like a Neanderthal—" Kash looks to King and Parker before shrugging "—we're game. But you don't act like that to either of them, or any other woman."

The guys' eyes narrow, but I catch him slink back slightly. "I'm not dealing with a bunch of street thugs," he quips.

"You want to raise your voice and get in someone's face like that, you should expect to deal with something a whole hell of a lot scarier than a street thug. I can guarantee if you do it to them again, that will be me." King's not much taller than the driver, but his head is tilted to look down at him.

Summer's shoulder brushes against mine, making me realize how stiff my muscles are, and I'm fairly certain they're also shaking slightly, vibrating with anger and adrenaline.

"Get your shit out of your car," Kash orders.

The stranger turns with a huff and retreats to his car, where Kash shadows him. King's eyes follow them, and Parker takes a couple of steps closer to the cars as if anticipating the opportunity to throw a punch.

"I should get my stuff too," Summer says, retreating to her car. King moves a few steps forward so that he's closer to her.

"What's going on?" Julio—one of the masterminds to the delicious food of Sonar—is breathless, his eyes alert as he scans the sidewalk.

"Nothing. That guy was just being a dick."

"Who are the other guys?"

"My boss and his brother, and their friend," I reply, wiping a wet piece of hair out of my face.

"Mia said he was yelling at you!"

"He doesn't like being wrong."

Julio laughs. It's loud and a refreshing contrast to the anger that just transpired. It makes my lips lift and my lungs expand with a deeper, fuller breath of air. "We've got it covered. You can go inside."

He reaches over and messes my hair up before retreating.

I release my ponytail and notice the guy turn and shoot an angry glare in my direction. My hands stop from securing my hair, falling to my sides. I raise my chin and eyebrows with a silent challenge, then Kash steps in front of him, muttering threats that don't reach my ears.

It takes only a few brief moments for the correct information to be shared, and then the guy is back in his car, mumbling something as he backs up and waits for a window in the heavy commute traffic to leave.

King's shoulders sink slightly as he watches the car disappear. Then he turns, his hand digging around in his pocket, and he sorts through a handful of its contents and flips three pennies to the sidewalk.

"What are you doing?" I ask, my brows drawing down as I watch one roll into a shallow puddle, because in Oregon, puddles are everywhere, including on the sidewalks.

King's face is still mostly tilted downward from watching the pennies when his eyes meet mine. "Call me the Genie."

"What?"

His shoulders roll casually in a shrug. "Sometimes people need a reason to think their luck is changing."

I hate that I find that so entrancing. He's right; people view lost pennies as a sign of good fortune, a chance to right a wrong, karma's nod of approval.

"Let's get something to eat. You guys need to warm up," Kash says.

"That's alright. I think I'm just going to head home," I object.

"No way. We're going to go get a drink after that," Summer says. I turn to her, another excuse already lined up, and she shakes her head, pursing her lips. "Don't even try it. Get in the car."

"I'm going to drive your ride," Kash says.

"What? It's not like he broke it! He just fucked up my bumper."

"Yeah, but if something happened—"

"Don't feed me that line of bullshit! You just like my truck better than yours."

There's a collective laugh as though this has been discussed previously.

"I've got my bike in the back. Since it's raining and I don't have my top on, we need to get out of here. Where'd you park, Lo?" she asks.

"I rode the bus."

All of them turn to look at me with a similar look of confusion that dissipates as the rain picks up. "Come on, Lo. You can ride with us," Parker says.

Kash tosses a small wad of keys across the space that Parker picks out of the air. "Don't let King drive. He's got a target on his ass."

King grumbles an objection but moves to the passenger door.

"Wait!" Kash shouts. He moves to the back of the car and lowers to a knee, looking under the vehicle. "We're leaking something."

King changes direction and gets down to look beside Kash. The two confer for a few minutes before Summer lets out a frustrated growl and the three move back over to us with Kash carrying her bike. He deposits it into the bed and then collects his keys from Parker and opens the driver's door. Summer slides into the passenger seat while Parker gets in the back. I stand on the sidewalk and release a deep breath before stepping past where King is holding the back passenger door open expectantly.

"How in the hell did you guys get here so fast?" Summer asks, turning in her seat to face Kash.

"I was calling to tell you we were coming and you didn't answer, so I called Lo. She said something about a situation and I heard that bastard yelling," Kash explains.

"He was a bastard," Summer says quietly in agreement. "But you should have seen Lo! Seriously! My mind is blown!"

"We saw," Parker says from beside me. "You were completely chill as you stood there. He was pissed you weren't intimidated."

"He was just trying to act tough," I say dismissively.

"Seriously though, you looked like you were ready to throw down with him." Summer turns in her seat to face me. "Like you wanted him to try something so you could hit him back."

A soft laugh breaks through my lips. "I prefer to go into situations like that with a pair of steel-toed boots. I knew this wasn't going to be anything."

"What?" she shrieks, giggling as her head falls back. "Don't tell me you know how to kick a guy's ass."

I smile in reply and then voice an honest *no* when they all turn, seeking an answer. "I've been known to stare too long when I people-watch. He was slow, in a suit which restricts movement and reactions, and his hands were super soft. There's no way he works out." I shrug. "He wasn't a big threat."

"You knew that from looking at him for like ten seconds?"

"Some people are easy to read."

"Have you kicked someone with steel-toed boots before?" Parker's voice is anxious with anticipation.

"No." I quietly laugh once more. "That was a joke."

Parker looks genuinely disappointed by my response and then moves his attention forward and questions Kash about Summer's truck.

"What's that?" King's voice is so soft it takes me by surprise. His index finger brushes against the blue ink staining my skin.

I look up at him, noting too many details in the few seconds of silence shared between us. "His plates."

King licks the pad of his right thumb and wraps his fingers around my wrist, bringing my arm to the small space between our legs. His thumb rubs across the sensitive area with an obvious intention, but it's gentle and slow in an attempt to not irritate the area. The friction he creates is warm and distracts me from everything being said and done around us. He rubs until his thumb and my wrist are both dry, the numbers slightly faded. I glance up at him when his thumb hovers over the most prominent of the characters remaining, and his eyelids lower, reflecting a pain that I don't understand. His thumb settles against my wrist with the slightest pressure. I work to remain casual and unaffected, but I'm sure he knows otherwise. I'm certain he can feel just how much he affects me while my heart thrums under his touch. Voices are light, joking as we go. I can tell based on the tones, but that's all that registers. I'm obsessing over why King is touching me, and if he would be if the shadows of our legs and night weren't cloaking so much.

As King opens the rear passenger door, his hand slides from my wrist and his body turns away without glancing back at me. He's out of the car in a second and slamming the door closed within the next. Why did I let him touch me? Why did I come back here? I already know the answer—it's because as much as I want to dislike, hate, even loathe King, I can't, and that's slowly making me despise myself.

Several hours later I'm sitting at my easel, wearing an old tattered sweatshirt and drawing King's hand holding my wrist, erasing that guy from my skin. Thoughts of his reaction to me for the rest of the night are intermingling with those moments, creating an ugly mixture of shades to be present.

Being ignored by King is nothing new, but it's beginning to hurt more and more.

"I don't understand why you're working so hard to change for some guy you don't even like."

My eyebrows crash down as I rear my head back from Kenzie's verbal slap. It's a weekend, and for the first time in many weeks, she's here at the studio, filling the space with unease. I don't know that many others would consider what I'm doing to be 'cooking.' I'm attempting to make a breakfast burrito and I've burnt the eggs, so they're now a rubbery consistency and no longer smell recognizable. "I'm not trying to change anything."

"You've never cooked, so why do you care now?"

I return her stare while considering her words. I care because of Mercedes. Because *he* posed a challenge and I loathe defeat. I'm learning because I can't eat boxed dinners for the rest of my life. Do I care what King thinks? Maybe. Probably. More than I wish I did.

She raises her eyebrows, recognizing my awareness.

chapter
FOURTEEN

Today has been one of those days that I wish I could have a free pass to erase and do over again. Nothing has gone as planned. I missed the bus to school. I was sprayed by mostly dirt from a car. Mercedes was in a mood that rivaled my own, bringing out an uglier side of both of us. And Charleigh has stood me up for the second time now to go out with a guy.

I head to the bus stop, avoiding the puddles with my ballet flats that I am hoping will return to their shimmery golden tan color. The rain has been one of my favorite things about Oregon, but today it's just annoying. The dark clouds in the sky are annoying. The puddles are annoying. The sound of tires splashing through said puddles is even more annoying because it forces me to move to the far side of the narrow road and brush up against the fir tree branches that I swear are reaching for me as they soak my leg from thigh to ankle.

The car stops beside me, and I look over my shoulder to see the tinted window of a silver SUV slide down, revealing King.

"What are you doing out here?"

I look ahead and then back to him as though the answer is obvious.

"Where's your car?" he demands.

"I don't have a car."

"You walk here? Every day?"

"Until they can figure out that whole teleporting idea."

"Get in."

"That's okay. I'm all wet and it's not that much farther." I turn to look down the road again and then back to the interior of the SUV, where King is looking at me with rounded eyes.

"Get in the car." His tone is calm and relaxed like this is merely a friendly suggestion, but the intense look he's giving me says he's going to follow alongside me until I get in.

I sigh deeply and reach for the handle of the passenger door. The warmth inside the vehicle makes my damp skin prickle as I slide in, the leather squeaking protests against my wet jeans, bringing King's attention to my lap.

"You're soaked."

"It adds to the conditioning. You know how swimmers go in with all of their clothes on to build resistance? I find this improves my calf workout."

"Why don't you ever ask for a ride?" he asks, dismissing my joke.

"Why would I?"

"Because it's dark and pouring down rain."

"It's not that bad," I lie. "I just have to get to the end of the road, and then the bus stop is a couple of blocks West."

"How did we not know you don't have a car?"

I look at King and raise my eyebrows. "Why *would* you?"

"Because you shouldn't be walking this every night."

"King, you're my employer. I'm not going to ask you or Kash to drive me to the bus stop. That would be unprofessional."

"No, what it would be is smart. And I'm not your employer." My mouth opens to retort and then I pause, watching him shake his head. "I don't understand why you're trying to avoid me. I'm not going to tell anyone about what happened."

I want to contest both of his points since he works just as valiantly to avoid me, but my mouth opens before my thoughts are done forming. "You already did."

King's gaze cuts to me so fast, it makes me nearly lose my focus. His eyes quickly move to each of mine, searching for what all I know. He drops his stare before looking out the windshield as though he's embarrassed. "I told Summer I met someone, way back in September. I never told her you're the same person."

"I know. She figured it out a few weeks ago when we met to discuss the work for the shop."

King closes his eyes and raises a hand to his face where he pinches the slight bridge in his nose. "Why didn't one of you tell me?"

"What was I supposed to say? I'm so confused by everything that involves you. Most of the time you act like a dick and completely ignore me. Other times you act like a nice guy. I didn't even know that night meant anything to you after I didn't hear from you. Then I found out your name isn't Bentley, and I was positive it meant nothing to you."

King drops his hand and opens his eyes to stare at me for several long seconds as the windshield wipers echo in the silence. "Most people around here know who I am. I tell people my name is Bentley because sometimes it's nice to just hang out and be me." He squeezes his right fist with his left, creating a symphony of pops. "I lost my phone that night. I had no idea where it went and your name wasn't in my backups." He swallows, his hands stretching, reflecting there's something more. "I asked everyone I knew at that party about you."

"I only knew my roommate and her friend."

We stare at one another for too long, each of us weighing thoughts and questions that feel louder than actual conversation. I break eye contact first, moving my gaze to the windshield to watch the rain in order to gain the strength I need to ask the question I've been agonizing over for months. I press my lips firmly together and turn back to him. King's eyes are wide, his mouth set in a grim line like he knows what I'm about to ask. "Did you want to be found?"

His shoulders curl inward as though he's relieved. "You have no idea how much I wanted you to find me."

I want to ask why he acted so surprised and cold when we met again, but the fact that he did makes this questions seem more inappropriate than my last. "We have to go. My bus will be there in a few minutes."

King's chest rises with a deep breath and his shoulders square again. He doesn't say anything more as we drive the distance to the bus stop. The rain is our music, loud and angry against the windshield and streets, amplified by the roof of the SUV. I hate that it reminds me of that night and lying beside King, getting lost in the rhythm of his heartbeat and the rain until I couldn't decipher one from the other.

"I'd offer to come get you tomorrow, but I have a feeling you'd say no."

"I would." I unlatch my seatbelt and slide closer to the door, gripping my messenger bag and pulling it into my lap. "Thanks for the ride, King."

"Lo." King's voice is loud and unsteady. "We don't have to go back to that night. We can just be friends."

I'm so relieved I didn't turn around when he called my name, because I'm certain my face is contorted with confusion and anger. I slam the door shut and head the few paces to the undercover bench where a woman I see here nearly daily is waiting. We don't make eye contact. We never do. I pull out my phone and sit beside her, ignoring King's stare.

chapter
FIFTEEN

"Where are you going?"

"The restaurant."

"But it's nearly nine. Aren't they closing soon?"

I shrug, my fingers fastening the final button on my coat. "I prefer to work when people aren't there watching me and asking questions every other minute."

"How are you going to get home?"

"The bus."

"Does Kenzie have that guy over again?" Charleigh's eyes drift upward as if seeking the answer herself.

"Yeah, apparently, they're dating or something. She's been bringing him around for the last couple of weeks."

Charleigh's chin snaps, nearly hitting her collarbone. "Kenzie's in a relationship?"

"It certainly seems that way," I say.

Charleigh takes three swift strides to the window and pulls the curtain with a rough tug. "Where are the flying pigs?"

Allie giggles and slides her eyes from the pattern she's meticulously cutting out. "I'm happy for her, but I'm also kind of bummed. I liked hearing about her different conquests."

"I wish she'd spend more time at his place," I admit, slinging the strap of my messenger bag over my neck.

I take a step back as they both laugh at my misery. "I'll see you guys tomorrow."

"Bye!" they call out in harmony. I shake my head with a small smirk as I pull the door closed behind me, their giggles echoing down the stairwell.

I slowly descend the bus stairs, shoving my phone and headphones back into my messenger bag. The sky is even darker tonight, filled with invisible gray clouds that are sprinkling the city, making the streets and sidewalk glossy and fragrant the way only rain can. "Shit," I mutter, gripping the railing as I step onto the sidewalk. The restaurant is visibly packed.

"Everything okay, miss?"

I turn to the bus driver and mumble my apologies as I release the rail and take a few steps forward, hearing the hiss of the bus's engine as it pulls away.

"Lauren?" I twist my neck to see Estella heading my way, a cigarette balanced between her index and middle finger.

"Hey."

"You forgot it was Tuesday." Her voice is a quiet acknowledgment. I did. With so much going on, I feel like I'm losing track of days, sometimes losing time altogether. Like it's passing without me.

"I can bring you home," she offers.

I look back to her after glancing at the crowded tables. "That's alright. I need to get some work done on the mural and I'm here."

She smiles warmly as she wraps a hand around my waist, pulling me closer to her. We walk side by side, my steps shorter to keep pace with her as the smoke from her cigarette lingers in the air. My dad has smoked Marlboros his entire life, but Estella's are clove, the scent slightly savory as it stretches and dances in the air before settling in my lungs.

"Did you come for tacos?" Mia calls, her lips stained the same bright red they always are.

"Maybe. I need to get some work done first."

"I'll hold some back for you. This crowd can *eat!*" Mia says with a bright smile.

I enter the dining area with my head down and my strides swift. It's amazing how many people will stop you when they think you're a member of the staff, even when it's apparent you're off duty. The crowd is alive with laughter and voices that have clearly been enjoying the drinks that are often accompanied by tiny umbrellas.

The underpainting makes me wish I were working in private. I loathe how it looks like a giant mistake rather than a piece of art. It's the base coat that will allow me to paint the mural, and because this wall is red, I had to use a light beige paint to allow all of the colors to show, making my underpainting that much more pronounced.

I lay out the old sheet I've been using as a drop cloth and unload my acrylic paints and supplies. Charcoals have always been my preferred method of art. I've been using them for so long they feel like an extension of my hands. Blending, sketching, shading, it's all done with the charcoal and a gum eraser, but with painting, I have to hold a palette that constantly gets in my way or begins to slant while I'm working, blending colors I never intended to mix. Plus, I have to constantly add more paint to my brush and always have to create more of a hue that I inevitably run out of. Therefore, I've always had to force myself to paint, and while these frustrations are faced each and every time I hold a brush, my love for the techniques, colors, and results sometimes inspire me to want to paint every surface I see.

When Estella and I first discussed me painting a mural, she wanted a beach scene, something that she could look at that would warm her through Portland's rainy season. I offered to post a want ad for her at school because I don't do landscapes; I never have. At least, not by choice. In school I've had to create them, like the ocean scene I was working on when I first met Mercedes, but I never like their results. Nature has many extraordinary secrets and gifts that it shares, and while I enjoy admiring them, it's people who draw my attention. Gapped teeth, bridged noses, wide-set eyes, full lips, thin lips, freckles, dimples, scars, it doesn't matter; everyone has beauty if people are willing to look and not get distracted by what they're taught to find attractive. Estella wasn't interested in having someone else. She insisted on having me do the work even if I couldn't create what she wanted. It left me unsettled for weeks as I contemplated what I could paint that would still evoke the same warmth she was seeking. When I came to her with a list of ideas, she shook her head and walked away, leaving me wide-eyed with confusion. She found me later that same day and told me she wanted me to paint what I felt in my heart. That made the decision even more trying because I wasn't painting a mural for me to look at every day; it was for her. It was less than a week later while we were closing up after a busy night like tonight that I knew what to paint.

I squeeze several shades of reds, browns, yellows, and oranges onto my palette and add large globs of black and white. Several paintbrushes go into my back pockets in order of their brush size, and an old shirt goes over my shoulder to be used as a rag. Terry cloth is impossible to use. You can't get a clean line with it.

"Hey, Lo, I brought you some water for the wall and coffee for you." I turn so I can smile my appreciation at Mia. "I wish I could see what's in your mind! I can't wait for it to be finished!" Her words translate to: whatever that is, it's hideous! I hope you know what you're doing!

I press my lips together. I'm trying to smile, whether to give her assurance or because I don't know my alternative, I'm not sure. It's not convincing her of much because she returns the tight-lipped smile before taking a couple of steps back and disappearing.

Her reaction makes the energy and passion I finally found recently dissipate. A long breath escapes me and my shoulders sag. I take a step back, turning my chin to look at the angles I've begun to outline, trying to see the still image as a fluid motion. My eyes close and the hum around me invigorates the emotion I'm working to capture. I pull a wide brush from my pocket and swirl reds with a touch of brown and orange. Then the noise fades along with my tension as new colors and lines are added to the wall.

"La, La, La, Lauren!"

I push a loose strand of hair back with the handle of my paintbrush and turn to see Kash, a wide grin covering his face.

"You were in the zone!" he cries.

I raise my eyebrows in question, and he laughs so hard he has to lean a shoulder against the wall for support.

"I was saying your name for like five minutes before you heard me!"

My smile is due to his amusement more than the fact that I find humor in the situation. It's a part of any sort of passion. We all zone out when we care about something enough. I'm confident he knows exactly what it's like to lose the world around you and find yourself in one where nothing exists but your craft. "Yeah, sorry."

"This is crazy! What are you doing here?"

"I used to work here."

Kash raises his eyebrows and juts out his chin. "You worked here?"

"For three years."

"No shit. What a small world." His last word is spoken softly, distracted by the mess of color I've applied to the wall tonight. "What are you painting?" he asks, still following lines to blotches of color that will be used as my outline.

"She won't tell us." Mia's response is delivered with her red-painted lips spread wide and a smile that I recognize from going out with her after work a couple of times—she's interested in him.

"Can we guess?" Kash asks.

"She only smiles when you do." Mia places a fresh container of water and cup of coffee on the table beside me. "It's a mischievous smile, like she wants us to keep guessing."

My lips climb because I do. "Mia, this is Kashton, my boss."

"I'm pretty sure Mercedes thinks she's your boss," he says, making me laugh out loud and causing my palette to drop down just far enough that one of my yellows mixes with a red.

"That's cool. She says really great things about you guys," Mia says.

"That's because we're pretty great." I have to turn away from where I'm adding some paint to an area I don't want to dry before finishing, to see if Kash is truly flirting or if his tone is just getting mixed in the chaos of the ensuing noise. His back is straight, his chin angled and eyes bright. I feel the urge to say something. Anything. I can't understand why he's flirting with Mia when Summer is so perfect for him.

"Do you know who's closing tonight?" My words are too fast and too loud to be subtle. Both of them turn to me, but my focus is on Mia, my eyes rounded in warning. Her eyebrows rise, telling me she's misreading my warning to avoid him as a staked claim, before she takes a step back and smiles guiltily at me.

"I'll find out. Do you need anything else? Some food?"

"No, I don't want to stop and eat right now."

She nods a couple of times and then turns, giving a brief smile to Kash before disappearing.

"King! Get over here! You were right!" Mia's departure doesn't seem to faze Kash as he yells through the restaurant, making me frown slightly. I've never appreciated when people disregard everyone else, and yelling in a restaurant doesn't seem courteous in the least. Then his words repeat in my head and each of my muscles grows tense. *King's here? He recognized me?* "King! It's Lo!"

Half the restaurant is now looking at me, and for the first time tonight, I'm looking at them. "Do you know everyone here?"

"Yeah." His gaze follows mine to the first couple of tables before he looks back at me and shrugs dismissively. "Just some friends." I'm pretty sure this is twice as many people as I actually know.

My thoughts stop as King appears with an arm slung loosely around Summer's shoulders.

"You didn't tell me you were painting when we were here." Summer's tone holds a slight trace of offensiveness, but her eyes are distracted with following my blocks of colors. "Your colors are beautiful." Her eyes find mine, and there's an authenticity behind them that makes me feel slightly sheepish.

"She won't tell anyone what it is yet," Kash explains.

"That's awesome," Summer says, her lips spreading into a smile that makes her nose crinkle slightly. It's an approving smile, and for the first time, I feel as though Summer is being genuinely accepting of me. Maybe she wants to be my friend after all.

"How often do you work on it?" Kash asks, his eyes once again following my paint.

I shrug and run my brush through a color on my palette I had created so a shell doesn't build over it from remaining stagnant. "When I get extra time. I've never done anything this big, so I don't know how long it will take."

"You're doing this in the shop!" Kash cries.

My heart is beating so fast I feel nearly dizzy with the thought. Painting on a wall is different from a canvas because of its permanence. Sure, someone may paint over it at some point, but for a period at least, my work will be present on Kashton Knight's wall for him and all of his riding buddies to see. The fact is intimidating. The shop is open and so bright and minimal that even if I were to use a gray palette, it would be impossible to miss.

"I'm serious," Kash says. "I didn't realize you were already contracting work out when we discussed you doing this. I want you to paint my shop. I want a Lo Crosby original." He turns to his brother. "King, draw up a contract tomorrow. I want this shit done before the Swiss team gets out here. I want everyone to see it, and have it be a part of the marketing plan."

My vision goes fuzzy with the onslaught of terror and pressure Kash just passed me. "I don't know how to do a logo. I can paint something for you, sure, but ..." My words fade because the only ones I have left are screaming *I can't*.

"Sketch some designs out. Create a portfolio of ideas, colors—the works. I want to see what you can come up with, and we'll all sit down and discuss it." Kash is in business mode, his thoughts precise and deliberate. I wish I saw him act more like this with Mercedes. "Can you get something ready in two weeks?"

The muscles in my shoulders and neck feel strained as I stare at him, my brush still. Thoughts of what possible doors this could uncover, and how badly I could possibly mess this up, make my jaw feel rigid.

"Two weeks." Kash nods, setting the date.

"Two weeks," I repeat in some form of confirmation.

"Now, come have a beer with us! King, did they bring more pitchers out?"

"That's okay," I begin. "I need to get some more work done on this before I leave, and my paints are starting to dry."

"We'll be back next Tuesday, see your progress." Kash says the words like an assurance, but they're anything but. I don't want the added pressure of having someone continually checking in to see the development of my work. It makes the tiny creative receptors in my brain shrink as my panic levels grow.

"You look nervous," King says as Summer follows after Kash.

I turn my attention to him and think of every previous tip I've used to relax. "I don't create logos."

King lifts his shoulders in a casual shrug that makes them look even wider. "You said you don't paint murals either, yet here you are."

"Yeah, but this will sit on one wall. Not on stickers and bikes, websites, and everywhere else."

"It will still become a part of this restaurant."

I shake my head. He's being ridiculous trying to compare these situations. As a part of Kash's business team, he of all people should be on my side.

"Eventually you're going to have to make the decision. There's a shit ton of artists out there. Are you going to be able to cut it?"

The fine hairs on my arms bristle though my cheeks heat. Only King can make me feel chilled with fear and heated with anger all at once. "I'll be sure to sign your copy."

chapter
SIXTEEN

"What are you doing, Lo?"

I feel each of my muscles contract from the concern of Kash seeing me looking like this, causing the load I'm bearing to briefly lighten as my imagination works to picture the mess I resemble. Turning my head to face them, I feel a muscle in my shoulder protest. Kash is standing in the hallway holding a large box. The sight of King standing directly behind him makes me feel slightly mortified.

"I'm just trying to make this fit in here." My voice sounds far away from the strain of having my arms above my head for too long.

"You're going to break your back trying to carry that by yourself," Kash objects. He sets his own box down and strides toward me, already raising his arms to the box though I'm several feet ahead.

I give a final shove before he can reach me, and watch the box slide into place. A loud sigh breaks the silence and my arms fall to my sides, tingling so badly it's hard for me to grip the top of the ladder.

"Lo, don't worry about this stuff. King and I will get it."

"It's no big deal."

"You're crazy." Kash shakes his head once. "Where's muchkin?"

"Her friend Paige is here. I hope that's okay. She said she's allowed over whenever. I think they both got tired of me hovering, so I thought I'd move some of these old files."

"Paige is cool and always welcome. Thanks for watching out for her, Lo." I see the edges of Kash's lips curl before he turns his back and grabs the box he carried in. His heavy footfalls echo in the direction of the living room as I slowly climb down the ladder, my muscles loose and fatigued.

"Hurting yourself because you're too stubborn to ask for help is stupid. Swallow your pride next time. Or is that something else you don't like to swallow?"

My eyes fix on King with a glare.

"Oh, does that look say you're starting to remember more?"

"Sorry, I don't obsess over something minor that happened months ago! Especially when it was nothing noteworthy."

"Then why do you still draw me?"

I drop my head back and move my attention to the ceiling to stop seeing the cocky grin that's covering King's face. "I don't draw *you*. I draw your stupid hands. Get over yourself." I should have denied, denied, denied. No one knows I still draw him. For some reason, the knowledge that I do so often completely overshadowed any chance of deflection.

"My hands?"

Before I can stop my head from turning, I'm watching him look down at his hands, his baseball hat sitting low on his brow so I can't see his expression, only hear his confusion in his tone. "Yup, your hands, *stud*."

My words are meant to be as condescending as they sound, yet he looks up at me with his smile stretched impossibly wide. "You did say my hands were amazing. You told me you loved how wide my fingers—"

"Dude, is the new gear here?" The rustling of coats has King and me both turning toward the front door where Summer and Parker are shedding their outer layers.

King's stare meets mine again. He tilts his chin and purses his lips like he's annoyed they've interrupted yet another one of our hate exchanges. "You told me to never stop."

"Never stop what?" Parker asks, pulling the box from King's grasp and lowering it to the ground. His focus remains on it as he pulls a switchblade from his pocket and flips the blade free. In one quick motion, he slides it across the box with a soft pop from the tape, and then he looks to King, holding both flaps of the box. His gaze quickly turns to me and then returns to King with his eyebrows arched.

"Never stop riding. His personality doesn't allow for much else," I say quickly.

Parker howls with laughter and Summer quietly snickers, but I can read the vengeance in King's narrowed eyes. "I thought you were the one that never wanted to stop riding?" King's lips press into a firm line.

"Dude, you aren't riding again without us, are you?" Parker asks, sounding genuinely shocked as he looks to me.

"I've just been messing around while Mercedes works with Summer. It's nothing big."

"You have to get your ass back out to the shop with us! I want to see you do the ramp. You've got ice in your veins! You're going to rock it."

"Yeah, ice in her veins and bricks in her head. Don't give her any more dumb ideas to try," King mutters.

My fingers tighten around the ladder that I'm still gripping for support. I wish it were smaller and lighter so I could throw it at him.

"Don't be a dick, dude. She won't go off the ramp again or any of the jumps until she feels ready." As much as I appreciate Parker defending me, I'd rather he shut up too so the conversation can be redirected.

"Besides, we might take off the training wheels, but I'll catch her if she falls." Parker's eyes dance and his lips spread wide with a smile that once again eludes to his intentions.

"Maybe we'll try the ramp tomorrow."

"Her long arms would probably knock you out." King's reply stings before I've been able to consider Parker's innuendo. The guys laugh with a mutual agreement that has my cheeks warming with embarrassment and my hands falling to my sides in an attempt to not appear so large.

"These are awesome!" The attention shifts to Summer as she pulls out a wad of fabric covered in plastic. She quickly pulls it open and shakes out a sweatshirt as I condense the ladder and disappear into the garage to put it away.

"Lauren, I didn't mean anything by that."

My muscles pull back as a reflex from being startled. My thoughts were so distracted I didn't hear him follow me out. The ladder misses the hooks. It falls with a crash and painful sear to my shoulder and hand as I desperately move to catch it so it doesn't hit Kash's car.

"Are you okay?" King's voice is raised with concern and only inches from me. He pulls the ladder away and leans it haphazardly against the wall, his attention fixed on me.

"Dandy," I reply, shrugging the pain off.

King closes his eyes and moves a hand to his face where he presses a thumb and forefinger to either side of his nose. I trace over him without thought. The scars across his knuckles, the veins and tendons that are stretched even with little movement, and the grease stains along his index finger—I see it all. I turn before I can move on to his face and stalk back into the house where Parker and Summer are surrounding themselves with shirts and plastic wrappings.

"Lo, what size do you need?" Parker asks, lifting a pink sweatshirt and digging for the tag.

"I'm good. Thanks though. I've got to go. I'll see you guys later."

Parker's hands stop, and he turns to look at me. "We'll see you tomorrow?"

"I'll be here." I grab my coat and look around for several minutes before recalling I left my bag out in the shop. My breath releases in a silent huff as I make my way to Mercedes' room, ready to leave. I knock twice, opening the door as I do, and find both of them sprawled out across the floor with a mess of magazines between them.

"Bye, ladies! Have fun tonight. I'll see you tomorrow." Each delivers a half-hearted wave that reinstates they're having fun and that Paige is a good kid. This small assurance lightens the weight on my shoulders as I head back to the front door.

"Night, Lo!" Kash yells down the hall.

"Bye, Kash," I call in reply, gripping the front door handle. "See you tomorrow."

It's cold out, the air heavy, saturated with a dampness that has created a low fog that is both eerie and beautiful. The gravel crunches beneath my feet for several steps as I ignore the sound of movement coming from the garage until King appears beside me, pushing a bike.

"I thought you were going home."

I am not going to look at him. I am not going to look at him. I am not going to look at him.

"Stalking me again?"

My head whips around and my narrowed eyes fix on King. He laughs loudly, freely, his head thrown back like the act is medicinal. It makes memories filter into my thoughts of that night and how we both laughed like this. Together.

I hate that he has such a great laugh.

I hate that he enjoys laughing so much.

I hate that he's laughing at *me*.

"I was just kidding. I knew you were ignoring me." He extends an arm and wraps it around my shoulder, gently jostling me. "Loosen up."

"I resent that you're implying that I'm uptight because you have a terrible sense of humor."

"My humor isn't that bad."

"It's not that good, either."

His lips curl into a small smile, barely showcasing the unevenness of his lips before I realize I'm breaking my vow and looking at him. I don't return the friendly expression. I look forward again, slightly surprised that the fog has become thicker.

"That guy the other night that hit Summer's car, his screaming like that, the anger, why weren't you bothered by it? You should have been afraid or angry, but you were neither."

"If I had, he would have dictated my emotions. I didn't give him that satisfaction."

The skin between his eyebrows draws together. "You've dealt with anger before." His words repeat in my head, working to verify if it's a question or statement. There was a slight inflection with the last word, but his eyes aren't asking, they're verifying.

"Don't we all feel angry sometimes?"

"I didn't say your own." My jaw sets. "You hang out with Mercedes all afternoon, and while you have definitely connected with her, she isn't the easiest personality to be around, especially when she's not getting her way. It never gets very far under your skin though. You know how to calm her down. I didn't really realize it until I saw you face off with that guy."

"Realize what?"

"You've dealt with some pretty difficult tempers, haven't you?" The concern in his tone turns knowing.

"I didn't have angry and abusive parents if that's what you're thinking." It is. "My dad is sort of a gruff guy, but he would never hit me. Make me muck stalls for a month straight, no doubt, but hit me, never."

"What about your mom?"

"What about her?"

"You said your dad wouldn't hit you, but you didn't say anything about her."

"She wasn't around long enough to know if I'd annoy her that much. Neither one of them were, really."

"What do you mean? Like they worked a lot?"

The gravel crunches under our feet as I look over at King and find what I was expecting: attentiveness. I could feel it. King's emotions are like drops of rain, and whether I want to or not, I feel all of them. First they tickle my skin, then coat me, refusing to be ignored. Finally, it seems they soak into me, reaching parts of me I don't think anyone has ever touched. I'm not certain how he's capable of doing so—I'm not sure he even realizes it. Sometimes it terrifies me that it's apparent with my reactions; other times, I really hope it is.

"My mom left when I was a baby." King's eyes tighten, as he listens to me divulge a fact about myself that I have rarely discussed. Growing up everyone just seemed to know I only had my dad and brother. No one ever asked me where she had gone, and it wasn't something I ever enjoyed discussing. "I see her from time to time." The times when I have told others about my mom, their faces relaxed when I explained this fact, but King's does the opposite.

"And your dad works a lot?"

I nod, turning my attention to the path briefly before looking back to him. For some reason, I want to see his reactions. "Yeah. I mean I know he loves me. He's just busy, and he doesn't like the whole art scene. If it was up to him, I wouldn't have gone to college. I would have stayed and worked with him."

"Doesn't he want more for you?"

My eyebrows furrow slightly. "What he has isn't less than what I want—it's just different."

"That came out wrong. I didn't mean that what he does isn't something to be proud of. I just meant that if art is what you love, doesn't he want that for you? Isn't that something we want for everyone we care about?"

"Sometimes people get distracted by thinking they know what's right for someone."

He nods once and then looks forward, a smile raising his lips. "How old are you again? Sixty?"

"Well, I grew up working with a lot of people older than my dad. That likely aged me an additional twenty years, so that makes me forty-two."

King laughs in response as we walk through a well-lit pocket. The light from the garage dances across his chestnut hair, highlighting and shading different strands.

"How old are you?" It's a question I've pondered several times but for some reason seems so trivial. So often people obsess about age differences, yet I could hear that King is thirty-five and I don't think it would change my feelings for him even if others think it should.

His eyes meet mine, and the humor is gone. "Twenty-seven." I keep his stare, not even blinking for several seconds while he waits for a reaction that I don't give.

"That means you're only fifteen years younger than me." Slowly, his lips climb into my favorite smile.

"You're home early." Allie's words interrupt my mental checklist, startling me.

"Yeah, I didn't work today because my mom's coming for dinner."

"I didn't know she was coming. How long will she be in town?"

"I'm not really sure. Hopefully through the weekend. I'd like to show her around."

Allie smiles thoughtfully, building my anticipation. "Think she wants to attend a modeling practice Friday morning?"

"I thought you were going to ask Kenzie?"

"No, you suggested I ask Kenzie, but I told you no. You're my muse, babe!"

"Muse?" My tone is doubtful, filled with humor while I secretly pray that she's joking. I can't say no to her if she really wants me there. As an artist I know how difficult it can be to connect and harness your creativity.

Her blue eyes widen, silently pleading with me. It's like a direct shot to my gut. I feel awful for making a joke when I had even the slightest doubt about her sincerity. "My mom would love model practice. Hell, she'll probably have some good tips. She modeled when she was our age. I'd tell you about it, but she'll likely repeat the stories five times over, so I'll save you the pain."

There's a lingering hint of embarrassment in her smile, but it fades after I reach forward and hug her. "Friday," I confirm. She nods, her confidence returning before I head up to my apartment so that I can start preparing dinner.

King's name leaves my mouth as a curse while I pull open the window. My eyes burn so badly from the onion I've just chopped, I can't even see straight. "Who in the hell thought eating these was a good idea after their eyes felt like *this*?" I cry, fumbling to reach for the sink so I can turn on the water. I blindly wash my hands and then splash cool water on my face, desperate for a reprieve.

My eyes are still tight, tears blurring my vision when I smell smoke. I turn around and find the pan that the onions are supposed to be sautéing in releasing billows of smoke into the small kitchen.

"No no no! What is going on?" I remove the pan from the burner, fanning the air with my free hand before grabbing my spatula and turning the onions. "I forgot the oil," I groan. The onions are dark but don't appear burnt, so I pour some oil into the hot pan and listen to the sizzles and pops fade before returning it to the heat. I release the handle as I scroll over the recipe again, making sure I'm not forgetting another step, and nearly drop it when a pain sears through my middle finger. I pull it back from the stove where it brushed against the burner and thrust my entire hand into the sink that's filled with lukewarm water and packed with several days' worth of dirty dishes.

A new pain hits my palm. It's a sharp, instant pain that fades quickly. I pull my hand from the water, confused and slightly fearful. A long white line leads from my ring finger to the pad of my thumb. I stare at it, dumbfounded, grateful that I must have pulled back fast enough or not hit the blade hard enough to inflict damage. Then the white disappears, replaced with maroon blood that makes my stomach curl. I grab the roll of paper towels and rip several off before clutching them in my fist.

The onions are popping, the oil splattering. I work to carefully reach around it so as to not get burned again, and shove the pan to the back burner with fresh tears in my eyes—these from defeat.

I head to the bathroom to find the brown bottle of hydrogen peroxide and cringe when I remove the stained paper towels. It hurts more to see the cut then to actually experience it. I douse my palm, ignoring the stinging sensation as I grab a clean washcloth to hold against it.

The kitchen is a mess. My dessert—a no-bake cheesecake—looks lumpy but still edible, and slightly appealing, even. After all, it's in a graham cracker pie crust. I release a deep sigh, focusing to hold on to this silver lining as I resolve to order a pizza. Wine, pizza, and cheesecake—we can make this work out to be something really great.

The pizza restaurant explains their specials to me, answering several questions that I knowingly ask on my mother's behalf before choosing one that I know she'll enjoy.

I'm almost grateful my palm is hurt, preventing me from working. If it weren't, I would be sitting at my easel feeling obligated and compelled to work on my portfolio with nothing but frustration and anger swirling for how badly things have gone and how uninspired I feel to draw anything other than *him*.

I flip on the TV and distract myself with two sitcoms before the doorbell rings and a smile covers my face.

"Why does it smell like pizza?"

I reluctantly open my eyes and discover a headache settling deep in my temples, making the temptation to close them again unbearably tempting. Kenzie is the last person I want to see most days, but especially tonight.

"Did you make a cheesecake?"

"Just throw it away," I grumble.

"Where's your mom?"

"Good question."

chapter
SEVENTEEN

"**W**hat happened to your hand?"

"Why are you wearing plaid again?"

King's eyes move to his shirt, and he shakes his head with annoyance before looking back at me. "What happened?"

"I cut it."

"Obviously. With what? A machete?"

"A knife that was in our sink. I didn't see it because I was trying to make the burning stop."

"The burning?" His eyebrows shoot up under his baseball hat, his eyes reflecting lighter shades of brown with the yellow and black plaid shirt I'd like to stain with bleach in an attempt to get it out of his short rotation.

A smirk curves my lips as I curl my fingers into a fist and lift my bandaged middle finger. He doesn't react like I had been expecting, making the act far less satisfying. Instead, he takes my hand in his and makes quick work of peeling the bandage off while I list off several objections. There's a large blister along the pad of my middle finger that still feels like the epicenter of hell.

"You need to put something on it that isn't going to stick. This stuff will make it hurt worse."

"I know, but it's all we had and I don't want it to pop. With my luck it will become infected and I won't be able to work for a month."

He keeps hold of my hand, rotating it from side to side to look closely at the swollen area that seems darker than appropriate against my pasty skin tone. "This is going to take a couple of weeks." I don't voice that I already know this. There's a scar across my shin that is a lasting memory of just how long burns take to heal. "We've got some dressing that will be better than this shit." King crumples my old bandage in his palm and lifts his chin to gesture toward the hallway.

He follows me down the hall while a hundred different ways to tell him I can take care of this on my own cross my mind. I should, but a sadistic part of me wants to see what he's going to do. Being around King is like having a tooth cavity; you keep biting down on the area to see if it still hurts even though you already know it will. I'm fairly certain they consider this behavior a symptom of insanity.

King pulls open the medicine cabinet and rifles around for several seconds before pulling out a few items. He washes his hands methodically and then draws out a clean towel from under the vanity. I watch as he prepares the bandage by covering it with an ointment, and then he instructs me to thoroughly wash the area. After drying my hand, I carefully extend it palm up, spreading my fingers wide so as to create enough space to wrap the tape.

"I thought you remembered how much you liked saying 'fuck me' that you were going to do it again."

"I was just showing you my burn like you asked."

He's still holding the bandage a few inches from my hand, but he looks up at me instead of my wound. His eyes are shadowed by the bill of his hat, but it's still apparent they're wide with sarcasm. "I remember you saying it plenty of times when we—"

I clear my throat loudly, drowning his words, and reach for the bandage that he pulls back as if anticipating my move. "I can take care of this, thanks."

"I'm pretty sure you enjoyed me taking care you that night."

"What in the hell is wrong with you?" My tone and eyes are lowered with a fierce anger that has me ready to quit my job so I never have to see him again, and tempted to bite down to see if it will still hurt. "I am not some cheap whore that finds your disgusting jokes humorous. Everyone else might think that because of who you are, you're entitled to say crap like that, but you aren't. That night meant nothing. I've been over it and you for a long time. Now you need to get over yourself." I reach forward and rip the bandage from his stilled hand and stalk out of the room, my heart beating so fast and powerfully I can feel it in my throat.

My hands feel unsteady as I wrap the dressing around my finger while my words run on replay through my head. I'm not afraid of him firing me, I'm not afraid of hurting his feelings, but for some ridiculous and inexplicable reason, I feel guilty for lying.

He really must be driving me to insanity.

"Why are you fidgeting again?" Allie's scolding is in the form of a whisper but still reaches my ears as a yell because I know by the sharp look in her eye that she's ready to stab me with a pin if I don't stop.

"Sorry," I whisper. I work to ignore an itch on the back of my neck and another on my shoulder. As I think about how much I hate standing still and why I didn't see King at all today though he always works in the home office on Fridays, I feel several more tickles across my skin that arise because I know I can't move.

My eyes scan over the large space that we're filling. There are at least two hundred other students in here, each with a model who, like me, is standing atop a crate, making a select few of us even more uncomfortably tall. Several people look perfectly relaxed as they stand completely still, their shoulders back and chins raised as though they're already on stage. My eyes trace over each of them, noticing their poise, boldness, and beauty.

"She's really pretty."

Allie's looks up at me with minimal interest. "Who?"

"The girl over there with the dark blond hair." I nod in the direction of where she's standing.

"You're an artist, Lo. She's definitely pretty, but her confidence is what makes her stand out so much."

Allie's comment makes me stare longer at the girl, noticing her eyes are a little too close together, and her forehead too short to be what is believed to be the definition of attractive. It brings me to hate those ignorant facts even more because she is beautiful, and I'm grateful she seems to believe so without meeting the dictated standards.

"Lo," Allie hisses in warning, making my hand drop from where it's rubbing across my mostly bare thigh.

"You should really consider asking Kenzie."

"I would have if I had known you have ADHD. What's with you?"

"I don't know."

"It's because you can't draw, huh?" My attention drops to Allie as she places another pin along the hemline.

"That's definitely not helping."

"When do you think you'll be able to hold a pencil again? Are your professors freaking out?"

"I don't know. I'm hoping by the end of this week so I can draw while I'm home for Christmas."

"Are you excited?"

Her gaze remains fixed on the dress as I raise my eyebrows, her question sinking into my thoughts. "I guess. I don't know."

"You don't talk about your family much." Allie's eyes dart to mine for just a fraction of a second, but I'm sure it's long enough to notice mine working to evade contact.

"There's not a whole lot to say."

"What happened to your mom this week?" I feel her briefly glance up again before moving her hands to a new spot where she begins measuring the fabric for the next pin.

"Something came up. I'm sure I'll see her after the holidays. You know how this time of year is."

She places a white chalk pencil between her teeth and nods slowly as if debating that it's the correct response. She frees it again, intently focusing on the fabric, and places a careful mark. "You aren't mad?"

I shrug, earning a glare from her that I return with a frown. Her lips fall open into a laugh. "You just need to focus on someone and mentally draw them; otherwise, you're never going to make it out of here tonight, at least not without a thousand pinholes."

My neck twists as I look around the room again. There are so many people in here. So much beauty, anticipation, desire, and passion: things I seek for my own inspiration, yet when I close my eyes and start sketching lines across my imagination, they don't make up anyone that's in here. I think I'd be surprised at this point if they ever do again. There are times like yesterday when I genuinely wish I hated him. Hell, he's been a jackass to me enough that I could justifiably say I do, and anyone would be able to understand where I'm coming from. Then again, that would also require having someone to discuss my feelings for and interactions with King.

I wish I hadn't been exposed to the kinder sides of him.

I wish I didn't see how he acts around Mercedes to witness his unconditional love for her.

I wish my memories of that night were fading rather than becoming clearer.

I wish I wasn't falling for this asshole.

I wish he'd fall for me.

chapter
EIGHTEEN

"Lo!" Mercedes' smile is stretched wider than I think I've ever seen it, and knowing this reaction is because she's happy to see me makes that maternal instinct inside of me burn like a flame. That light is such a welcoming feeling; to be missed and cared for is something I don't know that I've ever experienced to this extent, and while it's coming from a ten-year-old girl I nanny for, rather than a friend or boyfriend or even a family member, it makes me feel a slew of emotions that has my lips lifting into a smile and my eyes filling with tears that I wipe away as she hugs me.

"How was your Christmas?"

She pulls back from me, her eyes still bright. "It was so fun! We had four of them!"

Mercedes notices my gape and laughs. Braiding her arm with mine, she leads us into the living room where the tree is still standing. I was slightly concerned when I left ten days ago that they wouldn't remember to get one, or would bypass the tradition. Two bachelors living in a house, I could definitely see that happening, especially when I had witnessed their living conditions

BM: Before Me. If mounds of dirty laundry and unrecognizable objects weren't of concern, I figured a tree wouldn't either. I didn't know how to broach the subject without sounding like I was meddling, so I attempted my discreet intervention by using Summer as my liaison. Since our conversation took place via text, I couldn't see or hear her reaction, but she sent me a smiley face after assuring me one would be up and thanking me for pulling out the boxes of ornaments I had stored in the laundry room after realizing I was the only one who knew where they were. Sure, I told both King and Kash where I had moved everything, but neither one seemed overly interested, more just shocked at the transformation of their house.

The tree is tall and has wide gaps between branches, some spaced over a foot apart. The lights are multi-colored, and the ornaments, which don't match, primarily consist of homemade ornaments that I can tell were done at the hands of Mercedes over the years.

She wraps her small hand around mine, turning my attention from one of the first sights I've wanted to draw that isn't a person. "We did one here with Summer, and another one with my grandma, and one with my grandpa, and then one with Dad's work."

"That's like *Groundhog Day*."

"Like what?" She faces me with sincere curiosity.

"I just mean that's a lot of Christmas!"

"It was. But it was amazing! And now you get to open your gifts because you weren't here!"

"My gifts?"

Mercedes raises her eyebrows with a silent *duh!* and she heads to the tree, retrieving a single wrapped package from below the boughs. She sets the box on my lap, where I carefully inspect it with appreciation. The wrapping is covered with snowmen and is perfectly folded and taped—clearly Summer assisted. Mercedes slides it closer, her patience once again waning.

Inside is a pillow of tissue paper that Mercedes eagerly helps me remove. Below are several different pens, rubber erasers, charcoals, acrylic paints, oils, and brushes. They're an expensive artist's quality, too, not the cheaper student grade. I'm still eyeing the brushes when Mercedes pulls a smaller box free from the bottom and pushes it closer to me.

"There's more?"

"We each got you something."

My chin drops and I silently wait for her eyes to meet mine before asking her what that means.

"This is from King."

King?

I haven't seen him since snapping at him after he crossed too far over the asshole-line again that day in the bathroom. Curiosity is heating my entire body. It's going to be a joke, a gag, something utterly useless.

"Open it!" Mercedes growls then reaches forward without waiting and lifts the lid. Inside is a golden bangle. A delicate feather creates half of the bracelet, tiny marks and details reminding me of the one I held.

"I told him you were going to love it."

I am completely speechless because I do. It's beautiful and elegant while being chic and modern. Not only that, but while this could be an inside joke, I feel quite confident it serves as an apology.

"You love it … right?"

My fingers are still wrapped tightly around the bracelet as they fall into my lap, and I look up at Mercedes, my smile climbing impossibly wide. "I love all of it! Thank you!" Her arms fling around my neck, jostling the bracelet with her aggressive hug.

"I have something for you, too."

Her eyes are wide, gleaming with excitement for what those words promise when she pulls back, and I'm proud of her for not squealing like I can tell she wants to. I lean forward and lift the gift bag I had brought while still securely holding the bracelet.

I agonized over what I would get her. Champagne tastes on a beer budget became Cristal Champagne on a Pabst Beer budget when it came to shopping for her and the brands I know she adores.

With an easy pull of tissue paper, Mercedes pulls out a custom helmet I ordered with Summer's assistance, covered in a shell that is comprised of sketches I had to send in that include ones of her riding and several of the images I drew while she wore the bandages on her chin that now only shows the slightest red seam.

"I love it," she whispers, her eyes wide as her hands turn the helmet to see the other side again. "I love it." This time when she says the words, her eyes meet mine, and a warmth passes through me that has my eyes once again filling with tears.

chapter
NINETEEN

"What do you do on the weekends? Like party and shit?" I appreciate that Parker often begins conversations at a completely random point, skipping over customary greetings and diving right into whatever his question or intent is. Sometimes it makes my head spin as I mentally exchange the pleasantries out of habit before I'm able to respond, but I'm slowly adjusting.

"More like work and shit." I drop the dishtowel I was using to dry the counters and lean against the stove to face him. I've been here for over an hour, waiting for Mercedes. Summer picked her up from school to go get fitted for a new bike, something I didn't even know happened, leaving me to find something to do to occupy myself. I settled on deep cleaning the kitchen.

"But you're young! You're supposed to be having fun, making mistakes!"

"Yeah, that's just never been me. I don't know, maybe it's because I was raised in a small town where it was really hard to get into much trouble because everyone knew who everyone was and what they were or were not supposed to be doing. Like my friend got grounded for two weeks our freshman year of high school and she tried to sneak out on her last night of house arrest to help our friend get ready for homecoming, and she didn't even make it a mile before she was caught." I notice Parker's eyes widen with humor and nod, a trace of a smile on my lips. "It's pretty hard to walk too far out of line when you live on large plots of land without public transit and over a thousand local guardians."

"So you never did high school things? Like get drunk? Have sex?"

"I don't think there's necessarily an age tied to either of those events, but yes, I experienced those and other 'normal high school activities.'" My fingers quote his term and then drop when I realize I'm acting far too much like one of the thousand local guardians I just told him about. "I mean, we all did stuff, just not the kind of stuff I see in movies and hear about now."

Parker's phone buzzes and his eyes, still laden with humor, meet mine briefly before he frees it from his pocket. I'm pretty sure by the way this conversation has been going, if his phone hadn't rung he would be asking me more questions about my sexual experiences, but I'm hoping I'm wrong as I stand up and head over to where my notepad's lying on the counter. I feel the familiar energy course through me, the desire to open the cover and seek out a blank page. My mind is already silencing Parker's voice and selecting the illusion it wants to breathe life into.

"Sorry, Lo, I've got to run. Spencer and Kash are waiting for me to do a few retakes."

My lips press into a tight smile as I try to hide my relief. "No problem. I'll see you later."

"Yeah, I'll be by tomorrow."

"Sounds good."

He leaves, and I'm not sure if my sigh is physical or merely mental as I reach for my things and head to the table. I don't like drawing on a flat surface because the light falls unevenly, but I only have an easel at home and school, so I have plenty of experience with poorly lit level planes. I don't bother wasting the time to find the next empty page, simply flipping to one near the very back.

The need to draw has become a tightly wound ball of tension, and as charcoal lines are cast across the paper, the tangled web quickly relaxes, melting like a fine thread of sugar hitting the water until I feel nothing.

I turn my head as I work to see if the shading is correct. I'd lift the pad up to get a better angle, but that will only create a bigger mess from the charcoal dust that collects with shading. I use the side of my thumb to create a stroke of color and jolt when I realize I'm not alone.

"How did you do that so fast?"

I use the back of my hand to try and brush some hair out of my face. The same strands fall back across my cheek as I look to King. "It's one of the reasons I prefer charcoal." My mouth feels too dry as I swallow and turn my attention back to my drawing. "It's very forgiving, versatile, and fast."

"But that was like twenty minutes."

"It's not done. I haven't finished shading and blending, or softening it. I don't have an eraser with me."

"Do you always work that fast?"

I shrug absently. "Some take longer, others less. It depends on what I'm working on, if I've done it before, my mood."

King moves until he's directly behind me, never asking if I mind as he looks over my drawing. "What does it mean when you draw something in twenty minutes?"

"Are you asking if I've drawn you before?"

King doesn't reply, but I can feel him staring at me from over my shoulder, waiting for me to look at him. I'm reluctant to do so, but it's pointless. I'm the one who threw tact out the window by asking the question I knew he was alluding to. His brown eyes aren't teasing like I expect but intent, causing me to shift slightly in my chair before looking away. "I draw everyone I spend time with. It's easier when I'm familiar with people because I know so many of their expressions."

I expect him to make some sort of distasteful joke, but his eyes return to the drawing, and my fingers burn with the familiar itch to draw as I notice how much darker his lashes look when reflecting off his dark eyes from this angle.

"You should do this work for Kash. It could open doors for you. Who knows, you could get grabbed up by a huge company to design logos."

"That sounds cool and all, but I don't want to design logos. Logos are about being clever and creative. I never construct anything new. Everything that I draw already exists. I don't know how to draw something if I can't see it."

"How do you know unless you try?"

It's not necessarily fair that his question infuriates me, dredging up countless memories shared between my dad and me about art and the few doors it will ever be able to offer me, and the far longer hall of doors it never could. Still, I find the fact that he chose to give up his love and passion to ride to go into the business side of things a factor that will make it nearly impossible for him to understand why doing that seems like an impossibility. "You couldn't ask me to give up my art any easier than you could ask me to stop breathing. The end result would be the same."

He furrows his brow, catching me off guard. Then I watch his lips purse as the muscles in his jaw flex, like my thoughts were just delivered through osmosis or something, and he finds them offensive. "If you don't want to do the drawing, you don't have to. It's not that big of a deal. We can find someone else."

"No, I want to do this one. I just can't picture myself being stuck in an office talking to people about what their brand means and trying to somehow capture that with such minimal space and details. It takes me at least an eight-by-ten sheet of paper and sometimes several hours to show a single expression. It would be like you guys going from doing what you do to joining the Tour de France. Sure, you'd still be on a bike, but what you love about the entire sport would be absent."

King's eyes relax as they slowly shift between mine, making the desire to look away grow alarmingly fast with each second that he continues. "What were you thinking when you were looking at the pictures we were editing for the ad campaign?"

Once again, King's words tilt me off balance. While Parker skips right into the meat of a conversation, King never makes inconsequential conversation.

Each question or statement seems to be purposeful, like there are a million intents behind each.

"What do you mean?" I try to recall seeing them, blocking out his presence and how he worked to avoid me while I was in there. The memory distracts me from the question at hand, making me shake my head slightly in an attempt to stop thinking about them.

"You didn't like something about them."

"No, no. They were great. Really."

"But..."

"No buts. They were great."

King's eyes narrow again, brimming on accusation, but there's too much confusion in his expression. "There was something. I saw the look on your face."

"I'm sure it was just the shock of the stunts he was doing."

"No, it wasn't until the originals were up that your eyes focused like they do when you draw. But while you looked at them you had the expression you were making when you were shading here." King's finger hovers over his neck on my drawing, reawakening the frustration I felt while I was working on the simple structure. I kept picturing King's face in several shades of light and never took the time to focus on any one, causing the shading to all be slightly awry. I hadn't minded it until I got to his neck, and then the shadows seemed to make it appear too narrow, and then too wide, and then highlighting the errors on his face, making it seem less abstract and creative and more novice.

I press my lips together and think back to the pictures I stared at while in a reverse position to what I am in now with King. "Sometimes I think society depicts too much about what is beautiful. We remove details that are real and natural because we think they're unforgiving and repulsive. We remove and alter stretch marks, cellulite, blemishes, an errant hair, all to make someone look like no one truly does. Perfect isn't real. Some of the things that made Kash beautiful in those pictures were erased in an attempt to make him perfect. It made me focus on those spots because all I saw was what was missing. She created imperfections." King's eyebrows rise and the corners of his mouth tilt up. I pray he's not baiting me and plans to use this to make Summer hate me again. Regardless, I continue, "By trying to make Kash perfect, she erased the indentations along his spine, and the scar along his side, and the sweat and dirt that was there because he was working his *ass* off. You didn't see the tendons in his hands, or the expanded veins because of the adrenaline and tight grasp he had on the handlebars, or the focus and bliss that was written on his face with the way his brow was drawn, and his eyes were focused on something that you know only few can see."

"You need to stop questioning yourself."

I pull my head back with surprise. He doesn't clarify my obvious confusion, or elaborate further; he simply looks at my drawing of him again and then steps into the kitchen.

I can feel a growl of frustration climb higher in my throat. I am so irritated by his brush-off that I want to throw my piece of charcoal at the back of his head.

"Ready to learn how to make an alfredo sauce?"

"I think my days of cooking are over," I mutter, closing my notepad without dropping the particles of dust left behind by the charcoal into the trash. I know it will smear the picture, but I don't care. I want to rip it out and shred it into teeny, tiny strips and then burn them. Simply distorting it means I'm being civil, an adult, though his eyes are laced with humor and accusing me of being anything but.

"Your problem is you stick to things you're good at so you never know what it feels like to be uncomfortable."

My spine feels like a rubber band being snapped. I glare at him, wishing to explode and tell him how uncomfortable I feel stepping through the door every single weekday and some weekends, knowing he might be on the opposite side. Or how uncomfortably I have slept all week because Kenzie continues to bring over her special "friends," depriving me of not only my bed, but my easel, clothes, food, and solitude. Instead, I lift my hand and show the bright pink line that is a roadmap to my failed cooking attempts.

"You can't stop just because you had one bad experience."

I drop my chin, pursing my lips. The small smirk on his face tells me he knows I'm not referring to just this single incident.

"Think of cooking like art. The spices are your colors."

I shake my head, baffled by his comparison. "They're nothing alike."

"Sure they are."

"No. For me, art is … I don't know, it just makes sense. I know without having to think about it how things go together."

King's lips turn up into an uneven grin that makes my eyes narrow into a glare. He laughs and moves to pull a pot and a couple of pans out. "You see the same things that everyone else sees, yet you see what makes them beautiful. Art's instinctual to you, it comes easily. You're going to have to learn how to cook." My mind's still stumbling over his last words about how I see things and what that means, if anything, as he continues. "So you're really going to do the logo, huh?"

My head shakes as I wander farther into the kitchen, stopping when King smiles with triumph, making me briefly consider going back to the dining room table before I cross my arms over my chest and lean back against the furthest counter from where he stands. "I'm painting a picture on one of the walls in the shop, but as I've told Kash, I don't expect him to choose it as his logo."

"Do you know what you're going to draw yet?"

"Not a clue."

His grin is benevolent, friendly even, as he moves to the fridge and pulls several ingredients out. "You should come to the match next week, watch it all happen and see if that inspires you. You said you can't draw what you don't know." King shrugs as he drops a stick of butter beside the stove. "Time to get acquainted."

The fact that he's right makes my nose scrunch. Even when it's an obvious situation like this, I've never been great at accepting dictation.

"Come over here and grab the middle knife on the far right of the block."

An immature desire to remain rooted and voice my protest crosses my mind before I quietly sigh and move to do as he's instructed.

The knife feels heavy and awkward in my hand as I wait for further direction and watch as he fills a large pot with water.

"Grab that red cutting board and the package of chicken," King says, nodding to the counter beside the fridge. I feel him watch my movements, making each of them feel painfully pronounced and awkward.

"You're going to cut the chicken into small pieces, and then we'll put some spices on them and sauté them."

"How big is small?" I ask, unwrapping the paper from around the chicken and drawing out three breasts. I hate the feel of raw meat; it alone could easily convert me to a vegetarian.

"Bite-sized."

"For a horse or a toddler?"

"Since we don't have either of those, I think you've found your answer."

"Asshole-sized, perfect."

"Don't start a war you won't be able to finish," King warns, his movements stalling, ensuring me his sole focus is on me. The action isn't a taunt, it's a threat, and it burns a sudden level of frustration through me that only King can evoke.

I raise my chin as I turn my head to face him. Slowly, I release my grip on the knife so that it rests against the cutting board, removing my temptation to throw it at the back wall. "Go ahead." My shoulders roll, my knees bend, and my hip leans against the counter. My entire body is showing how little I care about what he has to say next. It's a lie, of course, but one that is crucial to maintain.

"What? Is Charlie going to kick my ass?"

Charleigh? How is Charleigh a part of this?

"I know all about Charlie. I don't know why you didn't just tell me you were dating someone. It's not like I was going to hold what happened over your head or something. It's not a big deal."

This is one of those moments where I so wish I had the capability to read minds. Clearly King thinks Charleigh is a guy, but that's all I'm certain of. Why he's bringing up the possibility that I have a boyfriend and the idea that I would pose a boyfriend as a warning against him makes me question if he's threatened. Jealous? Merely curious? I need an extra hour to sit down and sketch the expression on his face so that I can fully decipher what all he isn't telling me.

"Is that why he never comes over? Because he knows … about me?" If hope isn't tainting his words, I am completely insane, because I swear I hear traces of it. But his expression turns cold and stoic in an instant, shoving my thoughts of clarifying who Charleigh is to the deepest depths of my vocabulary.

"Why would I tell anyone? It's not a big deal, right?" I ask. King's words hadn't stung upon first impact, but playing them back in my head once more, they feel like more than just a rejection; I feel used. They shouldn't be causing this reaction. I've used these same words against him numerous times in the past; however, this time they leave a sour taste in my mouth that worsens now that I've repeated them back.

He squares his shoulders, the distaste obviously affecting him as well. To make certain my point is made, I shrug and raise my eyebrows before turning back to the chicken and carefully beginning to chop it. I never mention how much the feel of it bothers me, nor do I seek assurance that I'm doing it right. I simply do as he instructed, and once I finish, I place my knife in the sink carefully so as to not make a loud noise. If I dropped it, it would reveal I'm frustrated and still stewing over his words. I refuse to let that happen. After washing my hands three times, I dry off and head outside because I can't be around him a second longer without demanding answers to questions I'm still trying to make sense of.

I suggest to Mercedes that we hit the mall up the next day and then go to OMSI, the science museum, to prevent any chance of encountering King, with the promise this is the last time I'm going to avoid him. I'll let him continue working at it, but I'm done expending the energy on him.

"I'm so proud of you! That was insane, Lo! I need to take a picture so you can draw yourself doing this!"

I risk looking over to Mercedes as my tire rounds over the lip of the smallest of the ramps. They rarely use this piece of equipment, seemingly making it a waste of space, which seems fairly bizarre since so little of the shop goes without purpose and extensive use.

"Are you ready to graduate to the next ramp?" Parker's beside me, his eyes bright with excitement from finally convincing me to go on the ramp again.

"I think I need to master the small one first."

"Master? You were like the Jedi out there! The kid is right, you looked awesome! I can't believe you haven't been on a bike in over ten years!"

"Believe it." My muscles feel nearly buoyant as they accept Parker's praise, feeding off his enthusiasm and confidence. Mercedes and I have been riding a few times a week since the shop opened in October, but I've still shied away from doing much of anything, generally blaming my always inappropriate shoes for doing much else. Still, I've pushed so far outside of my comfort zone.

"You don't have to do it, Lo. We'd all understand if you're afraid." Summer's voice sounds sincere, yet I still feel as though I have something to prove to her, sealing my fate.

"Okay, let's try it." My brain is going into overdrive, working to make sense of this suicide attempt while trying to effectively order my feet to stop pushing me forward. My pride is louder than my sense though, and I keep going.

"*Woo hoo!*" Mercedes calls from the side. I know I've heard Parker echo the same call at least three times since I agreed to go, but hers is the first that really penetrates the haze of fear and excitement I'm surrounded by.

"I won't flip over the edge, right?"

"No, it's just like the small one; the momentum will glide you right over the lip. Just remember: you don't want to use your hand brakes. You'll be fine. You want to ride it out, just like a rollercoaster, baby." Parker's hand settles on my shoulder, feeling much like a lead weight, causing my shoulder to sag.

The loud pounding of my heart distracts me as I push to the edge of the ramp. The only thing I notice is the heat and weight of Parker's hand sliding away. With my first and last trip down the ramp, I just went. I didn't take the time to consider what I was doing. This time, I look down and across the space, more amazed by the distance of the smallest ramp now that I've crossed it and can see it from this angle. I take a deep breath, feeling the pressure of my heart in each of my fingers as I rest them gingerly on the brake so they're ready for when I get over the lip. My toes push off and the bike slides forward. The wheels spin so quickly I nearly lose my footing on the pedals. The speed builds fast. Too fast. My breathing is loud, but not as loud as my heart, and all of my muscles contract with fear, making my fingers squeeze reflexively. There's a startling stop from the front tire, and then an instant lurch as the bike falls forward and sideways all at once. My right arm is tangled in the bike, but my left extends to stop me from leaving a stamp of my face on the bottom of the ramp. It hits with an alarming explosion of impact, and then my helmet cracks against the cement. The bike falls on top of me with a crushing blow. I don't know how to move. I don't know if I *can* move.

Voices register, followed by the slap of shoes on the cement.

"Lo, are you okay?" I recognize Mercedes' cry over the others and slowly move in an attempt to straighten myself.

"Don't move," Parker instructs in a yell. "Your shoe is caught in the spindles." A hand holds my foot, and the warmth of it soaks through my ballet flat. The comfort seems vast in contrast to the cold, hard cement, and the pain that is starting to radiate through my body.

The bike moves next, and my entire body seems to sigh with relief. "What hurts?" Summer is beside me, brushing hair out of my face. "How's your arm?"

I slowly roll to my side, and the helmet clonks against the cement, straining my neck as I lie on my back. Parker reaches forward and makes quick work of releasing the clasp and gently settles my head back down.

"Shit!" Summer's word comes out in a breath as she drops to her knees beside Parker. "Can you move it?"

Her attention is on my leg. I don't want to try. It's throbbing and aching so badly I want to curl on my side and cry until the branding-iron-like heat dissipates. But the embarrassment and weakness that would reveal would haunt me worse than the face dive I just did.

"Video's up. They're showing Slim's newest—" The others turn as King's words abruptly end. I take the brief reprieve to squeeze my eyes shut and let out a deep breath that trembles, serving little comfort as an expression of the pain I'm feeling. "What happened?" His words come out with an intensity that matches his strides as he swallows the gap between us, briefly regarding Summer before returning to me.

"She started to panic, and her wheel caught the edge of—"

The skin between King's eyebrows crinkles as they draw together, and his eyes flash with anger as they narrow on me. "You tried to go down a ramp? You haven't been on a bike for thirteen years!"

"She was holding her own. Totally killing it in fact. You would have been impressed. She's got balls."

Parker's comment diverts King's glare. "You guys watched her try to kill herself?" His eyes round back to mine and then drop and search over me. "Fuck. That's gonna hurt." He takes a deep breath and shakes his head ever so slightly. "Mercedes, go get your dad. Tell him we need the insurance information for the hospital. Summer—"

"I'll watch Mercedes."

King nods and then watches Mercedes jog toward the doors of the shop.

"Don't move," King orders, stopping me as I raise my right hand to sit up. I ease back against the cool surface and release a quiet breath.

It's only a few minutes before Kash and Mercedes return, but it feels much longer. No one has spoken. They're standing around me either staring fixated on my ankle, or like me, completely avoiding it after looking in my general direction and wincing. King looks irate, his hands woven on his bent knee as the two approach where he's kneeling beside me.

"What in the hell happened?" Kash asks.

The desire to sit up consumes me once more. Feeling weak is one thing; looking weak is another level of awful. I avoid looking at him as I have King since he came in, though I'm still feeling his attention, more poignant than the others.

"Can you move your hands?" My eyebrows drop as I look to King.

"Yes." That was the first question I had too, and therefore the first thing I checked. He doesn't respond, drawing my attention from my torn jeans to Kash. His glare is harsher than King's, making me realize Mercedes likely inherited the cunning look from him.

"Her ankle might be messed up. Her foot got caught in the spokes." Parker's face appears over King's shoulder.

King doesn't ask permission. His hands move to my legs and then slowly run down each one, applying the slightest of pressures before he reaches my ankles and the slight gap between the bottom of my skinny jeans and ballet flats. His fingers prod with increased pressure around my ankles, and then he focuses on my right foot. My shoe is gently removed, and his hands envelop my heel. "It's already bruising."

"It's okay. It really doesn't hurt that much."

"That's the adrenaline. You'll feel it, believe me," Kash assures me.

"We need to take her in." King tosses my shoe to Kash and, without warning, slides his arms under my legs and around my back and lifts me. Pain slices through me as I stiffen, forcing me to try to settle against him. I've always been tall. Nothing about me screams petite, cuddle, or protect. I struggle with wondering if it will be easier for him to carry me stretched out with my weight disbursed, or huddled together so I'm not as long. My thoughts cease when

I catch sight of my ankle. There's a large lump surrounded by bruising, and looking at it amplifies the pain shooting through it. My breaths become more labored as I silently instruct myself to look away, but I can't. My entire body heats and the room begins to swim.

chapter
TWENTY

"She's lucky the bars didn't crush her arm." The irritation in King's voice is vibrant, nearly as much as the pain that's still ricocheting through my foot and leg.

"Hey, are you okay? You're alright?"

I nod in the general direction of Parker and close my eyes. "I'm going to be fine. I don't need to go to the hospital."

"We need to get X-rays of your ankle." King's tone is slightly softer, but his words are still clipped.

"It's fine. Just a sprain."

"And you know this how?" King asks.

"Because it just hurts a lot."

"And how do you think it would feel if it was broken?" he asks, his tone holding a new level of warning and sarcasm that makes a concoction I can't refuse to accept with a sardonic smile.

"It would hurt a whole hell of a lot."

Parker gives me a short laugh, mostly out of courtesy for my failed attempt at humor, but King's eyes are narrowed, lacking any trace of amusement.

"We're going to the hospital. Kash is getting the Suburban now."

I turn to object again because I know with near certainty that it's not broken. If my arm was able to handle the impact, my ankle is a guaranteed home run. The look on King's face stops me. It's intense, daring me to voice, or worse, act out an objection. His silent threat of being prepared to throw me over his shoulder caveman style is loud and clear. My lips close and I settle farther into the couch, looking away before I'm able to catch a glimpse of his satisfaction from my forfeit.

As always, the emergency room is a zoo. A zoo of sick people that makes me once again question the validity of King's cave-man threats. To make matters worse, they've refused me the right to walk. Parker carried me to the car, and Kash carried me inside the waiting room where I sit in an ugly and lumpy navy blue wheelchair, waiting to get X-rays while undoubtedly being exposed to things far worse than the parasites on a feather.

"Do you need new ice?" Kash looks down at my foot that's propped up with the support, covered with ice packs.

"They're still frozen." My foot went from burning with pain, to burning from being so cold, to now feeling nothing.

"I'm still on my dad's insurance. You guys don't need to wait around." Truthfully, I don't want to be here alone, but having them wait with me seems to make the time pass even slower. I can't admit to them that I don't know anyone else to call who would be willing to wait with me. I know Charleigh or Allie would but also know that neither can afford the time to be here when they're both struggling to find enough for their work, especially now that Charleigh is dating her mysterious boyfriend.

"I can't believe you went down the middle ramp," is King's reply. "And while wearing those shoes!" He motions toward my remaining silver ballet flat with a pointed toe. Parker told me I had some bad *bacon*, which had my face scrunching with confusion, prompting him to translate the term to road rash. He later confirmed my shoe had even worse *bacon*.

"It won't happen again, trust me."

Different expressions of objection are worn on each of their faces as they turn to me.

"You can't give up now." King's words beat the ones Kash was starting to say in a much softer tone.

"I'm pretty sure I can. My future depends on my being able to use my entire arm for drawing. Taking a chance to do something that has absolutely no benefit is stupid."

Parker laughs, King scowls, and Kash pats my knee a couple of times before smiling. "The benefit is the freedom, Lo. You'll learn to understand that with time."

I'm mature enough not to break out in a chorus of "I told you so," but not mature enough to miss the opportunity to shoot a pointed look to King as the doctor clears me of any breaks and informs me I've got a bad sprain that requires crutches for at least a week.

A week.

When I was little, the week before Christmas always felt like an entire year, yet now, this week sounds like ten. How am I going to get on the bus with crutches? How am I going to walk to and from the bus stop to the Knight residence with crutches? How am I going to get up three flights of rain-slickened apartment stairs with crutches? This isn't even counting school.

I'm never riding a damn bike again.

My ankle is wrapped and I'm back in a wheelchair, being taken out to where Kash is retrieving the Suburban. King is carrying my crutches while listening to the discharge nurse remind him that I need to be careful with both my ankle and left arm for a couple of weeks and should ice them frequently. They've also given me some antibacterial ointment for my first official *bacon*—something

Parker took several photos of and Tweeted while we were waiting for the results of the X-rays, stating I was official.

"She needs to take the ibuprofen religiously for the first couple of days to minimize the swelling. That and the ice will significantly help with the pain," she prattles on. I've had worse injuries; this isn't going to be a big deal. It's the commute that's going to be difficult.

The dark Suburban pulls up, and I grip each side of the wheelchair, ready to stand up before the nurse makes a cry of shock and puts her hands on my shoulders with just enough pressure that I know she's instructing me to stay put.

"Alright, why don't you help me." I twist in my seat to try to see who she's talking to. "She can wrap an arm around both of our shoulders and hoist herself up, and we can help her into the car."

Without waiting for King to agree, she's beside me, pulling my right arm around her neck and anchoring it in place by securely holding my wrist.

I feel completely dumbfounded and at a loss for words when King does the same with my left.

"Alright, one, two, three..." she counts, pulling me at the same time that King does so that I'm balanced on my right leg. "Okay, the easiest way to get in—wait!"

But I'm already free of her grip and being deposited into the Suburban behind the driver's seat by King. Thankfully he doesn't fish for my seat belt or situate me as though I'm a broken doll.

"Alright, so I think the best thing would be for you to stay at the house, Lo." Kash pulls away from the curb as he makes the statement. The pain pills that were lulling me into a comfortable haze of nothing, vanish. "You can take up residence in a guest room and just chill out for a few days. If you start feeling better, we can drive you to school. This week is empty. We really don't have much going on."

"Thanks, but that's alright. I think I would be more comfortable at my house."

"You live on the third floor," Kash objects, his eyes finding mine in the rearview mirror.

"Yeah, but I can't go anywhere for a couple of days anyway." I know my reasoning is faulty and weaker than my ankle at this point, but there's no way in hell I'm going to stay at the Knight residence.

Nell says I'm as stubborn as the day is long, but apparently she hasn't met King or Kash, because compared to them I'm easygoing. They entertained me with banter that at times made me briefly believe they were going to give in and take me home, but then it became clear that all they were really doing was stalling.

"How are you feeling?"

My eyes wander from the guest room to where King is resting my crutches on the wall beside me. "This really isn't necessary."

"Why is it so difficult for you to accept help?"

"It's not!" My reply is instant, my voice high, making King's eyes swing back to me for a second before he shakes his head.

"It's those that don't know when and how to ask for help that are weak."

"Why did you stop riding?" My question lacks accusation, and I feel certain as he searches my face he can tell I'm genuinely curious.

"I ride every day."

"But you don't compete."

"Who says?"

"Parker." He looks down but smiles. I'm struggling to make sense of if he's embarrassed, caught off guard that I know this, or is looking to change the subject.

"Parker has a big mouth."

I shrug in reply and tuck a few strands of loose hair behind my ear before my hand freezes, hearing Charleigh in my thoughts, telling me the useless fact that playing with your hair in front of a stranger is a sign of flirting according to psychologists. "I asked him if you ever had competed after I watched you do the course last week. I've never seen anyone look so fearless and happy at the same time. You just looked like you belonged out there."

My eyes stretch with shock. What are these painkillers doing to me? Why am I saying this?

"It's always been Kash's dream to do this."

"Why does that have to affect your dream?"

King shrugs, his eyes again diverting mine. "He's had too much taken from him. He doesn't need to not only lose my help but also have another person to compete against."

"What if you did different events? Two of my good friends are going to school to be fashion designers, and while there are times I can sense one of them getting jealous of the other because of attention they're receiving, or because they've excelled at doing something, the pride and excitement they share, is much greater than those times of being green with envy."

King nods three times, his head only moving an inch in each direction before he looks back at me and smiles his beautiful crooked smile. "Is one of them the friend you're doing the fashion show for?"

"How did you know I'm doing a fashion show?"

King shrugs that small roll of his shoulders that he does so often. "Mercedes tells me about her day every night while we watch the highlights on ESPN."

I don't question what they talk about, though I'm curious. Hearing that they share this time each night does nothing but place a cape across his shoulders in my eyes. A cape he doesn't need when I'm already working to ignore him. "Yeah, apparently she really digs the fact that I'm taller than most guys."

"You're tall, but you aren't *that* tall."

My eyebrows go up, and my eyes widen with obvious disbelief.

"Okay, maybe with heels you are, but normally you're not."

I huff a nearly silent laugh and turn my attention to the ice packs holding my wrist in place. Like bandages, the Knight residence has no shortage of ice packs.

"I also have really big hands and, according to Summer, a big head." The words leave me before I can edit them. I've just told King that I have a big head!

If he hasn't already noticed, I'm sure that's what he's going to be thinking about now when he looks at me. These painkillers are apparently a truth serum.

"I like that you're tall."

Looking back at King isn't even a question—it's a necessity.

His upper body shifts back and then slowly forward again. "I mean, it's not like I look at you and think it's cool that you're tall. I just don't even think about it. It's just you. The way you carry yourself doesn't make anyone think about how tall you are. It's probably the last thing people notice."

"My dad says I walk around like my head is in the clouds."

"That's because you're looking at everything, and rather than thinking about what is really going on, you're finding the beauty in it all."

"I do like to watch people."

King chuckles quietly, his chin drawing to his chest before he looks back to me with his lips still spread in a brief smile. "We should do this again."

"Do what again? Try to break my ankle?"

His smile grows as he shakes his head. "Talk. When we aren't trying to hate each other, we seem to get along pretty well."

"You consciously work at hating me?"

"I consciously work to remember you hate me."

"I don't hate you. I never told you I hate you," I object.

"Maybe not in those words."

"I told you to stop being a jackass because you were acting like one. That's not me telling you that I hate you."

"Do you know how many girls have called me a jackass before?"

"Do you actually keep count?"

"It's a pretty simple number when the only other one is my sister."

"That's because you're usually nice to everyone else. Well, I have seen you act like an ass once in a while, but I can usually predict it."

"You can predict when I'm going to be an asshole?" King's smile tells me he's amused.

"You get tense and avoid eye contact with people. You generally flip your hat around so the bill is backward, like you don't want anything to distract you. When you're in these moods, your smile is forced, making your jaw tighten. And you tend to pinch the bridge of your nose, like you're trying to massage a pressure point."

"You … I what? I pinch my nose?"

I lift my hand to my face, illustrating the same act I've seen him do on numerous occasions. "But you also do it when you're deep in thought, so it really isn't the telltale sign."

"How do you know all of this?"

"Never trust an artist. We can read emotions better than those hack psychics at the fairs."

"I'll remember that." His head dips slightly, but I can hear the smile in his tone. "So I saw your work at the restaurant last week. I thought you'd be there."

"I don't have a class in the morning anymore, so I've been going before they open."

"You really don't like having an audience."

I shake my head, confirming his assessment.

"Why?"

"I don't know. Does it bother you when someone watches you learn something new? There's a part of me that enjoys it. I like to see the wonder on their faces, but so often they see the beginning and lack seeing the potential." His eyes are on the bed, making me shift with unease. "Am I boring you?"

His eyes snap to mine, and his head shakes while a grin grows. "You should get some rest."

"You should find a more sincere way to end a conversation."

"You should stop being so defensive."

"And you should stop making me get so defensive," I huff.

My brain scurries in a million directions preparing my next *you should* comment because he's nearing the door, which makes this argument seem extremely unfair.

He turns when he reaches the doorway, one of his hands is in a loose fist in front of him while the other wraps around the door. His brown eyes find mine and a silent current of thoughts seems to pass between us. A tangle of sarcasm, secrets, and frustrations, along with something far more peaceful that I'm not able to identify because I'm still working to pick the right comeback line. "I'm glad you've been wearing your feather, Lo." Then he's gone.

My eyes drop to the duvet where my hands are laying, my left with an ice pack and my right encircled with the gold bangle.

Being put on bed rest always sounds appealing when you're really busy and obligations keep piling up without warning or preparation to make you go from feeling overwhelmed to not sleeping, living off caffeine, and riding the dangerous line of emotional imbalance. More than once over the past couple of months while I've been working to finish the mural at the restaurant, being a part-time nanny, going to school full time, and becoming the next forgotten model, I have wished to have a weekend in peace when I could do nothing but binge on Netflix and gummy bears and forget about doing any- and everything, including showering and getting dressed.

Now that I've been living the "fantasy" for three days, I'm restless, twitchy, and I stink. I took a shower my first night here and was able to replace my clothes with my art clothes that I had worn to school, but didn't wash my hair because when you have unruly hair that you work to straighten to try and create a façade of normalcy, you don't wash it every day. Instead, you wash it every other day, and in two hours, I am going to be on day four of having it gone unwashed, and it feels gross.

I've watched the entire first season of a show that I fell in love with and was disappointed to learn the second season wouldn't be on for several months, and haven't been able to find another that will hold my attention. I need to shower. I need someone to talk to. I need to draw.

My ankle objects as soon as I'm vertical. I can feel the blood pooling, increasing the throb that has been an unwelcome visitor. I grab my crutches that are leaning against the wall and clumsily fumble with each to get them securely in place. I've been sentenced to crutches a few times before, once when I was kicked by my horse, another when I fell off said horse, and a third for trying to do a cartwheel at my friend's and landing on a rock. It's the one story I rarely share and prefer to pretend never happened because really, how uncoordinated does that make me sound?

The rubber and metal make clicks as I navigate my way to the bathroom where the mirror confirms how badly in need of a shower I really am. I strip out of my clothes and have to sit on the edge, and then lift myself inside. I've felt like an intruder staying here, and felt worse when they've asked if I needed or wanted anything. I'm their employee, and they're now having to replace my ice packs, get me food and drinks, check and make sure I'm taking my required doses of ibuprofen, and sometimes just say hi. Mercedes spent most of her afternoons with me. I hadn't used crayons in so long that the coloring books ended up being my favorite distraction of the different gimmicks she brought in. It was fun to see what I could create with them, and only slightly frustrating when I was reminded how impossible they are to blend. Kash has been surprisingly doting, reminding me once again that although he sometimes forgets some fairly important parenting details, he won't ever fail at the task. He couldn't even if he wanted to because his heart is far too big. I've only seen King once, and that was when he walked by the open door. He looked inside, but that was as close to conversation as we've gotten.

Toweling off proves to be more difficult than I remembered, and I ultimately lay my towel over the toilet seat lid and sit down to finish and get dressed again, shoving my underwear to the very bottom of the trashcan because I refuse to put them back on.

After finger-combing my hair, I head out to the kitchen, the clicking of my crutches growing louder as I enter the living room. I've only been here on a few occasions when it's dark, but tonight, it looks different. I'm not sure if that's because it's past 1:00 a.m., or because I've spent the past three days being a houseguest rather than employee, or because I took my pain medicine less than an hour, ago and they're starting to make everything seem a little different, even myself.

I take a seat at the head of the kitchen table, my left foot elevated with another chair. I left only the barest of lights on so I wouldn't catch too many reflections on the long windows that line the room. My sketch pad is opened to the first blank page, my charcoal posed, ready to be given direction. The predictable fight to draw something else doesn't occur, not tonight. I simply give in to the energy flowing through me, allowing it to dictate what my mind sees—King—even when I'm looking at everything else. I don't consider what he means to me or why. The questions about what, if anything, that night meant to him don't enter my mind. I also don't work to decipher his recent comments about Charleigh, I just draw.

"Why do you pretend that I don't mean anything to you when clearly I do?"

My charcoal presses hard against the paper as my neck snaps up to see King. He's fully dressed, his usual baseball hat still on, flipped backward, and wearing a flannel shirt with the sleeves rolled to his elbows. Flannel is growing on me, but I won't tell him that. His face shows no signs of humor or teasing. If anything, he looks almost pained.

"Did you just get home?"

"Why did you pretend you wanted to know me? Why not just call it what it was?" His eyes narrow as his chin drops.

"Have you been drinking?" I know the answer before I ask the question. I can smell it.

"I liked you, Lo."

My heart races with too many possibilities and hopes, and not enough validation.

"You spend so much time trying to convince yourself that what happened that night wasn't real."

"I was drunk."

"You weren't drunk. I wouldn't have slept with you if you were drunk! I don't do shit like that. It's disgusting!"

"I don't remember large parts of that night."

"You remember more of that night than you're willing to admit." His eyes land on my drawing where he studies the image for several long seconds. I should have covered it as soon as I realized he was here, but it was too late from the beginning. It's of him—of course it's of him. And to make matters worse, he's shirtless. The scars he mentioned me knowing about are there, as well as the few tattoos most of the world is deprived of seeing. "Obviously you remember."

His words make my cheeks burn with embarrassment. He's right, but hearing that he's aware of this fact is both strangely relieving and move-to-Australia-tomorrow worthy. "You left an impression," I admit before moving my attention so I don't have to see his reaction.

"Lo, I haven't been able to forget that night either. I think about it all. The. Damn. Time." His words are punctuated, driving his message much further than just my thoughts. "I spent weeks trying to figure out who you were." I feel slightly guilty that his admission makes me so happy. For so long I have thought he avoided me, lied about his name and identity so that I wouldn't find out who he truly was.

"Why did we wait so long to be honest with each other?"

King's breath is a snicker. "We're only admitting a fraction of anything."

His words run through my head, lacing into several variations of what he actually means, still, I nod. "This conversation needs to happen. We need to figure shit out because I'm tired of trying to avoid you, and I'm really tired of you ignoring me."

"Aren't we kind of doing that now?"

King shakes his head as he closes the distance between us, then grips the table with his left hand and bends so his face is level with mine. "If I stay in here any longer I'm going to do something that would probably make me deserve getting slapped, so I am going to say this and then leave." King pauses. I can smell the scent of beer and peppermint on his breath, along with the warmth of his skin as his shoulders roll forward. His eyes are wide and bright, demanding me to pay close attention to his words. "I know you're tough. I know you can draw better than any damn person I've ever met in my life and most likely ever will. I know you love Mercedes and would never risk changing that relationship. But we like each other, and I don't know what in the hell that means exactly, but I know I want to find out. The question you need to ask yourself is, do you?"

King's throat moves, swallowing words we both know he's fighting with. Ones that would make things both better and worse. He reaches forward, his chest grazing my shoulder. I hate that I don't want to move. That I want to absorb the feel of King's warmth and convince him to admit truths we both know and bury on a daily basis in a sea of general politeness and attempts to avoid one another. But the truths are laid open with the innuendos, silent stares, and capitalized when we go out of the way to cross the other's path. King has become an exhausting and thrilling addiction that I don't know how to consider stopping or even changing at this point.

A long breath runs through my nose as King's dark eyes meet mine, exposing he's fighting his own battle: silently pleading with me to bring things up by making a cutting remark or joke about our night. I know he wants it because it's the only way we can both talk about it and relive it. It's apparent by the way his jaw locks and his eyes waver from mine that he also doesn't want me to respond. He's waiting for me to consider his words and come back. His arm flexes as he holds the table even tighter. Then he stands and stalks out of the room, leaving my heart beating so fast I feel like I just went down the largest ramp in the shop.

Holy shit.

chapter
TWENTY-ONE

I wake up to two missed calls and a dozen texts from Charleigh, the last one saying she's on her way.

Last night is still fresh in my thoughts, likely because I obsessed about it for hours before texting Charleigh and asking her to come get me and finally falling asleep.

Before moving to sit up, I wrap my hair into a knot that I know is accompanied by a halo of fuzzies since it air dried without any product. My mouth feels dry and gross from only having my finger to brush with, and my clothes all feel slightly stretched and worn from wearing them consecutive days. Clean underwear is officially at the top of my to-do list for when I get home as I stand up and hobble around the bed, working to straighten the duvet, though I'll need to wash the sheets.

"Hey, Lo, how are you feeling?" Kash is standing at the stove, a large bag of instant pancake mix beside him, confirming King isn't up yet. Summer turns from where she's perched at the island. A book of pictures sits in front of her with a rainbow of sticky notes protruding from the pages.

"Pretty good, actually. The swelling's gone down a lot."

"How's the burn?" Summer asks.

"It's not bad. That cream is amazing."

"She's a good liar," Summer says teasingly as she looks to Kash. She takes a drink of her coffee before shooting me a smile.

While mine is smaller than hers, I return the gesture.

"Do you want to make a list of things you want and I can run by your place and get them?"

I question if she's offering out of guilt or concern that Kash is still upset with her, even though it was my own decision to go down the ramp. Either way, her face only holds compassion. "That's okay—"

"Why didn't you wake King up, Dad?"

Mercedes stumbles into the kitchen, her hair looking similar to how I'm sure my own looks currently. Her eyes are still puffy with sleep, and her voice extra whiny.

"They're pancakes. They all taste the same," Kash says dismissively.

"Wrong." King's single word is like a small firework going off, lighting the entire house, creating more beauty, emitting bright colors, and making me fear for my personal safety.

Kash rolls his eyes and returns to the stove, but Summer's attention has completely left her book. She's staring between King and me as though she was present for our conversation last night. Maybe he told her?

"Why don't you take a seat and we'll get you some ice packs and pancakes, Lo," Kash offers.

I'm grateful to move my attention back to him. "That's okay, Charleigh's on the way."

"Right ... Charleigh," King says, his voice heavy with sarcasm.

I've been told before that the expression I'm giving King—with my eyebrows raised and my eyes wide—is condescending, and for once, I really hope it is.

"Are you still coming tomorrow to watch Daddy?" Mercedes' word choice makes me flinch slightly, but I still smile in confirmation.

"Yeah, crutches and all."

"Are you bringing Charlie?" Summer's voice is cautious and far quieter than her usual tone.

The doorbell rings before I can reply. King tilts his head, the outside corners of his eyes strain as he stares at me. Then he moves purposefully toward the front door and swings it open. As I walk up behind him far more slowly with my crutches, I notice his rigid shoulders fall slightly.

"Hi. Is Lauren here by chance? I think I'm at the right place. She said it was out in the middle of nowhere, but this place is *really* in the middle of bloody nowhere."

My lips tip up and down like a see-saw as I work to fight my laughter at King's reaction. He's staring at her with such intensity I can tell she's confused.

"You have neighbors, right? Or mates? Someone nearby in case I scream? Cause you're kind of freaking me out."

"Hey, Charleigh." I step up beside King and grab my bag that I deposited by the door last night.

"You really did get all banged up, didn't you?" Her eyes leave King and travel over me. There's little to be seen since my clothes cover most of the damage, and the Ace bandage covers the rest.

"Are you concerned about the stairs? Or is that just me?" she asks, the lilt in her voice a refreshing song, promising me the comforts of my own house.

"I'll be okay."

Charleigh's eyebrows go up, and they stay stretched as she lets out a deep sigh. "Alright, you ready to go then?"

"Yeah."

"Wait! I want to meet Charlie!" Summer's voice is right behind us. I turn because I want to see the look of surprise on her face as well when she realizes the error.

I take a step back and extend my hand to Charleigh. "Charleigh, this is Kingston, Summer, and Kashton. Everyone, this is Charleigh."

"And me!" Mercedes calls, sprinting in from the kitchen. "Hey, Charleigh!"

She smiles brightly, and I notice King, Kash, and Summer all look at her with surprise. Clearly they never considered asking Mercedes if she knew anything about Charleigh. She doesn't know much, only a few stories that I've shared with her, but still, they would have known she was only a friend, and a female at that.

"It's really great to finally meet you, Charleigh. We've heard a lot about you and it's nice to put a … face to the name." Summer elbows King in the gut. The move is subtle, nearly undetectable, but King releases a huff to validate it happened.

They have been talking about me.

King finally turns to me, his lips are pursed, his eyes bright with humor and something else that has him digging for his phone.

"I've heard loads about all of you as well. Though, I sort of knew what you all looked like."

"You did?" Summer's question makes the muscles between my eyes clench tighter. Leave it to Charleigh to reveal everything—to *everyone*.

"Sure," Charleigh replies, unaffected. "Haven't you seen her sketches? She draws nearly everyone she meets. It's amazing and awful, really."

"You've drawn me? I want to see! Do you have them here?" Summer's voice is higher, her eyes brighter.

"Easy there. Don't you have enough pictures of yourself?" King teases. He releases the door handle and takes a step back, opening the doorway.

"Not a hand-drawn one!" Summer's response isn't defensive or teasing. I know that if I don't bring one over, she will never drop it, likely because it's not the drawings of her she is interested in, but the few of Kash that I've done. I will have to dig through my notepads and bring a couple for her.

"I'll bring some over next week," I say, nodding forward, indicating to Charleigh it's time to go.

"It's really nice to meet you, Charleigh!" Summer chimes.

"You as well."

"We'll see you guys tomorrow!" Mercedes calls.

"Definitely," Charleigh says with a nod.

"Thanks for the care and help. Sorry again for being such a klutz."

"I'm thinking it was for the better," King says, a knowing smile spreading wider across his face.

"Alright, well, I guess I'll see you guys tomorrow, then. Thanks for the night off."

"I told you at the hospital it wasn't a big deal. It's still not a big deal. If you want next week off, just let me know. Or we can come get you and take you home. It's your call," Kash explains.

I give a small smile filled with appreciation and move to Mercedes. "Let me know if you need anything."

"I'll text you later."

"Sounds good." With that I move forward, shooting Charleigh a look to tell her to get moving.

"Who put a bee in your bonnet?" My eyes are wide as they wait for Charleigh to glance in my direction. "What?" Her voice is alarmed, genuinely surprised by my look that is intended to say *you know why*.

"You told them I draw them!" I hiss.

"You *do* draw them!" she exclaims. "Besides, I told them you draw *everyone*. Really, Lauren, you need to stop hanging around me and this angsty kid so much. Americans are supposed to be smiley and happy about nothing, and you're rarely happy about anything. It's not normal."

She doesn't look at me as we approach her car. It's probably best that she isn't because her words serve to do nothing more than remind me of what I've been told for most of my life: I'm different.

"Sorry I had to call you. I know you were out on a date last night. I hope I didn't make you cut it short."

Her face radiates with a smile as she maneuvers her car into drive and starts heading down the long driveway.

"I'm taking that look to say the date went well. What's he like?"

Charleigh's shoulders shrug like she's trying to remain indifferent, but her lips are pulling up at the corners as though she's stuffed the last piece of candy in her mouth. I don't push her for details. As much as I enjoy Charleigh, and like being around her, it's been clear to me since our friendship began that Allie is her confidant, the one that keeps her centered, her best friend. I try really hard to not be hurt by this since both of them are so accepting of me, and I know genuinely enjoy our time together; it just stings when moments like these occur.

Getting ready with crutches reminds me of how blessed I am to have been healthy for most of my life, regardless of being too tall and lanky.

Charleigh and Allie knock on my door thirty minutes early with matching faces of concern about me going down the stairs with my crutches. I assure them a half dozen times that I'll be fine before they stop encouraging me to go down on my hands and butt like a toddler. I'm on the last landing when the Suburban pulls up and King jumps out of the back with a similar expression.

"Lo, let King help you!" Parker yells from the driver's window.

"I've got it!" I yell back, my focus remaining on the stairs with determination.

King stops a few steps short from me, his chin twists, and the look of indecision mars his brows before he takes a step back, closer to the railing. He keeps pace with me, his hands precariously close to reaching out to me, though he never does.

I don't object when he opens the door, though my pride wants to, regardless of how inconsequential it seems. Before I get in, I turn to ensure Allie and Charleigh are still with us and go through a brief introduction before lifting myself into the car and watching King take my crutches around back to the trunk.

The girls are both restless, their smiles wide. I can tell they're excited to be riding with Parker and King, and while I hadn't been able to see their expressions when they arrived, I continuously notice them both looking from him and me and then to each other. It's worse than high school.

"This is crazy!" Allie says with a happy sigh. Her eyes are dancing over every exposed chest and bicep painted in tattoos. "I'm in heaven."

Parker laughs loudly only a few inches from her shoulder, sending her hand to her chest in surprise, leading his eyes to crinkle with an even deeper, heartier laugh. He leads us through crowds and teams that are gathered, discussing strategies and triple-checking everything with the bikes. I'm thankful we're inside because I can't imagine navigating through the Oregon mud, but even indoors is proving to be difficult with the large number of people.

I'm trying to focus on watching the event. Parts of my mind are even mystified, making my jaw drop and my eyes grow wide, though most of my thoughts are preoccupied with trying to understand King, and working to recall every minute detail of last night. Did I imagine the way lust danced in his eyes when he told me he was tempted to do something that would make me want to slap him? He did say that … right? Between my painkillers and his obvious drinking, maybe neither one of us can clearly recall what transpired last night. I thought we did when he arrived and was so valiantly ready to assist me with getting into the car, but now he's several seats and people away from me, and his attention hasn't veered from the stadium once. I know, because I've been staring at him so hard everyone between us has looked over at me at least a few times.

A throat clears from behind me, getting louder as they lean in close. "Take it easy. This is his passion. King belongs out there. He isn't ignoring you; he's just lost in his other world right now." I look back at Summer and she gives me a small smile, her lips pressed together with both apology and comfort, and I'm pretty sure it isn't all for King ignoring me.

I try to hide the vast relief her words impart on me, but her growing grin confirms it's apparent. This crush that I've had on King since a night that was laden with flirting, revelations of each other, and eventually a shared intimacy that I haven't been able to shake—or willing to move past—has torn off every cover I've tried to bury it under, revealing my feelings have been much larger than a mere crush for months, maybe since that very night if that's possible.

Her assurance grants me the ability to see the athletes more closely. I watch and listen as tricks and maneuvers are completed that stun me into silence. I am lost as I watch the joy and love for their craft pass over each of their faces, and absorb each expression as they finish. Though each is different, some filled with regret, others with pride, and a few with disappointment, I recognize the same fuel of energy and passion. Some have performed several times now in different events, allowing me to recognize their faces and expressions to where I know I'll be drawing them for days to come.

"Want some paper?" Charleigh reaches forward as she asks, gripping my bag before I can reply. She hands me a pad and a handful of charcoal pieces that I select two from before depositing the remaining pieces back to the bottom. She gives me a smile and then turns, gifting me with the attention to move forth and draw.

I sketch expressions of hopefulness, failure, excitement, anger, blissfulness, and camaraderie before I delve into the bikes and pedals, the irregular angles of their bodies, and gravity-defying stunts. Eventually, I stop drawing faces and simply draw figures, shades, and movements that equal each of the expressions I started with.

Summer's foot knocks against my chair, breaking me from my trance, and I hear the rustling of seats and greetings and turn to see Mercedes, accompanied by an older man who I recognize from his acknowledgments and waves that are directed my way a few times a week now: the man from the green house.

"Hey, Lo!" Mercedes' greeting doesn't divert my attention from staring at the man, wondering who he is, and how he fits into this picture.

His face warms with a smile that doesn't hide his amusement. "Nice to see you here, Lo," he says with a nod.

I blink several times, biting my tongue to tell him how strange it is to see him here of all places, since he obviously knows everyone, making a statement like that borderline rude. My eyes widen several times as different questions and things to respond with cross my mind.

"Lo, you know Robert?" I'm thankful to turn my attention away from the man and look to Summer.

"Sort of." I sound less sure of my words than the time I got caught sneaking out of my room in the middle of the night by Alan, Nell's husband and my father's right-hand man. That time I had been dressed, makeup done, shoes carefully gripped in my fingers so I could make as little noise as possible, and still I smiled at him without a trace of guilt or fear. At least initially I had.

"She walks by the house on her way to the bus stop," Robert explains. "The first day she passed by my house a dozen times before I finally asked the poor thing where she was headed and what do you know, she was lookin' for the Knight residence." His eyes are bright and smiling as though he's sharing a joke. "I knew as soon as I saw her that my granddaughter would like her. She's got spunk."

Granddaughter? She's Mercedes' grandfather? King and Kash's dad?

"I had no idea you were…"

"Of course you didn't. How would you?" I can't tell if Robert is teasing me or eluding to the fact that if I had taken the time to ask a few questions, I would have. "That's what made me like you even more. You're a smart girl."

"Wait until you see her draw. How are you, Robert?" I take a step back, angling my body so I can see both King and Robert. "It's been a few weeks. Every time I try to track you down, you're out. Up to some new *shenanigans*?" King draws out the word.

Robert's head falls back as he laughs. The gesture is familiar; he's done this a few times when I've spoken to him. It makes me wonder if this is his genuine laugh, or if it's a façade for both of us. "I just keep ignoring you, waiting until I see your bike turn up."

King's eyes tighten. I'm not the only one who notices, because Robert's eyebrows rise and he nods, confirming something that the two seem aware of while the rest of the group remains oblivious.

An introduction for Kash has us all sitting back in our seats, our attention shifting to the center of the concrete stadium. I have no idea who Kash is talking to as I catch sight of him before walking his bike forward. I'm curious to know why King, Parker, and Summer aren't down there but fear my question is rudimentary and ignore it. The movement of Kash shaking out his left hand catches my eye. I've seen him do this before but don't realize it until now. He wraps it around his handlebars and then does the same with his right hand before he glides onto his bike and kicks off. Many of the contestants seem to have a pattern, one which involves searching the crowds until they find their support group, as if reliant upon their encouragement. Kash never does.

My heart is in my throat as I watch his routine, transfixed by each of his movements. The more I continue to watch this sport, the more beauty I find in it. The connection, respect, and love between a rider and their bike nearly make me forget that it's an inanimate object.

We're all screaming and clapping as he rounds the edge of the jump with a finish. It's then that his eyes find us, and his smile goes from bliss—to elation.

"You hold a brush a lot different from your pencils."

People have been in and out of the shop all day, each stopping to chat with me and take in my work. I loathe people looking at the initial sketch. It's a shell, an idea that I can't fully translate until I'm able to add color and design, something I can't do on this large of a scale with a pencil. I just started adding color, and there isn't enough for attention to be welcomed. This is, however, the first time in two weeks since I've seen King. I accepted Kash's offer to take last week off after he said he would appreciate having a reason to stay away from work and hang out with Mercedes, and the last three days of this week, King has been absent. I've been working to convince myself it isn't suspicious. I was tempted to text him, debating on a joke or sarcastic remark that I knew would make him laugh, but all of them seemed like I was checking in, which is exactly what any of them would have been.

I look back at him as I dip my brush back into the black paint. I want to play this cool. I want to show him that if he has decided to regret his previous drunken admission, I am willing to let it pass as well. At least, I will try really hard to pretend that I have.

"I hold charcoals with all of my fingers because it allows more movement. I can use my shoulder and elbow, not just my wrist. I can do the same with paints on certain surfaces, but not on a wall like this. The texture makes it difficult. You have to be a lot more forgiving and try not to focus on adding too many details."

"Who taught you to do this?"

"I've always loved art. I've been told I used to paint with my food." I smile, and my shoulder lifts. "But I think every kid does that." King's lips turn up into an unexpected smile, and his eyes are steady as they gaze at me as though he's not looking for a reason to leave. "When I was eight, my dad hired a farmhand that liked to sketch. He'd sit out in the fields and draw different scenery. I swear, by the time he left five years later, he'd drawn nearly every single angle of the farm. He didn't talk a lot. He was older, and I think he had a lot of secrets he shared with his art, drawing darker shadows than what were present and clouds when the skies were clear." Explaining this brings me back to sitting beside him, the scent of hay as potent as the Oregon rain is today as I braved approaching for the first time while he was in the middle of creating the field of mares. "One day I couldn't stop myself. I knew he was out there drawing, and I sat right next to him and just watched. It was so different than what I had been doing. It was the first time I saw anyone use charcoal, and I fell in love instantly. "We rarely ever spoke. I just enjoyed watching him, learning techniques and his methods."

"I think if others took the time to listen and watch rather than speak, we'd all be a lot smarter."

"I think if people took the time to discuss things, there would be far less confusion."

King tilts his head. "But the problem is, the same people that always want to talk are rarely ready to listen."

"Are you insinuating something?" I've never been great at keeping my thoughts to myself, but with King I feel like my gloves are completely off, my base paint exposed. "I'm pretty sure you're the one that's been gone all week."

"Missed me?"

"If you didn't already learn from the last time you tried to tease and taunt your way into making me discuss things with you, it's not a great approach."

His hand reaches forward, encircling the feather bangle I have worn every day since receiving.

"Nor is claiming." I pull out of his touch and shoot a glare to send my point home.

"Dude, you ready?" A guy I barely recognize directs his question at King.

"No, he's not ready." The guys' eyes rotate to me, his head still facing King and his lips parting with unease.

"Um…"

"I'll catch up with you later," King assures him.

Without nodding or saying a word, the guy turns and leaves.

"I'm done playing these games with you. If you really want to hang out, or be something besides an annoyance in each other's lives, you need to cut this shit out. I'm funny. I'll laugh at your jokes, but I am sick and tired of being the butt of them."

"Your butt has never been in one of my jokes."

My chin drops. King's lips twitch before he stops trying to maintain his stoic expression. Then he nods. A loud breath blows between us and he moves a hand to his face, where I know, as I turn back to my painting, that it's pinching the bridge of his nose.

"I'm not trying to be an asshole. I just don't know … We're going about everything in reverse order. I feel like things are upside down and backward because I already know so much about you. I know what kind of person you are. I know that you don't give two shits about who I am or what my brother does. I know you are crazy cool and ridiculously talented, and while you can't cook to save your life, I'd be okay with eating it simply to spend time with you."

My brush holds no paint, yet I can't move it from the wall. After demanding that he change his approach, I'm so caught off guard with this one that I can't look at him.

"You know I like you. I think I like you a little too much, and it makes me forget I'm not ten."

My lips tug into an automatic smile that lifts higher when his hand brushes down my back, settling where my spine curves inward. "I'm going to stop being such a dickhead … or at least try. I'll warn you though: you have the ability to irritate me more than anyone I've ever met."

I'm no longer too shy to look at him. My eyebrows are drawn with my confusion and offense.

"Don't act surprised. I know I drive you crazy too."

"That's because you act like a dickhead."

"You guys are both stubborn and way too proud. Lo gets on drawing and painting tangents and King, you find every excuse to travel, or come beat the hell out of yourself in the shop."

"Thanks for that assessment, Summer." King lifts a hand and points to the door. "We'll see you later."

"As long as you guys both know that I know. Now when one of you starts acting like a jackass, I'll be sure to remind you to stop." Her smile is nearly as bright as it turns when she's spending time alone with Kash. Her blond hair fans as she whirls around and heads outside.

Before turning back to King, my eyes dart around the shop, studying each of the areas to ensure we're actually alone before continuing the conversation.

"I'm leaving tomorrow morning for San Francisco, but I want to take you to dinner when I get back. How about Friday?"

"I can't. I have model practice."

"How much longer is that?"

"Five more weeks."

King's eyes stretch. "Jesus. Okay, Saturday I have to be up in Seattle for a competition. What about during the week?"

"You do realize I see you like every day, right?"

King furrows his eyebrows, telling me my words are crazy. "That's not the same. Yeah, I like getting to spend time with you and just see what you're like and be in a relaxed setting, but I want to see you in heels and a dress. I want your attention focused on me. And I really don't want the Peanut Gallery to be around, adding subtext to all of our interactions."

A dress? Heels? I've been out on dates with guys before, but never while wearing that attire outside of a high school dance.

"I have to get some work done next week to complete my submission." I balance my paintbrush in my hand holding the palette so I can brush a few strands of hair back from my face, not caring when I think of Charleigh's assurance that it means I'm flirting.

"Submission? For what?"

"Italy this summer."

"You're going to Italy?"

"I doubt it. There's some really steep competition, and multiple colleges across the country are participating."

"What would it be for?"

"Art restoration."

"Next Saturday." He shakes his head when my mouth opens. "Next Saturday," he repeats.

"Next Saturday," I confirm with a nod.

His lips quirk up into his uneven smile, and without question or thought, mine follow. Confidence radiates in his steps and his eyes that are focused on mine, making me squirm and look back to my palette and the wall a few times before finally returning to King. He smiles even wider, revealing his perfect teeth that I had described to Charleigh, and then he leans closer. I can feel my pulse in my neck, and it increases when the scent of him blocks the acrylic paint and coolness of the cement that the shop always exudes. "Lo, close your eyes." His tongue wets his lips, and his eyes blink slowly, the weight of lust making them heavy. "You're studying me."

I shake my head so slightly that it's nearly imperceptible. "I'm memorizing you."

"Are you going to draw me?"

"Are you going to kiss me?" My voice is low, the anticipation making my lungs forget their primary function.

"If you tell me you're going to draw me."

"Probably a thousand times tonight."

"Good." The word barely slips through his lips before I lean closer and kiss him. If it surprises him, I can't tell, because there is no hesitancy, no awkward shifting that often happens when you're learning to kiss a new person. King's bottom lip covers mine and then moves to my upper lip, pulling, plying, massaging, and erasing every last thought and image aside from him. The palm of his hand is hot as it cups my jaw. Then his fingers gently press firmly into my skin as his other hand wraps around my back. Our chests and hips are close enough I feel the graze of him as he breathes. Everything is fluid, matched, perfect.

"What's going on?"

I turn to face Mercedes, my eyebrows stretched high in question.

"You did your hair today and you seem really happy, when all week you've been a stress case."

"I was able to get a lot done with my portfolio this week. I'm relieved that it's starting to come together."

"That doesn't explain the hair."

Touché.

"I'm just…"

"You know I know, right?"

"Know what?"

"Everything." She giggles as my eyes roll. "I might be ten, but I pay attention. I know you like my uncle King."

"That's…" Mercedes' fists go to her hips. "…true…" A smile breaks out across her face with my confession.

"Let's go out to the shop! He's out there riding right now." She takes my hand before allowing me the opportunity to object and pulls me to the front door.

I'm trailing behind her only slightly, my own excitement not allowing me to play it very cool. Each day that we've been in here this week while King's been gone, my eyes have landed on my painting before seeing anything else, scrutinizing it and reminding myself of things I need to change or do. Today my black and white creation isn't even a thought as my attention lands solely on King. He's mid-air, a euphoric expression highlighting his face.

He completes two more trips across the ramp before coming to a stop and looking our way. "I thought you were bringing her here as soon as she arrived?"

"She made me do my homework first. I tried texting you!" Mercedes cries.

My neck and face heat. I know I'm blushing, something I can attribute to my ever-white Irish skin. I shoot an accusing look to Mercedes that she reciprocates with a laugh.

"I knew already. King can't keep a secret. Not from me." Mercedes' voice holds a lilt from her obvious amusement.

"No gloating," King says, walking his bike up beside us. Mercedes' smile isn't affected by his words, but she does turn and get her own bike.

"Hey." My eyes stop following her and return to King, my pulse quickening. "Want to try getting on a bike again? We can go for a ride on the trails instead of in here."

"I have to be able to stand for three hours tonight. I don't think riding would be a great idea figuring what happened the last time."

"I'll help you. You can trust me. I won't let you do anything to hurt yourself." The sincerity in his eyes makes turning down his offer a little harder, but I'm not ready to get back on two wheels.

"That's okay. I don't want you to do it while you're nervous. That can lead to unnecessary accidents. Take your time, watch, and when you're ready, we'll go together," he says before I have to object.

"King's the best teacher," Mercedes chimes as she rolls her bike past us.

"At everything," he adds, his eyes lighting up with endless innuendos.

I smirk to hide my laughter, but his growing smile tells me he knows that I understand his silent insinuations. I've been holding on to our last kiss since Monday, four days ago, and it's making the teenage boy euphemisms and implications that are running through my mind seem far more entertaining than they are.

"Hey!"

I turn, hearing the greeting and find Isabelle at the door with a bag slung over her shoulder. It's too big to be a school bag or purse.

"Hey, Isabelle!" Mercedes calls out. Her excitement for seeing Isabelle makes guilt swim thickly through my distaste for her.

Isabelle's smile is a mixture of nerves and excitement as she steps inside, and while I know King has feelings for me, watching her actions makes me aware of how much she likes him and drowns the guilt with jealousy.

King steps forward, his chest meeting my back. His hand loosely clasps my left shoulder. "What's up, Izz?"

"I heard you were heading to Seattle tomorrow so I came by to see if I could bum a ride. A friend drove me down a couple of days ago but came down with the flu, and I'm worried about riding with her. Getting sick right now would really suck with classes."

I listen to the steady clicks of Mercedes' pedaling, the intakes of King's breaths, and feel the slight pressure as his fingers squeeze me closer to him so that as he starts to tell her he can if she's willing to get up early, I can feel the reverberations of his voice. Like everything about King, I feel it in every single cell, all the way to my toes. I want him to speak again, let me experience the sensation once more, and then Isabelle laughs and expresses a genuine appreciation that tears my attention to her. I tell myself to smile three times before my lips finally listen.

"Stand up straight. You have all of this beautiful height and long neck, and you stand there slouching like a tortured tortoise."

I purse my lips so tightly I'm sure it looks like a pucker as I force my spine into a rod and push my shoulders back. I don't care for most of my own professors, but having to deal with someone else's, who constantly ridicules all of the volunteer models in the class, is becoming my greatest challenge.

Allie gingerly pats my forearm. "Sorry. I think she's getting a little stressed out about things." I cock and eyebrow to ask if that's an excuse for her always acting like such a bitch, and Allie presses her lip together, one side going up in a hopeful expression. It forces my thoughts of her professor, and the sharp prick of a pin that she apologizes for sticking me with, to subside because it reminds me of King. I didn't see him as I left today because he was in the office with the door closed, talking to someone about the weekend. I had wanted to wait until he was done so we could sneak in another make-out session, but I was already pressed for time and after missing the last two modeling practices, I had to leave. My thoughts of regret wander to King riding in a car with Isabelle for three hours tomorrow. Both thoughts make my muscles contract, bringing me to stand a little taller.

"You okay?" Allie asks, her light eyes moving between the bead she's replacing and my face.

"I'm fine."

"Want to hang out Sunday? Maybe go see a movie at the discount theater? We haven't done that in months."

"You and Charleigh aren't doing your Sunday DVR marathon?"

She shakes her head, and I notice the edges of her lips press into a frown as she completes another knot in the tiny thread. "She has plans with that guy again—Brandon."

"That's his name?" Allie nods, her focus moving to the dress. "She must really like him." I watch as she processes my words. I'm sure my face has looked similar to hers now since earlier when Isabelle showed up. Tight lips and eyes: it's envy, tinged with loneliness.

"He's not at all what I expected him to look like."

"What does he look like?" I ask, straightening my shoulders as I catch the glare of her professor once again.

"Short and kind of scrawny," Allie explains. "He's got great hair and dresses well, but he kind of looks like he's sixteen."

My laughter makes her smile before she disappears behind me to inspect any additional missing beads or flaws. "Apparently he's not so scrawny in bed though, if you know what I mean. Apparently he was a virgin and is a very quick learner."

"A virgin?" My eyes are wide with disbelief.

"I know, right?"

"He isn't sixteen, right?"

"I went to a club with them, and the bouncer like quadruple-checked his ID, but apparently it was legit."

"Well, it's good that she's happy." I scan the room as I try to remind both of us of this fact.

"Yeah, but she dropped out of the show because of him."

"What?" The shock in my voice has several people turning to look at us. I think even my arms are flushing as I try to smile an apology to everyone.

"Yeah, she said she'd rather spend her time with him than doing this right now."

"But we're seniors. This is her last chance."

"She can try to get other internships, but it will definitely eliminate several opportunities." Allie's voice is forlorn, much like her expression, as she comes back around to my front.

"I can't believe she's willing to give up all of this after only knowing the guy for a couple of weeks."

"I know. But don't tell her that. If you do, she'll pretend you don't exist. I know from experience."

"Lame."

Allie looks back to me, her eyes crinkled with a smile. "You're so good with words, Lo." The air seems to lighten as we quietly laugh, adding another plank to our bridge of friendship.

When our dress rehearsal is over, Allie drags me to pick out two pairs of heels that, even with my many objections, she insists on paying for with the reasoning that I'm only getting them for the show. Before we leave, she lays on a thick layer of guilt that has me agreeing to wear one of the pairs home and promising to continue wearing them for the next two weeks.

My objections are drowned as we share a late dinner of enchiladas and margaritas, and then Allie watches as I paint until hours after the restaurant closes. Unlike many others, she barely speaks while I work, and when she does, it's never in reference to what I'm making, simply discussing plans, or stories about school, friends, and at times her family.

It's two in the morning when we say good-bye and I close the door to my apartment, noticing Kenzie alone in her bed sleeping. I peel off the heels that are already making my toes cramp and ache, and the rest of my clothes, replacing them with my skiing candy piece pajamas and an old sweatshirt. Neither my muscles nor mind is tired. I want to sit at my easel and sketch to see if I can capture the look on King's face from Monday before he kissed me.

A flashing light in my messenger bag distracts me, and I fish out my phone and take a seat on my bed as I swipe it on. Twenty texts and seven missed calls. My eyes widen, and I find seven messages and two calls are from King.

I roll onto my back, feeling the stretch of my cheeks as I open my missed messages.

King: I'm sorry I missed U. I didn't realize that call would take so damn long.

King: I know UR at model practice, but call me when UR done.

King: What do U do at model practice? Will U show me?

King: I'm not being a perv.

King: Okay ... maybe a little.

King: R U okay? It's late.

King: Sorry to sound like a stalker, but where in the hell R U? R
U OK?

I thumb through messages from Mercedes, Kash, one from Kenzie even, asking me if I'm okay, that end shortly after ten, around the time we got to the restaurant.

I hit reply to King and quickly type out an apology.

I'm surprised when my phone indicates a new message within less than a minute.

King: Do you always go off the grid when you work?

Me: Usually, sorry again.

King: Don't apologize. Just something for me to be aware of.

King: Can you stay up for ten more minutes?

Me: Yes ... why?

King: I'm coming over.

Me: It's 2 AM!

King: Yup

Me: You're supposed to leave for Seattle in 4 hours!

I impatiently wait for a response, hoping he's fallen asleep, and even more so that he's ignoring my protests because he's driving. I quickly change back into my clothes on the off chance he's really coming and sit at my easel, only illuminating the space with my small but bright lamp that's clamped to the top. I'm too excited to draw, but I sift through several pages, looking for the ones that most closely resemble the passion I saw on King's face before he kissed me.

A soft knock against my apartment door sets my heart into overdrive. It's been fifteen minutes, just long enough for me to confirm that it's him.

He's smiling as the door swings open, bringing a gust of chilled air and the scent of rain and King into the apartment.

"You're going to regret staying up so late in a few hours." His eyes are easier to see with his hat missing. The fact his flannel shirt is buttoned confirms he's been dressed all night. King's lips part, and the look I was just seconds ago searching for in my work makes my entire body swim with a desire and excitement that builds as his hand hooks around my hip and pulls me closer to him.

"Not even a little." His words are spoken with my eyes closed and chin tilted upward in anticipation, his bottom lip grazing mine with the slight movement, sending a chill through me. I wish I could capture this feeling with my drawing. The anticipation that makes me feel like I am going to separate into a million tiny pieces and float adrift because King breaks all rules about rational thoughts and convention.

My bottom lip is pulled between his as the hand behind my back pulls me farther forward. And just like that, I am a million floating pieces, wrapping around this kiss that is so unbearably perfect, it doesn't seem possible. My lips press more firmly against his, my hands digging into the fabric of his T-shirt after bypassing his outer layer of flannel. My chest is firmly planted against King's and I'm not even sure if it was me pulling or him tugging that brought us this close. All I do know is it isn't close enough.

My fingers braid themselves into the short wavy curls at the back of his head in an attempt to draw him nearer. I swallow his groan and feel the doorjamb against my back as his body settles more firmly against mine, his hips aligning with mine, making me wish there weren't two layers of denim between us.

His lips slow, the hunger receding. King plants a soft kiss to my upper and then lower lip, and pulls back.

"I'm going to be thinking about nothing but that kiss in a few hours."

I want to plead with him to ignore my roommate and come in. Strip off his clothes and properly study every single detail and nuance that makes up King, and then verify that sex with him is like nothing else because there's something about him that just fits every single part of me.

His nose skims mine and then he softly drops a kiss there as well. "I don't want to annoy the hell out of you or think something has happened, so just shoot me a text tomorrow when you start working so I know to leave you alone. I won't be home until late Sunday, but I'll call."

I nod, gripping his loose hand with mine while his other presses firmly into the skin above my hip. "I'd like to hear from you." The words are nearly casual, but the plea behind my tone makes it sound like a supplication.

King smiles, and squeezes more firmly against my flesh, making the thoughts of asking him to come in to return.

"Don't worry about Isabelle. Nothing will happen, I swear."

I'm grateful for the dim lighting on the landing because I know without a doubt how red my cheeks are stained as I nod and try to act confident.

"Lo, look at me."

My eyes take the long way to meet his, searching over our tangled fingers, his shirt, the night air, and then him.

"I need you to trust me. I travel a ton, and if you are going to be second-guessing my intentions, we aren't going to see what this really is."

"She likes you."

"It doesn't matter, Lo. Nothing matters but how I feel about you, and what you feel for me." His eyes bore into mine. "The rest is inconsequential. She knows I don't like her, and I've already told her I'm seeing you. She won't press things."

"It's just weird."

King nods, his lips pursing with understanding. "I shouldn't have agreed without speaking to you first. I've just known her forever. I swear, nothing has ever happened between us, and it never will. I don't have any feelings for Isabelle. I haven't felt anything toward anyone else since September when you finally stopped ignoring my stare and shook your head with that tiny smile that told me I had a chance."

"It's only because I had been drinking. If I had been sober, I would have looked away so fast I would have had whiplash."

"I specifically recall you saying you were going to struggle being able to see another person after that night."

"I did. I do. I think I have four notebooks filled with you. I would have looked away because you're … gorgeous."

"Don't hate me, but I'm going to have to remind you of this in the future. I want you to be prepared."

"I'm serious."

"So am I," King says, releasing my hand and gripping my other hip as he laughs. "Lo, you're beyond beautiful, and the more I see you, the deeper that beauty grows because it's not just your face, it's you. We have something, and I am blissed out to see where it leads. Just trust me, okay?"

"Alright."

His lips press against mine in a brief kiss that he breaks with a smile. "You really filled four notebooks with me? I must be hot."

"Go home!" I cry, shoving his shoulder and taking a step backward.

He catches my hand before it falls to my side and tugs me forward, his playful smile growing. "We're going to have really hot make-up sex one day when I get your panties all tied up in a knot like this."

"Don't count on it. Plan to make up for it with gummy bears and new charcoals."

"I can do that too." He kisses me again, the edge of the hunger returning in a much smaller degree that poses as a challenge, one I want to meet. Before I can, he pulls away. "I don't want to wake her up," King says, looking over my shoulder at Kenzie's bed. "Get some sleep and text me tomorrow."

"I thought you were calling me."

"I am." King moves his left hand from my hip and coasts it along my jaw. "Don't look at me like that. For six months I've wanted to see your name light up across my screen multiple times a day. Granted, there are many other things

I've been wishing to see as well … but we'll address those hopefully in the near future." His eyebrows do one quick dance to ensure I catch his intent that has me laughing.

"Thanks for coming."

"If you need anything while I'm gone—"

"I won't. I swear I'm capable."

His eyes tell me he wants to argue with me, but he obliges and gives me one last lingering kiss. "I'll talk to you tomorrow."

TWENTY-THREE

I try to ignore my phone to see if King texts me as I sit in the theater. I've carefully propped it in my bag so I can see if the little light goes off, alerting me to a message, but Allie spent the drive here and previews explaining to me how she's felt ignored and forgotten since Charleigh began dating Brandon. I hate that I understand both of their sides so intimately.

King knows I'm here and I doubt that I'll hear from him because yesterday when I told him I was going to be working on my portfolio, he didn't say anything but to enjoy and to send him a few pictures of my work afterward so he could share them. He remained silent for the four hours I worked, creating a picture of his face that I was only able to capture the slightest hint of the lust and longing his eyes had exposed. When I sent him a picture of it, he called within seconds and much to my surprise, we talked for hours. He explained that his meeting had been rescheduled for the next day due to a partner having a family emergency, and that he'd spent the afternoon wandering through Pike's Place Market, comparing my artwork to others who set up small kiosks and stands where people could have their face drawn for a small fee. We talked about my submission for Italy, and the heels I promised to wear for the next two weeks, into a slightly more substantial discussion about my design for the shop. There were durations of silence we shared as we sought new topics, but neither of us seemed willing to end the conversation. It didn't matter that we had nothing to share, or that the footing was slightly uncomfortable, sharing our silence was more than enough.

This morning he called after hitting the hotel's gym, something that is as foreign as Mars for me. Vacation has never equated a workout in my book. We were more flirtatious this morning, our comments daring to cross back over that slight barrier we've built up over the past six months until they were nearly forgotten.

I feel like I can't focus on a single thing other than him. Like every minute detail reminds me of him. I want to tell him about everything I'm seeing and doing. The buzz of anticipation of seeing King tomorrow has my muscles tight and my steps giddy. My chest feels tight with the expansion of swarming thoughts and thrills running through my imagination. New pictures of King are being painted and sketched at nearly every second. And I love every single bit of what I'm feeling.

"Looo."

I turn in my seat and blink several times to focus on Allie beside me. "Sorry, I'm in creative land."

"No, you're in King-dom." Allie sits back in her seat, her eyes reflecting a sad smile.

"I'm sorry. I swear, I'm having a good time. I want to be here with you."

"I'm not comparing what you're experiencing to Charleigh. She just met this guy; you've known King for months. Plus she and I have been best friends since freshman year."

I know she's justifying her thoughts verbally and that it shouldn't hurt that she's said what I've already known. But a piece of me envies their relationship. I wish I had someone I could share everything that I'm feeling about King with. "You should tell Charleigh how you're feeling. I'm sure she's just caught up in that haze that makes us all a little crazy at the beginning. I know I'm lost in that same fog."

"But you aren't giving everything up for him, and you actually know him!" The theater is emptying around us for the intermission between films, and while my mind is itching to see if I've heard anything from King, my eyes keep hers, seeing the pain this is inflicting upon her. "Plus, King's hot. Anyone would be lost in a fog with him."

"I think King could be scrawny and look sixteen and I'd probably be just as lost."

"You haven't seen Brandon, Lo. I'm not kidding when I tell you he looks young."

"I believe you. I just know that what I feel for King is so much more than physical, I don't think it would matter."

She huffs out a reply that tells me she wasn't looking for anything more than someone to listen to her woes, which makes me feel guilty because I understand that yearning. We don't always need someone to put things back together for us. Sometimes we just need someone to try to understand our pains and frustrations and validate that what we're feeling is okay.

"I'm sorry," I say, reaching across the double armrest and placing my hand on hers. "You're right. She's gone to some pretty hefty extremes, and your concern for her and her future is completely justified. You guys are best friends, and while she has a shiny new toy that is fun to play with, she shouldn't abandon everything else."

"Exactly!" Allie cries. "What if they break up in a month? What is she going to do? Even if it's in a year or ten years, she's still missed this opportunity to follow her dreams."

I don't allow the rebuttals in my head to become clear. I simply nod in agreement and settle back into my seat as the next movie's previews begin.

After the second movie, I take a little extra time in the restroom to check my phone for any missed calls or texts. There aren't any, and it makes Allie's previous sentiments more understandable.

I don't take the time to see who's calling before I answer. It's late, and though I'm not sure if Kenzie is home tonight, I feel bad that my phone likely just woke her. "Hello?"

"Are you okay?"

I scrunch my eyes and blink several times before narrowing them and focusing on the alarm clock that's too bright to clearly view.

"Lo?" The concern in his voice is heightened.

"I'm fine, just sleeping. What's wrong?" My groggy thoughts are beginning to shift at a quicker speed, traveling directly to Mercedes.

"You said you were going to let me know when you got home."

I look over to Kenzie's side of the room as I sit up further and see her bed is vacant. "Sorry, I was hanging out with Allie and then got some work done with my portfolio and just lost track of time." I'm lying through my teeth. After the third movie with Allie, we did spend some more time together, but my phone was set to the loudest ringtone, and then I went up to my apartment where I attempted to work as the phone stared at me.

At one point I got so desperate I went back downstairs and asked Allie to text me to ensure my phone was actually working—it was. I spent another couple of hours mindlessly flipping through channels until I gave up and went to bed.

"Lo." My name is spoken quiet and deep: a warning. "I'm twenty-seven. I'm not going to play bullshit games with you. I'll respect the time you want and need to spend by yourself, but I'm not going to call and text so you know that I'm sitting around twiddling my thumbs and waiting for you. We have a lot to still learn about each other, and while I know you're not into mind games, you seem to be playing one hell of a mind game with yourself right now, and unfortunately you're dragging me into it. I will always be honest with you. I won't take advantage of you, but I need your trust, and I need you to stop trying to set me up to fail. If you tell me you're going to call me, call."

My earlier convictions are a cold sweat, drying to my skin and making me feel dirty and contrite. "I'm sorry. I … I'm not used to this."

"I think I'm realizing there's a lot you aren't used to." His words have so many plausible meanings that I clench my teeth as my temper rises. "I have to stay another day. There's a store here Kash wants me to check out, and the owner can't make it in until after they close."

"Oh." My tone and heart turn poignant.

"I'll be in on Tuesday, though. I want to spend some time with you. I know we're going out Saturday, but stay late a couple of days this week. We'll watch a movie or something. I really don't care. I just want us to get past these last few months where we've been working to build up these defense walls, and remind each other who we really are. I know I keep saying this, but we have something, Lo, and I *know* you feel it."

"I'll burn some popcorn."

His laugh unwinds my muscles in a quick sequence. "I'll take care of the food. You just need to worry about letting your guard down, because whether by permission or defeat, I'm getting through."

My thoughts are a jumbled mess, causing a stretch of silence far less comfortable than ones previous.

"Goodnight, Lo. Sweet dreams. Call me tomorrow when you have some free time. I don't care if it's when you wake up or on your way to school or on your way to the house. Don't overthink it, just do it."

"You can't tell you grew up with the Nike headquarters in the same city."

King releases a sigh that is tainted with a laugh he's trying to conceal. "Goodnight, beautiful."

"I'll call you tomorrow."

"Don't talk yourself out of it."

"Just do it." I hear his heavy release of breath and can picture him shaking his head.

We sit in another silence. This time, the familiarity returns along with a giddy anticipation. I can sense his reluctance to hang up because I'm certain my own unwillingness to go is just as obvious.

"I want you to tell me about you. I wish I could be beside you and listen to your past."

"There isn't a lot to tell. What do you want to know?" I ask, sliding down in my bed, my feet greeting areas that have gone cold from my absence.

"Everything."

With the weight of his single word, I know I've just crossed beyond my crush status into something far more intricate and deeper than I've allowed my thoughts to travel. My heart beats with an equal measure of fear and exhilaration.

"Sleep well, Lo. I hope you draw another thousand pictures of me in your dreams."

"I draw much faster in my sleep than in real time. It will likely be a few thousand."

"Good."

"I'll talk to you tomorrow."

"Bye, Lo."

Several seconds later, I take a heavy breath and push end with the desire to call him right back dancing through my thoughts.

"Lo!" Estella cries as I enter the back of the restaurant with my bag filled with paints and brushes. Her arms encircle me before wrapping around my shoulder and walking me over to where Mia is waiting for an order. "Are you hungry? We just pulled out some chile rellenos."

"You know you can't pay me anything when this is done, right? Because I think I'm going to owe you for all that you feed me."

She laughs, patting my arm as she moves to the sink to wash her hands. "I'll get you a plate!"

I'm filled with horchata—a sweetened rice milk flavored with cinnamon that I've been addicted to since I was first introduced to it when I started here nearly four years ago—and the mound of chile rellenos Estella dished up for me, and painting a flourish of colors to a wide expanse of the wall.

"I thought you were supposed to be wearing heels."

Lowering my brush to my side, I turn to where King is sitting in a chair pulled up so he's within just a few feet, a plate of chile rellenos resting in one of his hands.

"How long have you been here?"

King shrugs like the answer is trivial. "I understand why you never learned to cook. I don't know if I'd have much interest in learning if I ate here every day, either."

"It's pretty amazing, right? How was your drive?"

"This might be one of the best things I've ever eaten. And thankfully, my drive was fast since that pain in my ass had to delay our meeting again." He cuts off another bite and looks at me with his dark eyes looking tired but anxious. "How was your day? And where are the shoes?"

We talked twice on Monday, both times the conversation flowing with a level of intimacy that proved we had been watching and caring about each other far longer than a mere week. What King and I have built between us is a mutual respect and friendship that was somehow kindled when we both were working so hard at finding every excuse to not like the other, and continually came up short.

"I can't wear them while I paint. Everything would be off." King grins, expecting my answer. "Today was kind of rough. I think those kids have been teasing Mercedes again."

"Those kids need their asses chewed."

"That won't stop them. Hatred doesn't stop hatred."

"Don't tell me you want to deliver each of them a plate of cookies." King's tone is a bite in itself as he rests his fork on his plate, waiting for my answer.

"Of course not." I stand straighter with indignation. "What happened to not acting like a jackass?"

He extends his arm to set his plate on a table in the corner and stands up. "Their words hurt her way more than falling off a bike."

"I know." My words are clipped with my annoyance for his previous comments, and now for insinuating I don't know how hurt Mercedes is from these kids.

He sighs loudly, his finger and thumb going to the bridge of his nose. "I know you know. Maybe we should transfer her schools or something. I'll talk to Kash about looking into it."

I shrug, hating the idea.

Recognize the war of patience that I often find with Mercedes visible with his raised eyebrows and wide eyes, I'm prompted me to explain my reaction.

"I think people often have to experience something in order to understand it." King's eyebrows disappear under his ball cap with a silent *I know! That's what I'm saying!* "But then you're no better than they are. You don't want to teach her to stoop to their level, and you certainly don't want to teach her that there are appropriate times to do so, because that line will become fuzzier and fuzzier every time she feels threatened or insecure from someone else."

"Then how in the hell are those kids ever going to experience it?"

"That's not our lesson to teach. Our lesson is for Mercedes to feel comfortable and confident with who she is as a person." King drops his gaze from mine and shakes his head, releasing a heavy sigh that is tangled with words of objection. "You aren't going to be able to fight off every bully she encounters, King. She would never allow you to and you know that! Mercedes is as proud and independent as you are. She barely shares these situations now. We have to make sure that the bullies she faces are simply external and are never her own haunting thoughts."

He shakes his head a few more times with one of his hands clasped to the back of his neck. "How do you propose we teach her how perfect she is?"

"Assurances like that, and one other idea I'm going to see if I can work out."

Slowly, he lifts his eyes, narrowed with curiosity. Then slides his lips together, processing thoughts and stealing my attention. "This isn't how I pictured tonight," he admits, regret heavy on his words. "I'm sorry I distracted you. You were obviously feeling it."

I shrug dismissively and shift to my right foot. My left ankle still isn't fully recovered, even if I refrain from admitting it aloud. "She's more important."

"You're important too. Your thoughts, your work, they all matter."

I swipe my brush through a shade of turquoise I've created because the intense stare paired with his words prevents me from being able to hold his gaze.

"Lo." King's voice is a commanding plea to look back at him, one that seems far harder to oblige than it should. "You matter. You're important, and not just to me."

I swallow because I don't have a reply. Have I ever felt like I've really mattered to someone, let alone be told in such a confirming way that I do? My eyes slide over his shoulder, my unease growing.

No, I haven't.

I force my attention back on King and feign being comfortable with a smile. "Mercedes threatened me today that I have to start riding again or she's going to start hiding my sketch pads at the house. I think her exact advice was: I need to grow some balls."

The intensity marring his face slips away, replaced by a genuine smile that makes my own lips turn up higher, which only causes his to follow suit. King takes slow, deliberate steps toward me and then runs his hand from my shoulder down to my elbow. "Are you ready to get back in the saddle?"

I know he means the bike, yet the way his hand is lingering on my arm and the energy that's apparent in his eyes make my heart jump nearly as high as my eyebrows.

King tilts his head back and releases a loud and throaty laugh, making my blush increase. He drops his chin forward, and a quiet rumble confirms he's trying to hide his amusement. "I like where your mind goes, Crosby." The shimmer of humor and lust makes King's eyes resemble waxed and polished ebony wood, with strains of lighter and nearly black hues winding together into a beautiful maze. "Speaking of Saturday..." My favorite smile spreads across his face before I can even give him the sarcastic reaction he's expecting, and he continues, "You told me the only thing you don't care for is seafood. Is that really all?"

"That's it." I shrug. "I'm pretty easy." My casual expression falls and my eyes squint with embarrassment. The heat that had just started to dissipate returns with a vengeance as King's tongue wets his bottom lip, working to fight a smile he loses to.

"I'm going to stop talking and get back to work now."

He nods a couple of times, still battling with his laughter, then presses a kiss to my mouth that makes me lean into him.

I crane my neck to the side, feeling a tightness that usually comes only after several hours of focus. It feels as though I've only been here moments, but looking over the amount of paint I've spread tonight, I know it's been longer. My head snaps to the overhead clock on the wall nearby, and my eyes widen with disbelief. I intended to paint only until the paint on my palette was gone, but I felt inspired by an energy that was absent for so much of the year. I still feel nearly drunk off it when it returns in these strong doses. It's past 10:00 p.m. The restaurant is going to close any minute. I've wasted our entire evening!

"I'm so sorry, King! I didn't realize ... I get in these ... zones, and I just lose track of ... well, everything sometimes..."

"Why are you apologizing? I get it. You need to get this done." King's shoulders lift and he stands from his seat. I don't think he moved at all while he waited. We didn't exchange words, only a few glances when my energy started to wane and I needed a new hit.

"I know, but we talked about spending tonight together."

"We are together."

"Yeah, but not in a way that we're getting to know each other any better," I argue.

"We're communicating on a level we both understand best."

"Silence?"

"I think I could lose myself watching you discover yourself."

I think I've already lost myself, at least the part of me that knows how to be an artist, and that's always been the side of myself I'm most familiar with, and the easiest for me to identify myself by.

chapter
TWENTY-FOUR

"Hey. Have you seen Mercedes? I can't find her anywhere."
Last night, King drove me home, where he hopped into the backseat, his hand encircling the feather bangle and pulling me back with him. The bench seat in the back made it much easier than the bucket seats up front to test the theory of making out in a car and whether it really fogs up the windows.

It did.

After leaving a dragged handprint on the back window as an ode to Jack and Rose, King walked me to the door of my apartment, my nerves growing. I questioned if I had remembered to shave that morning, what sheets were on my bed, how I would introduce King if Kenzie was home; if Kenzie wasn't home, the first two questions became far more important.

I appreciated that he walked me to my front door. It reminded me a little bit of home because there, if you didn't escort your date safely inside, you weren't looked at as being hip and cool but as a lazy jackhole. Small-town life does have a few perks.

King didn't give me the option of inviting him inside; instead, he pulled me against his chest, his back against the doorjamb, and kissed me until I forgot what I had been worrying about. My mind was made up when we parted; he was coming inside, even if my bed was made with old Minion printed sheets. But as soon as I unlocked the door and turned to face him, King smiled and told me to have a good night and asked to text him my schedule so he could come get me from class tomorrow.

A dozen oppositions were lining up in an orchestrated procession, beginning with those I hoped would be the most convincing to stay. I was ready to voice them, inhibitions aside, but he waved and picked up his speed.

King's desk chair swivels toward my impartial greeting, a hesitant smile on his face where his eyes are shadowed by the bill of his hat. I think he knows how disoriented I still feel about our relationship and my employment. Seeing him, I want to kiss him just as badly as I did last night, yet there's a trace of doubt with him having left that mixes with my unease of where we're at.

"Allie might be my favorite person," he says, looking at my shoes and distracting my nerves.

"She's lucky to have one person still in her corner." I jut my hip out slightly, and without thought, I'm striking a pose that I've been practicing each Friday in model practice. For the first time I feel sexy, in control of my body, confident even.

King's eyes don't miss my posture. He scoots his chair back and stands. "When we're done, we're going to meet Mercedes and Summer."

"Where?" My question should be *when we're done with what?*

His eyes follow his hand as it rests on my protruding hip, and then slowly climb to my face. The longing in his eyes makes me want to pump my fist into the air. I've never seen King so distracted and at such a loss. "You have a little drool. Right here," I tease, pointing to the corner of his mouth.

Unexpectedly, he turns and gently bites my accusing finger. It's shocking, sexual, erotic even—all things that are King. His dark eyes hold mine, making the act far more sensual than it would be if I tried to describe it to Charleigh or Allie later.

"King! You in here, man?"

I pull my hand back reflexively and move back several steps away as the office door is pushed open farther.

"You coming to ride?" Parker asks, oblivious to what was happening.

"No, I was just going to finish up some stuff and then take Lo to meet up with Mercedes." King's tone is so casual it's as though he's completely unaffected, while I'm still seeing the prospect of my clothes flying across the room every time I blink.

"Oh cool. Are you going through the video edits again?" Parker asks, taking a few more steps into the office.

King's eyes move to me and stay there while Parker pulls up a chair. "Sorry, man, I didn't realize how late it is already. We're supposed to meet them now. I'll show you the trailer later."

"Oh, no problem. I have to get those jerseys back. Do you want me to take Lo?"

He shakes his head. "Nope," King pops the last syllable and turns his neck from side to side, his ears nearly touching each shoulder.

The three of us stand in place, a curiosity spreading from each of us, creating more confusion to grow. Then King digs for his keys and nods to the hall, and we awkwardly traipse out of the room.

"Alright, well you guys have a good time," Parker says, veering toward the shop.

"This is going to be really weird, isn't it?"

"What?" King asks, opening the passenger door of his truck for me.

"Us."

"What? You think it's going to be weird to tell Parker that we're dating?"

"More like telling anyone." King closes my door and makes his way into the driver's seat before he looks at me with an expression that makes me a little nervous, because unlike so many that I can read with a simple glance, I don't know what it means.

"Lo, I already know what they all think."

"I just don't want you to feel obligated to tell anyone. We can keep work and our private time separately," I continue.

"Parker was just trying to root around and see if what he's heard is true. No way he hasn't already heard the news. I told you, Lo, I don't play bullshit games." He turns to regard me as we travel down the driveway. "Are you bothered by others knowing?"

"No!" The word bursts from my mouth as I shake my head. "No, it's nothing like that. I just ... I work for your brother."

"You're acting like you're the help and that somehow puts you below us."

"Not below you, just an HR liability. My dad never hired women because he said it would be a distraction to everyone else, and I always hated that."

"Welcome to Oregon, babe. Here, if someone treats you different because you're a woman, you get to sue the fuck out of them." King's voice is a jumble of frustration and contrition.

"I wouldn't sue you guys..." My eyes close for a moment with the ugly place this conversation has gone.

"They're excited." King shifts uneasily in his seat before looking over to me. "Everyone likes you, Lo. They know you aren't in this for status, or to get with Kash, or anything else."

"Get with Kash?" King's eyes round on me and his brows are raised. I never even considered that people would attempt to use him to get to Kash when in my eyes, King *is* the main prize. I hope Summer kicked their asses.

"So how do we interact at the house?" This question seems far more important than King's casual shrug and quiet laugh warrants.

"You can't jump me in the kitchen or in the living room, but maybe the shop, depending on what everyone else is doing. The office is a pretty safe bet too."

"King!"

His laugh grows louder while his grip on the steering wheel relaxes. "You can greet me however you're comfortable. Just know that my returned greeting is going to involve kissing you, and possibly an ass grab."

My cheeks lift into a smirk, appreciating he wants to kiss me when I've been wanting to kiss him every day that I've been working at the Knight residence and have seen him. Yet I know already that my ten-year-old counterpart and near sister is going to heckle the shit out of me.

"Why didn't you send me your schedule?" King's question doesn't fit with my line of thoughts that are considering Mercedes' reactions, causing my eyebrows to draw down with confusion. "You were going to text your schedule to me so I could come get you."

"I don't want a chauffeur."

"Think of all the time you would save." Low blow. Time is a constant shortage. "See, you would be able to spend more time on your portfolio and whatever else you want."

"This is going to sound kind of crazy, but I sort of like the bus." King sends me a silent look that says bullshit. "I like to see all the people. I need that inspiration when I start hitting lulls."

"At least a third of the people that ride that bus talk to themselves."

"It's better than them trying to talk to me."

He sends me another look of disbelief that's colored with the slight hue of acceptance, or possibly defeat. It's tough to tell which it is because he's focused on parking.

King flips five pennies throughout the mostly empty parking lot and then speeds up to keep pace with me. His fingers lace with mine as we approach the doors. It feels good to hold someone's hand. Growing up, I held hands with all of my friends. It was an acceptable show of love and friendship, like we were so giddy and happy to be together, we needed to be fused by our fingers. With age, holding hands somehow changes in definition. It's no longer something you do with any friend. The acceptable list shrinks, which translates the action to hold a deeper sentiment. You hold hands only with people you're sexually attracted to, like it's a claim or a promise. I wish it were acceptable to hold hands with friends again, because while I feel a thousand tiny transmitters of emotion and lust being lit by holding King's hand, it also brings me back to running through fields and pastures, giggling until I can't breathe, sticky popsicles melting down my fingers. I'm mentally noting that I'm going to hold Mercedes' hand tomorrow, knowing how likely it is that she never holds hands with anyone, when we step inside.

"What is this place?" I ask, looking up at the extensive sign as we enter the large space with the air conditioning running on high, regardless of the cool temperatures outside.

"Somewhere you can overcome your fear of being airborne," King replies as my eyes dance over the large room filled with trampolines. "Come on, we need to get some socks."

"Welcome to Fly High. Have you guys been here before?" A man who's several inches shorter than me greets us.

"We're virgins … at least for doing it *here* we are."

Rolling my eyes to him, I drop my chin with annoyance. It only serves to make him laugh.

"Alright, well, you'll both need to fill out these liability forms, then." He gestures toward two monitors.

"Oh good, signing my death waiver is helping already." My tone is dry, filled with a half-truth.

King chuckles and shakes his head as I sign my safety away. "You're going to love this place."

We climb the stairs and discover a vast area covered with trampoline panels, bridged by padded sections that extend to walls stretched with even more of the buoyant material. There are large foam pits to the side, a basketball court, a climbing wall, and more areas that I can't see from where we're standing.

"Ready?"

I look over to King with wide eyes. I can't remember the last time I jumped on a trampoline, and feel the adrenaline rush of an eight-year-old me that was stirred awake in the parking lot, become fully awake. His lips pull up into that uneven smile that inspires me late at night, and he nods forward before stepping onto one of the rectangular trampolines. He bounces slowly without his feet ever leaving the surface. The energy in me rises as I step onto the one beside his and bend my knees, rolling my weight to my toes. My feet push off and I gain several inches of air beneath me. I land and push off a bit harder, feeling my heart race. I push further until I'm weightless, fearless, utterly lost in joy. I bounce to another rectangle of the mesh and bounce in a pattern only my feet seem to recognize. It leads me to a large mat that makes my body shift as I land on the solid surface, similar to the feeling one gets after riding a horse for several hours.

It leads me to the massive pit of foam where I stand, fixated. The thought is instant. I go from wondering to doing and within seconds, I'm crashing into a mess of soft foam that sinks below me. I'm laughing, pumped with energy and the desire to do it again as I lie weightless for a few long seconds.

King hits the foam less than a foot from me. His smile radiates to his eyes, and before either of us seems to question or realize what I am doing, I'm clumsily moving, shifting and climbing through the short separation and kissing King.

We spend the entire afternoon and most of the evening jumping, climbing walls, daring to cross bands extended mid-air that promise a cushioned fall of foam, and allowing our competitive spirits to spark through the relay race section. I think I surprised both of us when I beat him the first round. He didn't make the mistake of taking it easy on me again. I may like fashion and sit with nearly weightless tools for my favorite pastime, but growing up like I did, I can still manage to be a force to be reckoned with.

My muscles are tired, and soreness teases my calves and hamstrings, but I can't stop smiling. I want to come back and do this again tomorrow and the next day and the day after that. Immersing myself into a world where there is no portfolio competition or modeling practice, I don't have to fret over my roommate's sexual activities, or what I'm going to do in a few months when I graduate.

I look over to King as we make our way out to the parking lot; Mercedes and

Summer are ahead of us. Sensing my glance, he turns and bestows that radiant smile I have drawn so many times that I now know every single curve and crinkle, and with it comes the feeling that perhaps I don't need to be bouncing on trampolines for hours to feel this euphoria. Maybe I just need this: King, Mercedes, Kash, and even Summer.

chapter
TWENTY-FIVE

A rt has always been my main point of both stress relief and stress enhancer. I love sitting down in my private bubble and getting so far lost in my work that the world seems to pass by without even a whisper or trace. However, showing my work to someone and now creating this portfolio to mail off to be viewed and judged to see if I possess the necessary talents to do this internship is keeping me awake at night, requiring additional hours of drawing that I'm starting to feel more prominently in my wrists and hands, and I'm pretty sure the beginnings of an ulcer. Still, it pales in comparison to my long walk down the Knight driveway as I prepare myself to meet King and Kash's parents and sister. King sprung it on me last night, trying to act nonchalant as he mentioned he was going to be cooking prime rib and to bring my appetite. I smiled, the thoughts of a stay-at-home date brewing in my imagination, and then abruptly blown away with, "they'll probably arrive before you, but if you want me to come get you"—insert pointed look—"you'd be here first." I was nervous, expecting him to announce one of the people from Switzerland, or the infamous Spencer, I've yet to meet, prompting me to ask who.

"My parents and sister." He said it so casually, as if this was just a single step forward rather than leaps and bounds. Sure, in Montana I knew the parents of my previous boyfriends, often times their siblings, aunts, uncles, cousins, and entire life story. But that's because I lived in a really small town and grew up with most of them.

My shock must have been evident on my face because King quickly explained they were coming for a birthday dinner for Kash—another fact I was surprised to learn.

It's cold today, the wind whipping rather than blowing through my hair and the surrounding trees, making the walk seem even longer.

I'm halfway down the driveway when I try to call Charleigh and reach her voicemail. I don't leave a message because I'm seeking a hit of confidence, one that a later returned call will not be able to soothe. I call Allie and sigh with relief when she answers on the third ring, her greeting sounding almost confused.

"I need your help."

"What's going on?"

"I'm going to meet King's family. His *entire* family."

"Don't you already know them all? I mean, you work for his brother."

Frowning, I lower my head and keep walking against turbulent weather. Clearly she doesn't understand. "Yeah, but tonight I'm meeting the elusive sister and parental units."

"You need a drink. Did you stop and take a shot?"

I shake my head, fighting a smile. The gravel crunches beneath my steps, and the wind howls even louder. I might have to take King up on a ride back to the bus station today. My carefully selected outfit that's intended to show I'm mature and sophisticated, and not a gold-digger, but ready to play because that's my role, consists of dark denim skinny jeans that feel far too thin to be real denim, and a lightweight purple sweater with an open stitch that requires the use of a jacket.

"No, I didn't think smelling like alcohol would help my case," I say with a laugh.

Allie laughs, and I hear the slight rustling that had been present in the background stop. "You're going to do fine, Lo. Just be you."

"I'm an artist," I cry. "They're going to look at me the same way my parents did when I announced I was going to art school."

"Lo, Kash is an artist too! Deep breaths!"

"Yes, but Kash is a *successful* artist." That word makes all the difference. Anyone can say they're an artist, but until you're either published or have works in multiple museums, people say the word artist in a demeaning tone, often accompanied by an eye roll.

"I know. Stop going down that path though. It's not going to help. Hold your head high, and know you're just as good as anyone else, artist or otherwise. Our titles and jobs don't define us."

I heave a deep sigh. "You're right."

"Of course I'm right. And just remember, King chose you, Lo. It doesn't matter what the rest of his family thinks. It matters what he thinks. Plus, you've already got Kash and Mercedes on your side. This will be a cakewalk."

"I'm glad I called you. This helps."

"I'm glad you called too."

"Are you working on one of my dresses?" I hope she doesn't feel I'm asking out of guilt. I genuinely am interested in what she's doing and worry that she's been too focused on work.

"I'm working on the dress that is going to make me go down in fashion world history. You better practice your smile. It's going to be seen everywhere when they see this dress."

"Whitening strips, got it."

Allie laughs, and behind the swishing of the pine branches, I hear the rustle of fabric once again. "You're going to do great, Lo. If you need anything, call or text me. I'll be home all night."

"Thanks, Al."

"I want to know how it goes. Stop by when you get home!"

I laugh my agreement and hang up. Taking a deep breath of the Oregon rain that is hanging on every surface like a coat of lace, my lungs quiver, still not fully convinced.

The lack of additional cars in the driveway fills me with relief and confusion. Did they decide to go to dinner? Are they late? Maybe they're like my mom and don't know how to honor a commitment.

Like every other time over the past six months, I use my key and head inside. Postponing this meeting would be ideal. I don't feel ready to meet the rest of King's family, yet it oddly fills me with a sense of disappointment and an even larger dose of irritation. Why wouldn't they have called to let me know? Is he embarrassed to have them meet me? Did Kash decide it was a bad idea? Questions are swimming through my mind, triggering emotions to fire off left and right, softening the sounds of voices until I'm met with their source. King, Summer, Kash, and Kenzie are standing in the kitchen, their stiff postures reflecting that none of them are comfortable. I stand in the doorway, staring at them as a group, and then slowly each of them individually. Their hair, though varying shades, all has the same chestnut undertones, their skin sharing a dose of additional pigment that reveals their bloodline is from further south on the equator, and while they all look drastically different, there's a striking resemblance that slaps me across the face. How could I of all people have missed this? I study people's faces! I have been taught to see similarities, to recognize the minor resemblance they all share. I've drawn each of them!

I can't hear their words as they all turn to look at me, my eyes settling on Kenzie, who is projecting a silent scream of shock.

"But, you have different last names," I sputter, shaking my head as I take a step back.

"Lo." My name is barely a whisper. Kenzie is just as surprised by my presence, which confuses me that much more since she's who got me this job. "I didn't realize … I've been meaning to tell you … Lo…" Her face tinges with embarrassment. I've never seen it before. With all of the mornings she's faced

228 • MARIAH DIETZ

me after having a visitor, she's never looked even slightly uncomfortable.

"You didn't realize I was referring to your brother when I asked about him *ten thousand* times?" My heart is beating erratically, but my voice is surprisingly calm, holding on to a thread of hope that I am clenching with both fists.

Her eyes shift under the weight of my stare. "I was just trying to help him. He loves Isabelle. He was starting to realize that, and then he met you and forgot. I needed him to understand why you two would never work." She takes a few steps closer to me, her shoulders raised with conviction. "You're from small town nowhere, and you don't know anything about the BMX world or our family. Isabelle grew up with us. They're meant to be together."

My mouth feels tight, like the muscles are yearning to form an objection or scream, but my breath doesn't seem to climb any higher than my chest. I stare at her, imploring my words to return.

"I hated you when I found out you guys slept together. I hated you even more when he asked about you. I thought for sure that when you started working here, you'd both understand that things could never work between you. I never in my wildest dreams imagined you two would start dating. Never. I thought you would get tired of how stubborn and rigid he gets, and I thought your carefree ignorance would drive him insane. Now you're just going to break each other's hearts because you're going to Italy in a few months, and King is finally starting to talk about racing, and those worlds—they don't coexist."

"What?" King's words barely register as I think of all the times Charleigh, Allie, and I discussed him. Discussed him *with her*. Just last week Allie and I were talking about him while Kenzie was in the apartment.

Kenzie's gaze remains on mine as I absently catch King shaking his head and the fact that he's muttering something. "Isabelle's my best friend. They were supposed to realize how perfect they were together at that party. He wasn't supposed to have feelings for someone else!"

"Are you out of your goddamned mind, Kenzie?" King's been speaking, working to divert attention and intervene, but these words are the first to succeed because they are so loud it makes my heart stall for a second with surprise. "You told me she wasn't interested in me! That she liked another guy!"

"I was trying to help you."

"Help me?" King bellows.

"She drives you crazy!" Kenzie continues. "You've said so yourself."

"Kenzie." It takes me several seconds to process Kash's voice but an instant to realize he's touching me. He has wrapped a hand around my shoulder with a firmness I know is meant to be comforting, but right now, it produces the opposite effect.

"I can't believe you." My words are too quiet to sound like a threat. I shake my head and take a deep breath to fight my emotions from breaking through.

"Lo, I'm sorry. I didn't know how to tell you after you started dating. I knew you guys would eventually—"

"Kenzie, just shut up!" King yells. His face has turned hard, his eyes a darker shade of brown, and while I expect his fingers to be pinching the bridge of his nose like they do when he's upset, they're fisted at his sides. My eyes get distracted by the movement of his T-shirt, exposing his breaths, which are coming in quick heaves. Everything about him portrays anger.

My body feels too large, my arms and legs too long as I order them to move.

"Lo, wait." Kenzie's face is haunted. I don't doubt for a second that she's regretting what she's done. The tears streaming down her cheeks express more than just the guilt for the deception.

"I can't believe you. I can't believe you had the audacity to lie to my face countless times. Then you decided to hate me and treat me like a goddamned leper. You're the most selfish person I've ever met. You need to get out of your own head and look the hell around." Shaking my head, my thoughts sift through curses I want to scream at Kenzie, but I know that would make me no better than her. "Why in the hell did you encourage me to get this job? You basically gifted it to me on a silver platter."

"Because he wanted to find you. I was afraid he wouldn't stop. Don't you understand? Isabelle's my best friend. He needed to get over you." Kenzie's eyeliner and mascara run with her last few words.

"It's none of your business, Kenzie. You don't get to be like Mom and control this shit!" Kash objects.

"Kash, it's Isabelle."

"I know that, Kenz. I know you're not trying to hurt people, but—"

"Get out Kenzie," King orders. "Your entire life you've blamed Mom for meddling in your business, begged Kash and me to help get her off your back. She never pulled a stunt this sick and twisted. Never. You want to know why you hate her? It's because you're just like her."

The fact that I've never met their mom or heard any of them mention her in detail doesn't matter. I can sense the harshness of his message in the way Kenzie's narrow shoulders fall, and her eyes are glassy with tears. It causes my emotions to somersault with the need to stand up for her, while the urge to condemn her is still actively present in my thoughts. "I need to go."

"Lo, we need to talk." King crosses the distance between us with intentions clear in his eyes. His hand swallows the golden bangle along with my wrist. "Kash..." He doesn't say more. I don't know if it's because they're both already aware of what's going to transpire next, or if he's simply passing the baton to him, done with his turn in the relay.

Emotions are running rampant, shooting out accusations and questions before King has the office door closed.

"Why didn't you tell me? Why didn't you ask me?" The questions burst through my lips, nearly as angry as the ones I had directed toward Kenzie.

"Because I thought you were dating someone else! I thought you were just like so many others that didn't give a shit about me, only my name."

"I've never cared about your name!"

"I know!" King's words are still too loud, like he can't manage to get his own emotions in check.

"That's why you thought Charleigh was a guy."

"Of course that's why I thought she was!" He dips his head, closing his eyes.

"Do you love Isabelle?"

King's head snaps level again, his eyes bright. "No!" We focus on one another, a silent conversation passing between us that consists of his plea for me to trust him, an insult for my insinuation to a question he's already answered, along with an apology that I'm having to ask again.

"Never. Kenzie's right, I did grow up with Isabelle. She's like a sister to me. There was never a time I even considered liking her as anything more."

"This is really…"

"I know."

"What if she's right?" I don't bother specifying which part she may be right about. Every one of them would be awful, and I hate considering any of them.

"We can't think about it like that. What if she's wrong? If you go into something already thinking you're going to fail, what's the purpose of doing anything in life? You wouldn't be going to school to have an art major. I wouldn't be considering stepping into competition. We'd still be thinking the world is flat, fearing we'd fall off the edge if we got too far out. But I'm not going to let that fear ruin my chance at having one of the best things happen to me."

My chest feels heavy, like I have too much air, or too much blood, or maybe my organs have suddenly tripled in size. I knew that I mattered to him; I just never realized it could be this much.

"I need you to go back to being an asshole for a few minutes before I say something I'm not ready for."

"I wasn't that bad." King looks like he wants to smile by the way his cheeks move up, but it quickly becomes a wince. "Was I?"

A smirk pulls at my lips as I nod. "You were a class-A asshole at times. It was easier when I could hate you."

"I don't want you to hate me."

"I don't want to care about you this much," I admit.

"I don't want you to stop." King's eyes are warm, gentle as they hold mine. The desire to have him hold me and fix this, fix everything, is so tempting.

"All my life people have been there when it was convenient, when it benefited them."

"I want to be there for all of it, the good, bad, ugly, and everything in between."

"That's easy to say now."

"The last six months have been anything but easy and good. Still, look where we are. Look where we're going, Lo." King's voice is calm and assured as he takes a step closer to me, not even slightly deterred or defensive about my concern. It makes something warm and tingly to spread through my entire body.

"You need to go talk to Kenzie."

"First I need to make sure you're okay. I want you to tell me you aren't going to let what she's done affect us."

"It won't. It might make living with her more difficult, but it doesn't change anything between us. Besides, I get off on proving people wrong." Eyebrows raised, he struggles to conceal his smile. "Don't even," I say, raising a hand. "That wasn't intended to be dirty."

"Yet it was. I like that you think dirty. No need to hide it."

"Go talk to your sister."

"Going." He doesn't move though. King's hand curves around my waist, pulling me closer to him as he takes a step forward. We kiss for several long moments, and while it leaves me breathless and with the promise of all he can make me feel, it isn't a hot kiss filled with lust. It's packed with passion and sincerity, ensuring me that everything is going to be okay.

chapter
TWENTY-SIX

I haven't seen Kenzie for two days, not since King came back into the office, where I waited for him to sort through his family drama, and told me Kash was giving her a ride home. I didn't pry … much. I knew by his tired expression that he was feeling remorseful for what he had yelled at her. I feel a little guilty that I'm so relieved to not have seen her. The inevitable conversation between us in an attempt to iron things out is without a doubt going to be awkward and forced.

The doorbell rings, distracting me from going through the contents of my closet once more.

"Here," Allie says, shoving a garment bag forward as I open the door.

"What is it?"

"Your date with King is tonight, right?"

"Yeah…"

"This is what you're going to wear."

"What is it?" My hands are already pulling down the zipper, not patient enough to wait for her reply. "Allie!" I squeal, pushing back each side of the bag.

"If you get anything on it, I'm going to kill you," she threatens as I lift the beautiful handmade dress so I can fully admire it. It's one of the pieces she's going to present during the fashion show. I recognize the color, but that's all. There have been two dresses she's been working on that I have barely seen, this being one of them.

"Are you sure?

"Of course I'm not. But I am sure that this is a big deal to you, and therefore you need to be dressed to the nines."

"This is like the twenties."

Allie smiles with pride and drops a bag on the kitchen counter. "Let's get you ready."

The dress is like a second skin. A flawless, shimmering, surprisingly heavy second skin. It's emerald and falls several inches past my knee in waves of hand-sewn beading. When she initially shared the idea, I regret to say I looked at her with wide eyes, trying to hide how unattractive the idea seemed. Now, I'm amazed. The waist extends for my height and curves to my body, knowing of my bust and hips perfectly.

I leave my straightened hair around my shoulders, and while it feels wrong to hide any of the dress, Allie insists it will allow me to be casual enough to fit into nearly any restaurant that King chooses.

"Shit! He's early!" Allie cries. She's only a few steps behind me, watching over my shoulder as I apply another coat of mascara.

I take a deep breath as Allie moves to the front door. She turns, looking over her shoulder for me to confirm I'm ready before pulling it open.

"You clean up nice," she says.

Curiosity has me moving forward around my easel and beside Allie. She's wrong. He cleans up to look like a Calvin Klein model.

King is dressed in charcoal gray slacks and a navy blue shirt that both fit him so well I wonder if they were tailored to fit him. At the very least, I know Summer was involved. I'm staring at his hands, mesmerized by how even accompanied by fancy dress clothes they reveal hints of tricks gone bad, grease, and hard work. It makes my desire to have them on me—all over me—become my sole thought.

A sharp elbow to the back of my ribs has my eyes darting up to see that King is just as lost.

"Fair-y godmother," Allie says quietly. "Don't order anything with a cream or red sauce. They stain."

King's eyebrows raise, but Allie doesn't notice. She's packing things back into her bag. She slips around me and behind King and doesn't turn around again, making her way downstairs.

"No red or cream sauce?"

"She made this dress. It's the least I can do."

His eyes widen, peering over it once more. "She's definitely climbing the charts to favorite person status. First heels, now this." His hand sweeps down the length of me but several inches away, making that yearning for his touch grow more prominent.

I'm grateful I've been forced to wear heels lately; otherwise, I know I would be as nervous about them as I am this dress as we head down the stairs, my hand resting in the crook of his arm. It's cool outside, the black shawl draped over my shoulders barely serving as a barrier, but thankfully it's dry.

"How are classes going?"

"Good," I answer while attempting to fasten my seatbelt and sneak another look at him before the dome lights dim. It's starting to stay light later, but the sun still set a couple hours ago.

"Did you get your submission in?"

Since mailing my portfolio I've felt a heavy weight in my chest each and every time I consider the possible outcomes. "Yeah. I mailed it on Tuesday."

I catch the slight lurch of King's chin and his hand tightening around the steering wheel. "You're going to love it. Traveling and working on paintings from artists you've studied. It will be like a dream come true."

"They haven't said yes."

"They won't be able to say no."

I don't know which possibility scares me more.

"There's this restaurant in Florence, it's called 13 Gobi. When you get there, you have to go. Their food is like nothing you've ever tasted before. It's where I first started to really appreciate eating and wanted to learn to cook."

"I doubt it will leave the same impression on me."

King flashes his smile, the dim lighting from the dash and passing cars teasing at what they expose, hiding so much that my imagination draws most of it.

"You haven't asked where we're going yet," King says as we pull to a stop at a light.

"Call me weird, but I like surprises." Not to mention it seems rude to ask him. I fear he's going to spend an obscene amount of money going anywhere our attire is set for.

"Goes with your theme of surprising others with your work, huh?"

"Something like that. I feel like people don't have an appreciation for waiting any longer. As a culture we're so used to being able to get any and everything at the tip of our fingers: we need it, and it arrives the next day. People no longer spend time thinking about the perfect gift. They simply go online and order whatever's popular. We don't want movies that leave us thinking; we want things spelled out. Popular books have spoilers online because people want to know what they're walking into. Couples buy their own gifts. If something doesn't load within seconds, people complain and leave the site, or call their phone and carriers crap."

"This coming from the self-proclaimed food assembler."

"Yes, but I don't have a great appreciation for food. If I did, it would be different."

"That sounds like a double standard."

"It probably is. After all, I am a part of this culture as well."

King glances over with a smile of amusement. "Wait until you get immersed into Italy's culture. By the time you return you, won't know what to do when you see a line, or understand why our dining experiences are so fast when there they savor not only the food, but the time together."

"Impatience for the tedium and great amounts of patience for what they love. I can appreciate that to a point."

"To a point?"

"Maybe if we all appreciated the fact we get to do tedious tasks, they wouldn't seem so tedious."

"The glass is half full."

"Sure. Otherwise, what's the point? If all you want to see is the pain and suffering, why live?"

"A friend of mine said artists are all sad. That their work is how they express the grief they feel."

"We have to know sad in order to know happy, pain in order to feel pleasure, fear to teach us safety."

"You told me that same line that night at the party."

"Even while drinking, I'm deep. It's a gift."

King's silent, navigating us through the busy Saturday evening traffic. He doesn't even look my way. I have a feeling if his hands weren't both on the wheel, one would be on the bridge of his nose and the other tightly fisted at his side. Though my words are light, I can tell by his reaction he was hoping I'd share in reminiscing. He isn't mad. He's disappointed.

"I remember meeting you." My confession is so quiet my own ears strain to hear it. "I had only drunk a glass of beer before you arrived. Granted, that was enough to make me pretty tipsy since the glasses were ridiculously big, and I pretty much never drink, but I remember."

"You were talking with Kenzie. I noticed you because you weren't hanging on her every word and giggling. You guys were actually having a conversation. Kenzie has always sought out people that just want to have a good time. I knew then you were different."

"You had a crowd of twenty girls around you. I didn't even know you were at the center until you started moving forward, and through a mess of hair, I saw you." I smile, recalling my piqued curiosity, and the sympathy and confusion I felt for each of the girls. "I expected you to be a complete asshole. I *wanted* you to be an asshole. There was no way I was going to join that group, and then I went out to get some air, and there you were."

"Did you sleep with me because they were interested in me?"

King's question sends a flash of anger through me. A bold insinuation, one that I hate to admit I've questioned myself about several times. "You walked right up to me and introduced yourself. I thought you were going to be one of those guys that just assumes everyone is going to fall head over heels in love with them. Then you made that joke about the rain in Oregon and how it's always just a cloud away and how glad you were because it weeded out the people that were afraid their façades would wash away. It just seemed so honest. Granted, now I know you lied about your first name ... but I'm willing to let that slide, now that I know the reason behind it."

"You told me you loved the rain, and I couldn't tell if you were being sarcastic or trying to flirt."

"Neither," I say, surprised he considered those were the only possibilities. "I really *do* love the rain, but I am glad it isn't raining tonight. I doubt Allie would approve of me getting a single raindrop on this dress." *And hopefully my nerves won't be reflective under my arms when this date is over. She definitely wouldn't appreciate sweat marks.*

"Where are we...?" My words pause as King pulls into the parking lot of Portland's Art Museum. "You know it closes at five, right?" I shift in my seat when he doesn't reply, feeling guilty for my reaction. "I mean, this was a really sweet idea, and I would love to come another time..."

"Do you think I would have brought you here without looking into it first?"

My eyebrows that were already raised dance higher, eliciting an amused laugh from King. He ducks out of the truck and is around to where I'm sliding out, offering me his arm once again. Without delay, he strolls to the main entrance of the museum where we're met by a man wearing a suit and museum badge. He nods to King with a courteous smile while bidding us good evening, and then waves us in.

"If you have any questions, please find me in the Sculpture Court," he says, locking the entrance doors. He gives us a parting smile, and then his shoes echo across the tiles, where we hear him far longer than we can see him.

"If you're trying to get in my pants tonight by impressing me, it's not going to happen. Allie sewed the dress on."

King's head tilts, his eyes growing larger. "She what?"

"There wasn't time to add the right closure, so she sewed it on. I'm not drinking anything while we're out tonight. I don't think this skirt will go much higher than mid thigh."

King bursts out laughing. "You're kidding."

"I'm as serious about it as I am my love for the rain."

He moves behind me, sweeping my hair to the side and brushing his fingers down my spine, making chills run across my arms even with the casual touch. "You guys are crazy!"

"Says the guy that hangs upside down while midair on a bike."

King's still shaking his head, but he's laughing, I'm pretty sure mostly at me. "Come on." Taking my hand, we set off through a maze of halls that I've been through dozens of times while surrounded by other viewers. Being here alone with King, the rooms seem far more expansive, the silence an ode to each of the works of art. We walk slowly through the first two galleries, stopping in front of each picture or object to admire it.

"You like this one?" King asks from over my shoulder. We've been standing in front of the picture for several minutes. Neither of us has shared our thoughts on any of the pieces thus far.

"I don't actually know what I'm looking at," I admit.

His hand catches mine and he laughs so hard, I feel his weight against me. "This has to be the ugliest thing I've ever seen. I feel terrible saying that, especially with you here since you understand the time and energy that goes into each, but that is just fugly."

"I respect all art and the artists that create it, but that doesn't mean I like it all. I imagine it's like you with food. You know how much work goes into certain meals, but your tastes don't always match."

"I followed you."

I shake my head as my eyes slant with confusion.

"At the party I saw you motion to Kenzie where you were going. Then I told everyone I was going to the bathroom, and I followed you." King maintains eye contact with me while explaining himself, his eyes bright with intensity. "I was drawn to you and knew I wanted to know you. I know Kenzie lied, and this entire week I've been going through periods where I've been so pissed off at her for it, but in some perverse way, I'm kind of glad. If you hadn't started as Mercedes' nanny, you would have been working at the restaurant, and with me being out of town and busy so often, and you doing school and working full time, I fear we wouldn't have been able to see each other very often. And as much as I hate to admit this, there are things about each of us that if we saw without getting the chance to know each other, they probably would have driven us both crazy."

"I've thought the same thing. I don't plan on telling her that, however."

King shakes his head, his lips spreading into a smile. "Hell no."

"I'm glad you followed me."

"It was one of my better decisions."

We spend several more minutes in front of the painting King deemed fugly, neither of us acknowledging it as we kiss until we're both tempted to test Allie's sewing job.

"We just made that painting a whole hell of a lot more attractive," King says while gently stroking the pad of his thumb under my lower lip. "Come on."

We go to the door where special exhibits are set up, a room that has been closed off the last few times that I've been here. King opens it, and inside the sizable room, the lights are dimmed, the spotlights turned off completely. Our shoes echo even louder in this space. There's nothing inside but a small table adorned with several white tiered candles that appear to have been lit for a period of time based upon the wax dripping down their sides, and two plates covered in silver domes that I've only ever seen in movies. A single red rose lies in the center, tied with a thin twine to a feather in varying shades of blue.

King pulls out my chair and then gently slides me closer to the table before uncovering the dish.

My eyes widen and my stomach growls. "You remember."

"When you told me you could eat dessert as a meal, I wanted to think you were referring to me since, you know, we'd finished round two and you were completely relaxed. Your eyes closed as you told me pie was a waste of calories—you preferred cake with extra frosting, and dessert to any meal—but I thought, what the hell."

The smirk on my face falls away as I inspect my plate. There's a large slab of chocolate cake nestled between a crepe covered in whipped cream and strawberries, and a chocolate-covered donut that's sitting beside a dish filled with chocolate mousse. A bar that's several layers of sin high and a slice of tiramisu both look flawless and almost fake they're so pretty. Slices of fresh fruit are artfully placed around the plate so that only the rim reveals that it's a made of white porcelain. I only need a single finger to count the number of times I've eaten off fine china, being that it was only once when my mom's sister invited us over for Christmas. My dad sent me while he and my brother spent the day with Nell and Alan. I'm not sure why or how I became the sacrificial lamb that year, but I recall the heavy plates and the way my aunt's eyes seemed to zero in every time anyone lifted one to get more food.

I shove the memory aside and look to King. "This is perfect!"

The smile he responds with is flawless. I see the relief, anticipation, and excitement in his eyes, and for the first time in my life, I feel like someone gets me. More importantly, I feel like he wants to.

TWENTY-SEVEN

"Hey!" I call, catching a glimpse of Charleigh as she heads to her car.

She stops and turns toward the stairs as I rush down the last few. "Hey, I heard you and King went on your first official date."

I'm sure my smile is a giveaway, but I still confirm it.

"I'm happy for you, Lo."

"Thanks, I really appreciate that." We stare at each other, the last several weeks of not seeing each other causing a wedge of discomfort to fill the space between us. I have no idea what she's been up to or how school is going. I still haven't even met her boyfriend yet or heard her accounts of him. "How is everything going with you?"

"Good, really good."

I nod, unsure of how else to respond. "Allie said you dropped out of the show."

"Don't go there, Lo. I don't want to have this same conversation with you."

"Go where? I was simply asking."

"Yeah, and then you're going to tell me I'm throwing away my future for some guy."

"Actually, I probably would have told you you're alienating your best friend *and* throwing away your future for some guy."

"Isn't that cheeky. You're learning to cook for a boy, going to modeling practice every week, painting on the wall of a restaurant for free, and sitting at home waiting all night for your mum to show up, even though she never does. You sit around waiting for everyone to make you into whomever they want or need."

"I know who I am. I also know that sometimes you do things you don't want to because someone needs you."

"You're too scared to say no. You don't ever want to make yourself stand out too far. Otherwise, someone might realize how tall you are, how good at art you are, how much time you spend on that damn bus. You're so afraid to be in the spotlight, you just sit in everyone else's shadow."

"And what in the hell are you doing with dropping out of the fashion show?"

"Saying fuck you to everyone and doing exactly what I want to. I'm twenty-two! I want to have fun and make mistakes and have loads of orgasms before I lock myself into a room to try and compete with thousands of other struggling artists that can't even remember what the bloody sky looks like, or what a good night's sleep feels like. I deserve to have some time to myself!"

We glare at each other, accusations and hurt making our eyes wide and our lips pursed.

"You need to stop living for everyone else and live for yourself a little. Maybe then you'll understand." She stomps to her car and peels out of the entrance lane rather than exit.

"Do you have any idea how hard it was for me to come out here to go to art school?" I mumble. "Of course not, because you have your head shoved so far up your own ass, you don't care."

I stalk to the bus stop, my thoughts still on the argument with Charleigh, a thousand more appropriate responses running through my mind. Some of them are witty and would have been so much more rewarding, while others are far calmer, bringing me to regret the anger I allowed to respond to her initial accusation. I'm grateful I only have one class on Mondays. Otherwise, today would royally suck.

Though the rain is coming down in heavy sheets while the wind howls like two of mother nature's tools are at war with one another—causing the rain to seemingly come at me from every angle—I smile when I hear King's ringtone from my coat pocket. I pull my hood up a bit farther and my umbrella a bit lower before I reach for my phone and press it close to my ear so I can hear him over the current losing force.

"Where are you? You aren't walking in this, are you?"

"Conditioning, remember?"

"It sounds like a fucking hurricane." With that prompt, the wind howls even louder, folding my umbrella so it's now collecting water rather than repelling it.

"I'm nearly there. Are you home?"

"Not yet. I'm at Spencer's. How far out are you? Why don't you call Summer, see if she's there?"

"It's okay. I'll be there in just a few minutes. This wind is pushing me along, making me go faster. It's kind of cool."

I hear a man's voice in the background asking if he's talking to his girlfriend, followed by a dozen kissing sounds.

"What are you, twelve? She's not my girlfriend. Get your label fetished mind out of here, and get back to work."

I know King's words would hurt me regardless, but they seem to compound Charleigh's previous accusations, causing them to burn even deeper.

"Sorry, Spencer's a pain in the ass."

"Yeah, you've said that. Alright, well it's kind of hard to hear you, so I'm going to let you go."

"Are you upset?"

"No, why would I be upset?"

"You sound upset."

"It's just the storm. I'm fine. I'll see you later." I hang up before he has the opportunity to reply. Saturday night I was disappointed my dress required Allie's assistance to remove. If it hadn't, I have few doubts I would have ended up sleeping with King again. Now, I'm so relieved I could kiss her.

I beat Mercedes home. Knowing her carpool is set to arrive at any minute, I set a pot of milk on the stove to boil for cocoa, confident the marshmallow cream I just found in the pantry will at least make my stomach feel better.

Mercedes arrives with her carpool friends unloading from the minivan, and a yelled promise that they won't play too late as they head toward the shop. The mother of one of the girls shares a cup of hot chocolate with me, making things awkward when she starts asking too many questions about Kash.

When the weather worsens, the mom compiles the girls, and Mercedes and I spend the afternoon watching shows made for young teenagers that I am ashamed to admit I've grown quite fond of, even anticipating watching them with her to see what's going to happen next. I'm pretty sure this is another sign that I need a best friend, one who was at least born in the same decade as me.

"I'm going to put a load of laundry in really fast," I say, standing from the couch as Mercedes delays the next show so she can text someone on her phone with no opposition.

"Lo!" Mercedes screams as I push start on the washer.

I take the stairs two at a time to the main level and find her at the top, waiting for me, her arms crossed over her chest and face pale.

"What's wrong?"

"Did you hear that?"

The house lights up, quickly followed by a loud crash of thunder that has Mercedes jumping.

"It's okay. It's just the storm." My voice is too quiet and unsteady to assure either of us, but she doesn't object.

I reach out and lock the front door as we pass it, and lead her back into the living room, turning on more lights. The rain seems to be actively trying to find a way inside as it pounds against the windows and roof. Rather than wait for Mercedes to consider what we should do, I sit her back on the couch and reach for the remote, flipping through the DVR to the lightest, most comedic and usually obnoxious show that I can find.

Four episodes later, the storm still seems at full force, the thunder and lightning dancing to a terrifying melody that the rain makes every attempt to interrupt.

"Do you think my dad and King are okay?" I hate that she's bringing to light the same question I've been working to avoid all night.

"Yeah, I'm sure they're on their way now."

"You won't leave, right?"

"No. Of course not! Storm or no storm, I won't leave you if they're not home. Ever."

Mercedes jumps as another loud clap of thunder sends a slight vibration through the house. "It's getting worse." Impossibly, it is.

With all of the cleaning I've done in this house, I can't recall having ever seen storm supplies. I try to hide my concerns and take a deep breath. "Do you guys have flashlights, Mercedes?"

"Yeah, why?"

"Just in case the power goes out."

Her chin juts back as though my words have slapped her. "No." Her glare is set between anger and refusal. "The power can't go out! I don't want to be alone in the dark without my dad."

"It's okay. It probably won't. We're just going to be ready."

"Being ready sucks," she mumbles. Her movements look reluctant as she drags her feet slowly across the wood floor in the direction of the office.

"They're all in here somewhere," she says, opening a drawer of the desk.

My lips draw down in a frown. It's King's desk of all places we're going to be digging through. Another roar of thunder, followed by a flash of lightning that illuminates the yard, quickly buries my indecision, and I step beside Mercedes and start rifling through a drawer.

We find two large flashlights and a much smaller one with a keychain that I consider leaving before I flip it on and notice the beam hits halfway down the hall. I pocket it and push the button on each of the larger flashlights to find that both are thankfully working.

"Let's go make some dinner, and then we'll play a game or something."

"You totally think the power is going out, don't you?" Mercedes doesn't even look to me for a response. We both seem to realize this storm is going nowhere anytime soon.

"I don't know." My shoulders bunch and my eyebrows rise to reflect how unsure I am. "I just think that if it does, it's probably a better idea that we get some food cooked. Unless you want to test out that magical wand I found."

"Funny, Lo. Very funny." Mercedes' mouth is pulled down in a frown and her eyes shut before she shakes her head. A few months ago I would have found this reaction to be rude and annoying. Now it makes me laugh and reach forward to tickle her.

"I'll show you funny."

"No, Lo! Don't! I'm sorry!" she squeals, grasping my arms with both of her hands. "I'm sorry!" A soft laugh follows her words and has me staring at her features, seeing both Kash and King in her high cheekbones. I have only seen a few pictures of her mom, but I know that her green eyes and lashes that seem impossible with how long they reach, are from her. Mercedes' smile spreads wide and then she falls against my side, wrapping both her arms around my waist and hugging me tightly.

I'm the youngest in my family of non-expressive lovers. Hugs were rarer than the occasional 'I love you's,' yet holding her to me like she's mine to shelter and care for is natural and even feels good.

"What should we make?" I ask.

"What will you not burn?"

"Hey!" I protest, snaking my hand to her armpit. "I haven't burned anything in a few weeks! Give me some credit!"

She giggles as my fingers find their target and wiggles to get free.

"How about that pasta you made last week with the weird green stuff?"

"The pesto and sundried tomato *stuff*?"

"Yeah."

I don't make any attempt to hide my smirk as she looks at me and then nods. "Yeah, we can make the weird green stuff again."

Mercedes makes herself comfortable in the living room as I scour the fridge, pulling out the ingredients I used last time and some new ones that I think may be a good contribution.

I'm adding the cheese to the sauce when the door shuts with a cough of complaints and the rustling of fabric. Without thought, my hands release the grater and cheese, my feet migrating to the quickest path to the door where Mercedes meets me.

"King!" She throws herself against his chest, though he's visibly wet. "Where's my dad?" She pulls her head back, desperate for assurance.

His eyes scan over her, a hand settling in the middle of her shoulders. "He's at Summer's. Roads are closing. He'll be back in the morning." King scans the room as he finishes assuring her, settling on me. He's staring at me, searching for something

"He's not answering his phone," Mercedes objects without wasting a moment.

"They're starting to re-route calls. I'm sure it's in case anyone needs help, but I'm positive he's there." King moves his hands to her shoulders and squats in front of her, waiting until she meets his gaze. It takes a few seconds, but slowly Mercedes' head turns to face him. "He's going to be okay, monkey, I swear."

Slowly, she nods her agreement.

"Come help me finish the sauce. You can tell me if there's enough cheese." She turns to me, revealing the frail measure of strength she's struggling to maintain. I don't smile because I know she would find the gesture to be patronizing rather than supportive, so I tilt my head back toward the kitchen and lead the way with the hope that she'll follow.

Thankfully, she does.

"You cooked?" King's question plays through my head a few times. It isn't filled with sarcasm or shock, but pride that has me ducking my head a little farther as I return the last of the ingredients in the fridge.

"Sort of. It's more like my usual assembling because I mixed premade stuff together, but we made it last week while you were gone, and it was pretty decent." King's infamous uneven grin has me staring at him for several seconds though I've sketched this same expression so many times, I know the right pressure and angle to use.

"It's fab! You'll love it, Uncle King," Mercedes chimes, her mood slightly uplifted, giving me hope that she's going to relax as I move back to the stove to stir the sauce and pasta together.

"This looks and smells amazing, Lo." The sincerity in his voice makes me want to turn and face him again, to smile with his praises. To laugh with some absurd joy he's instilled in me. How can I feel so weak and ridiculous while also being so happy and content?

I drop the ladle on the spoon rest and turn to face Mercedes. "Positive thoughts. Remember, everything is going to be fine. I will see you tomorrow, okay?"

Her eyes grow wide with objection.

"You can't leave. Didn't you hear me say they're closing the roads? I'm sure the buses are all stopped. I'll take you home tomorrow once it quiets down," King says.

I shake my head before I can formulate the right words. "No, I'm not sleeping over."

"You can sleep in my room." Mercedes states her offer like a well-thought-out plan, her eyes growing with ideas.

"You're like sleeping with an octopus with a vendetta," King says, pulling Mercedes' back to his side and putting her in a playful headlock.

"I am not."

"You are." King's tone is missing the teasing inflection, and his eyes barely acknowledge either of us, conveying something is bothering him. Whether it's my lack of interest in staying or his disinterest in me being his girlfriend is the question burning in my mind.

"We left the shop open," Mercedes cries after another burst of thunder reigns the night skies.

"The shop's open?" King asks, rubbing a hand over the back of his neck as he looks to the large picture window. "Where are you going?" he calls, but I'm already pulling my jacket on. "Lo, you can't go out in this."

"I didn't check to make sure any of the bikes used went back, and they went out in the yard for a while."

"I'll go. Stay here."

"It was my responsibility." I have no desire to go out in this weather, but the idea of King cleaning up a mess that was a part of my job grates on my nerves.

"You need to learn to accept help from others."

"I don't *need* help." I don't mean for my words to be defensive, but my voice has deepened, and my eyes have narrowed.

King opens his mouth, I'm sure with a retaliation, but I don't hear it. I'm already heading toward the shop, using the small flashlight I discovered in King's desk drawer that I had pocketed. The rain is coming harder and faster than I think I've ever seen it, hitting every surface with so much force that it bounces back into the air as if doing a choreographed dance that makes my shoes squish and squeak with each step.

"You're so damn stubborn! I would have done this and you could have stayed warm and dry. Your pride wouldn't have been touched."

"I'm not worried about my pride."

"Bullshit! Since the first day I walked into this house, you've worried about your pride. There are times you try to fight with it and let me see sides of you, but let's face it, Lo, you are so caught up with not needing help from anyone, you become a liability to yourself."

My head snaps back. The lights from the house and shop cast just enough light for me to see King and the reflection of thousands of raindrops continuing their torrential dance. We've stopped, and the fact surprises me. I can't recall making the conscious decision to face him and listen to his accusations.

King lowers his eyebrows and runs a hand along his jaw before clasping the back of his neck. "Why are you so damn afraid to ask for help?"

My eyebrows slant together, slitting my eyes. "I'm not. I just don't need it. If you want to talk about being a liability to oneself, you need to look in the mirror! You people are all crazy!"

King's chin dips toward his throat, lowering the bill of his baseball hat so I can hardly see his face. "Us people?"

My hands swing around the empty yard. "Yes, *you* people. You guys are all adrenaline junkies. You think that by being crazy and reckless you are being an individual. Someone true only to yourselves. Newsflash: It's not unique! People have been being stupid long before you guys started."

"Just because you're too afraid to be yourself, afraid of who might judge you, doesn't give you the right to point your damn fingers at others. I don't give a shit if people know who I am."

"You just lie about your first name to everyone you meet, right?"

King's eyes narrow. "Why in the hell are you so pissed off at me?"

"Why am *I* so pissed off?" I ask incredulously. King nods, rain dripping down his face. "I'm trying to do my job and you're accusing me of being a fraud."

"I'm not accusing you of being a fraud."

"You did! You are! By saying I'm afraid to be who I am. Do you understand what it took for me to move out here? My dad has basically written me off. My brother—who didn't like me to begin with—now loathes me. They feel as though I've betrayed them because I chose my dream over theirs. I live with ... God, I live with your sister of all people, who, let me tell you, just in case you aren't aware, is a giant pain in my ass! On top of that, I'm losing one of the two friends that I am closest to, and just learned through hearing you tell someone else that you don't want me to be your girlfriend."

"You heard what?"

I don't see what reaction accompanies his response. I've turned, moving closer to the shop again, refusing to go down this road and admit just how sour my mood became after overhearing his words. Granted, how could I not have? It seemed almost as though he intended for me to hear them.

"Is that why you're so pissed?"

"This isn't all about you!" I screech, turning on my heel and nearly running into him, approaching me with long strides to keep up.

"Titles are stupid, Lo. They mean nothing! That's like having to deem someone your best friend. Your best friend could change tomorrow, next week, or in ten years, but likely, it won't be who it is today, so why bother with such pettiness? To make them feel better? To make you feel better?

"Why do you need to call me your boyfriend? Will it change your feelings toward me? Will it make me more attractive? Or does it simply justify you sleeping with me again?"

My eyes are flaring with anger, I'm sure of it. I want to slap away his expression that's waiting for my reply as though it's a valid and appropriate question. "Do you know what I call my mom?" I shake my head to reflect I don't want him to even attempt to answer. "Linda. I call my mother Linda because shortly after she had me, she decided she was done being a mother. She doesn't want to be a mother. She doesn't want to be my mother.

"It doesn't matter if the person that is your best friend today isn't your best friend in ten years, because right now they are, and ten years from now, they still would have been. You'll still think back and most of your stories will include them. You'll still have pictures with them by your side. And who knows, maybe that person would be your best friend still if you took the time to appreciate them and not write them off as just another person because of the chance that you might grow apart. That's like refusing to call Mercedes your niece just because one day you may not live under the same roof and be her favorite person." I shake my head again, frustration rolling off me, making my muscles ache with tension. "Sometimes I feel like you understand me so well.

Like you're looking at me and hearing everything that I don't know how to explain, and then other times you come out with bullshit like this, and I feel like I don't know who in the hell you are, and I feel confident you don't know who I am either."

"That's because you want me to give you everything to give me anything!"

"You're impossible!" *And flipping crazy!* It takes so much willpower to not throw those words into the fire we've built, that it makes me feel physically weighted with exhaustion as I turn around and head toward the shed once again. I hear his steps matching my anger as they splash against the sodden ground. The fact that he seems angry at me for initially being angry makes my blood boil, warming me though the temperatures are low enough I can see my breath linger with the rain.

I spin on my heel, making my hair whip and slap my neck. "I can't believe you think you're justified in being upset and don't think I should be. This is so hypocritical."

"I don't even know why we're fighting. I had to take twenty detours to finally find a route that allowed me to get here because I thought you would be freaking out, and I get home and you're chomping at the damn bit to leave."

"Horse jokes aren't cute. They're insulting."

"I didn't mean…"

"Yes you did. It's you, King. You always mean something with your words. We both know that."

"Are you only pissed because of the comment I made to Spencer?"

I hate that he threw the word *only* into his sentence, but I release a deep breath that I try to shove the thought out with and wipe a hand across my forehead to push back the loose strands of hair the rain is plastering to my face. "I don't want to be a convenience for you. I don't want this to be something casual where when it fits into your schedule things are great, and when you're too busy…" King is always busy, with crazy things that range from marketing, to taping for Spencer, to now preparing for his own biking career. "…I want…"

King takes two long strides and slides his palm across my cheek. "You deserve to be significant to someone. You shouldn't feel bad or embarrassed to ask for that." My gaze drops to see his feet glide closer so that our toes are touching. "Lo, if you want a title, we'll use them. I'm not trying to be an insensitive dick." My eyes drift up when he doesn't continue, taking in the rain that's making trails down King's face, touching and feeling places I've been tracing with stencils and have been anxious to feel again with my own skin. "My mom's been married six times. *Six* times," he repeats, heavily emphasizing the number. "She loves to use titles. When she introduces Kash, she lists off every award and title that's ever been used by the media." I can tell by the way his eyes darken and then close that there's something behind how she introduces him as well, but I'm not sure if he's upset that it's accompanied by titles or a lack thereof.

"I want you to be my boyfriend, King. I don't want you to be my BMX-riding, brother-of-Kashton-Knight—" My eyes travel to the side because I was just about to say sex God, and really, that would have both been awkward and untrue. I *do* want him to hold that title. "I don't care about those things."

"I like the ring it has when you say, 'My boyfriend.'"

"If you're patronizing me…"

King's hands fly up to his sides, drawing my attention to the water sliding down his widely stretched palms. "I'll call Spencer tomorrow and re-clarify things."

My head snaps to the side and then I turn and tromp the few remaining feet to the shop where the door is propped open and three bikes are out, sitting in mud puddles that are forming around them.

"What? I'm kidding. I'm just … bad at this … Clearly."

"Clearly," I agree.

"Titles aren't something I'm a fan of."

"So you've said," I state, making his eyebrows rise with a silent challenge.

"You really aren't the kind of girl that has angry sex, are you?"

I raise my eyebrows and purse my lips.

King's eyebrows match mine, but a small grin appears on his face. I hate it because it makes him look more desirable matched with his wet hair and long-sleeved tee that is currently clinging to every line that I've tried to re-create and, I'm now realizing, have failed at. "Clearly *not*." His tone is friendly, playful even, but I'm frustrated. I've just revealed things about my family that I hadn't intended to and don't think he understands the significance of either the fact that I'm trusting him with it, or how much it bothers me that my family has never truly accepted me. I turn and head toward the bike that is the farthest away.

It's slick, and my feet keep getting stuck in the mud. There's no way I'll be able to wear these shoes again, even washed. I know after being submerged this many times in the dirt they'll never come close to clean. As I pull out the bike, my left foot slides deeper into the muck. Thankfully my hands are on the brake pads, and I'm able to use the bike as an anchor, but when I pull my foot, my shoe is stuck, encompassed in the sludge.

I struggle for several seconds, muttering every curse word I know and damning this weather.

King's hand disappears into the puddle up to his wrist, clutching my foot. He tugs my foot loose with a squishing sound as the muck loses suction with my shoe. "You love the rain. You can't hate it just because it doesn't always do what you want or expect. We all have ugly sides."

"It doesn't mean I have to like it right now."

"No, you don't."

I turn with the bike and head to the shop, my left shoe filled with grit from the puddle that rakes painfully against my heel and the top of my foot.

King is behind me with the other two bikes. I'm not sure how he managed to get both of them when he had just freed my foot, and both were covered, but I don't ask. I'm not into pointing out that I've acknowledged both his speed and strength. He flips on the lights and goes over to the lockers where he retrieves a stack of old rags. Without asking for help or giving direction, he starts toweling one of the bikes clean.

I watch him carefully for several seconds, noting how dark his hair looks when it's wet and the width of his muscles around his shoulders as he moves. In modeling sessions I've been looking at many backs with the numerous strapless gowns and have realized that it may be one of the most beautiful parts of a human. However, most of the women modeling are thin, lacking much tone or definition, while King is corded with thickly defined muscles. Watching him makes my body heat and my pulse quicken.

His dark eyes flash up as though he knows what I'm thinking and I swallow, moving my attention to the pile of rags. I grab one and take a few steps back. It's crazy the simplest thing on King seems to have such an effect on me. I know he caught me staring at him. I also know he reads me well enough to have known that I was admiring him, but he doesn't say anything. Neither of us does. We simply dry the bikes and put them away before shutting off the lights, closing the door, and making the wet and muddy trek back to the house.

"What took you guys so long?" Mercedes cries as we step inside.

I don't move. I remain huddled in a small corner of the extended doormat, feeling the warmth of the house slowly sink through my layers of mud and rain, causing shivers to run through me.

"You guys left three bikes out. You know the rules," King says, stepping in behind me and kicking off his wet shoes.

"I know. I'm sorry. It won't happen again, I swear," Mercedes assures him, her eyes avoiding eye contact with him.

King shakes his head and runs a hand over his face. "Put your dishes in the sink, and go watch a movie or something."

I follow Mercedes down the hall, relieved to have an excuse not to talk to him while I'm feeling so off kilter.

"You can borrow some of my pajamas," Mercedes offers, opening her closet.

"I think I'll stick to my jeans, thanks."

"You can't sleep in those. You're all wet." Her face twists in disgust.

"I'll dry." While she changes, I retrieve a couple of towels from the bathroom and return to where she has flipped on every light, including her closet, desk lamp, bedside lamps, and floor lamp that has five single shades spaced out, shining in each direction.

"There's this great old movie you probably haven't seen, but they sing during a rainstorm like this."

"No," Mercedes says without thought.

"Want to dance?"

"Dance?"

"Yeah."

"Are you serious?"

"Come on." I pull her from the bed and pick up her phone from the nightstand, flipping through it until I find a music app. I turn it up so loud I can't hear her objections, and then I begin to dance.

I'm a terrible dancer. It's an activity that I vehemently avoided while growing up because I was never able to find enough confidence or comfort in my own body to move freely, especially not in front of others. Each time my friends somehow managed to convince me to go to another school dance, I'd mingle, finding people I hadn't talked to in semesters, sometimes years, that were getting a drink or taking a break. I took the opportunity to chat with them—act like it was a great coincidence that we had run into one another—and would catch up until the music would pull them back to the floor. Then I'd go in seek of my next long-lost friend. I even avoided turning in circles with slow songs, discovering the entire process of finding a dance partner to move in mercilessly slow circles with extremely painful. I shut these thoughts down and proceed to let the music carry me. My moves are exaggerated, my voice nearly as loud as the speaker, and my eyes are closed, not caring that I'm showing Mercedes a side of myself that I'm slowly becoming more comfortable and familiar with.

It feels silly. It feels freeing. It feels great.

I open my eyes and see her standing on her bed, a hairbrush in one hand as she belts out the lyrics with me. I'm smiling so wide I can hardly see her, and then I'm moving again, my heart pumping in rhythm with my feet and hips. I'm sure I look ridiculous, but I don't care, and neither does Mercedes.

"You need to go to bed," I say, still fighting to convince my lungs to expand enough that my breaths don't come out in short bursts. We danced for an hour with only short breaks to laugh, or change songs when Mercedes vetoed them.

"I can't go to bed, Lo. I need to wait until my dad gets home."

"Everything's going to be okay, I promise."

"I need him to be home *now*."

"He's coming home," I insist.

"What happens if he doesn't though, Lo? What if something happens?" Her words waver and then she gasps and buries her head in my shoulder.

The warmth of her forehead makes my arms, which are still damp, prickle with goose bumps.

"He's going to die."

I squeeze her as my heart races with confusion and shock from hearing her words. "He's not. He's not going to die, Mercedes."

"I can't lose him, Lo."

"You won't. I promise."

Mercedes pulls away from me, her hands extended to reveal she doesn't want me to come closer. "My mom died because she lost control of her car during a storm." Tears run down her cheeks that have turned even redder than they were moments ago from our dancing. I had no idea. It makes me feel guilty that I didn't know how she had passed. I just never knew if it was okay to bring her up when Mercedes never does. "She hydroplaned right into a tree." *Trees rarely lose to a car* is a line my dad used repeatedly when either my brother or I ever left to go somewhere on a weekend or evening.

"Mercedes." My voice is so quiet I feel as though I should try again, but still, she looks at me, her eyes round and glossy with tears. "I'm so sorry." Her head moves jerkily with a nod, her walls rebuilding rapidly as her posture becomes more rigid. Before she can completely erect it, I wrap her in a hug, ignoring her arms still stiff as I attempt to take every single one of her desires to become distant and defensive with me. When her arms don't wrap around me, I squeeze tighter, pressing my cheek to the top of her head. "You don't have to do this alone."

"I want a mom. I want my mom, but I want someone that actually understands me, someone to get pedicures with, and do girly stuff that I can't do with my dad and King. What's going to happen to me when I start my period? What about bra shopping? What happens when I get my first boyfriend? Or worse, when I get dumped?"

I hold her even tighter.

"I don't even remember her, Lo. I don't remember what her voice sounded like, or how she smelled, or what kind of music she liked. Everything I know about her is stuff people have told me." I'm amazed by how strong her voice is, only cracking twice as she admits this to me as though it's her greatest fear, or possibly regret. "In some ways I'm really glad—I think it would hurt so much more if I could remember her—but other times, I think it makes it worse. I want to have something of her that is just mine. Something I can remember."

My eyes fill with tears. I understand this predicament so thoroughly and still don't know which is the better option, or if there is one.

My fingers constrict to the point they ache.

"I can't lose him too."

"You won't, I swear."

Her sobs are so quiet, and her body so still, it's nearly impossible for me to tell that she's crying until she gasps, trying to catch her breath.

I wish there was something for me to say. Some significant words that could grant some relief or at least impart some wisdom. I have nothing. The BlueCross Babysitting classes that I attended years ago never taught me how to even make a meal for the kids I would take care of, let alone discussed distraught pre-teens who lost their mother and don't know how to discuss their feelings. I take a deep breath, smelling the sweetness of her shampoo mixed with the scent of the shop and dirt that I'm pretty certain is coming from me, and press my hand to the side of her head so she's completely against me, and I cry with her. I cry for her.

TWENTY-EIGHT

My eyes are sticky and dry when I open them, feeling a hand on my shoulder. It takes me two seconds to realize that it's King, and another two to realize I should be startled since nothing about this scenario is within my comfort zone. First off, I'm cuddling, and although it's with Mercedes, it's not something I do. Secondly, I'm wearing soggy clothes and sleeping in Mercedes' bed—an atmosphere I only see during the day.

"Come on. Let's get you some dry clothes," King says quietly.

I look back to Mercedes and find her in a deep sleep with both hands tucked under one side of her face. She looks so peaceful I fear moving.

"She sleeps like a rock," King says when I hesitate.

Still, I pay close attention as I move ever so slowly to get free before I follow King to the well-lit hallway.

"This way." King tips his head and moves toward the basement. I follow him slowly, still feeling the urge to head to the front door and hike through the rain to my apartment. I allowed myself to be so vulnerable, and while a side of me relishes in the fact because I've found so few people I can reveal my darker sides to, I hadn't anticipated doing so tonight, certainly not in that setting.

I know most of the basement is set up for King. There's only the laundry room and a large closet down here that I've ever accessed. There was never a stipulation put in place that I couldn't enter his space, but even now that we've been dating for a couple of weeks, I haven't been down here. I'm assuming it's because it resembles the rest of the house BM: a disastrous mess.

My eyes widen in surprise as I follow him through the door that bridges his space. We're in a living room where a large overstuffed sectional sofa is cozied up to the far wall, across from an expansive TV. There are three bikes mounted to the walls and several framed black and white photographs that I know without asking were taken by Summer. The floors are a dark cherry like the upstairs, and the walls a muted gray. A desk with a computer sits near the door. It's sleek and industrial, tying in with the metal and hard lines of the bikes and black frames, softened by a large white area rug. The contrasts remind me of King, who's currently opening a door off to my right.

I'm curious to follow him. Since there are only two additional doors and he came to get clothes, I have a pretty safe assumption he's gone into his bedroom, and the urge to see it is increasing by the second.

Before I can move more than two steps, the light is flipped off and he reappears. "Here."

I accept a handful of clothes and quietly muster a thanks before King directs me to the other door: the bathroom.

The walls are a dark espresso, and while the pedestal sink needs to be cleaned, I can tell it was washed within the last couple of weeks. It explains why the kitchen was the only clean room in the house when I began.

It takes me several minutes before I finally manage to get my jeans off, tight and sticky from being wet. I pull on the soft cotton of King's sweatpants with relief. They slide low on my hips and end slightly past my heels. I then pull on his T-shirt. The hem reaches the top of my thighs, and the sleeves go down just past my elbows. It's so rare for me to ever feel small, yet I feel that way now, petite even.

I pull my hair free from the collar of the sweatshirt he gave me and head back to the kitchen when I find his living room empty. The house feels so different at night. The large windows that line the dining room and usually allow the muted Oregon sunshine and shades of green to brighten the house are dark, revealing faded reflections that make my eyes continuously dance over shadows. The wood floor is cool under my bare feet as I cross to the fridge. I pull a glass down from the shelves, admiring the flash of lightning that dances across the surface like a firework, and turn at the sound of quiet footsteps. King stops when my eyes meet him, and he freezes. It's apparent with the way his eyes are searching mine, he's looking for some sort of clarification on where things sit between us.

"Do you remember that song? It was popular when I was a kid I think, so I don't know, but you're older. You may remember it."

"Are you calling me old?"

I shrug. "Maybe."

He laughs, and the sound is nearly an acceptance.

"The lyrics talked about how the rain sounded angry, and I never get that when I listen to it. To me it's just peaceful." Silence extends around us. We're both listening to the dance rain leads with every surface outside.

"Do you know what I like about rain?"

I turn to King, my curiosity piqued.

"People can try their damnedest to avoid it—add extra layers, umbrellas, boots—but you can't escape the rain. It will always get you wet, even if it's only a few drops." His account is so true. I know from working to avoid it on numerous occasions myself that it's nearly pointless. "That and girls at parties tell me it makes my face look like a sculpture that inspires them to paint."

His comment sparks another memory from that night. I recall following a raindrop down the side of his cheek with my finger, twisting his hair and feeling the contrast of cool and warm. "Girls?" I ask, stretching the s.

He shrugs. "Girl. There's only one girl that has made me feel comfortable in my skin. Like it doesn't matter what my name is, what mistakes I've made, or whether or not I'll ever live up to my brother." King takes several steps, closing the gap between us until there are only a couple of feet.

"You and I both have a negative history with titles, but you shared something with me that I didn't respond to like I should have. You opened up to me, Lo, and told me something personal about your past that I know you don't share with others, and I should never have thrown my mother into the mess like it was a valid reason to void your experience. It doesn't." His hand travels to the side of his jaw, and I hear his nails catch on the short stubble.

I shake my head, uncomfortable with his apology though it offers a salve to my previous embarrassment and rejection that I hadn't realized was there until now. "I'm only going to be here for a couple more months. Using the terms girlfriend and boyfriend isn't necessary for something that we already know is going to end."

King's eyes widen. "You got accepted?"

"No. I haven't heard from them, but if I'm not, I'll likely head back to Montana and work there until I figure out what to do next."

He looks at me with patience in his wide brown eyes. "Let's go downstairs," King says, nodding toward the foyer.

I follow absentmindedly, wondering if he's trying to convince me to stay.

He turns to face me after flipping on a floor lamp. We stand near the sofa, but neither of us sits. "Can't you figure out what to do next, here in Portland?"

"Portland's expensive. Kenzie's moving to Seattle in June and I don't want to find another roommate to live there with me. I've realized studio apartments really are made just for one person."

"We can look outside of the city, Hillsboro, Vancouver…"

"I've thought of that, but…"

"We can figure it out."

My lips part with an objection and King takes a step closer to me. He wraps a hand firmly around my hip and his eyes bore into mine. "A lot can happen in a couple of months." King's eyes become darker, unfamiliar, yet I recognize them so clearly from that night back in July. It's been seven months since I last saw him look at me like this, and the memory it brings forth has every cell in my body brightening, strengthening, anxious.

"We've only gone on one date," I murmur into the darkness of King's living room.

"We've known each other for months."

"We hated each other for most of them."

"Lo," he whispers, and I feel fairly confident it's to make me shut up by the sternness that makes his voice slightly deeper. "I want this."

"What?" I ask. "What is this?"

"Us."

He steps forward, allowing my eyes to see him a little more clearly. His hand falls from my side and fists the hem of the shirt he loaned me, making my heart rate bolt. He hesitates, and I nearly protest. Instead, I lean forward and kiss him. His lips are soft and warm, familiar as my own brushstrokes, but realizing that I'm going to sleep with King again—completely sober this time—stops me from falling into rhythm with him and my teeth crash against his, making a sound as revolting as nails on a chalkboard.

King grips my shoulders and pulls me forward, a lazy smile on his lips. "I've already seen you naked. In fact, I've…"

I press my fingers against his lips, silencing him. But then I move them, curious as to what he was going to say. "You what?"

"Lo."

"Yes?"

"It was better than you remember. I'm going to make you remember everything tonight that you've been working to forget."

My heart thrums, an excitement that makes all of my limbs feel suddenly different, more alive and aware. My eyebrows rise and my lips set into a smirk. "Promise?"

His lips meet mine and his hands travel under the baggy layers of his shirt and sweatshirt, gripping my sides with a reverence that makes me feel claimed. I've never been someone who has ever wanted to be a possession. I want to be a strong, competent, capable woman, never needing anyone, especially not a man to make me feel whole, or of merit, certainly not a possession, but the way King handles me like I'm necessary for his own survival, makes me want to be every title, every significance to him, because he's become so many of mine.

King's hands trail higher, tracing the line of my bra and then over my clavicle, making me shiver and shift with impatience.

"I told you I'd make you remember. I didn't rush this then; I sure as hell don't plan on it tonight."

"King." My voice is quiet, nearly uncertain of what all I'm about to reveal. "I remember that night with such perfect precision. I have several notebooks of you that I will never be able to show others."

The air between us thickens with the magnitude of my admission. "For months, I was desperate to find out who you were. Charleigh and I asked so many people about you, about your tattoos, scars. I couldn't forget any of it. It was as though I was constantly reliving that night. I never expected you to walk through that door. I was so upset with you…" I'm not sure what I'm about to admit. That I was angry with him because he was even more attractive than I had managed to remember? That I felt used? Embarrassed? Elated? Terrified that he had forgotten me?

"You felt everything shift," King says, tightening his hold on my waist where his hand rests just below my ribs. "I'm pretty sure it took me a week to convince myself it was really you."

I'm tempted to tell him how much he means to me, but I don't know how to unwrap my words from my lust. We slept together twice that night. I had laid in bed completely naked, tracing lines and scars over his body while laughing and revealing secrets about myself I'm fairly certain I didn't even know about prior to that day. But it's far more than that. I know King. While that night back in July was void of inhibitions and packed with trust and comfort, I now realize that part of that was simply an image that we both created and fostered. While neither of us has any idea what would have happened had his number not rubbed off or had Kenzie not meddled, I feel that we never would have become what we are today. I know how much he loves his family, the extents he would go to for his friends, and how much attention he's been paying to me when I never even knew.

My hands glide over his chest covered by the thin barrier of his T-shirt as I take a step closer to King and slowly tilt my head, smiling as I do as if to pronounce my intentions. The right side of his lips rise with the uneven smile I now consider mine, and his head tilts forward, his chin tilting to prevent another collision. Our lips move slowly, tracing over each other with the intention of imparting every detail of this night to memory. With each ridge my hand travels over, the muscles in my stomach get tighter. King's hands are stretched wide as they travel under the cotton layers. I feel the pads of his fingers pressing into my skin like they don't want to let go, and the reverence they possess as they slide across my ribs, my stomach, my lower back, making me move even closer to him, knead my fingers deeper into his skin, press myself flush against him. It elicits a groan from King that I trap with my mouth.

His hands are spread against my back, searing their memory into my skin while mine run over his shoulders, tying him to me as our tongues trade promises.

King releases me slowly, sliding down my sides and fisting my sweatshirt and T-shirt together. His tongue presses more firmly against mine, the stubble on his chin deliciously sharp as his head moves forward with the intensity of his kiss that only lasts a moment before he draws back and pulls the shirts from me in one fluid motion.

The lighting is muted, yet King stares at me as though I'm a fine painting being showcased with impeccable light. As his eyes slowly trail down my body, I step forward and place a hand on his chest and tilt my head forward. King leans his upper body back and rips his own shirt free before pressing his warm chest against mine.

His lips graze against mine, but before I'm able to kiss him back, his hands are gripping my thighs, encouraging me to lift them to wrap around his waist. Thoughts of being too big, heavy, and awkward for this to happen make an ugly appearance that King amplifies by bending and not giving me the chance to consider things. My knees bend only out of the absurdity that comes with seeing them both sticking out at uncomfortable angles. He carries me through his bedroom door, where we're encompassed in darkness.

King's lips are leaving hot paths along my jaw and down my neck that I can't reciprocate because my mouth is level with his forehead. I'm considering ways to convince him to set me down that won't require words, when his hands shift, one running a teasing trail up my spine and stopping on the clasp of my bra. His mouth doesn't leave my skin, licking, sucking, tasting as his fingers deftly release the clasp in a single motion. The magenta fabric slides down my arms, resting in the crook of my elbows. His tongue traces a line to the hollow of my collarbone, sending my heels to dig into his sides and my head to draw back. King's hand rests on the bare space between my shoulder blades, and as his teeth graze over the tender skin that follows my collarbone. His hand slides down my shoulder, taking the strap of my bra with it so it hangs from just my right wrist, and his palm covers my breast, lifting the weight and compressing as his fingers glide back down to my nipple, and run over the sensitized peak with just enough pressure to make my thighs constrict.

"There you go, baby. That's my girl." His words are quiet and throaty, and his lips tickle the bottom of my ear as they're spoken before he slowly runs his teeth along the same area. His fingers compress more tightly, tugging on the tips of my nipples as his teeth catch the very edge of my skin, creating a sensation I didn't know my earlobe could produce. My hands run up through his finger-length hair, my nails lightly scratching his scalp, pulling him closer to me. I want King to do that to every inch of me.

His hand returns to my back and his lips to my neck, distracting me from the fact that we're moving until he's laying me against a down-feather comforter that sinks under my weight. King slowly stands, pulling my bra completely free and discarding it somewhere in the dark room. I can barely see his silhouette, let alone his expression, as his fingers brush from my shoulders, over my breasts, and along my stomach, to the elastic bands of my sweats and underwear. I can't recall which pair I wore today, but it doesn't matter. They, along with my pants, are gone with a second that stretches as King's hands push them down while his palms glide down the outside of both of my legs, continuing all the way to my toes. His hands create a new path on their way up, gliding over the tops of my legs, over my stomach, and slowly over my chest before coming back down, where his hands trail the insides of my legs. My hips lift inadvertently with his touch. King's hands stop on the inside of my thighs, his fingers massaging the skin as he hums a quiet approval and drops his head to kiss me. "Every inch of you is beautiful. Every. Inch. Don't hide from me, Lo." His fingers slide up, running along the area where I am now in need of his touch. My hips lift again, a quiet gasp breaking through my lips with relief and desire. Too quickly, his hands fall back to my thighs and continue their journey to my ankles, returning along the underside of my legs and clenching both butt cheeks before moving around to my stomach and tracing up along my breasts. This time, he doesn't continue up to my neck; he kneads both nipples with enough pressure I'm confused if it hurts or feels like nirvana.

My breaths come out shallow and uneven as he applies more pressure, my body writhing under his touch. He stops, and my throat groans with protest.

"King." I mean for his name to serve as a warning. A threat that he can't stop at this point because I feel the buildup like a punch to my stomach.

"I remember that sound," he whispers, his lips sliding along my jaw. "You're almost there."

"Then why did you stop—"

King's mouth moves to the apex of my legs, his tongue meeting the promises he made to my mouth as he massages every nerve ending with his tongue. My hands fist the comforter, my hips lifting off the mattress, pressing against him. His movements are slow, rhythmically moving higher and higher until he's kissing my stomach.

I hear him pull his nightstand drawer out and wrap my hand around his arm stretched forward. "I'm still on the pill, and I haven't slept with anyone but you since…"

King's head drops and his teeth connect with my thigh. "God I'm glad I wrecked you as badly as you did me." He stands up, spreading my legs, and I stop.

"Do you have a lamp?"

"What?"

"I want to see you. I want to be able to draw this."

A small stained glass lamp with milky panels and small dragonflies creates a dim light that allows me to see the bright gleam of lust in King's eyes, and his hair, tousled by my touch.

He watches me for long seconds, and then drops his hands to either side of me and kisses me. His chest is pressed firmly against mine as his lips move with a reverence and need that I reciprocate. King presses one last kiss to my lips and stands up, linking my legs over each of his arms he pulls me to the edge of the bed and slides into me so slowly, I'm lost between frustration and bliss until he pulls out and does it again at a slightly faster pace. He repeats the movement until I make a guttural sound in my throat, and then King takes me to every edge as he burns new memories and fuses previous ones to this night, making every inch of me feel beautiful and sated as only King can.

"I have known you for only a few months, and already it feels like you know me better than anyone." Using his finger, he slowly traces my cheekbone.

"You should let more people in."

I look down as his wide fingers press firmly around my hand. I look back to his face, and his eyes are wide with patience. "It's not that I keep people out. I can tell twenty other people the same stories that I've shared with you, and they still wouldn't understand." He lifts his free hand and cups the back of his neck, dropping his head. "This sounds so lame. *I* sound so lame. I'm not saying you're … I don't know what we are, Lo. All I know is that six months later, you're in my head more than ever. Hell, that's saying something because I didn't even know who you were for the first two, and I would still feel your skin when I was trying to sleep. I was thinking about what makes you laugh when I was supposed to be working. I didn't even know you. Something about you just buried itself inside of me. Initially, I thought it was because you didn't know who I was. You treated me like I was just a normal guy. It wasn't until a few months ago that I realized it's not *something* about you, it's *everything*."

The next morning I stand in the kitchen, surveying the coffeepot. I may not know how to cook many things, or use kitchen gadgets with much success, but coffee I can do. I've been an addict since I was eight. Apparently I was either meant to be well over six feet, or it truly doesn't stunt your growth.

I set the machine to brew as I lean against the counter, appreciating the soreness of my muscles. King and I fell into an exhausted state of euphoria last night, and if I hadn't been so tempted to draw him this morning, I would have woken him up to do it all over again. Instead, I dressed in his borrowed clothes again and grabbed my bag from upstairs, preparing things in case he was a light sleeper before I made my way back down and sat on the edge of the bed so I could still see him while my hands went to work. I worked for over an hour, until my lids felt heavy and my shoulders ached from slouching, making coffee a necessity.

"Hey." King rests his cheek against mine. I feel his chest slide against my back, memorizing the heat and friction, the width of him against my frame, before his arm wraps securely around my stomach, overwhelming me with sensations.

"Did I wake you?"

He shakes his head slightly. "No, but I was disappointed you were gone."

"I needed some fuel."

"I can help with that. Let's go back—"

"Is Dad home yet?" Mercedes makes her way into the kitchen, her hair in a million directions and her eyes still blinking with sleep.

King sighs, his hips shifting against me slightly before he moves to stand behind the bar.

"Not yet, but it's still early," I say. It still looks gray outside, but I checked the news when I first woke up and reports informed me that crews worked late to clean everything up.

"Want some coffee?" I ask, turning to King.

"Please." He leans forward on the bar. "Are you the kind that drinks their breakfast?" Curiosity pulls his eyebrows up.

"Not always, but it is what makes me approachable." He laughs as I pull two mugs down and face him. "How do you like it?"

His eyes turn bright, his lips curving into a smile that makes them nearly even.

"Your coffee," I say, shaking my head.

King's lips stay pulled into a smile as silent innuendos pass between us. "Two sugars," he says finally.

I'm distracted by his silent insinuations, picturing images of him from last night that make my movements feel slow as I reach for the coffeepot. The sound of the front door closing has me turning to the foyer where Isabelle's now calling out a happy greeting. Her eyes land on me and grow wide with calculation before she smiles again and wanders farther into the kitchen, stopping to hug Mercedes.

"Hey, Isabelle," King greets her. Rounding the bar, he hugs her and then stands behind me, his hand resting gently on my hip. "I'm going to take a shower."

I nod absently, not certain if I prefer him being around while she's here or not. He disappears down the stairs as Isabelle takes a seat next to Mercedes at the bar.

"How are you hanging in there, monkey?"

"I'm going to go try calling Dad again." Mercedes slides from her chair and looks back once before also disappearing.

"Is she okay?" Isabelle's tone is filled with a sincere concern that makes me feel worse for not liking her.

"Yeah, the storm last night spooked her, but I'm sure as soon as she talks to

Kash she'll be fine.

"It's so great you're getting along so well with the family. It surprised me a little to hear about you and King, but I'm happy he's happy."

"They're a great family." I feel as though I should say something more profound, or something to verify I'm worthy of their time, as pathetic as that seems. "Would you like some coffee?" I lift the coffeepot in question.

"Sure, that would be great." I pull down another mug and fill it. "Is that for King?" she asks as I pull the sugar bowl forward.

Arching my eyebrows, I nod.

"He likes brown sugar."

"In his coffee?" I ask.

She nods with a shy smile that ties my stomach in knots. It exposes secrets, truths about their relationship that, as benign as I know they are, still burn.

I want to find out what else she knows, but the front door opens and Kash and Summer make their way in with rushed movements, showing they're just as anxious to ensure we're all safe.

While I would prefer to ride the bus home, King insists on driving me. We sit in silence, one of his hands resting on my thigh while the other drums against the steering wheel. He's relieved and happy, forcing my interaction with Isabelle to the recesses of my mind.

TWENTY-NINE

"I thought we talked about this smiling thing. I've only seen you down a couple of times: that first time we met, a few times early on when I knew Mercedes was giving you a run for your money, and now." Robert's voice is clear as he calls to me from his porch. I left early, before King got home, because I couldn't face him. Not today.

"The good news is these downs remind you that you're living. If life doesn't offer both good and bad, we've lost our reason for existence." His words replay in my head as he makes his way down the cement steps, his smile widening as I take a couple of steps up his narrow driveway.

His comment makes me think of the conversation King and I shared weeks ago now, and I attempt to smile though the thought makes me want to cry. "That attempt at a smile is a little pitiful. What's bothering you?"

"It's complicated," I say with a sigh.

He shrugs noncommittally, and I'm suddenly curious about how often he and King speak and how detailed their discussions are. "Likely, you're making it confusing." He scratches his cheek that still looks too young to be capable of holding the title of grandpa to a ten-year-old. "You didn't get accepted to Italy?"

I raise my eyebrows and stretch my hands out, feeling the tightness in my muscles and tendons stretch with a painful reluctance. "No, that's the problem. I was."

His eyebrows go up, clearly caught off guard. "You're afraid to leave."

"I finally feel like I'm in a really good place. I care about them. I can't ask King to give up on his dreams and come with me."

"No," Robert says, slowly shaking his head. "You can't. Just like he can't ask you to stay. If either of you did, that wouldn't be love."

I press my lips together, feeling the burning threat of tears.

"My dad used to say that people generally start something out of love, but then it becomes a rat race. We lose our focus, our passion, our drive to complete our initial mission because we get so caught up in the competition, the bright lights, the distractions. You need to think about what your mission is and focus on it. You're young, Lo. Don't throw away your dreams because you're afraid you'll lose someone. All that will do is lead to later resenting him, and that won't be good for either of you."

"You guys need to talk about bikes, or ... whatever it is you guys used to talk about before I stopped to ask for directions."

His eyes reveal more humor than his faint smile. "He cares very deeply for you. Don't doubt that."

My lips roll against my teeth as I nod. "I know."

"Do you? Because you look like you're trying to convince yourself."

I blink several times, unsure of how to respond. Instead, I numbly nod in response and fish out my phone to see what time it is as a casual way of finding an excuse to leave. "I've got to go. I'll see you."

"When you're sad, everything seems worse. Stop looking at things through jaded glasses and look for some rose ones."

I lift my chin once in acknowledgement and then turn, taking two steps before he clears his throat. "The world needs smiles like yours, Lo. Don't deprive people."

Sometimes like now, I'm fairly certain he's crazy. I've always lacked the enthusiasm that perpetually optimistic people seem to maintain regardless of what the world delivers. I much prefer to sit back and watch everyone, memorizing eyes and how they often reveal answers that lips rarely do, arms and how they can be so defensive and possessive with simple and slight differences, postures and how when you're too far to see someone's face clearly, you can generally read the excitement in someone's bounce, or sadness with the roll of their shoulders.

I stop at the bus stop and search the cloudy skies that are a dark enough shade that I'm amazed it's still dry.

I change buses and head south, getting off at Sonar, the restaurant that has been a constant during my time here in Portland. The air is warm and spicy with the hint of freshly baked tortillas that makes my stomach rumble.

Without taking the time to greet the others, I set up my supplies and fill the container I've designated for water in the restroom so as to get straight to work. There's white noise behind me, but I easily block it out without even an ounce of thought being applied to it. I'm lost in a haze of familiarity with colors, textures, lines, and shading that blocks even the thought or concern of time.

I make a final sweep with my brush, smoothing a line, and take a step back. It's done.

I've been working on this for months, and now it's complete. The swell of emotions that has my eyes blurring and my lips breaking into a wide smile surprise me as much as they overwhelm me.

Several moments later, I step closer to the painting, selecting a fine brush that I use to make minor corrections that most would likely never notice. This deserves to be as perfect as I can make it. I want Estella to feel as warm and loving toward it as I do about her.

Sighing, I drop my brush on the tray I converted into a painting tray and step back to look over it again.

"You were made for this." King's soft words don't surprise me. Not in the least. I think I subconsciously felt him here the last few hours.

"I can't believe it's done."

"It's amazing, babe."

"King."

His eyes sweep over me, hearing the emotion in my voice. They're focused and tender, yet determined.

"Let's go back to your house."

"Is it hard to leave it?" he asks, running a hand over my shoulders.

I nod. I don't know that I'll ever be able to fully explain how I'm feeling. I imagine it's much like a mother sending a child off to college. This is my first and largest wall mural, and while I completed Kash's first, there is something so significant about this painting. I've spent hours upon hours creating this wall that is now covered with a large group of people dancing to a song I could physically feel and hear as I painted. There is a beach in the distance, an expanse of sand that's been stamped with people coming and going. Love and happiness are carefully etched across each of the people in the picture, reflective in every last detail. The emotion I feel about leaving it scares me about the prospect of how many works I'll be leaving an ocean away next fall.

Time freezes, but my heart accelerates. Have I already decided I'm going?

"Let's go," I say, plunging my brush into the water and quickly swirling it clean before grabbing my other brushes and dropping them in their case.

"Estella's still here. I think she's waiting for you."

"Art is meant to be looked at alone. No expectations."

"You don't want to see her excitement?"

"Not this time." I don't. I can't. Another emotion isn't able to fit in my head right now.

King wraps an arm around my shoulder again, his warmth causing my head to naturally recline back.

We step out into the cool spring air, and King digs in his pocket. I watch him flip two pennies on the sidewalk before we reach his truck.

"Are you excited for your event Saturday?" I ask, reaching forward to turn down his music that is always loud from when he rides alone.

King looks over to me, his lips drawing up into that perfectly imperfect smile I love. "It's insane. I can't wrap my head around it all."

"You're going to be great. I need Summer to take a ton of pictures. I'm going to make your logo so sick, you will freak out."

King's eyebrows draw up faintly, his lips still raised. "You're going to design my logo?"

I feel slightly embarrassed, uncomfortable by my presumptions.

"Swear. Swear to me you'll do it," he says, grabbing my hand.

My eyes are on his, which are wide with an intensity that makes me wish he had bench seats. I want to be as close to him as I can.

"I swear."

"I didn't want to ask you because I knew you'd feel obligated, but seriously…"

"No, I'd really like to do yours."

"I'm going to give you the orgasm of your life tonight."

"You already did that on Saturday, remember?"

"You're going to see stars tonight for sure," he says with a grin, making me regret telling him what Charleigh used to call him.

"Can I ask you something?"

King looks over at me, his eyebrows high with surprise. "Am I really always that great in bed? Yes. With you, definitely yes."

I roll my eyes, feeling my cheeks heat with how to phrase my question so it doesn't come out as an accusation. "How does Isabelle know how you like your coffee?"

King's eyes flash to mine and then the street that is unusually busy for how late it is. "What do you mean?"

"She corrected me Saturday when I was putting sugar in your coffee."

King lifts his shoulders and reaches across the small space to hold my hand. "She's like a sister, Lo. I get how you could take that to mean something, but I can guarantee you it doesn't. She was around a lot when I was growing up. She's gone on vacations and camping with us."

"She gets along with everyone so well, and she's beautiful, and smart…"

"Are you trying to convince me to date her?"

My eyes narrow in annoyance, although he's right—I do sound like I'm trying to up-sell her. "I just don't understand."

"Isabelle is a great person. Some guy is going to be very lucky one day to be with her, but that guy will never be me because I don't feel anything when I'm around her except for friendship. I don't want to be in a relationship with someone I care platonically for. I want someone that is going to make me think and will constantly push me to improve. Someone that distracts me while I'm in boring-ass business meetings without even being present because I can't stop thinking about the way her hips move and the many things I want to do to hear those sounds again."

"What sounds?"

King shifts in his seat, his eyes returning to mine for another fleeting second. "Tonight you're going to have to stop watching so much and listen."

My back is pressed firmly against King's chest, our legs intertwined down to our ankles. I definitely saw stars tonight, an entire sea of them. After we had both been exhausted and sated, I curled up in the large chair in King's room wearing a pair of his sweatpants and an old T-shirt as I sketched the outlines of five different expressions of King that I wanted to ensure I would never forget. I don't know why I did it. I know without a doubt I won't forget them. Even if I tried, I don't think I could. He's become a part of me.

"I thought you were exhausted?" he asks, brushing his fingers over my arm.

"How'd you know I was awake?"

"You're a loud thinker."

I shift to my back so I can see him, but it's too dark to make out more than the faintest of outlines of him.

"Want me to close the window? Is the storm too loud?"

I shake my head, nestling closer to him. "I love the rain."

King kisses the tip of each of my fingers, pulling them back slowly, deliberately so that they drag across his bottom lip.

"You're like the rain," I whisper, turning so that I'm completely facing him. "No matter what kind of barriers I tried to put up, you slipped through all of them. You've coated every last part of my skin and have worked your way into every depth of me, parts I didn't even know existed."

"Everyone else hates the rain."

"Good."

"Good?"

"Are we speaking metaphorically?" I ask, suddenly confused and slightly flippant since I was trying to be sweet, and I'm pretty certain he's trying to be a pain in my ass.

"I thought we were talking about the rain."

"You're so freaking annoying." I shove King and roll to the edge of the bed. The floor is cold beneath my feet, making me even more angry with him because I was warm and comfortable mere seconds ago.

"Where are you going?"

"We fight. Like all the time. That's not healthy. How can we be in a relationship when you constantly see the left side of the map while I see the right? That's setting ourselves up for a collision."

"We barely fight anymore. I, for one, kind of miss it."

I lower my chin and glare at him even though I know it's too dark for him to see. The light beside his bed flips on and I squint, completely ruining the effect.

"People only fight with those they either really hate or really care about. Everyone else no one gives two shits about. We started fighting because you wanted to hate me. Now we fight because you don't want to love me."

My eyebrows rise and my eyes stretch wide with disbelief. *Love?* "You're crazy."

"When it comes to you, I'm in need of an institution. You get so damn stubborn, and you do things that aren't safe, or even smart—"

"You do tricks on a bike for a living! I'm not the one living a life of danger."

"You're so difficult, and as much as it drives me crazy, I love it." A heavy breath blows through his open lips. His brown eyes close for the briefest of seconds and then settle on my own. "I love your passion. Your passion to be right. Your passion to be independent. Your passion to help others. Your passion for art." He smiles widely, erasing that slight variance of his lips. "In case you haven't caught on, you're really passionate about everything."

"Except cooking," I add, lifting a shoulder.

King raises a fist and puts it in front of his mouth as he laughs hard enough his eyes close. It causes that warmth in my chest he's brought to life to swell and a smile to spread across my own lips. He nods once and lowers his hand. "Except for cooking," he agrees. "I don't care if you ever learn to cook. Or if you don't get accepted to Florence. I just want you to keep painting the beauty in this world that so many forget to notice. You can paint it on canvases, or walls, or with spray paint on abandoned buildings, or chalk downtown, I don't care. You can paint every square inch of the shop and this room.

"You wanted labels, I gave you them. Now I want you to start realizing that what we have isn't going to end in June."

My heart aches. Physically aches. I wish I hadn't opened that letter today. I wish I didn't know I was accepted to Florence.

"I love you, Lo. This shit isn't going anywhere, certainly not in a few weeks."

Tears course over my cheeks and my nose runs. I can't see King clearly, but I hear the sheets shift and feel his arms encircle me seconds later.

"You got in." There's no inflection to his words because they aren't a question. He knows. "Lo, you can't be upset, babe. This is great! It's amazing! You worked your ass off for this!" He briskly runs his hands up and down my arms as if trying to spark some enthusiasm.

"How am I going to leave you?"

"You aren't," he says adamantly. "You're going to go on a work trip, and then you're coming back. We'll figure out where you're going to live, but you're coming back to Portland. And while I think long-distance relationships seem like hell on earth, we're going to walk through the fire together, and we're going to come out on the other side. I don't care how hard it is. I don't care that it's going to be a fucking pain in the ass to find time to talk because you're going to be nine hours ahead. You and me, Lo, we can do this. We've got this shit."

"I love you."

"I know you do, and that's how I know we're going to make this work. We'll figure it out."

"King, I love you. I love you, I love you, I love you. I love you."

"Now tell me you believe we can do this."

chapter
THIRTY

Saturday arrives too fast. I'm sitting in the stands between Summer and Mercedes, waiting impatiently to see King for his first event. He's just been announced, and my heart is beating a mile a minute with anticipation and nerves.

"He's gonna kill it," Summer says, changing the lens on her camera. "The cocky bastard is going to create a name for himself today."

I see Kash first, his bright red hat visible in a sea of helmets and other baseball hats.

"This is going to be epic." Mercedes is calm, poised in her seat, ready for things to start, fully confident in King's abilities.

"Alright, any special shots or you just want as much as I can do?"

"The latter."

Summer laughs softly and brings her camera to her face, obscuring the expression I know is mocking me.

King rides along the top of the rink a couple of times and then proceeds to bounce the bike in place a few times on the back tire. I've seen him do this a hundred times and still I'm captivated, watching the fluency he has with the bike. He slides down the ramp and does a single flip, landing seamlessly on the next one, which he pedals down with a fierceness and determination that I can feel in my own muscles. He goes up and rotates so many times I lose count before he lands again, this time securing to the concrete with only the front tire and swinging the bike around as he stands on a peg, precariously close to the edge. The crowd is insane. They're cheering and screaming, so amped up on the show he's delivering that I'm realizing everyone is feeling the adrenaline rush he's creating. He bounces the bike a couple of times and then soars back down the ramp, landing and then flipping along with the bike so that it looks like the bike is doing a back handspring with him along for the ride.

It's perfectionism in motion. Not a single thing could have been done more flawlessly, and the crowd knows it. Their cheers grow louder before he lands his final stunt and moves so that he has both tires firmly on the ground. Then his bike is down, his eyes wide.

"Go!" Summer demands, pushing me out of my seat. She points with one arm, still holding her camera with the other, and I don't ask. I go.

King must see me as I hedge against the rail to the aisle, because he's running toward me, his fingers releasing his helmet. I climb over the wall that holds the audience back, and Kash is on the other side, offering me his hand, but I don't need it. I hop down, and the moment I do, King is there. He's sweating and his muscles are vibrating with adrenaline and excitement that I know is going to make him crash later, but right now, I want to bask in it with him. My hands are fisted in his shirt and my lips are sealed with King's, giving and taking in a kiss that clearly states we wish we were alone and could ride out this high, pushing each other to the very limits.

When we part, King holds either side of my face and presses his forehead against mine. "Thank you."

"This was all you, babe."

"This was all you believing in me."

"You owned it, King. It was flawless. I've never seen anything so beautiful."

I don't know if he can hear my last words over the announcement being made and the deafening crowd. Still, I yell how much I love him, and hear him yell something in response, and though I can't understand it, I know he's saying the same.

Although it's Monday, I have a bounce in my step as I make my way to the Knight residence. My hair is being unnaturally even-tempered for how damp it is, and I don't have to work at the restaurant or shop. I essentially have the next six weeks to finish school, watch Mercedes, and spend time with King. Not to mention I'm starting to feel comfortable with my decision to go to Italy for the summer. I've never been abroad, and in this case I will not only be going to a beautiful city filled with culture and beauty, and as King assures me, delicious food, but I am going to have the opportunity to work on some of the amazing art that fills the city.

I bound up to the door with a smile stretching my lips wide and check to see if the door is unlocked. It swings open, revealing someone is home. A song is playing in my head, a sketch occurring in my mind as I shed my coat and bag and then stop, hearing soft murmurs followed by a sound that has become nearly foreign. My feet take me down the hall until I reach Mercedes' room, and I stop in the doorway, where my heart lurches to my throat. I don't think I've ever experienced anything wreck me like watching Mercedes cry. It creates a chaotic mess of emotions that make me think of the time I tried splatter painting, which involved dipping a paintbrush and then using sharp, jerky movements to splatter paint across a canvas. Lights covering darks, hues that didn't belong together comingling, undefined shapes and borders. It was too messy for me, and I feel like that now. My anger is peaking. My eyes are heavy, stinging with tears. My need to make her happy and laugh is pushing me to forget the other emotions, and it ends with me staring at King, whose eyes have lifted from Mercedes to look at me.

"They all hate me, King. I can't go back."

I watch his throat move as he swallows words and threats I know he's experiencing because I am as well. "They don't hate you. They're jealous."

"They aren't jealous! There's nothing to be jealous about. That's what people tell others so they don't feel bad. They *hate* me! They hate everything about me!"

"There is nothing about you that anyone could hate. It's not possible. They're being assholes to get a rise out of you. It's people like that you should pity. They don't see the joy in life. All they see is the threat they offer, and to try and maximize that threat, they act like a bunch of assclowns and attack. They're vicious and heartless. You have to..." King's words drift off, and his brows furrow in pain. He isn't sure what to say. I'm sure his instincts are providing instructions on how to be a bigger asshole in return, but something is stopping that advice, and it turns my stomach because although I hate the thought of her being equipped with how to be the bigger bully, I loathe seeing her in this kind of pain and feel subsequently responsible for prolonging it.

I take a step closer to the bed to ensure she will hear me when King doesn't speak. "You don't want to become them, Mercedes. You want to be like Summer: talented, strong, and loving. Those girls at your school are never, *never* going to be like Summer, not even half as good because they're going to get so distracted in their lives by trying to ruin others, they're going to miss their own opportunities."

King releases a deep breath and closes his eyes, making it unclear if he believes my insight or hates that he does.

The afternoon is slow. My previous mood has, like the rain, washed away, but as many rainbows as I try to create, Mercedes refuses to see any of them. I can't blame her. Sometimes we all need to respect and acknowledge the pain we're experiencing. Otherwise, it just festers. Sadly, King vanished shortly after I arrived, and I hate wondering if he's upset with me for interfering.

I set up the stairs of my apartment complex, my hand reaching for my phone to see if King's sent me anything, and stop when I see Charleigh on the landing, her movements stalled, waiting to see my reaction.

"Hey," I say, taking the last step so I'm standing on level ground with her.

"Hey." There's a faint smile on her lips.

"So, I'm sorry. I don't know what happened exactly. I think I just got a little jealous of you spending so much time with your new boyfriend, and you not introducing him or telling me about him, that when I heard you dropped out of the show, I was so shocked I didn't know how else to really react." I try to trace back to that day and what all we said to each other. "I understand why you've made the decisions you have."

"Because of King?"

"Not just him. Because of Mercedes, and Kash, and Summer, Allie, and you. You guys have all taught me about love and how life is too short to waste it doing something you don't love."

"I'm sorry I blew up on you. I never meant to hurt you or Allie. You both mean so much to me, and I just got caught up in things. I want you to meet him, but I also want to spend some time with you, catch up."

"I'd like that."

"Have you heard back from Italy yet? Are you going to be saying things like *ciao*, and *mi scusi*?"

I take a deep breath and nod. "I'm hoping my accent will be better than yours, but yeah."

Charleigh's eyes grow wide, lacking a reciprocating smile. "You're going?" The lilt in her voice makes it difficult for me to decipher between it being a question or disbelief.

"June second."

"But it's good ... right?"

"I think so. I hope so."

Charleigh's eyes are still wide as she nods, her motions stiff and forced, making it clear it was disbelief.

"Hey, if you don't have anything going on Thursday, I was wondering if you and Allie could convince a few of your stylish people and models to do a field trip?"

"A field trip?"

"Yeah." I take a long breath, glancing at the clouds heavy with rain. "Mercedes is having a really rough time with a couple of kids, and I am hoping we can share a little sense with them."

"We're twenty-two. Are you sure we have sense to share?"

My lips curve into a smile. I've missed her. "Hopefully we do collectively."

I step in front of the class and ponder if I should have told Kash or at least King that I was planning this. I shake my head and remember I should have told Kash since he's her dad. But the teacher is introducing me and moving to the side of the room, queuing that it's my turn to attempt to resolve this issue that is not only breaking Mercedes' heart and spirit, but all of ours as we watch her endure it.

I press my palms together. They feel sticky and too big like they often do when I stand in front of a group, especially one consisting of small and obviously judgmental girls, ready to make fun of me for any slip. I remind myself three times that I don't care what they think of me when one whispers to a friend, eliciting a snicker. I take a deep breath. "My name's Lauren Crosby, and while none of you have ever heard of me and may never again, it doesn't matter because others will. I'm an artist." I look to the far right of the classroom where there's nothing but empty desks because the students are all gathered around the large blue area rug, facing me as a small laugh gets caught in my throat. "I'm a really good artist, and it's taken me a very long time to admit that to anyone, including myself." I press my lips together and feel a confidence carry my gaze back to the group. "You see, all my life I grew up thinking I was going to work with my dad and brother on our family farm." I swallow, keeping my gaze on no one. "I never thought I'd leave Montana because so many of my friends and their families never did. I thought I was Lauren, dairy farmer, tall, skinny, too young to do most things I wanted, and too old to do the others. But then I took a chance. I decided I wanted to see what other potentials were out there, and have learned that those things that I thought defined me, these arbitrary numbers that so many of us allow ourselves to be described as, are nothing but a bunch of numbers that mean absolutely nothing, unless you allow them to.

"Height, weight, age, they're all just numbers. Numbers that make you feel inadequate because they're always either too high or too low. You will never be the perfect weight. People will either find you too thin or too heavy. You'll be too young to understand or too old to relate. You are too tall or too short because everyone always bases the height of others upon their own. You can't let a bunch of bullshit numbers define you. All they do is tell you what size of clothing you need and your shoe size. That's it. The rest of them mean nothing."

I hear a giggle followed by a whisper that clearly contains the word bullshit, and guiltily look toward the teacher and mumble an apology.

"We need to forget about numbers and where we come from because we have the ability to change perceptions. To mold ideas. Challenge society. You guys can be anything you want to be if you have the right drive and focus. The thing is, breaking others down is never going to make you feel better. It might for a few minutes, maybe even through your years at school, I don't know, but I can guarantee that while you may think it's making you stronger, better, and smarter than the person you're putting down, it's not. It's distracting you from what you need to be focused on. There are a hundred people waiting to show they're better than you, and chances are, many of them will be, but you have the choice to focus on what you want to accomplish, or on them.

"But here's the real kicker. You guys have it tough. There's a ton of responsibility on your generation and mine. We're supposed to clean up the planet, find alternative fuel sources, control knowledge that continues to grow for both good and evil, *and* differentiate the two. Women are supposed to be more independent, gorgeous, and powerful, yet we tear each other down as soon as we see another as a threat. We want them to be good, just not as good as us, certainly not better. Men do it too. You have to walk a fine line between being affectionate and masculine, so you never know if it's appropriate to share or discuss feelings. It's confusing! And it's ridiculous. We have to stop listening to these absurd notions and just live for ourselves with the objective of making the world a better place by being a better person.

"Being nice isn't hard. Life isn't a competition against another person. It's a competition against yourself. You are working to be the best version of yourself possible. And I'm not talking about being the thinnest, fastest, smartest—those are numbers, and again, they mean nothing compared to sincerity, genuineness, compassion, and humanity. That's what we *all* need to be pushing ourselves to be the best at."

I can't tell if my words are making sense to them, or if they're working to digest them, or are still stuck on the fact that I clumsily said the word bullshit at the beginning of my speech, but I pray that a few of my words will get lodged to the inside of their brains and one day they'll make some sense. Or maybe one or more of the others will be able to speak to them on a level they can connect with. That's why I invited several people. I wanted them to see people of all shapes, sizes, and professions so they could recognize that although we're all different, we're still the same.

I take a few steps back as Allie moves into place. She is comfortable, confident as she introduces herself, and then blows me into next week when she clearly states her continued struggle with an eating disorder I've never known about, all because of the years she was teased and tormented creating an internal fight she still has to bear.

Whether the stories truly become more emotional and gripping or my heart just feels heavier with each one is debatable. But by the end of our hour, the faces of the students in Mercedes' class makes me feel hopeful that we've been able to curtail some of the damage that has been spreading.

"That was one hell of a defense," Allie whispers as the teacher leads the class in applause.

"That was my offense," I reply, gritting my teeth because my emotions are still torn between smiling and crying.

chapter
THIRTY-ONE

My phone rings as I get off the bus at my stop, and while I consider ignoring it because I know King's busy tonight, for some reason I dig through my bag to find it.

I shuffle and apologize as I nearly make a man behind me stumble from stopping so suddenly, and answer the call, hating that I become so discombobulated from seeing her name.

"How are you, sweetheart?"

I haven't been sweetheart in years, not since I was too young to appreciate the term of endearment. "I'm well. How are you?"

"I'm great! I just spoke with your brother and he said you're doing some modeling. I'm so proud of you! I always told you you should use that height for something. You'll likely have to go on a juicing diet, make sure you shed any extra fat, but I bet you have the potential." The way her tone changes, her voice quieter, it makes me wonder if she's questioning herself.

"It's nothing serious. Not like for an agency or a company or anything like that. I'm just helping out a friend that's going to school for design."

"But you realize who goes to these shows, right." There isn't enough inflection in her tone to make it a question. "This is a big deal, Lauren. This could change your entire future."

"I'm not looking for it to change anything. I'm going to Italy this summer for art, and then I plan to come back to Portland and—"

"Do you understand the opportunity here?"

"I got accepted to go to *Florence*."

"Lauren, you're old to begin modeling now. If you're scouted, you must accept. This could do huge things for our future!" *Our future.* The words are a dagger. A million broken promises.

"I've got to go." I do. Otherwise, I might change all my future plans because of that one stupid word that has never been shared between us: our. I know she won't stick around, but the small promise of it is so alluring. It shouldn't be. I shouldn't have to be a model or successful for her to consider me her daughter and make time for me, and I know that, which is the only reason I'm able to hang up.

My mood dampens further when I see Kenzie's car in the parking lot. I haven't seen her in weeks. I have no idea where she's been staying, and while I've been a bit concerned, I know she's been in our studio apartment because clothes and bags have come and gone.

As soon as I unlock the door, I feel her eyes watching me. I refuse to look her way, something that is more difficult than I thought it would be when I came to this conclusion on the stairs. Our apartment is so small I can't help but look at her a few times as I change and get things set up to draw.

"Your phone keeps flashing." I keep my attention on my work as Kenzie grumbles her acknowledgment. "Are you going to answer it?"

My hand pauses and I look over to her. "You can flip it over if it's bothering you."

"What if it's something important?"

"It's just my brother."

"No it's not."

Her reply makes me furrow my brow in question. I muted my phone after his third call, knowing he wouldn't be deterred until he had successfully filled my voicemail. I reach toward my bed to lift my phone, and see three missed calls from King, two from Mercedes, and one from both Summer and Kash. Without giving Kenzie a thank-you or explanation, I call King back and press the phone to my ear, trying to block out the sound of my blood pumping harder with concern.

"Lo?" His answer takes me by surprise because it's filled with relief. "Are you okay?"

"Yeah, I'm fine. Are you?"

"What are you doing?"

"Drawing, why? Is everything okay?" I repeat.

"I'm coming over."

"Now?" The shock in my voice is evident.

"I'm already in my truck." I don't reply, waiting to see if I can hear anything to confirm that he is. "Pack a bag."

"For what?"

"Do you want to wear the same clothes to class tomorrow?"

Other than the night of the storm, we haven't done sleepovers. Spending the night there still feels like I'm doing something naughty, like even though Kash knows we're dating, this just confirms we're sleeping together, and while it's ridiculous that I find myself embarrassed to make it so blatant, I am.

A banging on the door stops my thoughts and causes me to drop the charcoal I'm still holding.

"I already know you're home." King's voice is quiet because he isn't yelling through the door. He's still on the phone.

I'm fairly certain Kenzie is more uncomfortable by having King here than I am. The two barely acknowledge each other, their greetings barely cordial, but I don't focus on it long because King is radiating with an energy that I feel through his hand that has been firmly on the small of my back since I opened the door. He's glowing with it, and it makes me feel anxious and happy for the first time today.

Without delay, I pack some clean clothes in a bag and then slide away from King so I can retrieve things from the bathroom. I'm only gone a few moments, not long enough for a lengthy conversation, but there isn't even a single word shared between the two.

"Ready?" he asks as I place a couple of sketchbooks into my bag.

"Yeah." I look toward Kenzie. She's filing her nails, but I can tell she's bothered. I'm pretty sure I wear that same expression most times I'm with my own brother. "See ya, Kenzie." I don't look to see if she turns her head. I'm not saying it for me.

King and I descend the stairs at a fast pace, his energy returning as soon as the door is closed.

"You seem happy," I remark as we clear the last stair.

King looks over to me and a sly smile lifts only the right side of his lips, and then his hands are holding my jaw with an unfamiliar timidness and his lips are against mine. I don't notice the softness of his lips or the sharpness of the short stubble on his chin against mine. It's muted by the heat of his breath, and the pressure that counterbalances the tenderness of his hands. Then I forget that too and wind my arms around his neck so I can pull him closer to me. His fingers constrict slightly as a sound far too similar to a purr is made in the back of my throat, and my hands fist in his jacket. It only serves to send the scent of him in the breeze, making this energy that he's passed on to me multiply.

A car horn stretches, and King's head snaps back. I doubt that either of us would have given it a thought if it weren't a foot away from us. A man waves his hand dismissively, his eyebrows drawn and mouth plastered into a frown, showing his frustration.

I glance down and laugh before grabbing King's hand and pulling him out of the parking spot.

"What an asshole," King mutters, standing beside the car as the man parks.

His shoulders are wide as he stands slightly in front of me.

I jab him with my elbow and move toward his truck, hoping he won't say anything to the guy but knowing this is the best deterrent I can offer.

"Have I told you how incredible you are?" His words are nearly as soft as his steps, startling me. Then he wraps a hand around my waist, bringing our hips together for the short distance to his truck.

"You weren't even going to tell me, were you?" he asks.

"About today?"

"Yeah, about today."

I shrug. "Only later if it worked. Then I would have gloated."

"You're such a liar."

"How is she?" I was a little nervous about her going to her friend Paige's this afternoon with everything transpiring, but she was sure she wanted to go.

"She has her head so far in the clouds, I think those girls could say anything they want and it wouldn't touch her right now."

I stop and lean my back against the cold metal of the door, sighing with relief. Although I felt it had gone well, I was still a little concerned it would bite her in the ass, and even more concerned she would hate me for embarrassing her.

"You were right, Lo. She's too good to stoop to those levels. And your words about numbers, and how they don't mean a damn thing—I think she really understood your message."

"I talked a lot. Hopefully a couple of words got stuck in each of their heads."

"Your words needed to be said. They're going to be better people from the message you left with them today."

"I said bullshit in the middle of it," I admit.

King lets out a quiet laugh, his eyes sparking with that energy the car horn dimmed. "I don't think it was the first time any of them had ever heard it. But your cheeks turned red, and you looked really cute."

"How do you know?"

"Mercedes taped it."

"What?"

"We watched you on the big screen, baby." He's teasing but sincere, making it both sweet and maddening.

"If you mock me…" I warn.

King's eyebrows shoot up. "Babe, you're cute when I mock you, and I like getting you playful and feisty, but I would never mock you for this. You went above and beyond, and your love for Mercedes, and even those other kids that you're trying to help, makes me respect you more than I already did, and I didn't know that was even possible. I'm going to take you home and worship you."

King's practices increase along with his media coverage and invitations. It isn't long before he's gone more than he was while trying to get things sorted with the PR team in Switzerland for Kash. This time it's both easier and harder. We're getting better at communicating, touching base even if it's only for a few stolen minutes between conflicting schedules. I'm so immensely proud of him and know with how often he reaches out that we're on stable ground, both of us fully invested. I also miss him somehow more than I did then when I would get moody and depressed from not seeing him. Now I'm mopey. Mercedes keeps me busy, and modeling practice has moved up to three times a week in preparation for the show Friday. But I have a bigger project that hours of my day keep getting lost to: King's logo. Summer has taken so many pictures of him, but I already know which image I'll be using, and it isn't in a photograph.

I reach for my phone to check the time. I'm supposed to be meeting Charleigh in five minutes at the restaurant. I'm excited to see her yet still slightly nervous because of the turbulence we experienced. Relationships have never been my forte, even friendships, so I like to think this is just natural progression, a required growth that will make us stronger like Allie has said.

The restaurant is warm and fairly sparse since it's just after four. Mercedes is with Robert today, giving me hours I've rarely seen since summer.

"Lo!" Mia calls warmly as she winds around the small desk. "How are you?"

My smile is an instant reaction to her. I think regardless of how much time spans, I will always think fondly of this place and the people here.

"Your mural is unreal, Lo! I can't believe how good it turned out! You wouldn't believe how many people ask about it! Estella is absolutely in love with it! When we don't see her for a while, we come out here and she's just staring at it. I can't believe you haven't been around!"

"I'm really glad you guys like it."

"Like is an understatement. I mean, we all knew you could draw, but girl, you can *draw*," Mia says. "And paint too, apparently," she adds with a small laugh.

"Don't fill her head too high; she has to be able to walk back out of here."

Mia and I both turn to see Charleigh, her hair in a large bun and her cheeks rosy from running in the rain.

"Hey, stranger!" Mia calls.

"Hi, Mia."

"You guys here for an early dinner?"

"I'm starved," Charleigh answers, following Mia to a booth near the back that sits against a window. They all know about my love to people-watch.

"Lauren," Charleigh says after Mia walks away.

I slide my menu down and slowly move my gaze up to meet hers.

"You don't hate me, do you?"

"No!" The word pops from my mouth. I'm shocked it was even a question.

"I know we both apologized, but I couldn't stand for you to hate me. I know I said some things that were a little forward, and I didn't mean to hurt you. Your relationship with your mum is something that I know is none of my business, but it really bothers me. She shouldn't treat you the way she does, and it upsets me that you allow her to. And while I think you should have kicked Kenzie's arse a couple of times this last year, I know that's not you…"

Charleigh rubs a hand across her forehead. "Dammit, I'm doing it again. I'm shit with giving advice, especially here. You guys are all so sweet with your … what do you call them? Word sandwiches? The positives covering a negative thing you all do. It's bollocks, really, because I think the negative can easily get lost, or more importantly, people don't hear the positives at all, but whatever. I'm going to do this the British way and just tell you how it is. You need to stop worrying about your mum, and everyone else, and do what's best for you right now."

I watch her eyes that are wide and set on me. There's an appreciation I've always had for Charleigh because she doesn't feed anyone a line of bullshit. If she doesn't like you or something you're doing, she never has a problem stating so. Maybe she's right—maybe we have gotten so lost in trying to be so nice and protect everyone's feelings, that we've lost sight of how destructive it is to have negativity laced within a compliment. Like having someone insult you and then deliver a laugh so that you're not positive they've really insulted you, or if they are merely joking.

"That means a lot to me."

Charleigh smiles, but it's reserved, hiding something that I can tell she's prepared to affront me with, but Mia arrives with a large platter filled with appetizers—Charleigh's and my favorite way to eat—and her attention is instantly averted.

"So what's this mysterious boy of yours like? Are you ever going to introduce him?"

"He's coming to the show on Friday with me."

"Really?" My curiosity is piqued, and I can tell by her smile that she knows.

"You're going to be surprised. He doesn't look like other guys I've dated." I've only met two guys that she dated, and neither left a big enough impression for me to create a class of guys that she likes. All I know is she liked pictures of guys with big biceps, licking them and claiming them like it meant something significant. "He's perfect though, and he's funny, and … he's perfect"

"I'm glad. I know you wouldn't settle for less, and you shouldn't."

Charleigh's smile begins from my words and then transgresses into something personal, like she's celebrating something only she's fully aware of. I'm envious of it initially, and then I think of King and feel my own lips curling. I understand what those stolen kisses and soft touches, tucked pieces of hair, inside jokes, and shared knowing smiles equate to. They aren't something that can be explained because like many things in life, words do not equate.

"So, I've told my mum and dad that I'm staying for another year. They went ballistic initially, but I think they understand now."

"Does that change your immigration status?"

"I've applied for my F-1 Visa, which allows me to stay another year after graduating. In that time, I'm hoping I'll be able to find a job or something that will allow me to stay longer. This one usually goes fairly fast because it's specialized for students graduating. I'm hoping it comes quickly though. Otherwise, I have to go back, then apply. If they lapse, it gets a lot more complicated."

"But you've got everything in?"

She nods, stabbing a large bit of taquito with her fork. "I think this is the right thing. I mean, I love fashion, and I'm hoping I can do something with it, but for now, I think just getting to enjoy life is what I'm supposed to do."

"We're late! We're late! Let's go!" Allie is barreling down the stairs, garment bags folded over her arms.

We aren't late, but I know from previous dressings that on time equates to late to many of these people. I follow her to her car and help load things into the trunk.

"Where's Charleigh?" I ask.

"Meeting us there. Where's King?"

"Same."

"Are you ready?" Allie asks, smoothing a loose hair back into her braid. For how stressed out she's been and was just mere moments ago, she seems composed, relaxed—the complete opposite of me. I'm pretty certain if she pays attention long enough, she'll see that I'm shaking, all of me, like I'm the epicenter of an earthquake. She nods once and opens the driver's side door. "Let's go."

Once we arrive, we're led to a large hall filled with stations, dresses, people, and more lights than I have ever seen before in my life.

"You're fine," Allie says. Taking my hand, she pulls me through the room until we reach a spot that has her name taped across a garment rack.

"What are these if the clothes are already here?" I ask, adding the garment bags we hauled through the crowds.

"Backups." She doesn't even look my way as she responds, straightening the additions and moving to plug in a steamer.

"What should I do?"

"Go get a cup of ice."

"For what?"

"You need to start sucking on it."

"Why?" My brows draw low in question.

"It will lower your body temperature and make you stop sweating." I glance down, wondering if my nerves are visible under my arms. "You aren't yet, but you will." With that assurance, I head off in search of ice.

As I stand in front of the mirror—my hair and makeup completed by Charleigh—I realize Allie was never harnessing her talents; she was unleashing them, stepping outside of all comfort zones to create something that is beyond imaginable. I feel nervous to touch the first dress, let alone wear it. How will I move without possibly harming it? Even a crease seems tragic to this beautiful piece.

"You can't sit or eat or drink, and please don't sweat."

I look to Allie and feel the temperature in the room rise by ten degrees.

"Here's another ice cube," Charleigh says, offering me a plastic spoon.

They've been dropping them into my mouth to prevent me from ruining my lipstick.

"Don't lock your knees. You want to remember to lean forward with your chest, chin up, and weight on your toes," Allie instructs as her fingers trail the dress, seeking any slight imperfections that we all know don't exist.

I recite the instructions twice more in my head while keeping my arms propped out like a doll, another measure to prevent sweating.

"Alright, Lo, you've got to get in line," Allie says, grabbing the bottle of hair spray. She's sprayed me down from head to toe already, and still she does it again.

We walk—me stiff, them relaxed—to where others are starting to get in order. People with headpieces that link from their ear to walkie talkies are checking sheets, instructing us on where to go.

"You're going to do great. Take a couple of deep breaths and just look to the bottom right when you get out there. They're all waiting for you." Charleigh gently squeezes my hand, holding on until I feel my nerves start to subside.

The lights are bright, heating me like a dozen suns shining on me. They also make it nearly impossible to decipher anyone's face. I'm fairly certain the crowd is loudest on the right, and I reckon it's where King and the group are sitting, but I can't pause long enough to confirm it. I recite the tips again in my head. My face is cool with my chin tilted up, my chest forward, my weight balanced on my toes in a pair of shoes that I will do a celebratory burial for once this is over, and my knees are slightly bent as I make a final pose at the end of the runway where a sea of cameras are pointed toward me.

I feel slightly guilty for feeling exhilarated by the energy that is pumping through me as I descend the back stairs and head to where my next dress is waiting for me along with Charleigh, Allie, and two girls I've never met that strip me like a doll. I've been saying looks don't count, numbers are irrelevant, yet I'm parading around like they do. Still, this is such a huge step for Allie that I try to forget about the thoughts until later and ignore the fact that people are seeing me in nothing but a skimpy pair of underwear, and let them work their magic.

Five times I walk down the stage that thankfully seemed shorter with each pass. I was never able to pick out Mercedes, or even King from the crowd, but I don't doubt for a second that they missed the show.

"You were amazing!" Allie cries, flinging her arms around me when I step backstage. "You rocked every single dress."

"I should. You made them to fit me."

Charleigh grins, but Allie is so lost in a blissful happiness that is preventing her from taking in much of anything at the moment.

They strip me once again and I dress in my own clothes that feel loose and light in contrast to the dresses. I roll my shoulders, appreciating the range of motion being restored, and my feet sigh as they slide into a pair of ballet flats. Allie has vanished, whisked away to go take a bow along with the other designers and their professor who managed to give me the tightest of smiles before my last trip down the runway.

"Loooooo!"

I look up and see Mercedes running at me with a bouquet of red roses fisted in her hand. She launches into my arms from a foot back and hugs me so tightly it catches my breath. Charleigh smiles, and it tells me how happy she is for me and the close relationship that Mercedes and I have built and will always share.

"You were so beautiful!" she cries as Summer steps up behind her with a matching smile. "They won't let any boys back here," Mercedes continues, then looks to her left. "But there's already…"

"They're with the design teams," Charleigh quickly explains as two men brush past us. They had, I watched as they applied makeup like artists with a paintbrush.

Mercedes doesn't care. She's already peering around at the models and dresses, loving the commotion and energy that is still filling the room.

"Your mom thinks you're going to be the next big thing," Mercedes chirps. "I think she's right."

"My mom?" I don't mean for the question to be verbal, but they all look at me, Charleigh sucking in a deep breath to confirm she knew she was out there. I'm glad she didn't tell me; it would have made me obsess over everything, which is likely the reason she didn't.

"She's waiting with Kash and King," Summer says, her voice even and her face careful, like she's expecting a reaction.

Without asking her to, Charleigh takes my hand and leads us out to the hall that is filled with people. We don't have to go far. A hand catches my arm and within seconds I smell King in the air, moving around me as he advances, and then I'm wrapping my arms around his shoulders.

He's silent, or my thoughts and the crowd are too loud. I'm not sure. I don't hold on to him for long. I need to see that she's actually here, introducing herself to my friends as my mother.

It's not just her; my brother, Josh, is standing on her other side, clearly uncomfortable and reproachful of the situation. I don't know how to greet either of them because I don't call her Mom, not to her face. "Hey." My voice is quiet and strained, and I resent her being here more than I thought possible. I feel like they're intruding on this moment and time with my friends.

"Lo, you looked like a natural up there!" Kash says, awkwardly wrapping an arm around my side that King isn't still pressed against. "You seriously killed it! Summer has some awesome shots! I know you don't draw yourself, but you have to do at least one."

"Let's go to dinner! We have to talk about things!" my mom says. I look over her once more. She looks heavier, but she's trying to disguise it with a busily patterned skirt and black blouse that looks stark in contrast to her light skin that matches my own. Her hair is maintained at the same dark shade it always has been, nearly raven, and her eyes are too green, enhanced by contacts. I don't look anything like my mother aside from our shared skin tone and shape of our hands, something few people would ever notice. I don't look like my father either, nor my brother. They all have the dark hair and varying shades of green eyes. They're also all slightly shorter than me, even my dad. It's never bothered me. We are as different inside as we are physically. And because we've spent so little time together, I doubt we share even a single mannerism.

"You're always sexy," King whispers in my ear as we move to the exit. "Always."

I'm glad so many people drove because it gives me three excuses not to ride with my mom and brother, and ultimately, I choose to ride with Charleigh and her boyfriend, Brandon, who does look surprisingly young.

"I'm sorry I didn't mention it to you. I just thought—"

I wave a hand dismissively. "No, I'm glad you didn't. It would have distracted me."

"We don't have to go."

I've never told Charleigh much about my mom. The sordid details of our past are so meager and infrequent that I know what others' thoughts are when I share them. Still, she seems to recognize my discomfort, and always has when it has anything to do with her.

"It's okay. She never sticks around for long anyway."

"You were awesome out there, Lauren. Focus on that. You were so beautiful and confident. Everyone was watching you out there."

"I don't want to model."

Charleigh swings her head to look at me twice and then releases a deep breath. "That's what she wants? Why you're bothered? Just tell her no."

"Watch how well that goes."

She turns to look at me as she slides the key from the ignition, but I'm ready to get this over with. I slide out of the car and find King waiting for me. He wraps an arm around my shoulders, and with the tightness of his grip, I can tell he knows something is off.

"So, King, I was reading an article about you online that says you're starting to compete just like your brother, Kash," my mom says as soon as pleasantries are completed again, following another round of compliments from my friends. I wish Allie were here to accept some of them, but she had other plans with her family.

"I am," he says, sitting back in his chair. He's dressed in a pair of dark slacks and an olive-toned shirt that is once again rolled to his elbows. I think he feels suffocated in them, and the small gesture somehow makes him feel less restricted. The small gauge in his left ear catches the light, dancing across the starched tablecloth. I don't stare at him long because my brother is on his other side, and he has been staring at me with a look of disdain that I refuse to acknowledge.

"What kind of span is one generally able to compete? I noticed many in the field are in their teens."

My back bristles. She has always known how to take the upper hand in a conversation.

King's hand tightens around mine and then tightens even more, bringing me to look at him. I'm expecting to see the fury I'm feeling in his expression, but he's relaxed, his eyes looking lazy, his lips twitching with a grin. "That depends on so many variables; there really isn't a clear answer." He wets his lips with his tongue, and leans further against his chair, looking almost relaxed. "I plan to do it until I'm either tired of it or it's not a safe risk."

"Is it ever a safe risk?" she asks.

I can only see King's profile, but I'm certain he's sharing my favorite smile with her. It angers me even more. "Without risk, you will never find reward."

"Death is a reward?" Josh asks.

King's head turns slightly away, but his thumb strokes along mine, silently assuring me. "Only for some."

I glance to Mercedes, seeing her eyebrows are raised over wide eyes that are volleying between King and Josh.

"I assume you travel a lot with the profession," my mom continues.

King threads his fingers through mine, stretching and then clamping around my hand that continues to flex with irritation. "Some."

Her response is a smile that's tainted with malevolence.

"It's really great to meet you guys. Lauren has become very dear to us all." Apparently Charleigh senses the malice also.

My mother's eyes flicker to her, calculating, measuring. "We've been waiting to come for graduation, and then I heard Lauren got accepted to a program that requires her to go to Europe for the summer, so I thought we'd come and see how things were going. This modeling certainly seems far more promising than painting. You guys all thought she was really great. I think it's a very promising possibility." Her eyes turn back to me. "You'll need to start toning and drinking more water because your skin is visibly dry. Are you using a moisturizer? You aren't wiping your makeup off with a towel or your hands, right? We'll need to find an agent. Tomorrow we can start calling."

"Mom, I'm glad you got to see the show, but only because it will be the only time I walk down a runway. I don't want to model. I was uncomfortable and nervous, and feeding into an image that I don't believe in."

"Of course you were nervous! This was your first time. And the clothes weren't professional grade. You haven't been properly conditioned. Once you lose some weight and have some training—"

"I'm not modeling," I say firmly, my eyes wide and fixed on hers.

A waiter appears looking clearly uncomfortable as he clears his throat and asks us if we're ready to order. Fearing someone will ask for another minute, I confirm we are.

Nothing on the menu sounds good, though my stomach is growling from not eating all day. I order a salad without even thinking about it. This is the only meal my mother and I have ever ordered when out together since I turned ten.

Old habits die hard.

King orders manicotti, extra garlic bread, and two tiramisus that he requests to be delivered with dinner. His gesture is sweet, thoughtful, and manages to fracture the dread that's been silencing the group since I heard my mom was here.

There's an unavoidable silence that follows our waiter that has everyone reaching for their napkin or glass.

"Lo did an amazing job tonight. Really, she was spectacular, but with all due respect, it pales in comparison to her art. Nothing compares to what she's capable of when she gets a piece of charcoal or a paintbrush in her hand. Hell, we've seen her create art with a feather." I want to give Summer an appreciative smile, but my mom's eyes are locked on mine, awaiting my response. If I look away, it will appear that I need the help. Whether I do or not, I can't show her.

My mom swallows, waiting.

"She's created a logo for my marketing campaign that people are amazed by," Kash adds, not realizing that right now the best way to help me is to simply be quiet.

"Lauren, you're not going to Italy." Her words are said with an authority she for some reason believes she still possesses.

"This is stupid," Josh mutters. "This whole thing is so you, Lauren. Always needing attention."

Their words don't bother me. Growing up, my personal tormentor who teased and mocked me relentlessly was my own blood. My brother and I have been at odds since I was born, and nothing over the years has managed to do anything but intensify it. However, the fact that King, Mercedes, Kash, Summer, Charleigh, and Brandon are hearing them being said to me, bothers me a lot. I'm fairly certain everyone's back has just gone straight, but I'm looking at Josh, noticing his flexed jaw, and out of the corner of my eye, King's breaths coming faster, stronger.

"This really isn't a conversation to be having here. Clearly you both have concerns about Italy and art as a whole, and we can discuss them later. At my apartment."

"You're so selfish! God, you're so stupid!" Josh says the words so quietly, I'm not sure who can even decipher them.

King clears his throat and sits forward, turning visibly as if in a silent threat to continue.

"You don't think about anyone but yourself. Everyone else is working their asses off, and you're here doing what? Doodling? Walking around for guys to think you're hot? God." Josh closes his eyes and shakes his head. "You're so dumb."

King's chair goes back and my hand squeezes. "You're so out of line right now. So. Far. Out. Of. Line. You need to apologize."

My heart is beating so hard and fast, it's difficult not to focus on it as my entire body warms with anger. These verbal wars do nothing but end ugly.

Josh looks at King and then rolls his eyes before leaning back in his chair so he can see me through the barrier King is trying to create. "You need to stop calling. You've already left the family. You think you're so much better than everyone else. Woo hoo, my name's Lauren, and I did good in school. Look at me!" His hands dance and wave in front of him and his voice goes ludicrously high, making me temporarily fear that I might sound that ridiculous. "You want to be some independent, failing artist, then do it. Don't expect us to be there for you when you fail."

"You need to leave." Josh and I both turn at the sound of King's voice. His eyes meet mine. They're wide and questioning before they turn back to my brother.

"Who in the hell are you, anyway?" Josh asks, his tone aggressive.

"Who in the hell do you think I am? I introduced myself as Kingston, Lauren's boyfriend. How many more dots do I need to connect for you in order for that to make sense?"

Josh doesn't acknowledge King's reply or irate tone. I doubt he even heard it over the words he's clearly ready to spew. "You need to stop being a bitch and start thinking about someone other than yourself!" Josh continues, his belligerence making others in the restaurant turn, though his voice is still decently quiet.

"You aren't seriously going to let him say that to her!" Mercedes shoves back from the table. "I'll punch him if you guys don't!" She only makes it past Brandon before Charleigh stops her with an arm.

"You need to apologize," Mercedes demands. Her fists are stuck to her small hips, her chin raised high.

"You're dating someone with a kid? This is great. Mom couldn't stand you. That's why she left. Now you're trying to be a mom?" His laughter is colder than his words that fall too easily, without a second of thought behind what pain the callousness of his words brings.

"She's my nanny, you jerkface!" is screamed from Mercedes, but I don't see her. My attention is on King, whose head turns quickly, his fist even faster. His knuckles connect with Josh's cheek, making his head whip.

"I don't give a shit who you are. You don't talk to her like that."

Josh laughs and it's filled with a mocking enjoyment.

The entire restaurant has turned to face us. Everyone at the table is now standing, even my mom.

"Lauren, what are you doing?" she asks as I turn and grab my purse.

"Leaving."

"What's new," Josh mutters. "She'll leave you too, man. Get out while you can." King whirls around, his hands both fisted. "Ask her," Josh prompts, the muscles in his neck straining. "She doesn't need anyone. She's never needed or wanted anyone. She isn't someone you can hold on to and expect to be there for you when you need her."

Kash grabs King's arm, holding it firmly to his side and saying something so quietly, only King hears it. Then he turns and faces the table. "Lauren has been one of the greatest blessings our family has ever experienced. She has taught all of us about life and love and following your dreams. You guys should be embarrassed and ashamed. Don't step back into this city again with all this crazy shit. You aren't welcome." His hand is against my back, King's on the back of my neck.

"We're the city of weird, not rude," Mercedes says, her hip jaunting and eyes glaring. It seems like a million years since it was me on the opposite side of this reaction.

chapter
THIRTY-THREE

The parking lot is far worse than standing in front of everyone while modeling today. Far, far worse. Everyone is off balance with what to do or say, creating an awkward energy that has us all looking down at the pavement rather than each other.

"I say we get a drink. Are there any good pubs in the area?" Charleigh breaks the silence, looking to King and Kash for direction.

Kash rubs a hand along the back of his neck, exposing a long scar on his forearm. His eyes dance over each of us, focusing on me before looking back to Charleigh. "We could head back to the house. We've got all kinds of shit from different things."

"You want to ride with us, Lauren?" Charleigh asks, her voice high, revealing a hopefulness that makes me even more embarrassed.

I shake my head and look toward the street to gain my bearings. "I'm going to head home."

Mercedes looks my way, and I instantly turn my head. I feel like a coward. I've encouraged her to open up and speak freely with me about the tormenting she has endured at school, and now that we're in reverse rolls, I can't even look at her.

"We need to properly celebrate and get that awful taste out of our mouths." Charleigh's voice is hopeful and shaded with sympathy, which I loathe hearing.

"Yeah, I'm tired. I need to study for my math final, and I feel sticky and gross from all that hairspray."

"Let's just go for one round," Kash suggests.

"That's alright. I'm not in the mood either," King says, taking a step closer to me.

I notice Brandon shift uncomfortably and feel even worse. I haven't even introduced myself to the guy and he's already been thrown into the crazy circus that is my life. No wonder Charleigh went AWOL. I understand it. I completely get how life can be so distracting and crazy that sometimes it's more tempting to leave it all behind for a while and just enjoy something that makes you feel good.

"I'll see you guys on Monday," I say, taking a long step back.

King moves with me, his weight shifting in tandem with mine. I look to him, confusion knitting my brows. His draw down as well, and then he shakes his head just once, and I see a trace of pain cross his features before he drops his head. He remains in step with me though, a hand resting on my hip. I allow him to guide me to his truck, though I'd prefer to be on the bus tonight. I want the distraction of nameless faces and the lull of white noise.

When his driver's side door closes, he inserts the key and then drops his hand to his slack-covered thigh. The slacks he's wearing because of me. "That's the anger you were referring to. It wasn't your mom or your dad; it was your brother."

For several seconds my jaw stays flexed, my attention trained on the passing cars. Then I look over to him, my lips still firmly together.

"I don't know what you're thinking. I can't tell if you're sad or angry, or even worse, embarrassed."

I narrow my eyes, puzzled. "Why is embarrassment the worst thing?"

King's eyes shift between mine, still searching for recognition. "Because you deserve to be angry and sad, but there's no reason for you to feel embarrassed. You didn't ask for them to act like that. It's not your fault they were being assholes." He moves a hand to his nose, his thumb and forefinger applying pressure to the slight bridge there. His hands look cleaner than I've ever seen them, scrubbed to the point there's only a hint of grease along some of the deeper grooves on his fingers. Last night I had to alternately soak and scrub my hands until the charcoal was gone except for the small callus on the knuckle of my middle finger. I think it's imbedded into my skin at that spot.

"I knew ... I could feel it." My attention moves back to King's face. His dark eyelashes are fanned, his eyelids scrunched with thought and frustration that has his head shaking nearly imperceptibly. "Everything about it seemed off. You hadn't mentioned them, and Charleigh looked so annoyed ... I knew you weren't expecting them, but I thought ... I hoped ... they were there to support you. I so rarely hear you talk about them, I thought maybe it would be a good thing." He opens his eyes but doesn't meet my stare. "Something was off though, and I could tell things were going to go to hell in a hand basket."

"There's nothing you could have done to stop it." I don't want to say these words, because I fear that they are like when he told me he wasn't trying to insinuate that I was stalking him. I don't want him to even consider that he is somehow responsible for this night, yet I see it. I hear it. Being that it's King, I can even feel his guilt. It makes me nearly loathe them.

"Has he always been..."

I don't wait for him to discern which adjective to use. Rude, mean, offensive ... there are so many words and expletives to fill the awkward blank, and none of them would be appropriate alone, and I have no desire to discuss them. I fought hard to never lower myself to my brother's level and return the hurtful things he so often delivered, but that doesn't mean they didn't scar.

"An asshole?" My fingers stretch—constantly tight—and I shrug. "I think he blames me for our mom leaving. Well, clearly he does..." I shrug again, uncomfortable for talking to him when I intended to avoid this subject at all costs. "I mean, I get it. She was overwhelmed—"

"Of course she was overwhelmed! Kash was a fucking head case when they brought Mercedes home! Let me tell you, that attitude you've seen, it started at birth. She came out screaming." King's brown eyes are wide, looking as dark as my charcoals with the setting sun. "Her leaving had nothing to do with anyone but her. And that's fine. Maybe it was for the better." King's words make my breath hitch. Better? I've never had anyone say that, and while there is likely logic behind his words, emotion drowns reason out and all I hear is that it was better for her to leave. "But it doesn't matter if she left or not. These are your decisions to make, and regardless of what you choose, you deserve nothing except their support."

I shift in my seat, hating that his words have made my nose and eyes burn with tears. Long ago I concluded I wouldn't cry for them.

"Babe, tell me how I can help. I hate this."

I brush my cheek with the back of my hand in an attempt to make my tears go unseen and release a slightly garbled laugh because my throat is tight with the need to cry. "I just want to go to my apartment, eat something, and go to bed."

He nods, blowing a long sigh out of his nose as he reaches forward and starts the truck. We ride in silence. It's not even raining tonight to create a soft distraction, leaving me to repeat the ugly evening again and again in my head.

King pulls into an empty spot and slides out of the truck, not waiting for me to give him permission to see me in. I appreciate it because I think we both know I wouldn't have tonight. He doesn't stop at my door when I turn ever so slightly to say goodnight either. He walks past me, straight into our small studio apartment, and flips on the lights. It's messy as it usually is. The only way this place could ever truly look clean would be for us to get rid of half of our belongings. King doesn't comment though. He moves into the kitchen as though he's comfortable in the space and opens the fridge.

I lock the front door, curious about his intentions, but still wallowing in too much self-pity to safely ask without exposing how thin my façade is. I sit on our single couch and watch as he rifles through the fridge and freezer, already knowing he won't find much.

Not once does he ask for direction or for my approval on what he's making. He simply sets to work, opening drawers and cupboards that he digs through, rarely showing any emotion. It helps to watch him. The focus in his eyes and tightly sealed lips, the speed of his hands as he dices and cuts, and the movements he makes between the stove and his workspace all remind me of watching him in the shop. There's an intensity when King sets his mind to something, an impenetrable focus that I respect and admire because I understand it so intimately. I wonder if this is what I look like when I work. I hope it is.

It's not long before he delivers a plate to me with scrambled eggs filled with sautéed onions, a pepper I didn't know we had, sun-dried tomatoes, and cheese. I never would have even considered adding the tomatoes, but they, like King, are unexpectedly my favorite part.

Once our plates are cleaned, I give King a shy thank-you, grab a pair of pajamas from my dresser, and close myself in the bathroom—the only area of space in the entire studio apartment that has four walls and a door.

I stand under the stream of the water and think of the show, recalling my steps, the sway of my hips, the weight on the balls of my feet, how tall I stood. It all filled me with a confidence I never knew I could possess. A beauty and power that somehow felt tangible even if I was the only one who truly saw it. I hold the memories through shampooing and conditioning my hair, and then think of the mural I recently finished at Sonar, the large painting of Kash riding on the wall of the shop and how I'd like to add all of the others beside him. I think of the first sketch I ever drew with charcoal, and receiving my acceptance letter to college.

The power I felt while on stage was exhilarating, fun, fresh, new, but in comparison to the feelings I experience when I complete a piece of art, they all pale.

Why can't my family see that?

My hair is still wet, pulled up into a bun when I make my way back out to the apartment. I had wanted to be alone, yet now all I want to do is lie down beside King. Thankfully, he knew not to leave me and without me asking, he steps forward and pulls me into a hug, holding me so close to him I can feel each of his breaths and every beat of his heart.

chapter
THIRTY-FOUR

"Lo!" I hesitate before turning around to face him, knowing he's going to have accusation and pain in his brown eyes as well as frustration. "Why are you avoiding me?" He isn't supposed to be here, I know. I heard him working through his schedule with Parker after he let me cry on his chest. His phone rang and went to voicemail four times before he reluctantly answered.

I recognize the anger in his stance first, quickly followed by the accusation as his fists move to his hips just like Mercedes. "I'm not. I've just had to get stuff done this week."

"You've left early every day this week."

"You've gotten home late," I reply.

"I'm busy. Things are crazy with PR and all of the last-minute shoots and interviews."

I nod, hoping I look understanding rather than unhappy.

"I've been thinking about Italy," King continues.

"So have I."

He raises his eyebrows, waiting for me to continue. "What are you thinking?"

"I think we should take a break while I'm gone." Narrowing his eyes, he flexes his jaw, making me continue even faster. "We're going to be busy. You're going to be on a different schedule and traveling, and—"

"Why in the hell do you think that's a good idea?"

"I'm trying to explain that to you."

"We've talked about this shit. We both know it's going to be difficult. Do you think I'm looking forward to having to see your face over a computer screen for three months? Not hearing your voice from beside me, but two countries and an ocean away? Do you think I don't know how much this is going to fucking suck?"

"All of my life I've waited for others. I waited until my dad wasn't too busy, or my mom wasn't distracted by some new boyfriend. Whenever it suited them, I was their daughter. This whole art thing has always been a hobby to my mom and a crazy obsession according to my dad. He still hasn't even taken the time to look at my portfolio. He has no idea if I suck. I doubt he'll ever know because he doesn't care.

"We aren't going to be able to be there for each other. I can't be there to support you ... You're getting ready to unfold some of your biggest dreams, King, and I am too, and we're going to miss every single moment of it for the other, and I think it will tarnish our own successes."

King shakes his head dismissively. "Loving someone doesn't mean you have to give up on your dreams. Whenever I'm able to attend things, I will, just like you will for me."

"Conveniences build pain and resentment. Love is only made to bend so far."

"Dude, come on! We're late!" Parker calls from the front door.

"You need to go," I tell him.

"I need you to stop thinking of me like your family. That's them, not us." King sweeps a hand across the room, his forearms flexing and his eyes bright with anger.

"I'm not saying you are."

"Like hell! Lo, you're worth it. I'm willing to put everything into this. You need to decide if you are."

I nod, but can't look at him. I want to believe the conviction in his words so badly. The trouble is—I don't.

King brushes a kiss to my temple, a gentle squeeze to my sides. "I'll call you later."

My footsteps are slow as I leave the office in search of Mercedes. I told Kash I was accepted the day after I told King. He didn't seem surprised in the least, but he did appear sad. I asked them both to allow me the chance to tell Mercedes, knowing the news would be difficult for her to hear from anyone, but especially if it came from someone other than me. I find her in her room, finishing homework.

"Took you long enough. Were you guys playing smoochy face this entire time?" Her eyes remain on her notebook, but I see the sarcastic smile in the tightening of her cheeks and temples.

"Want to go on a walk today?"

She moves her head up to face me, narrowing her green eyes with speculation. "Why?"

I shrug absently. "It's nice out."

"No it's not."

"Let's go." I lift my chin in the direction of the door.

"You aren't breaking up with King, are you? I mean, I know he didn't handle things right at dinner, but I really think he was just trying to figure out what was going on. You know King. He would never let someone hurt you."

I look to the side but keep my face mostly forward. "This has nothing to do with King."

"Are you going to tell me about your brother?"

"There isn't much to say," I lie.

"Then why are we going on this walk?"

"Fresh air."

Her eyes are slits of disbelief, but she doesn't push me for any more. I'm grateful because I still don't know how I'm going to tell her.

We pass by Robert's house, and I note that all of his lights are off. I think Mercedes does too, as her attention seems to linger for long moments, searching for a definite conclusion.

When we arrive at the bus stop, I don't have a destination in mind, so I ask Mercedes if there's anything she'd like to see or do.

"Let's get on whatever bus comes next."

I raise an eyebrow in question, knowing that there are areas of Portland I would never willingly bring Mercedes to. I reserve the right to disagree until the bus comes and the lights inform me we're headed to downtown. We find a shared seat near the middle. Mercedes sits tucked in beside the window, and we both stare out at the streets of Portland. It's starting to drizzle, the skies darkening. It makes some people scurry, attempting to reach their destinations quicker, while others pull out a prepared umbrella or hat. Several, however, keep their pace. The rain is like an old friend to them, or perhaps they, like King, realize you truly can't hide from it. Can you really hide from anything?

I know there are several reasons I have delayed telling Mercedes about going to Florence, the first being I know how much it will hurt her. She has been left by so many, and I hate choosing to be another that does the same. The second and selfishly more prominent reason is that each day that passes, I find more and more reasons tipping the scale to stay, but I still know I need to go. This is my dream.

"Didn't you say Charleigh works at the greatest donut shop in Portland?"

I close my eyes to rid my thoughts and look to Mercedes. Small dark hairs are curling and sticking out near her temples. I'm sure mine are doing the same, and it makes me smile. "Yeah. You want to go get some?"

"I think we both need one."

I suck in a deep breath through my nose. *You have no idea.*

Then again, this is Mercedes. She likely does.

Although it's past four, there's still a short line in front of us. Blue Star Donuts is never empty. Their lines attest to how truly delectable the elaborate yet simple concoctions are that fill the glass cases.

Mercedes wanders to the far end while I stand in line, her eyes growing as she looks over the platters and names of each donut.

We order an odd number of the confections, neither of us able to commit to any one, therefore selecting over a dozen. "We're going to have to hide these. Parker doesn't even taste his food. He just inhales it," she tells me.

I smile, my mouth full of an apple fritter that is melting over my tongue, sending happy sugar shockwaves through my taste buds directly to my brain. It dulls the thoughts of leaving, of staying, of last weekend, and of breaking her heart.

"How did it go?" Kash asks as Mercedes drags herself down the hall to change out of her damp clothes.

"I didn't tell her." I can't look at him as I admit the words. He doesn't reply, and his previous movements to unload the dishwasher stop.

"Are you second-guessing going?"

I shrug, still not able to look at him. "No. I just don't know how to say it without making her hurt."

"You'll be back."

"But I'm still leaving, and she's going to have to get yet another new nanny. I don't think you understand how difficult this will be for her. How much she has loathed going through nannies."

"I know my daughter." Kash's words are a warning, one I should likely follow.

"Obviously not as well as you think you do."

Kash drops his chin, his eyes wide. "What is that supposed to mean?"

I'm picking a fight with him. I realize this, yet I can't stop it. I need someone to yell at. I need someone to yell at me. Hopefully it will be loud enough to try to dim the screaming in my own head. "What's your deal with Summer? You do know that Mercedes wants a mom, right? And I'm not suggesting you up and marry someone because of it, or marry her tomorrow, but—"

Kash shakes his head. "She's a child. She receives more love than half of the kids on Earth. Last Christmas she asked for a chimp." Kash's eyes grow wider and he extends a hand palm up. "Should I have given her one?"

The irritation in his voice baits me to continue, but the sorrow in his brown eyes that are pleading with me to stop makes my tone softer. "You have to give her some credit. She's ten, Kash. She loves you so much and is absolutely terrified of talking to you about her mom because she thinks it will make you sad. She loves Summer. Summer loves her, and Summer loves you."

Kash's gaze and shoulders fall toward the floor. "I can't. I can't go through the idea of losing someone again. It may not be death this time. Maybe it's divorce, or another guy. How many couples stay together these days? Once I'm in, I am all in."

"Summer hasn't dated anyone in five years. Five. Years. Kash." My head shakes with how obtuse he's being. "It doesn't get any more *in* than that. But if you don't do something soon, you're going to lose her. She's eventually going to resent always being here for you, and you never appreciating it or noticing how much she's giving, and just as importantly, what she's trying to give to you."

"What if—"

"There are an infinite number of what ifs but only one choice to make. You need to decide if you're ever going to be ready to let someone in, or let her free."

Silence stretches, hanging heavily in the air, beckoning me to break it. I swallow the desire as Kash's gaze travels back to mine, his chin tilted and attention focused. "Are you going to break up with King?"

My attention drops faster than a blink.

"Lo, it's just a summer."

"My career has no direct ties. I could end up anywhere."

"You're being a coward!"

I look back to him but can't keep his intense stare, so I move between over his shoulder and over his head. "I haven't made a decision."

Kash blinks heavily as his eyes grow wide once again. "You haven't decided on what? On not going?"

"Almost anything," I answer truthfully.

chapter
THIRTY-FIVE

T he next week goes by slowly. I'm no longer working to avoid only King. I'm working to avoid everyone and everything because the thought of saying goodbye is starting to threaten my certainty for going.

"Why are you ignoring everyone all of a sudden?" Kenzie's arms are spread between both railings, her eyes wide, demanding a response. I've been so careful, yet I wasn't even paying attention as I wandered up the stairs, trying to think positively about Italy for the first time all week.

"I've been avoiding you since September," I reply honestly.

I note the way her eyes look away for a fleeting second before returning to me. "Not like this you haven't."

I shrug off her response and take another step forward to signal I'm done. She allows me to pass, following close behind as I unlock the door to our apartment. Kenzie drops her purse to the ground with a thud, closely followed by her coat.

"Is this because of the fashion show?"

Through narrowed eyes I watch her closely, trying to read what all she may know about the situation.

"I know what it's like to not feel accepted by your family," she continues. "I've always been the black sheep. King and Kash were older and always off doing stuff with their bikes, or off on some adventure that I wasn't invited to. I never wanted to be home. I hated that place. It was huge and always empty, yet I was never allowed to leave. I felt like I had manacles around my ankles and wrists for *eighteen years*. Believe me, I get it."

I've never shared my personal feelings about anything with Kenzie. Perhaps it's the timing, or that I'm feeling vulnerable, but my head shakes with defeat. "The people that are supposed to love me the most, unconditionally..." My lungs feel weighted yet empty, and my throat too tight. I don't know if it hurts so much because I'm finally admitting this to someone else or because I am finally acknowledging this truth myself. "They don't love me. My dad needed another son. Someone to stay and carry on the family business with my brother. I can't remember the last time he hugged me. Hell, I can't remember the last time he told me he loves me. And my brother. God, my brother has hated me since I was born. Everything about me he hates. The way I look, the way I act, what I go to school for, the fact that I lived there, the fact that I'm now gone. And we can't forget about my mom." I take a deep breath as a strange energy creeps through my veins that has my fingers trembling, keeping tears at bay though they burn at the corners of my eyes. "You don't understand."

"Then tell me."

"I don't understand why you even care."

"I told you I messed up. I know I messed up. Eighteen years living with Queen Bitch taught me a lot of nasty habits. Ones I still don't even recognize until they're pointed out to me. We are really different people, but I know how much my family is starting to love you, and if I can do something to make this right, I will. Anything."

I press my lips together to stop them from quivering. "My mother left when I was two months old. She has never wanted me." My voice wavers and my eyes gloss with tears. "If they can't love me, who will?" My chin trembles violently and the gloss becomes smears as tears glide down my face.

"People who say that blood is thicker than friendship have never known what it's like to have an asshole as a parent. It's a bunch of bullshit. Too many families stick together out of pure obligation." Kenzie's throat moves as she swallows. Her lips and chin quiver as she opens them to speak again. "We don't get to choose our families, but we do get to decide who we make our families. Sometimes they're blood, and sometimes it's something much deeper."

"What if there's something wrong with me?" My voice is strained and hoarse.

"There's something wrong with all of us. It's a matter of finding the people that can accept those faults and love them as much as your strengths. Too many people want to be Wendy. They want to find the Lost Boys and be their savior— the reason for them to change their ways. People don't change, though, at least not permanently. Eventually, those bad habits will return because like it or not, we are all born with weaknesses."

I wipe my cheeks with the back of my hand and smile at her though my lips are tipped downward with the desire to cry. "I feel like we need to follow this up by singing *Kumbaya* or something."

"You're worse at having a deep conversation than my brothers," Kenzie says, shaking her head as her face travels up in an attempt to hide her own tears.

"I was raised by men. It's to be expected."

"I'm sorry I lied to you, and I'm really sorry I didn't tell you about King. I swear, it wasn't because of you. It was because of Isabelle, and I know that doesn't make it right or fair. I just hope you can sort of understand."

I nod, brushing yet another stray tear from my cheek. "I get it. Sometimes we do crazy things for the people we love."

"I won't butt in anymore," Kenzie says with a firm nod. "Your business with King is your business, but you really should go talk to him."

"So was this an attempt to make your conscience feel better, or a favor to King, or..."

Kenzie shrugs, her shoulders rolling in a way that reminds me of King.

"Maybe all of it, but, although we may never be close friends, I don't want you to hate me, Lo. I really did like you at the beginning of the year, and as much as I hated you for sleeping with King, I hated you even more because I still liked you."

There have been multiple times this year that I've loathed Kenzie as both a person and roommate, yet her saying this still makes me shed more tears. "I'm leaving in ten days."

"Don't waste them."

I wrap my arms around Kenzie in an aggressive hug that she reciprocates with a stunned pat, and then I move to the door, grabbing my messenger bag on the way out.

King is in the shop when I arrive, his face contorted with frustration and focus. His moves aren't as fluid or graceful as they always have been previously, and I know with certainty that it's because he's distracted. It doesn't take away from the beauty of watching him, however. He is still fearless liquid motion as he moves in impossible ways.

"Dude, you need to take a break. You're going to break your leg or your bike," a guy insists when King fails to land the same move for the third time. King scowls at him, but I take it as my cue to move closer.

He notices me at the same time I catch sight of his shirt. It's a black T-shirt with my logo printed in the center: a large bicycle wheel kicking up mud with spindles that are both iron and feathers. It pinches my heart.

"Can we talk?"

"That depends," King says, holding his bike beside him, his shin bleeding from hitting the edge of the ramp. "Are we going to discuss how we're going to make this work, or are you still feeling stubborn?"

"I'm pretty sure you called that my passion and you said it was one of my better attributes."

"I never said it was one of your better attributes. I said I loved it. But it's one of your worst attributes when you get so damn stubborn you can't listen to reason."

The guy who instructed King to take a break stares at me, clearly trying to interpret the situation and my intentions. "Want to go to Waterfront with me?"

"Now?"

I shrug, my eyes moving back to the man still staring at me. King follows my gaze and then leans his bike against the wall. "Let's go."

We ride in silence for the short distance to reach downtown, and I hate that it reminds me so much of two weeks ago after the fashion show.

As King parks, I notice his movements becoming slower. "What happened? Is it us? Your family? School? Italy?"

I take a deep breath, trying so hard to keep eye contact with him rather than look over his shoulder. "I'm so afraid we're going to hurt each other, King."

"Stop, Lo." He turns in his seat to face me, his hand finally extending across the cab to touch my leg. "It's three months. That's it."

"Three months of you competing in a world you love."

"And I know you want to be there, and that's enough for me."

My eyes fall at the thought. Is that enough? Why have I never considered it like that?

King nods toward the window. "Let's walk."

Generally when I walk Waterfront, there are so many people, my mind whirls with images, colors, textures, and infinite other details, but today I see only him. Even the noisy band that I had previously seen people turn their heads toward with a myriad of emotions ranging from joy to annoyance has ceased to exist. This only happens with King. I am exhilarated. Nervous. Inspired by all that is King, because only he is able to make the world disappear.

I'm also terrified, realizing he's carrying so much more than just my hand. What if he meets someone new? What if this doesn't work? What will happen to my world?

"We have a little over a week left. I don't want to waste it." His eyes close as he shakes his head ever so slightly. "I want to spend every second with you until you're so sick of me that getting on that plane to Florence is a relief."

The burn of tears threatens my eyes, but I force a smile on my face and shake my head when I realize the tears are coming regardless of how hard I try to fight them. "That won't take a full week."

King's lips pull up into a smile at my joke, but his eyes are unfocused, reflecting the same emotion I've been experiencing since opening my acceptance letter: loss. He wraps his arms around me slowly as though he's hesitant maybe from rejection, or because also like me, he knows this is the beginning of a short train of good-byes. He pulls me flush against his body, and I feel his heart against my chest, conversing with my own. It's a crazy and messy mixture of pleas and fears that my heart relays back as I hold on to King with everything inside of me.

The ring of a bicyclist is the only reason we eventually part. Otherwise, I think we would have tested how long we could both go without food or water. His jaw clenches and his eyes close, making my heart thunder and my eyes heat with tears. I understand what he's feeling; I know it so well. It is as though we are made to be together and time keeps mocking us. It hurts. It hurts like hell.

"Let's get some dinner," King says, threading his fingers with mine.

"I need to tell Mercedes."

"She'll understand."

I nod sadly. I should be relieved that he's ensuring she'll be okay, yet, whether it's for fear that she won't or fear that she will, my eyes cloud with tears once again.

We walk into the house holding bags of takeout. I requested Chinese when King asked, thinking about Allie and what she had told me about food and the comfort it brings. Summer and Kash are already in the kitchen, looking over new images she's taken.

"Where's monkey?" King asks.

"In her room." Kash looks to me as he answers, already knowing I'm late for this meeting.

I smile reproachfully and head down the hall.

"Hey," I say, leaning against the doorframe of her room.

Mercedes looks up, her long hair a curtain around the magazine she's looking through. "King has a centerfold in here."

My lips pull up in a smile and my feet lead me into the room with little thought.

I sit on the edge of her bed, and Mercedes sits up, tucking her feet under her so she's nearly as tall as I am. "Are you going to tell me about your brother?"

I hadn't intended to. Ever. "Do you want me to tell you about him?"

Mercedes stares at me for several seconds and then shrugs, but I see that she has questions before she asks, "Was he always so mean?"

My first response is to shrug in return, but I stop as my shoulders rise, and swallow. "Yeah, he has."

"Does it bother you?"

I rub the length of my arm because I'm covered in chills from the thoughts she's evoking. "At times."

"How do you make it stop?"

"Stop what? Caring?"

Mercedes nods.

"I don't know if I ever stopped caring. I just realized that his words were intended to make me feel as badly as he does, and I didn't want to be miserable like him."

"I'm sorry he's such a jerk."

"It doesn't matter anymore. The fact that they don't believe in me does nothing but fuel me to be better, push harder."

"You're an amazing artist, Lo."

"And you're an amazing person," I say, inching my fingers forward and covering the back of her hand.

"I have something to tell you," I begin.

"You got in." Her eyes leave mine, inflicting a sharp pain to my chest. "I already know. I knew as soon as you submitted that you'd get in. So did you, remember? I was there when you got your passport picture."

"I kind of hoped they'd turn me down."

Mercedes shakes her head, but she still doesn't look at me. "Don't say that, Lo."

"I'm coming back in September, though. Allie and Charleigh are both staying in the city, and I'll stay with them when I return until I figure things out."

She nods, sniffling as her fingers tighten into a fist below my hand.

"I wish I could take you with me."

Mercedes launches herself at me, knocking me off balance so I'm sprawled across her bed with her on top of me, her narrow arms locked around the back of my neck. I wrap mine around her back as we both cry.

"Lo?" Mercedes asks in a shaky voice after both of us have calmed to the point we can breathe evenly again.

"Yeah?"

She shifts, lying her head on my shoulder and reaching for my newly freed hand. "You remember telling me we have to appreciate what we have?"

"Yeah…"

"You forgot to say, we have to realize what we have in order to appreciate it. I'm glad I have you, Lo."

My nose tingles and my eyes burn from the quick return of tears. "I'm glad to have you too, Mercedes." As my words dance across the sounds of our breaths, she snuggles closer to me, her hair tickling my face. I want so badly to brush it away, but I don't. I wouldn't move right now for the world.

chapter THIRTY-SIX

"I hate that you came," I say against King's shoulder.

"I'm not wasting a second. I told you that."

"But this makes it so real." I imagine few are watching us as we cling to one another outside of the TSA security gates, thinking they know and understand what's happening. But they don't. They don't know King, and I'm positive they have no idea how impossible saying goodbye to him is.

"No less real than it would have been if we had said goodbye last night."

We had a small party at Sonar to celebrate last night. Charleigh attended with her boyfriend, Brandon, and I was glad I had the opportunity to speak to him for a few minutes sans drama to learn that his love for Charleigh was just as deep as hers for him, possibly deeper. I understood before that moment why she had chosen to drop out of the fashion show, but seeing them together made falling asleep last night nearly impossible.

Allie was there along with Mia and Estella, Summer, Parker, a few students from my class, and even Kenzie. I spent most of my time with King and Mercedes, knowing that I would miss them the absolute most. But I had asked all of them not to come to the airport. The idea made it seem so final.

Tears are already skating down my cheeks from the far corners of my eyes, my throat tight. "Why couldn't I have gone last summer?"

"Stop, Lo." King's hand between my shoulder blades presses me tighter to his chest. "I want you to go with the expectation of loving it, not hating it. It's going to be hard, but we can do this."

I nod, the wool of his plaid shirt scratching my face. I can't make a verbal response without choking on my tears.

"Everything is going to be okay. *We're* going to be okay, alright? We've got this."

I nod again absently, fighting the cry about to break lose.

"I love you, Lo." His voice is softer, pressed against my ear, playing through my head like a catchy tune. My fingers ache from squeezing the fabric of his shirt so tightly.

"I love you more."

He shakes his head. "Not possible."

"What are you guys doing today?"

King rolls his shoulders dismissively. "Summer has something planned," he says, but I understand that he has no intentions of allowing her to try to distract him.

"Estella invited you guys to the restaurant for happy hour."

King doesn't say anything, just grips me tighter.

"You remember the name of the company you're getting a ride from?"

"Yeah, it's in my bag."

"And you have your power converters and the euros?"

I nod, my throat closing again. He's preparing to say goodbye. "I want to hear all about your competition tomorrow."

King nods, moving his lips to the side of my head and softly kissing me. "I'll tell you everything."

"I have to go," I whisper as my tears become heavier, now running down both cheeks in multiple trails.

King nods, his throat moving as he swallows.

"I love you."

"I love you," he repeats back to me.

I look back at King several times as I go through the maze of nylon fences, each glance making my vision more obstructed with tears until I'm being beckoned forward through the metal detectors and can no longer see him. Then I lose it.

The flight to Italy is long, punctuated by a change of planes in Newark, where I ignore my growling stomach and pull out my phone to call King.

"Hey, baby." His voice is soothing, making me smile and tear up again as I wander in the direction of a food sign.

"Guess what?"

"What?"

"Only eighty-five days until I come home."

King laughs quietly. "I thought you were going to study your Italian keywords on the plane."

"You're a way better distraction."

"I'll have Mercedes create a countdown."

"I already miss you."

"Only eighty-five days, babe. It's going to go by so fast. You're going to eat Gobi and paint, making pictures more beautiful than people can imagine, and then you're going to be home."

I take a deep breath, fighting to believe his words. "I have to find a restroom and grab some food before my next flight. I'll try to call you again before I leave. Otherwise, I'll call you tomorrow, okay?"

"I love you, Lo."

"I love you more."

I wander around yet another airport with tear-stained cheeks, ignoring the world as I pick through my lunch.

Me: 4 the first time ever, my plane's early.

King: UR going 2 love Italy.

Me: Not as much as I love U.

King: Good.

Italy is more beautiful than any of the pictures have portrayed. The architecture, the colors, the people, even the cobblestones have me entranced. I want to sit down and draw everything I see. Being away from those that I care so deeply for makes being here bittersweet, but for the first time since learning about this adventure, I feel motivated and excited for what I will see and experience this summer.

I'm impressed with myself as I navigate my way into the hotel, never having issues with getting through immigration, finding my bags, or even the correct car company to get me to my hotel.

The man at the front desk is thin, his hair long and attention set on something behind the counter that I can't see. When he hears me, he smiles warmly, revealing with thick lines around his lips and eyes that he's older than I had assumed upon first glance.

"Bonjourno!" He greets me merrily, his arms lifting as high as his smile.

I can't help but smile in return as I pull out the documents I received that have all of my confirmation numbers.

"Ah, you're from America!" he says, his voice rolling over the syllables, making them sound like an art.

"I am."

"My daughter wants to go to America. She's in love with your country. You'll have to learn me new words for me to tell her. Her English is much better than mine."

"Sure," I say, smiling at his eagerness.

"Come, I'll show you your room. It's good you are staying with us. We have a lift." I'm relieved to hear this. King made a comment about how few elevators there are in Europe.

We walk through the hotel, tiled in a terracotta colored brick, the walls a soft red-clay color. There are paintings on several of the walls, all famous Italian monuments that I hope to discover while I'm here.

He leads me to a door and then gestures widely for me to enter with the sweep of his hand. The same terracotta bricks are inside, along with a gold-framed bed that's covered with a comforter in shades of forest green and mustard yellow. There are two nightstands, each adorned with a matching gold lamp, a dresser, and an older TV. The room is cold, ugly, but endearing because of the host that is proudly showing me how the few things inside are operated.

I am left to unpack, but instead I pull out my computer and phone to get set up, and while they power on, I draw.

chapter
THIRTY-SEVEN

My phone startles me awake. I reach for it, hoping it's King even though it's a ridiculous hour. I wanted to stay up to see how things went, but I fell asleep. I sleep soundly here from the thousands of steps and stairs I take each day, and the food that is packed with glutinous wonders that have ensured me peaceful dreams. I've been in Italy for two weeks. I've eaten at 13 Gobi—the restaurant King told me inspired him to cook—four times already. It truly is the best food I've ever tasted. I've also seen The Duomo twice, The Pitti Palace, and lost an entire Saturday in the Ufizzi Gallery where I met the statue of David in person.

The sight of Kash's name across the screen confuses me, but I don't hesitate in answering it.

"Lo?"

It's 4:00 a.m. I know by how early it is and the hesitancy in his voice that something is wrong. So does my heart. It's twisting along with my stomach.

"Lo, are you there?"

I shake my head and quietly respond. "What's wrong?" I ask when Kash doesn't immediately respond. I feel the tightness in each of my muscles as my mind races to prepare for what he's going to say.

"King crashed. He crashed hard, Lo." My breath is gone. I shouldn't be able to cry, yet I am. "He's in surgery."

My head shakes again. Maybe it never stopped. "What happened? What are they saying?"

"Not a lot yet."

"What do you mean?"

"He's in surgery, Lo. All we know is they have to reset his shoulder and elbow, and his hip was fucked up, and…" Kash takes a deep breath, and my tears stream faster.

The tiled floor is still eerily warm under my feet as I begin shoving things into my suitcase, balancing the phone between my shoulder and chin with nothing but stretched silence between us with occasional deep breaths and attempts to get our noses to stop running. I go into the bathroom and quickly shove everything in a plastic bag I paid for earlier today when I forgot my own grocery bag, and drop it into my suitcase as well.

"Tell him I'll be there as soon as I can."

"He's going to be pissed you're leaving."

"I don't care. I can't stay here."

"I know."

I slump to my bed. I don't know what about Kash's words hurts me so much. I think possibly it's the pity, like he understands this from his own experience. Refusing to think of the similarities, I push myself forward and sit up straight.

"Trains and planes are all going to be off for the night. You should get some sleep. I'll get you a flight out first thing in the morning."

"You're not—"

"I am. Get some rest. I'll call you in a few hours with the details." Kash hangs up.

A deep-seated pain is rising higher in my chest, magnifying every distinct reaction to this news. My heart is pounding as it races, my hands are shaking, my legs feel unsteady. I shove away from my bed with determination. There's no chance in hell I'm going to be able to sleep at this point. Instead, I finish packing my last remaining items away, tugging a pair of jeans on, and tennis shoes without any socks because I can't find any in the mess that is crammed into my bag. I'm lucky to find a bra and hook it into place and grab my jacket before shoving my portfolio into my bag. My messenger bag is filled last, my chargers, power converter, sketchpads, charcoals, and camera all jumbled together. I pocket my phone and head to the door, taking one last look at the hideous bedspread before making my way out into the warm evening in search of a cab.

By the time I'm loading the plane, I've only been in the airport for a couple of hours. Kash called an hour later, informing me he booked me on a seven o'clock flight. My feet feel gross from not having the soft barrier of socks, and I briefly wish I had dug for another shirt besides the one I slept in, because it's several sizes too big.

Flying home is the longest fourteen hours of my life.

Ever.

I don't bother to call Kash when I finally make my way through immigration. I take a cab to where I know they all are.

The elevator moves too slowly. I want to take the stairs so I don't have to keep waiting for people to file off and on at each floor, but still having my bags, I don't. I swallow my impatience with an angry huff and watch the numbers slowly climb.

The front desk only informed me of the floor, which has brought me to a long white hallway that makes me yearn for terracotta tiles. I reach for my phone and hit a few buttons to reach Kash and press it to my ear, trying to balance my bags and ignore how hot I feel.

"Did you land?"

"I'm here."

"At the hospital?"

"On the right floor, I think."

Kash emerges from farther down the hall, and I hang up, grabbing my things and pushing them in his direction. He moves toward me, wrapping his arms around me, knocking my bag from my shoulder.

"How is he?"

"He's good. He's a tough sonofabitch. They put pins in his shoulder, and they had to put in a chest tube because a rib punctured his lung, but he's going to be just fine."

I sigh as tears course over the well-made paths on my cheeks. "Can I see him?"

Kash nods, reaching for my two suitcases and leading me to a door marked as ICU that makes my skin prickle with a wave of fear.

"You can't bring that in here," a nurse says from a desk.

"Can we keep it somewhere? She just flew in."

"You shouldn't be in here if you just got off a plane," she says disapprovingly.

"King would take the bubonic plague over missing her."

The nurse's blonde curls shake and her lips purse, but she stands from her desk and moves toward the end of the counter. "You can leave them there for a few minutes. You need to wash your hands very well before you touch anything. And if she's going to be a guest, you need to fill out another form so I can get her a bracelet." She looks to Kash with her eyebrows raised in a V as though she's challenging him.

I hadn't considered that I could be a risk to him, and it makes my hand pause on the handle of my bag as I lower it from my shoulder.

"I'll do whatever you need, but I'm going to take her back first."

Kash places a hand on my shoulder and gently coaxes me forward, and my fears of going dissolve.

The sight of King stops my breath. He has so many tubes, wires, and bandages wrapped around him that my mind instantly believes Kash lied to me about his positive prognosis.

"The drugs have him sleeping a lot, but he said he's feeling okay."

I look to Kash, my eyes wide with disbelief.

"Where is everyone?"

"They went to grab some food downstairs in the cafeteria."

I nod and then move to the sink, washing my hands three times before I dry them with a scratchy paper towel. Then I move toward his bedside, pulling a chair from the corner so I can be as close to him as possible. Kash slips out the door, closing it behind him as a tear falls down my cheek. My fingers hover over his hand, looking for a safe place to make contact without pulling on anything, and eventually rest on his forearm.

Then I tell King about nearly every single second that has passed since I've been gone. He's already heard most of my stories, but I repeat them again, sharing minute details about things he already knows about like the creaminess of gelato versus ice cream, and how prego means far more than just you're welcome as the guidebooks had told me. I discuss the piece I've been tasked with restoring and how I was so nervous to begin, I had to paint a small replica before I could convince myself to actually make the minor additions to the original.

I'm not sure how much time has passed when Kash and Mercedes enter the room. She smiles at me, though her own cheeks are red from tears, and wraps her arms around me from the side so I don't have to move away from King.

"It feels like you were already gone for eighty-five days."

I nod, holding her with my free hand, and turn when she calls out King's name.

His eyes blink heavily as they move around the room, confusion making them grow wide. "Shit," he hisses. "What in the hell are you doing here?"

I stare at King for several moments, trying to read the scowl on his face.

"You had to have surgery."

"You're supposed to be in Florence."

"I'm supposed to be here, you jackass."

"You're throwing away your future," King barks.

My heart thunders in my chest, doubts filling me with concern. I have to remind myself a dozen times that he isn't upset about me actually being here, but about potentially harming my position with the program before I can respond. "I don't care about any of it right now."

"You need to!"

"Stop being a jerk," Mercedes orders. "You need to appreciate what you have and stop being so rude. I know you've been in a bad mood since she left, but you're supposed to be happy now—she's here!"

King and I both look to Mercedes, then to each other.

"I don't want you to throw away your dreams for me," he says.

"I'm not. This is more important. You are more important. If they can't understand why I need to be here, then I don't want to be in their program."

King flips his hand over, revealing another IV port in the crease of his elbow. He reaches for my hand still sitting on the bed and holds it. His fingers that are normally so warm, even with the Oregon rain and constant cloud cover, are cool as they wrap around mine, but his eyes slowly warm with an understanding that makes tears once again return to my eyes.

King is released from the hospital four days later, a cast around his entire left arm and a slight limp from severely bruising his hipbone.

"When do you have to leave again?" King asks while I stand beside him, posed to help as he slides into his bed.

"I'm not."

"You're not what?"

"Leaving."

"Like hell you aren't!" King yells, sitting up.

He has been grumpy since he woke up in the hospital. Mercedes and Summer have both assured me this is tame compared to the past couple of weeks, which seems surprising and so unusual for King.

"I nearly didn't leave."

"What are you talking about?" he demands.

"I didn't want to go. Yes, I thought this would be great, and I wanted so hard to prove to my family that I was good enough. But I didn't want to go. I love art, but I'm never going to work in art restoration. I don't *want* to work in art restoration. I want to paint and draw and create. I just got scared. I thought if I didn't go, I'd resent you later—resent us."

"What's to say that won't happen now?"

"Because the second my phone rang, I didn't think once about art or Italy. All I could think about was how upset I was that I couldn't be here with you. I will always have art, and I'll keep working to be the artist I want to be, but I'm not going back."

King relaxes against his pillows, watching me carefully with his brown eyes. "What if we both go?"

"What?"

"I'm going to be in a cast for eight weeks, which is going to make Italy a royal bitch, but if anything can heal me, the steaks at—"

My eyes narrow and he laughs, folding my hand within his. "I want to go with you, Lo. I want to be there and watch you succeed. After Italy, we can come back to Portland and figure out what's next, but this is your time to shine."

"That hardly seems fair."

"I'm not kissing my dreams goodbye. I'm not sacrificing anything. This hardly seems fair to you. I'm not giving anything up and gaining so much."

"What about doctor's appointments?"

"What about them?"

"You'll be in Italy," I say, barely able to contain my patience with his aloofness.

"So, that's a yes?"

"Is what a yes?"

"You want me to go with you?"

"Are you serious?"

"Weren't you just inviting me?"

"I swear, if you weren't casted and bandaged right now..." Shaking my head with annoyance, King laughs harder.

"Everything happens for a reason, Lo. I'm going to come to Italy. We can figure out all of the details, but I'm going with you this time."

"You're serious?"

"I love you, Lo. The last couple of weeks have been hell for me because all I can do is think about you. I am so sick and tired of missing you, and counting nine hours ahead to figure out what time it is where you are, and wondering what you're doing. I can't focus when you aren't around. I don't enjoy riding, or cooking, or even Kash because I am so preoccupied with thinking about you. It's been like the first couple of weeks after I came home and found you, and I hate it.

"I'm going with you to Florence, and we will travel across Italy, seeing every cathedral, castle, and monument, sample tiramisu from every restaurant, and fill ourselves with wine and coffee, but most of all, we'll be together, and that's all I care about."

"What about your obligations with Kash?"

"He'll understand."

I shake my head as a laugh bubbles up through my throat. "This is going to be like trying to escape the rain, isn't it?"

King's head shakes, his lips parted ever so slightly, causing my eyes to trace over them with the desire to both kiss and draw them. "The rain's got nothing on me."

EPILOGUE

"**M**aybe we should see if we can find an elevator." She turns, scanning the large hall in hopes of finding a sign or line.

"I've got this, babe." I place a hand on Lo's shoulder, wishing it were bare so I could feel her skin. Her eyes turn to mine, wide with worry. Worry for me. I would likely find this concern annoying from anyone else, but not from Lo. It makes me feel loved and cared for on a level few understand. I know that I am always in her thoughts, not only because my face is what graces nearly every page of her sketch books—even here in Italy—but because of all the small things she does that mean more to me than I can ever put into words. It's sending postcards to Mercedes twice a week. Collecting photographs for Summer each time we pass a small stand. Bringing me coffee while I'm still in the shower. Triple checking that I have my pillows set up before we go to sleep. Sending packages filled with fabrics and packaged treats to her friends. Remembering Kash's birthday, even though we're on the other side of the world. Every single day she shows me how much she loves me by working for her dreams, loving life, and trusting me to love her back just as deeply. And dear God, I do. Everything I see and do reminds me of her. I want to give her every flower I see in the shops we walk by. I want to cook her every meal that makes her moan with delight. I want to show her every beautiful secret and monument in the world to watch the way her eyes light up. And I would like to spend countless hours pleasing her because I can never get enough of the sounds she makes and the way she makes me feel.

She doesn't argue, though I see the hesitancy in her eyes. Instead, she nods and moves in the direction of the spiral staircase that she stared at in silence for several minutes when we arrived.

I knew she would love the Vatican. There are few places more impressive than this small country. However, seeing her take in St. Peter's Square made me wish I could take pictures like Summer. We had to wait for over an hour to get inside, but she never once complained. She was lost in a trance, one which makes me feel lost as I watch her.

We descend the stairs slowly, not because of the slight limp I'm still struggling with but the vast line in front of us.

The air is warm and humid as we make our way outside, and I appreciate the way her eyes travel over the square again, absorbing the scenery rather than searching for the right tour bus like everyone else around us is doing.

This summer has been nothing short of amazing. Watching Lo excel in her passions has given me a new appreciation for my own. I'm looking forward to getting home and starting physical therapy so that I can begin riding again, but like Lo, I'm not in any hurry. The weight of our love is greater than anything, and it will always be just as the rain: inescapable.

ACKNOWLEDGEMENTS:

I have to say, I'm really glad I'm such a terrible procrastinator sometimes, because there are so many people to thank, and waiting this long has hopefully ensured I can remember everyone! If I don't, I am truly sorry.

First off, I want to thank my amazing family! They deal with my moodiness when I can't write, or am writing and can't make things mesh, and my absences for while I'm either writing or lost in bookland. You guys are my foundation and my life, and I couldn't ask for a better or more loving husband and boys. I love you too. Grandma Cyndi for being so excited and willing to read whatever I write! And my dad, you've been one of my biggest cheerleaders. Maybe I should have listened earlier when you said I should be a writer. I love you guys so much!

Lisa Greenwood, I don't know how to put into words what you mean to me. I feel as though I've known you most of my life rather than a couple of years! Thank you for your endless support and encouragement, and for always being willing to kick me in my "loaf of bread." Your cockney threats don't scare me, still, but they greatly entertain me. I'm sorry for always babbling about books, and complaining to you on days my OCD gets out of control. I hope one day I can be as great of friend to you, as you are to me.

Sarah Pinkerton, I will always have you to thank you, because the day you told me my books left a larger impact on you than Twilight, I really believed I could do this. I love that you don't care at all about what I write or choose to do, you accept me for me, and that's all that has ever mattered.

Terri Peterson, I love my Terbear so stinkin' much!!! Thank you for … how do I even explain what all there is to thank you for? Your heart is so big and beautiful. Thank you for investing endless hours into my crazy thoughts. You are just as deeply implanted under my skin, as my words are on yours.

Jenna Chianello, thank you for taking a chance on me and becoming one of my closest and dearest friends. And thank you Katie Ross, for introducing me to both Terri and Jenna, and so many others. But, I want to thank you even more for just being you, because when I see a message from you, my entire day brightens—you have that effect on people.

Lucy Mae Enderby, I missed you for this book, but seeing you becoming a mom has been far more rewarding than finishing another book. Give sweet Maddie a kiss for me!

Dawn Nicole Costiera, your helpful advice and support means so much to me! I can't tell you how flattered and appreciative I truly am.

To my sweet and loving beta team that is much more than just a beta team, you're my friends, and I love you guys so much! Katie Ross, Lisa Greenwood, Jenna Chianello, Becca DawnTerri Peterson, Katie Mazur, Jessica Frider, Samantha Lloyd, you guys are such an essential part of this process, and I hope you know how much I appreciate and love you all.

CM Foss, my first and only critique partner—did I mention you're stuck with me?? THANK YOU!! Your humor and compassion have led me to never leaving you alone … ever. I am so anxious to see you in person this spring and give you one hell of a hug!!

The Bossy Babes—we changed our name from the Bosse Babes to the Bossy Babes, because we weren't ready to lose the Bosse sisters, and I doubt we ever will—you ladies ROCK! Your love blows my mind daily. Sometimes several times a day.

Giovanna Bovenzi Crus, Shell Williams, January Apted—you guys are amazing. I still am shocked people read my books, the fact that you guys encourage people to read them after you all do, shocks the hell out of me. It's very surreal, and it's incredibly awesome. I cannot thank you enough for all of your time and support. I hope I get to meet you all one day to squeeze you!

Lisa with What Lies Within These Pages, Becca and Candy with Prisoners of Print, Bianca Smith with Biblio Belles Book Club, Stephanie Powell with Night and Day Book Blog, Roxie Madar with Schmexy Gil Book Blog, Lisa Marie with A Risque Affair Book Blog, Terri, Katie, and Jenna with The Review

Loft, Becca Manuel with Becca the Bibliophile, Stephanie DeLamanter Phillips with Stephanie's Book Reports, I know I am missing more, I know, and I am so sorry, because bloggers, I can't thank you guys enough! Your love is what all writers dream of! You guys share your passion for reading with others, and I know how inundated you all are with requests, and the fact that you've all taken the time to read MY book is something I promise to never ever take for granted. Thank you. Thank you. Thank you!

Murphy Rae for editing and answering countless questions! And Hang Le with By Hang Le, thank you so much for creating what very well might be my favorite cover thus far, and for always dealing with all of my indecisiveness with professionalism, and grace! I wish I could hug you!

Max Dobson with the Polished Pen, thank you for doing the fastest proofread ever, and for continuing to always be my mentor and teacher. You are the greatest.

Emily and the gang with E.M. Tippetts Book Designs! You guys are miracle workers, and I swear, next time I will give you more time! I swear! Thank you for fitting me in and as always creating such a beautiful book!

And every single reader—thank you from the bottom of my heart. I appreciate each and every single one of you and welcome you to contact me with any questions or feedback!

ABOUT THE AUTHOR:

Mariah Dietz lives in Eastern Washington, with her husband and two sons that are the axis of her crazy and wonderful world.

Mariah grew up in a tiny town outside of Portland, Oregon, where she spent the majority of her time immersed in the pages of books that she both read and created.

She has a love for all things that include her sons, good coffee, books, travel, and dark chocolate. She also has a deep passion for the stories she writes, and hopes readers enjoy the journeys she takes them on, as much as she loves creating them.

Contact Mariah or learn more about her at:
http://www.mariahdietz.com/

FB: https://www.facebook.com/pages/Mariah-Dietz/317058868472780
Goodreads: http://bit.ly/1Mm6AdF
Instagram: http://instagram.com/mariahdietz
Twitter: https://twitter.com/MariahDietz
Email: mariahdietzink@gmail.com

Made in the USA
Lexington, KY
02 October 2017